# The Twelfth Rose of Spring

Crossway books by Doris Elaine Fell

## Seasons of Intrigue Series

*Always in September*
*Before Winter Comes*
*April Is Forever*
*The Twelfth Rose of Spring*

SEASONS OF INTRIGUE

BOOK FOUR

# The Twelfth Rose of Spring

Doris Elaine Fell

CROSSWAY BOOKS
WHEATON, ILLINOIS • NOTTINGHAM, ENGLAND

*The Twelfth Rose of Spring*

Copyright © 1995 by Doris Elaine Fell

Published by Crossway Books
        a division of Good News Publishers
        1300 Crescent Street
        Wheaton, Illinois 60187

Cover illustration: Chuck Gillies

Cover design: Dennis Hill

First printing 1995

First British edition 1995—ISBN 1-85684-123-5

Production and Printing in the United States of America for
CROSSWAY BOOKS
Norton Street, Nottingham, England NG7 3HR

**Library of Congress Cataloging-in-Publication Data**
Fell, Doris Elaine.
    The Twelfth Rose of Spring / Doris Elaine Fell.
        p.    cm.—(Seasons of intrigue: bk. 4)
    I. Title.   II. Series: Fell, Doris Elaine. Seasons of intrigue; bk. 4.
PS3556.E4716T9 1995    813'.54—dc20        95-10375
ISBN 0-89107-861-4

| 03 | 02 | 01 | 00 | 99 | 98 | 97 | 96 | 95 |
|----|----|----|----|----|----|----|----|----|
| 15 | 14 | 13 | 12 | 11 | 10 | 9 8 | 7 6 | 5 4 | 3 2 | 1 |

*Therefore if any man be in Christ, he is a new creature:*
*old things are passed away;*
*behold, all things are become new.*

—II Corinthians 5:17 (King James Version)

# Prologue

Nicholas Caridini gripped the side rails and fixed his gaze on the sun filtering through the hospital window. The windowpane, misted with yesterday's dust and rain, could not blot out the majestic Austrian Alps, the mountains he had come to love and call home. A late spring storm had painted the slopes with layers of white and the forest with frosty patches of snow. Sun-streaked rays added their blazing pink trails along the snowdrifts.

He tensed as pain surged through his lanky body, his bare toes tingling in revolt. He grabbed the call light, one thumb on the black button. But he resisted. More medication would only dull his senses, making him vulnerable to confessing the guilt and secrets that raged in his soul. His hair felt clammy; the pillows were drenched with his perspiration. As the waves of discomfort eased, he elevated the head of the bed and leaned back, his eyes once again on the Alps. Death no longer threatened him. He would welcome it as the ultimate escape. But the cancer cells multiplying inside him would forever rob him of these mountains.

A marginal smile touched his cracked lips as bittersweet memories engulfed him. He had arrived in Austria under the guise of an Olympian contestant in Innsbruck's second Winter Olympics. Ten years ago? No—almost twenty.

From the moment he rode in over the Brenner Motorway and finally into Innsbruck itself with its crisscrossing expressways and shiny railroad tracks, he had been struck by the charm of this town. Innsbruck lay tucked between Alpine ranges, flags from thirty-seven nations fluttering in the crisp mountain air.

In spite of the shadow of terrorism that had clouded the Munich games, throngs converged on Innsbruck. A million and a half spectators and more than a thousand young athletes arrived; Nicholas, the aloof Soviet assassin, came with them, carrying a forged passport. He had billeted in the Olympic Village. His sleeping quarters faced the steep, new bobsled run, but he wasn't there just as an alternate on the bobsled team. His political target was a powerful West German official named Klaus Zimmerman. Nicholas found it almost impossible to avoid the Austrian police, who far outnumbered the Olympian participants, but he worried more about avoiding Drew Gregory, the American agent who had tracked him to Innsbruck.

By the end of the first week, Nicholas had spotted Zimmerman. He stalked the man over snow-crusted streets, finally stopping him to ask directions to the ice-skating venue. As Zimmerman turned, fear lit in his eyes; he had no time to cry for help. The cyanide pellet exploded in his face, and his heavy body collapsed on the ground, making slush of the snow beneath him. His eyes remained fixed, sightless. As the crowd pressed toward the lifeless form, Nicholas recognized Drew Gregory among them.

"The man's had a heart attack," a woman cried.

Gregory knelt down and sniffed Zimmerman's blue lips. "I don't think so," he said quietly.

Nicholas moved quickly. He poked his pellet gun into the nearest snowdrift, raced toward a clothing store, and pocketed his goggles as he entered. Safely inside, he reversed his parka and tucked his skull cap and gloves beneath a display of expensive knit sweaters. Then he hurried back to the Olympic Village.

Before he could pack or formulate plans to escape, he fell ill with the flu spreading among the Olympians. For two days the only competition he experienced was the race for the bathrooms. But at last, while the Austrian Franz Klammer took the gold in the downhill, Nicholas pulled himself from a sickbed and fled to Brunnerwald, a Tyrolean village that clung to the lower mountain slopes—and from there safely into East Germany.

Now as he lay in his hospital bed at the Landeskranken-haus, he remembered the aching muscles back then and how a raging fever had ravaged his body. But it seemed nothing compared to the weakness and intermittent pain that gripped him now. Once again it was like lying in a body that was not his own, one fatigued and drained of all physical strength. He was midway through life's cycle and worn out, his once-sturdy six-foot frame an aged shell before its time.

Nicholas heard the door of the room open. He waited until it closed again before turning to face his doctor. Deiter Eschert came swiftly toward him wearing that familiar loose-fitting lab coat with pens and a stethoscope protruding from its pockets. Eschert presented as a quiet man, mellow in appearance, of medium build, the dark beard well trimmed. His surgeon's hands looked much stronger than his smile as he lowered the side rails and sat on the edge of the bed.

"Deiter, give it to me straight," Nicholas urged.

Eschert allowed a professional pause. "I've studied your films again. I could open you up and remove the new tumor."

"A cure, Deiter?" Nicholas wheezed.

"Palliative. It would take some pressure off your diaphragm. Let you breathe easier."

"For what purpose then, Doctor?"

"To give you a few weeks, maybe months."

"So I can put my house in order?" he asked lightly. "Do you think I'll make it to my fifty-second birthday?"

"Not without more treatment."

Nicholas studied Eschert's steady hands. Twice he had trusted the scalpel in them. "No more surgery, Deiter."

Eschert whipped the stethoscope from his pocket. "I thought we had licked it, but it's metastasized to your liver."

Nicholas thought of the years of vodka and champagne, the prestige and privileges that had gone with his career as an intelligence officer, the life that Eschert knew nothing about. He put his thin hand over the doctor's. "It's not your fault."

"Johann should have sent you back before it turned inoperable."

"Johann tried to persuade me, but I've been busy."

"It's time you did something for yourself. Take a vacation. You never give the sun a chance to tan your skin or kiss your face."

"My parishioners depend on me."

"The sick and the elderly?"

Nicholas smiled. "It's been a good life."

Eschert's narrow shoulders arced and fell twice. "You and Johann have buried yourselves up on that mountain. Johann I can understand. He never liked the city, hated it even back in medical school, but you—for fifteen years you've turned down every promotion."

"Bishop of Innsbruck? Archbishop of Vienna? They don't sound like me. I like the simple life, Deiter." *Where else could I hide?*

Eschert plugged his ears with the tips of the stethoscope and placed the cold disc against Nicholas's sunken chest. "Take a deep breath. Again—"

The effort started a coughing spasm. Nicholas fought it, swallowing in vain. The choking reached his throat, bursting in a dry, exhausting hack. A flushing heat burned his cheeks.

"I'll have the nurse bring you something."

"No," Nicholas protested. "I'll be all right."

The doctor's eyes grew more serious. "We'll want to do another lung scan, maybe try more radiation or chemo—"

"No, Deiter, the last rounds made me dreadfully ill."

"So did the last surgery." Eschert traced the red-rimmed stitches that ran along Nicholas's rib cage to his abdomen. "Looks like I gave you a brand new zipper. You'd never know there was an old scar beneath it." A fresh burst of curiosity brightened his blue eyes. "You've never said why they left that shrapnel in you."

"You never asked." It had been too risky, Nicholas remembered. Too far from a medical center, too dangerous to seek help. And when he finally did, they had done little more than an exploratory. "Don't worry, Doctor, it didn't cause my present problem."

"It didn't help your lungs either. Nicholas, I find it hard to believe that was an old hunting accident. A single rifle shell. Your insides still look like you were peppered with Rhino bullets."

He tried to process the seminary rules—celibacy, chastity, no weaponry, but he said, "Even priests go hunting, don't they?"

"Your old wound looks more like you were the hunted."

*You're dangerously close to the truth,* Nicholas thought. *What else have you guessed about me?* He made a mental note not to come back for more medical follow-up, not to risk a break in confidentiality or face more of Deiter's probing questions. Even talking about them left Nicholas heavy with fatigue.

Deiter shoved the stethoscope back into his pocket. "Would you like me to notify the bishop or the Vatican?"

Nicholas laughed. "Am I that bad?"

"I'm just trying to be helpful. Don't you have a family?"

"My family would be gone now," he said quietly.

"There must be someone. The nurse tells me that you cry out every night for Galina."

"Do I?" His voice cracked. "That was my mother's name."

"Let me send for her, Nicholas."

Cold sweat dampened his neck again. He turned toward the sun-blessed mountain slopes, streaked now with more glistening pink trails—their peaks capped with billowy white clouds. Far beyond the Alps lay the seacoast town on the Baltic Sea where he had grown up. Again bittersweet memories rushed him, the face of his widowed mother pushing away the years. It had been a harsh boyhood. His mother barely eked out a living, rarely complained, always smiled. He winced at the vivid image—a gentle, worn-out face with deep ridges by her faded blue eyes and a softness around her mouth.

He remembered the rough hands, the curved back, the

gold-tinted rosary that she hid in her apron pocket. Galina had wanted him to be a priest. Years later when he became a staunch Communist, he had tried to turn her in; but at the last minute party loyalty lost out to her love for him.

"There's no need to contact anyone, Deiter. No one."

"Then I'll send my findings to the doctor in Sulzbach. It's professional courtesy. Besides, you know Johann is an old colleague of mine."

Nicholas heard a measure of respect in Deiter's voice and a hint of disappointment as he mused, "Johann could have been a great surgeon. He gave up so much for so little."

"Did he?" Nicholas asked. "What about the skiers and hikers who owe their lives to Heppner's search-and-rescue team?"

"He's genuinely concerned about you, too."

"Doctor, he's more concerned about losing his chess partner."

Eschert's smile turned whimsical. "You're still good for a few games." As he stood, he pulled a pair of bright red socks from his pocket and dropped them on the bed. "Johann sent these for you."

Nicholas smiled as he fingered them. "It's a joke between us. He calls them the mark of a bishop."

"So he told me. I'll be in to see you in the morning. We'll talk about more treatment then."

"No, I've decided to leave today, Deiter."

Eschert controlled his agitation. "You're not strong enough to climb that mountain."

"I'll rest in Brunnerwald a few days. But I must get back to Sulzbach. I have work to finish." *A confession to make. A letter to write. A replacement to find. Another game of chess to play.*

Eschert's voice slipped to anger. "You're a stubborn man."

"As you are, Doctor. You've done your best."

"I'll be here, available when you need me, my friend."

Nicholas's banter turned serious. "And if you need me—"

"I'll remember that, Father Caridini." Deiter twisted the doorknob. "Are you certain there's nothing I can do for you?"

For a moment Nicholas considered confiding in the

doctor and confessing the deception that blotted his soul. He hesitated a second too long. The door opened and closed.

Alone, Nicholas lay against his pillow twisting the lapel of his silk pajama top. How could he tell the people in the village he was dying? Or merely confirm what they already suspected? Should he tell them at once and confess that he had deceived them? He ran his hand over the pouches beneath his eyes and tugged at the skin flaps. Would even his mother recognize him with his hollow cheeks and sallow skin? Everything inside Nicholas clamored for the chance to return to his native land. But Austria was his country now. His burial ground.

A tap came at the door. Before Nicholas could respond, a young man in white entered, grinning, a razor and basin in his hand. "I'm Herman. I'm to spruce you up a bit before you go home," he said cheerily. "Doctor's orders."

Herman skidded across the room and cocked his head. "Guess you don't like the open-back hospital gown?" he teased.

"I don't." Nicholas brushed his hand against the blue pajama top. What he didn't like was being depersonalized, robbed of control. He had become, after all, a modest man cloaked in simplicity and secrecy. He dared not bare his back or soul to anyone.

In swift, jerky motions the orderly lathered the prickles of a beard on Nicholas's chin. As he came down with the razor blade, Nicholas stiffened at the memory of a sharp knife in his own hand.

Moments later Herman slapped aftershave lotion on Nicholas's smooth cheeks. "Somebody meeting you?" he asked. "If not, I'm to see you to the train. Dr. Eschert's orders."

"That won't be necessary." To prove his point, Nicholas forced himself to stand on unsteady legs. He braced himself against the bed and swallowed his pride. "If you'd get my clothes—"

Herman cut across the room in four quick steps, youth in his favor. He yanked the clerical garb from the closet and picked up the Roman collar and black shoes from the shelf. When he turned back, he said, "I'm sorry, *Pfarrer*. I didn't know who you were."

*No one does,* Nicholas thought as he discarded the black socks and laid out the bright red ones to wear. *No one ever will.*

Marta Zubkov walked alone, undisturbed by the crowds milling along the Maria-Theresien Strasse. She had left her comrades in Eisenstadt, insisting that they travel to Innsbruck separately. Werner Vronin and Yuri Ryskov had argued heatedly against it, but when the elusive Peter Kermer failed to arrive on time, she went on without them.

Now she had two days for window-shopping before she met the others, forty-eight hours to gaze at the pretty clothes she longed to possess. On impulse she stepped inside the nearest shop and allowed herself the luxury of holding a sea blue gown against her leather jacket. Marta flushed as it fell softly with the curves of her body; she smiled at her mirror reflection, pleased with the transformation. Behind her the saleswoman with the upswept coiffure held out a silk mocha brown dress. "Perhaps this one," she suggested. "It accents the color of your skin and the golden glow in your eyes."

The harsh lines around Marta's mouth softened. "It's so expensive," she whispered. But she knew it was the perfect gown to impress the aide from Mitterand's cabinet or the staid Dudley Perkins in London.

"Try it on," the woman offered.

Marta calculated the hidden funds at the bottom of her pocket, money that was not her own. Her lifelong contempt for capitalism and Western culture, her hatred of the bourgeoisie class, wedged their way into her thoughts. The old party hard-liners opposed the fashionable clothes and the Porsche mentality of the rich. But she must own this dress—must hide it at the *pension* that she kept here in Innsbruck. At thirty-eight, with the threat of exposure always stalking her, she wanted just once more to have something that made her feel beautiful.

In the dressing alcove, she kicked off her boots and baggy pants and dropped the leather jacket on top of them. As the clerk fastened the dress at the neckline, Marta admitted to herself that it made her look feminine, attractive, desirable. Forty minutes later she left the gallery, nylon panty hose twisting against her ankles, two-inch heels squeezing her feet. Her whole personality felt uplifted by the mocha dress and the seductive quality of the wide-brimmed hat that tilted toward her dark-lashed eyes.

She left the main boulevard and cut along a side street to the hair stylist and from there to a city park shaded by towering trees. An elderly couple made room for Marta on the park bench.

As they sipped their cups of *Kaffee mit Schlag*, the woman asked, "Are you traveling all alone?"

Marta smiled at the woman's lifted brows. "Yes, but I'm meeting friends in a day or so and going on with them."

Right now *her friends* were conferencing with a Croatian minority near Eisenstadt, mapping out a takeover plan for Yugoslavia that would put that still war-torn land under Russian power again.

Marta turned her eyes toward the Alps, to the higher peaks where the snow never melted. "I so enjoy your mountains."

The woman nodded. "You're a tourist then? British?"

*Yes, that's the passport I'm using this trip.* "I'm on staff at a private girls' school near Kensington."

Her English accent was a good cover for a Russian agent who had just fled across the border to escape the fragile Serbian peace. But the older woman's curiosity turned to a musical ensemble preparing to play—four musicians in lederhosen and colorful Tyrolean vests, a chubby-faced violinist in the foreground. As the Strauss waltz filled the air, Marta's thoughts drifted back to Peter Kermer and their escape into Burgenland.

She had met Kermer five hours from the Austrian border. He was a tall, powerfully built man with curly brown hair and dark eyes that never smiled. When she caught a glimpse of the Star of David dangling against his bronzed skin, she feared he might be an Israeli agent, an imposter carrying Peter Kermer's papers. Yet the man used the right codes, the exact identity. She had to trust him; he knew the safest route to Burgenland. But when they missed their intended border crossing and ended up in Hungary, he refused to turn back. Instead, he led her across miles of Hungarian farms into Burgenland. *Odd*, she thought again. *Wouldn't the real Kermer know that I was in command? That I—Marta Zubkov—gave the orders?*

The woman beside her nudged Marta as a priest walked wearily toward the bench across the walkway from them. He was coughing fitfully, his fist pressed against his mouth. "He doesn't look well," the old woman whispered.

The priest slumped down—his back toward the bridge over the River Inn. He crossed his long legs, his foot trying to move to the beat of the music. Marta's fixed smile faded as he lifted his ashen face and mopped his brow. Through her dark sunshades she recognized that familiar face—so drawn and taut in illness now. She bent the brim of her hat lower so he wouldn't recognize her.

*Nicholas. Nicholas Trotsky!*

Her senses quickened. The remembered scent of Nicholas's spicy aftershave filled her nostrils, tantalizing her, the recollections wafting through her mind like autumn leaves caught in a skittering breeze. Her eyes teared, blurring his once-handsome features. The hairs on her skin prickled the way they used to when he pulled her to him. She could still recall the feel of his tweed jacket against her cheek, the strength of his body, the warmth of his lips on hers. And she could hear the sweet, hypnotic promises that he had made so long ago. The broken promises.

Fifteen years of missing Nicholas, of burying and reburying him—only to find him here in Austria! Alive! When threats of recall to Moscow had erupted, he had spoken of going back to Innsbruck and taking Marta with him. She was twenty-three then and madly in love with the striking, handsome Trotsky—Captain Trotsky when she met him—a KGB colonel when he disappeared. She never questioned his frequent trips out of East Germany, never doubted that he would come back again after he hunted down the American agent Crisscross.

Now she studied Nicholas leaning against the park bench, his thin face pinched, those sad eyes turned her way. Still the man across the walkway gave no sign of recognition. Had she been mistaken? Yes, that was it. She was imagining the impossible.

Finally the priest stood—tall like Nicholas had been—and walked slowly away. He stopped to smile at the violinist and to slip a schilling into the man's hand. The smile belonged to Nicholas.

Marta followed at a distance, cursing the new shoes that cramped her feet. She lost him in the crowd and then spotted him again resting by a lamppost. She forced herself to pass him and waited in an alcove until he had the strength to go on.

The rest seemed to renew him. As he neared the station, his pace quickened. Marta boarded the commuter train and took the compartment just beyond his. She sank into the cushioned seat and cried as they sped toward their destination.

At three they reached the village of Brunnerwald nestled in the foothills of the Alps. Brunnerwald! The place where he had once hidden. *Where he still hides,* she thought bitterly.

Again Nicholas's energy level seemed to build as he turned onto a narrow cobblestone road and made his way toward the blue-and-white *gasthof*. Marta ducked behind a tree as the door swung open.

A young woman greeted him warmly. "Oh, you're back," she exclaimed. "But you're exhausted. Come in. Come in." She pulled Nicholas gently inside.

Standing those few yards away, Marta knew that Nicholas was no stranger in Brunnerwald. The pain of his rejection intensified. *Why? Why?* she cried. *Why did you leave me?*

Hours later in the seclusion of her *pension* in Innsbruck, she placed a call to her old "Kremlin" contact. When he came on the line, she pressed the phone against her ear with her slender, nail-polished fingers. "Dimitri," she whispered, "I've just seen Nicholas Trotsky."

# Chapter 1

Lyle Spincrest rode the underground toward downtown London, his attention only vaguely on the swaying motion and rattling sounds of the speeding train. For all the labels that he wore—thirtyish and analytical, industrious and capable, attractive and available—he still wanted more. He despised being pigeonholed on the job as Dudley Perkins's boy. But not for much longer—not when he had the good fortune to know that Dudley Perkins had started to play with fire, and her name was Marta Zubkov.

Perkins, a scrawny man with listless eyes and a thin smile, held the safety of Britain in his hands and held the position in MI5 that Lyle coveted. As the train sped along, Lyle sat erect, eyes forward, his mind set on charting a course for the future, his narrow, tanned hands gripping the briefcase on his lap.

Routinely he spent Saturday mornings playing a fast game of tennis with Drew Gregory at the American embassy, but Gregory had gone on holiday with his family. Or was he keeping a low profile, trying to avoid the black cloud that hung over his career with American Intelligence?

Gregory's downfall infuriated Lyle. He found Gregory a likable man—serious, well-groomed, highly motivated. In the next few months, Lyle intended to replace Dudley Perkins as the director at MI5—to become the youngest man ever to hold that post. Currying favor with an American contact like Gregory would be advantageous. But that plan had come to a screeching halt when a scandal erupted in CIA circles—the Breckenridge affair, they had called it—with Gregory smack in the middle of it. Still Gregory knew the political scene and the intelligence community in a way that could prove useful. Spincrest smiled inwardly. The next month of Saturdays were already marked off on his calendar—tennis and lunch at a local pub with Gregory.

The underground train vibrated as it roared into Victoria Station. Sparks flew on the tracks when it jolted to a stop. Lyle sprang to his feet, determined to be first when the creaking doors slid open. As he stepped out on the platform, he brushed past an older passenger, gave her a polite but charming smile and made the escalator in quick, easy strides.

As he came up to the street level, he shoved his rimless glasses back from the tip of his nose, sidestepped a London bobby, and struck out at a rapid pace for the office. The empty building would allow him time to search the locked files for Dudley Perkins's chart. All he had to find was one major flaw in Dudley's character, one blot in his otherwise impeccable record. Lyle's pace quickened, his solid thumping footsteps beating a determined tread on the sidewalk.

London—his town, his future, his walking turf. He had cut many a well-worn path strolling through this magnificent, bustling city, her history as old as the Roman Empire. Again this morning he had taken his usual 5 A.M. constitutional with a three-minute time out by the River Thames. He enjoyed the imposing view of the Houses of Parliament and Big Ben and, beyond that, Buckingham Palace. Lyle took pride in British ceremony, often watching the dismounting of the Palace Horse Guards or the Chief Warder doffing his Tudor bonnet in a nightly ritual at the Tower of London.

He'd grown up on the south coast of England near Dorset, but his boyhood dream had been to live in London and be the king. He was almost ten when he realized that he had no royal blood flowing through his veins, no ties to the palace, no chance at kingship, nor any right to unearned riches.

The bitterness of that childhood moment still galled him. So he took second best, capitalizing on his photographic memory and keen intellect. It paid off with top scholastic standings at the university and a tap on the shoulder by British Intelligence. By Dudley Perkins himself—a senior officer at the time. Now for seven years, Lyle had thrived in the good life under Perkins's tutelage: the Victorian theater, shopping at Harrods', bidding at Sotheby's auction house for Perkins's wife—and browsing alone among the priceless paintings at Somerset House, a long-stemmed umbrella in one hand, a black derby in the other. He basked in this city where he had equal footing with Churchill and Chaucer. But he longed for position or knighthood that would grant him entry into No. 10 Downing Street and even into Buckingham Palace.

He stopped abruptly, shocked at his own carelessness. Perkins always insisted on a "dry-cleaning" trek between points A and B—going in and out of department stores and tube stations to avoid any surveillance. He immediately feigned interest in the shop to his right.

Reflected in the window was a Gothic spire-topped church. It reminded him of Westminster Abbey which housed the Tomb of the Unknown Warrior. Carved on the crimson-poppy grave marker were the words: "They buried him among the kings." Lyle felt that way about himself. He coveted the recognition that would allow him to be buried with the kings. But for now he wanted only to outlive Dudley Perkins.

A half block later Lyle turned into the building, the rumble of double-decker buses and commuter tubes behind him. He passed the Saturday security and let himself into Perkins's drab office with a duplicate key. As he shoved the door open, Perkins swung around to meet him, his leather chair squeaking in the stillness.

Lyle froze. Perkins glared back. Miles Grover, a note pad stretched out over his bony knees, shifted nervously. "Did you forget the courtesy of knocking, Mr. Spincrest?" Dudley asked.

Lyle wiped his mouth with the cuff of his Austin Reed suit.

"You weren't expecting us, were you, Spincrest?"

"No, sir. I thought I'd catch up on some back work."

"I thought you reserved Saturday for a game of tennis."

Lyle wiped his mouth again. "Gregory is out of town."

"It's just as well. Avoid him for now. That Breckenridge affair damaged his career. I'd just as soon we didn't take sides."

Grover twisted uneasily, his gray moustache twitching. "It was Porter Deven's suicide that stirred the fire."

"Grover's right. But find yourself another tennis player."

Lyle forced a grin and nodded. "Yes, sir." He hesitated in the doorway. "Should I leave, sir? I could come back later."

"When we're gone? No, you're here now. Come in. You might as well explain why you came down here on a Saturday."

Lyle slithered across the room to a chair and put his brief-case on the floor beside him. If Perkins pushed him too far, he'd mention Dudley's recent dinners with Marta Zubkov or maybe suggest that Mrs. Perkins was concerned about Dudley's long hours at the office. "I h-had work to catch up on," he stammered.

Unexpectedly, Perkins tossed a manila file across the desk. "I have a more urgent problem. Top Secret," he said. "Read it. You'd be in on it by Monday anyway."

Frowning, Lyle scanned the pages. "Nicholas Trotsky?"

"An old KGB agent—before your time. We thought he was dead until an hour ago when one of our agents called. Trotsky was a cold-blooded political assassin. He took out three of our agents. Almost got the prime minister shortly after the Olympic games in Innsbruck."

"Twenty years ago?"

"About then."

Grover folded his hands over the note pad. "Trotsky dropped into oblivion a few years later. Rumor had him dead in an avalanche in Austria. That's when we closed our file on him, but the Americans didn't accept that rumor. They lost some good men, too."

"Why the concern now, Perkins?"

"Trotsky was just spotted in Austria."

"And you still want him, sir?"

"Moscow will. And the Americans, particularly your tennis-player friend. Seems like Trotsky was Drew Gregory's nemesis." Perkins's thin-lipped smile widened. "Gregory is bound to get involved. We'll send out some bait. To Langley first and then to their new man in Paris. If they nibble—if they go fishing and Gregory shows up, we'll send someone in, too. *You* maybe."

Lyle shuddered. "You can't do that, sir. Austria is out of our jurisdiction. MI6 would be right on us."

"Lyle's right," Grover said. "We'd have the prime minister and the Joint Intelligence Committee on our heads at once."

"It'll be an unofficial investigation. I'll send someone to Brunnerwald just to keep us informed."

Grover Miles groaned. "Who can we trust?"

"Uriah Kendall's grandson."

"Perkins, he won't do any favors for MI5."

"He will to keep his grandmother's reputation unsullied."

"Threaten him that way, and what's to stop him from turning on us when he gets to Brunnerwald?"

"That's a possibility, but I'm counting on the Kendall loyalty to protect one of their own."

"I think he's preparing for the Tour de France. Isn't that what it said in last Sunday's news. He can't be hired on."

"Stop worrying, Miles. We won't hire him as an agent. No money will pass between us. We'll keep no records. Leave it to me. I'll check with Jon Gainsborough. He's sponsoring Kendall's team."

"Gainsborough, the steel magnate?" Lyle asked.

"Yes. He likes to keep on my good side. I'm certain I can persuade him to release young Kendall for a few days. It's just a simple matter. He'd go to Brunnerwald and keep us informed on Drew Gregory and any CIA activity. He may recognize Gregory."

"Then Gregory would know him."

"All the better. Just a casual meeting. Kendall could really keep us informed then."

"If Trotsky's alive and gets wind of it, the boy's dead."

"Miles, we will have to take that risk. Trotsky is one KGB

agent that I want credited to our account—not to MI6 or the Americans." He looked back at Lyle. "I'll send you to Brunnerwald as young Kendall's contact."

Lyle squirmed. "What makes you so certain that Trotsky is still alive?"

Perkins's gaze steadied. "You're wondering who my informant is?"

"Yes, sir."

"My dinner partner of a few weeks ago—the woman you saw me with." Dudley's eyes turned hard. "She thinks me a lonely man. I'm depending on that. She may prove useful to me, Spincrest."

Lyle wiped his mouth with the cuff of his sleeve again, his dreams of promotion slipping away. He waited, the tips of his ears turning scarlet as Perkins glanced down at Lyle's briefcase and said, "Her name is Marta Zubkov."

🕉🕉🕉

In Paris Troy Carwell ran his hand over his freckled forehead, spreading the strands of gray across a bald spot that constantly irritated him. As the new CIA station-chief, Carwell was anxious to curb the rumors surrounding Porter Deven's death, but all he had done was inherit the troubles. Morale had hit a new low since Porter's suicide, friction among the men mounting. One resignation from a good case officer lay on Troy's desk, and threats against Drew Gregory erupted daily.

No one was thanking Gregory for the spy hunt that exposed Porter's years of treachery. Carwell didn't blame the men. The intelligence community preferred Company loyalty to public disgrace. Porter's espionage had rocked Langley and the White House, but the vibrations seemed worse here in Paris.

Carwell's contacts with French Intelligence had snarled like a traffic jam. In spite of Porter's miserable personality, he had been well received in Paris. Now Frenchmen at the top worried lest their own classified documents had slipped through Porter's hands. But Carwell wanted an open policy with the host government. It had worked on his last two assignments. In Paris he had quickly identified himself as the new CIA station-chief and established an office at the embassy on Avenue Gabriel. But so far, all efforts to promote friendly relations with French Intelligence had met with chilling results.

Now Brad O'Malloy had just informed him that Zachary Deven refused to leave the embassy until Troy met with him. Troy forced a smile at the man across the desk, trying to hide his displeasure at Brad's stone-washed denims and arrogant smirk. They shared a thinning hairline and a liking for Gucci watches but little else.

"Porter Deven's brother, eh? What's he doing in Paris?"

"He lives here. Still owns the Devenshire Corporation, an export-import business that depends on government contracts."

"So what does the man want from me, O'Malloy?"

"He wants his government contracts back."

"That's not my problem."

"Zachary Deven thinks it is."

As Brad plopped his feet on the desk, Carwell made a mental note for a memo on dress code and ethical courtesy, his third one in this first month on the job. He prided himself in his own neat appearance and expected it of his men. Troy always wore a rich brown Canali suit or English tweeds and topped that off with a beige Hathaway shirt, a matching silk tie, cap-toed oxfords, and a dab of Tiffany scent, his wife's latest choice.

He glanced at his Gucci. "How did he get past the front gate?"

Brad's sleepy eyes drooped at half mast. "He knows the system. If you send him away, he'll be back. This thing with Porter is ruining his business. Porter set him up with government contracts. With Porter dead, State has canceled all of them."

"Not our fault."

"He thinks the Agency is behind it. The brothers weren't close. No one was with Porter. But Zach ran a clean business."

"He didn't know Porter was selling out his country?" Brad's lips went white. "None of us did."

"Have him talk to someone else here at the embassy."

"He insists on a CIA contact. Says he has a right to talk to the man who turned his brother in—and that's Gregory."

"That's impossible. Drew's on leave with his family. After that, Langley wants him back at the embassy in London until things calm down here. Then he'll resign."

"But not before they figure a way to promote Gregory for toppling Porter. Zach Deven won't like that. Nor will I. I'm surprised they didn't make Drew station-chief here in Paris."

Coldness crept into Troy's answer. "My appointment was Langley's decision, not mine. My wife went ballistic when she heard we were moving again."

"I didn't know there was a woman alive who wouldn't want to live in Paris."

"Nothing against Paris, but Maggie had her fill of me heading up stations in Moscow and Latin America. We'd just settled into life in Washington, and then this came up. Maggie knew about the scandal. She didn't want me to get involved."

"Sorry about that, but what do I tell Porter's brother?"

Troy straightened his tie. "Okay," he said. "Let's give this Zachary Deven ten minutes of our time and get it over with."

🌑🌑🌑

Zachary Deven was a squat man with a build like Porter's, a bit on the stocky side. The long nose and taut lips resembled his older brother's, but Zach's hair was thicker and wavy, the dark eyes anxious and direct—not a crystal blue like Porter's had been.

Deven bypassed the formal greeting and said angrily, "Mr. Carwell, your Agency is ruining me. My brother is dead, my wife went back to the States to avoid any more humiliation, and now you're trying to wreck my business. I have nothing left."

Carwell motioned toward a chair, but Deven was too agitated to notice. "Carwell, Porter gave you the best years of his life, and now you've accused him of treason."

"Porter sold classified documents to other countries. Mr. Deven, your brother made that choice."

Zach's burgundy turtleneck sweater seemed to choke him. "I don't believe you, Carwell. You're making all of this up."

His tongue-lashing stilled for a moment as his gaze darted around the room, settling on nothing until he noticed O'Malloy. "Why, O'Malloy?" he asked. "Why my brother?"

"No one knows why. But there was a woman."

Zachary looked surprised. "Porter and I never discussed his personal matters, O'Malloy. We didn't get on that well, not even as kids. But I felt sorry for him, what with Dad always booting him around and kicking the gut out of his dreams. It was Porter's idea to start a corporation in Neuilly. I ran the business; he just had an office there. Said it was safer in his line of work."

"His line of work damaged our national security."

"But why cancel my government contracts?"

"We had nothing to do with that, Deven."

"And nothing to do with Porter's death? Gregory pushed him to it. It was Gregory, wasn't it? They were always at each other. Just like Porter and Dad. I'll find Drew," he muttered as the red emergency phone on Carwell's desk flashed.

Troy signaled to O'Malloy. "Check with the ambassador or State Department. Try and get some answers for Mr. Deven."

Zach shook off O'Malloy's strong grip and glared back at Carwell. "If you don't get me some help, I'm ruined."

As the door shut behind them, Troy took his Langley call. He listened intently to Chad Kaminsky's voice on the other end, then said, "Trotsky? Nicholas Trotsky still alive?"

"Yes, that's the report just in. We want him, Carwell, and we want him before the Russians get to him." Chad's voice turned raspy. "Trotsky was KGB—may still be. As far as I'm concerned, the KGB is just as active as ever. And if they're not, we can't risk them rising from the ashes."

"Sounds like the old PHOENIX PLAN, eh?"

"That's about it."

"Chad, I filed that Phoenix report back in the days when I was a case officer in Moscow."

"I've got it right here in front of me. A splinter group from the old guard trying to reinstate the iron-fist system."

"Maybe I mentioned it in my report—they got their start toward the end of Leonid Brezhnev's days. Gorbachev was a member of the Politburo by then. Maybe he blew the whistle."

Troy heard the rattling of the pages over the wire as Kaminsky flipped through the file. "Nothing about Gorbachev or Brezhnev here," Kaminsky said.

"Just guesses, Chad. And Nicholas Trotsky was a star in the ranks back then. He could have been in on the planning stages. A good choice actually. Quite capable. Definitely revolutionary."

"Then you knew him, Troy?"

"No, I just knew his reputation. Rumor had Trotsky being recalled around the time two of the leaders of the Phoenix-40 were executed for a failed coup. Maybe his disappearance was planned after all."

"No wonder the Russians want him. And if Trotsky turns out to be an agent-in-place, Gregory will go bananas. We've got another problem, Carwell. I had Langley patch me through to Dudley Perkins, British Intelligence in London. He'd been trying to reach me. Seems like he's well informed about Trotsky's reappearance."

"Do we sit tight and wait on Perkins?"

"No, Carwell. I want to keep one step ahead of those boys in London. Put someone on it right away. Send him to Brunnerwald."

"I should go. I'm best informed about the Phoenix rebellion."

"We can't spare you, Carwell," Kaminsky warned. "You're just getting a handle on things there in Paris."

Troy let that one pass—no need to confess that morale was lower than when he first arrived. "Brad O'Malloy is available. What do you think?"

"No. Send Drew Gregory. Gregory's the only one we have who can recognize Nicholas Trotsky."

"Gregory? I thought we had him blacklisted."

"Send him."

"Should I brief him fully on the PHOENIX PLAN?"

"No, let's hold back on that. Going after Trotsky will be motivation enough for him."

When Troy hesitated, Kaminsky asked, "Should I fly over to Paris and head this one up?"

"No, Kaminsky, I can handle it."

🜲🜲🜲

By three o'clock Brad O'Malloy was back in Carwell's office for their third confrontation that day. He came into the room pulling his charcoal gray sweater over his unbuttoned shirt, slumped into a chair uninvited, and flashed a brash grin.

"Didn't you read my memo?" Carwell asked.

"The dress code memo? Figured you wouldn't implement that until after the embassy party on Saturday."

Troy eyed the younger man, his voice calm as he asked, "What are you wearing to the dance, O'Malloy?"

"It's black-tie all the way."

"No jeans? Then you won't mind being in proper attire when you report to work tomorrow. Make that a suit and tie."

In the thirty-second silence that followed, Brad reversed his slouched position and planted his scuffed gym shoes firmly on the floor. He offered a mock salute and said, "I hear you. Will you and your wife be at the dance?"

"Maggie considers that part of the good life in Paris. Almost as good as living at the de Crillon for another week or two. By then she'll drag those well-slippered feet of hers at the thought of moving to a more permanent residence in the suburbs."

Their tension eased. "What do you have for me, O'Malloy?"

"I turned Zach Deven over to State Department, and I got a lead on Drew Gregory. He's on vacation."

"Be more specific."

"I put in a couple of calls to London. Gregory's secretary said the family was vacationing together. Vic Wilson narrowed it down to doing Austria, city by city."

Carwell suppressed a snarl. "We need Gregory in Brunnerwald now, not ten days from now."

"Wilson said Gregory had tickets for the Vienna State Opera."

"We're getting closer. But when? Today? Next week? It'll take too long to check the registry of every hotel in Vienna."

Brad nodded. "Gregory's courting his ex-wife these days. She has lavish tastes, so it won't be the cheapest hotel in town."

"Any suggestions on finding him, O'Malloy?"

"We could send Vic Wilson to Vienna, but he hasn't been well lately. Or we could try to reach our agent in Burgenland. Peter Kermer came out of Sarajevo and Zagreb a couple of days ago, but we can't be sure of him now."

"Can't be sure? What's that mean, O'Malloy?"

"Kermer mixed up his codes in his recent transmission to us."

"He's still our best shot?"

"I think he is, Carwell."

"Then get in touch with him."

O'Malloy hedged. "The order should come from you, Troy, but there may be a bit of a problem. Gregory ran into trouble a few years ago in Croatia. Kermer is Croatian, and if he knows anything about Gregory, he may not help us."

"We'd pay Kermer well. What's wrong?"

Brad hesitated as if he were chewing on the possibilities. "I'm still worried about those mixed codes. Kermer's maternal grandparents were Russian. We encouraged him to work for the Russians when they contacted him—to pass information on to us."

"He's an agent. He understands the risks, so what's wrong?"

"Kermer may be running double. I've got this gut feeling that he's feeding everything we say back to Moscow."

Troy swore. "A double agent?"

O'Malloy's answer seemed slow and drawn out. "Not if he's the real Peter Kermer. But this is our chance to find out."

# Chapter 2

Drew Gregory stood in the Imperial Hotel lobby, hands thrust deep into the pockets of a dark blue blazer, his thoughts on his ex-wife, Miriam. She was late coming down from her room, so characteristic of her. It didn't matter. Except for the muddy, gray waters of the "Blue Danube," she had loved this trip to Vienna. He hadn't seen her so happy since those early days of their courtship. Drew's spirits had lifted. The despondency over Porter Deven's death and his own rejection by the Agency were almost forgotten in the pleasure of Miriam's company.

He had chosen this hotel for its elegance and fine dining, knowing that Miriam would glory in its luxury and in the magnificent paintings that graced the walls. But what delighted him most was the music of Haydn and Schubert, Mozart and Strauss wafting softly throughout the hotel.

Reflected in the sparkling window glass, he saw his daughter approaching. As she blew on the back of his neck, Drew turned and smiled down at her. "Good morning, Princess," he said. "Where's Pierre?"

"Getting directions to the Prater. He wants us to see Vienna from the Ferris wheel."

"Count us out. Your mother never liked flying."

"Poor Pierre is sick of museums and palaces. He refuses to see another one." She looked apologetic. "He wants to take in the U.N. and see whether it compares to the one in Geneva."

"Pierre's choice," Drew said curtly.

Drew's son-in-law was a strongly opinionated man, Swiss to the core. Pierre was anti-political and too often anti-Drew, yet he was tender and committed to Robyn.

"You're not offended, Dad? About Pierre, I mean. He's been good about the trip so far. He just doesn't want to see another stuffy art museum." He heard the childlike concern in her voice.

Drew still had trouble thinking of Robyn as twenty-six, married, happy. The image of Robyn at ten had fixed itself in his mind, constantly reminding him of the lost years of her childhood. He knuckled her chin. "I love you, Robyn."

"I know."

She lacked Miriam's exquisite beauty, having been burdened with the Gregory features. But on Robyn they held a special charm, an innocent beauty—wisps of auburn hair that always seemed windblown, honest, bright eyes, the pudgy nose that she hated, a slim figure that even surpassed Miriam's.

"Princess," he said, "after last night I planned on a more quiet morning for all of us."

"You do look tired, Dad."

"I should. Your mother and I tried to waltz the night away."

"Even after Pierre and I left you in the lobby?"

"Yes. When we got our second wind, I suggested slipping away to the Cafe Sacher for *kaffee* and the *Sachertorte mit Schlag*. After that we went dancing, Viennese-style."

"All night?"

"Almost." He glanced eagerly toward the grand staircase, anticipating Miriam's graceful descent.

"Dad, would you like some more time alone with mother?"

"You wouldn't mind?"

"I have Pierre's company. He'll be relieved that we don't have to stop at every art gallery in the guide book." She reached up on tiptoe and kissed Drew's cheek. "Be good to Mom. Pierre and I will be watching you from the top of the Prater."

"And you two save some energy for the opera this evening."

She gave Drew a Gregory grin. "Pierre's been fussing about the cost of my gown for days, but wait until he sees me in it." She cocked her head. "Why don't we meet at St. James Cathedral at two? We promised Mother we'd go to Dorotheum's auction with her."

"A-ha! I knew we had a reason for coming to Vienna."

His teasing netted him a hug, and then Robyn was off, running to meet Pierre. As she reached him, she turned back, pointed toward the stairs, and blew Drew another kiss.

Miriam came lightly down the spiraling stairway, that precise half-smile touching her lips. Drew pushed his way politely through the crowd, his heart racing as he assisted her down the last two steps. "Did you sleep well, *liebling?*"

"Soundly, but not long enough."

Her lilting voice sounded like the old days. If only she would stay on in Europe. Then he could persuade her to marry him again.

She looked around. "Don't tell me Robyn isn't up yet."

"Up and gone. Pierre wanted to show her Vienna from the Prater. I told her you'd prefer a view from the ground level."

She feigned a shudder. "You're right. I hate heights. But, Drew, why did the children go off on their own?"

"Robyn and Pierre are not children, Miriam," he reminded her. "They had some things they wanted to do without us."

"Drew Gregory, was that your idea?"

"No—Pierre's. But I wanted to spend more time alone with you."

He braced for her fury. Instead, she returned his smile. "You old romantic, you. But you didn't forget, did you? I have an appointment at the auction house this afternoon."

"But your morning's free?"

"Yes. And my evening is full." Her face brightened, aglow like her reddish brown hair without a gray strand in it. "I've looked forward to going to the Vienna opera with you for years—ever since Paris."

"Yes, I promised to take you on our honeymoon, but I got tied up in Paris. Married to the Agency, you called it."

"It's all right, darling. We're here now. Finally."

"Breakfast?" he asked.

"No. I ordered in my room. I knew you'd be up early downing three cups of black coffee with your head buried in a newspaper and your get-up mood at sub-zero."

As he led her away from the stairs and out of the flow of traffic, she asked, "You did warn Robyn to be back in time for the opera, didn't you? We bought new gowns to wear."

He rubbed his jaw, groping for a smooth answer.

"Oh, Drew, you didn't forget to pick up the tickets?"

"No, I bought four of them. Two in the fourth row. Two farther back. First class all the way."

Her frown threatened trouble. "Robyn will be disappointed if we don't sit together."

"It was our daughter's brainstorm."

His fingertips barely touched her smooth ivory cheek, but he pulled back quickly. He had promised himself not to force his way. Their times together were too fragile, too special for anything to disturb them. Just being with Miriam was thrill enough.

Her half-smile widened. "So what did you and our daughter plan for us this morning? Or—did you arrange something?"

"I hired a *Fiaker* all to ourselves."

"A what?"

"Horse and carriage. You saw them yesterday, remember?"

On impulse she kissed him. "How perfectly old-fashioned."

"A queen's carriage for a lovely lady."

"You are sweet." She blushed, her deep-set eyes no longer wounded when she watched him. "You sound like the old Drew."

"The one who rushed into the Metropolitan Museum of Art and swept you off your feet?"

"I thought I swept you off yours. You stood there gawking at me like a schoolboy."

"You were so beautiful, Miriam."

"And you were a handsome rogue then."

"And now?"

"I haven't quite decided. You're different somehow."

*Guarded*, he thought. *But, no, I was always guarded until I met you.* "I would have married you that day, but you told me we needed a blood test and had to observe a three-day waiting period."

"We could have run off to Elkton," she reminded him.

"Or flown off to Las Vegas." He'd been the one who had opted for a simple ceremony by the local justice of the peace, anything to avoid a church full of strangers. He had to get back to Europe on an Agency assignment, so he had promised Miriam a honeymoon in Paris. A selfish move on his part that left them with only Uriah and Olivia Kendall standing up for them. Drew hadn't even invited his own mother, and she lived barely three hours away. Fresh regret nagged him. *"Liebling*, you deserved better than a civil ceremony."

"I've always regretted not having a church wedding."

"The next time—"

"No next time. I have an art gallery to run, remember?"

All too well he remembered Miriam's Art Gallery in Beverly Hills. *Odd*, Drew thought. *Miriam's career stands between us now. Thirty years ago it was my job, my secretive life with the CIA.*

"I'm sorry, Drew. That was unkind." Abruptly she twirled around in her sleek black frock. "Do you like it?"

"It's lovely, but you'll need flat shoes."

"I thought we were going in a carriage."

"We are, but we'll browse around a bit, too."

She tugged at a black pearl earring, the one he had given her so long ago. "I can't believe my good fortune. Yesterday it was castles. Tomorrow more museums. Oh, Drew, I am so happy."

"That's what you said in Salzburg, Miriam. And Linz."

"And Innsbruck. And we still have Graz to see." Her eyes twinkled. "I can hardly believe we have ten more days left in Austria. Let's not let anything spoil our time here."

"You worry too much, *liebling*."

"I'm afraid Pierre's vacation will end before we see it all."

He hated telling her, but he wanted to be honest. "My leave is almost over, too."

"I thought you were retiring."

"Langley and Troy Carwell have tabled my resignation—until the Porter Deven affair dies down."

"Now who's worrying?" she asked, her fingers cupping his chin. "Let's not be sad. I love it here in Austria."

"Enough to live in Europe? Switzerland maybe? Or Scotland?"

A shadow crossed her face. "Please don't rush me," she whispered.

"I won't. You're worth waiting for."

She turned embarrassed. "I'll get my sandals."

Drew watched her go, her figure as lovely as it was the day he married her, her face and body sculpted like the goddess in one of the paintings she admired. He had rushed her then and married her six weeks after meeting her. Gregory the bachelor robbing the cradle, his friends had said. It wasn't quite like that. Miriam kept assuring him that eleven years didn't make that much difference. Did they now?

He ached thinking about the ugly divorce, the sixteen silent years without Miriam. He had grown old without her. No, that wasn't quite true. He was still physically fit, vital and virile with hair only sparingly gray, his features firm and strong, his awareness of beautiful women easily rising to the surface. But those years had been lonely ones; he never loved anyone the way he loved Miriam.

❦❦❦

Miriam leaned against the cushion of the black, gold-trimmed carriage, sitting so close beside Drew that there was no space between them; yet she sensed his distance, his vulnerability. Always before, she had needed Drew. Now she felt he needed her strength in this scathing aftermath of a spy scandal.

Dear Drew. He seemed to be bearing the brunt of another

man's treason. Yet he had made every effort to make this trip to Austria special for all of them. But the foreign headlines kept blaring the scuttlebutt from Washington. Congress and the FBI were screaming for the closure of Central Intelligence, arguing that in this post-Cold War era, intelligence gathering belonged exclusively to the military— not, as the article suggested, in the blundering hands of the men holed up behind the gates of Langley.

A year ago, even two months ago, she would have cheered the suggestion, waved a flag at the dismantling of Langley. It sounded so much like her own arguments in those first twelve years of a rocky marriage. No, no. The first five years had almost been smooth sailing. Drew's absences on Agency assignments were often softened by eleven red roses sent from around the world to remind her that he loved her no matter where his career sent him.

Back then it had been the Cold War, two superpowers vying for supremacy, both countries confident that a spy lurked in every corner. To Miriam, it seemed that Drew had committed himself to winning the battle on his own; she constantly pulled at his loyalties, wanting him solely for herself. Patriotism be hanged.

*No,* she thought as she stole a glance at him. *You have always been patriotic. That's one of the things I admire about you.*

Impulsively, she leaned over the open carriage and beckoned to a street vendor. "One rose," she said. "A red one."

She pressed the schillings into the young man's hand and turned back to Drew. Deftly, she tucked the rose into the lapel of his dark blazer. *The twelfth rose,* he had always called it.

"What's that for?" he asked, pleased, surprised.

"For you. The twelfth rose," she whispered.

A rare grin cut across his face from ear to ear.

"Drew, you are a handsome rogue when you smile."

The driver in bright-colored pants and fancy vest lifted his rein. Drew signaled him to wait. Then he called out to the flower vendor, "Eleven more roses. Red ones for my wife."

*His wife.* Yes, to Drew she was still his wife. This marvelous mosaic of a man—she wanted to brush his cowlick into place, those gray-streaked strands of hair that gave a boyish quality to his sixty-plus years. That firm Gregory profile—Robyn looked so much like him. His serious face that found it so hard to break into a grin, still smiling. The gentle, tender Drew who wanted desperately to regain the past, the lost years that would never come back. She wanted to recapture them as intensely as he did. She turned away quickly and gazed up at the towering spiral of St. James Cathedral, a magnificent edifice, the focal point in old Vienna.

Drew leaned closer. "When we get back from our ride, I'll take you to the top. There's a winding staircase inside with 343 steps. You'll feel like you're on top of Vienna."

"Oh, Drew, I'd never make it."

"Ready now, sir?" the driver called down from his high seat.

"Ready. I want my wife to see the beauty of Vienna."

The driver tipped his bowler hat and mumbled, "She'll miss it. She has eyes only for you."

They felt the jolt as their driver tapped his horse with a gentle prod. The carriage moved away slowly from the curb, stirring a slight breeze that caught the man's wide flowing tie.

"Miriam, this is so much nicer than my first visit to Vienna. St. James was a bombed-out mess then, the roof shelled so badly it had burned and collapsed."

She met his gaze. "I'd forgotten you were here after the war."

"Before your time, *liebling*. You weren't even old enough for bobby socks."

"You were young, too. A brash eighteen if I remember correctly."

"Brash and cocky at the privilege of driving an army officer around on a recovery detail, searching for lost and stolen art collections. So many of them belonged to Austrian Jews. They lost everything they had. A whole generation of culture destroyed."

He pointed to one renovated building. "Vienna was ravaged by aerial bombardment in the last days of the war, but the Viennese are a tough lot. They came back up fighting and rebuilt their city."

Miriam felt as though she had stepped back in time—listening to the clippety-clop of hoofs—as their horse-drawn *Fiaker* took the bend in the Ringstrasse ahead of the trolley car. Everywhere she looked, old Vienna was clothed in Baroque and Gothic styles: the opera house, the elegant parliament buildings, and expensive boutiques. Their driver stopped at their command, allowing them to leave the carriage for a closer view of art galleries and later for a quick glass of lemon and water to quench Drew's thirst at a quaint sidewalk cafe table shaded by a parasol.

At two thirty they reached St. James Cathedral again, their noses sunburned, their fingers entwined. As Miriam stepped from the carriage, the horses twisted in her direction, and the driver once again tipped his bowler hat.

"Mother. Dad. We're over here," Robyn called.

Robyn and Pierre ran toward them—Pierre tall and athletic; Robyn small beside him clutching his hand. Miriam felt a catch in her throat just watching them—Pierre's dark sable eyes, Robyn's brilliant ones, their faces vibrant with the joy of each other.

"We were getting worried, Mother," Robyn chided. "You're supposed to be at Dorotheum's auction house in thirty minutes to bid on some paintings for your gallery."

"Yes, dear," Miriam said as she allowed her son-in-law to take her packages and the wilting roses. "I guess we are late, but your father and I had a simply marvelous time."

# Chapter 3

As Peter Kermer stole along the brick walkway to the crowded condo on the outskirts of Vienna, he feared that Jacob and Hannah Uleman would be gone. Dead before fulfilling their lifelong dream of going back to Israel. But when he rang the bell, he felt a surge of relief. Hannah's lace curtains still hung in the window.

The door creaked back, and Jacob Uleman's gray head appeared cautiously in the narrow opening. His aged face lit with pleasure when he saw Peter. "Shalom," he cried out.

"Shalom, my friend."

The firm handclasp turned to a warm embrace. The two men stepped back and studied each other. There were tears in the older man's eyes. "And what do I call you this time?" he asked.

"Peter. Peter Kermer."

Jacob chuckled heartily as he pulled Peter inside. "That's a bit more Jewish."

Peter sighed. "It's a far cry from Ben Bernstein, but someday I'll be me again—back with Sara and the family permanently."

"Go back now, Ben—Peter," Jacob urged. "Before something happens to you. Sara would be lost without you."

Pain shot along the nerve tracks to Peter's ears, his jaw almost locking. "You worry too much about me, Jacob."

"You're practically family. Come, travel with us. We'd like your company." He pointed to the boxes on the table, the stacks of castaways on the floor. "I'm taking Hannah to the Holy Land. We don't have many years left."

"None of us do," Peter told him. "The Messiah is coming back again. I'm convinced of it."

"And someday He'll plant His feet on the Mount of Olives once more. I want to be with Him when He does that."

"So do I."

"Then why travel so much, Peter? Where was it this time?"

"Sarajevo and Zagreb."

"In a land of ethnic cleansing—why do you take such risks?"

"For our nation. For Israel. Our people always face the threat of annihilation, Jacob."

Jacob's shaggy brows notched together, his pale, pensive eyes sad. "Germany all over again? Your grandfather always said it could happen in some other country."

"My grandfather was right. It's erupted again in Eastern Europe and the Caribbean." Peter looked into the old man's honest face, not daring to admit that he had just escaped with his life by skiing over the higher slopes of the Slovenian Alps.

Jacob shuffled over to an open crate and plowed through it, his gnarled hands digging furiously. He came back clutching a tattered picture from his boyhood. His stubby finger pointed to each face. "That's me," he said, adjusting his dirt-streaked glasses. "Runty and half-blind even then. And this one was your Uncle Josef the year before he died at Dachau."

Jacob's finger rested on the handsome figure to the right, the eyes a fiery brown beneath a visored cap. "That's your grandfather, Peter. Aaron was a good man. You're like him."

Peter looked away. He had no real memories of the dark years when the Nazis invaded Austria, only the disturbing stories handed down by Jacob Uleman. The Fuhrer being welcomed to the Heldenplatz, those destined for Dachau watching helplessly; Jacob's friends rounded up for the extermination camp; Peter's grandfather smuggling his pregnant wife to safety and then going back to Vienna to risk his life for freedom. How many times Jacob had rehearsed the unbelievable war count. In a country synonymous with music, the somber dirge of death took over—more than a hundred thousand Austrians executed or killed, almost three-fourths of them Jews, Peter's grandfather among them.

Rough fingers caressed Peter's face. "Aaron believed in fighting for freedom. You are like your grandfather, Peter. He would be proud of you." The hands slipped away. "But if the Serbs knew you were Israeli Intelligence, they would have executed you."

"No one found out."

Jacob peered out the lace curtain. "Were you followed here, Benjamin?"

"No." He'd made certain of that, but the real Kermer had followed him through the back alleys of Zagreb. Ben had crouched in the midnight darkness, his ears tuned to the rustling in the bushes. When he heard the scream and someone running away, he had crawled back. "Jacob," he said quietly, "a few days ago I found the real Kermer dying from stab wounds in his chest."

"Were they meant for you, Benjamin?"

"Possibly."

"Was he Croatian? Serbian?"

"I don't know, Jacob. That's what I expected, but when I leaned down beside him, he was gasping in a mixture of German and Russian. He looked so pathetic, so frightened. He begged me to get him back to Vienna. 'Who are you?' I demanded. 'Austrian? KGB?'"

"Did he tell you?"

"He gave me a twisted smile and said, 'Marta. Find Marta. She's waiting for me at the hotel—go. Stop her.' I searched his pockets, grabbed his identity papers, and headed for the hotel he had mentioned."

Jacob's eyes sharpened. "You're a fool, Peter."

"What choice did I have? Kermer had followed me, Jacob. I didn't know why. There was little I could do for him, so I got out of there. When I found Marta, she accepted me as the real Kermer."

He hesitated, then risked saying, "Marta seemed angry

that it had taken me so long to link up with her. Even threatened me with recall to Moscow. I played along. We needed each other to cross the border safely into Austria."

"Russian! How long can you fool her, Peter?"

He shrugged. "Long enough to find out whether the old Russian hard-liners are trying to set up another Communist state in Yugoslavia. If they are, we must stop them."

Peter rubbed the week-old start of a beard. "There's another problem, Jacob. Kermer had contact with the Americans, too."

"Russian? American? Croatian? Which side was the man working?"

"I don't know, Jacob. All of them perhaps."

"Peter, go home to Sara while you still can. You would be safer in your father's clothing business."

"I was never very good at that, Jacob."

"But you had an eye for style."

"Did I?" He brushed at his threadbare jeans. "My sights were on flying and foreign languages, not on dressing up, Jacob."

Hannah came slowly into the room with a tea tray, her still-beautiful face marred with wrinkles, those blue eyes alert and twinkling. "Benjamin," she said delightedly.

"Peter Kermer this time," Jacob corrected.

The twinkle dulled. Peter went to her at once, took the tray, and kissed the well-rounded cheeks. "Shalom, my lovely one."

"My dear Benjamin! Are you flying to Jerusalem with us?"

Gently, he led her to a chair. "I'll come later."

"Oh, Benjamin, will we be happy there?"

He had to calm the alarm in her voice. "Sara is."

"Is it peaceful?"

"It will be when the Prince of Peace comes."

"But not now?"

He caught Jacob's warning frown. This was not the moment to speak of the constant feuding over boundary lines. *All right,* he thought, *I will not tell Hannah about the military buildup, women and men preparing to defend Israel.*

Peter held Hannah's trembling hands, smiling to reassure her. "You will be peaceful, Hannah, no matter where you are." He thought of the Torah, the prophets, the Christ. "They are readying the temple, Hannah. Everything is being prepared for its restoration. It's a good time to be going home."

"Overnight with us and tell us more. Your room is ready."

He patted her hand. His little room, the room she always kept for him. Aaron Bernstein's picture still hung above the bedstead—a tie with the past for Jacob and Hannah, a haunting image for Peter. He glanced at Jacob. "I don't want to impose."

Uncertainty shadowed Jacob's face. "Nothing must threaten our departure next week."

"I won't let it. I'm just here looking for an American."

"Would the real Kermer know him?"

"I don't think so. But apparently Kermer took orders from the Americans before. Paris gave me a detailed description of the American. I'll have to risk finding him. He must be a music lover, Jacob. He's in Vienna to attend the State Opera."

"If there's music in his heart, then he's all right."

"It's urgent that I start calling the hotels."

Worry lines pinched Jacob's mouth. "Everything you do is imperative and top priority. The phone's in the kitchen, same place it's always been. Hannah and I will go on packing."

Peter touched the old man's shoulder. "Jacob, I wouldn't ask this favor, but I'm pressed for time."

"And you need a safe place to be. What better refuge than with friends? Isn't that right, Mama?"

As Hannah fretted with the teapot, Peter said, "The only way to keep my cover is to do what Kermer was asked to do. I must put the American in touch with Paris."

The pinched mouth tightened. "There'll be no mercy if Moscow or the Americans catch you impersonating Peter Kermer."

"For the sake of Croatian Jews, it's my job to find out what Kermer was doing in Zagreb—and why he had both Russian and CIA contacts." He squeezed Jacob's shoulder as he passed him. "As soon as I find the American, I'm leaving for Innsbruck to meet Marta."

The two stared at each other forlornly. "If something happens to you, Benjamin Bernstein, what must I tell Sara?"

"That I loved her. Now—just give me a few hours, my friend."

Jacob's hoary head bobbed. "Yes, of course. Your grandfather gave me much more than a few hours when he saved my life."

❂❂❂

Robyn Courtland felt growing concern for her mother as they took their seats in the front of Dorotheum's auction house. Miriam seemed rattled as the auctioneer put a Titian painting on the auction block, but by the time the van Gogh went up for bidding, she was showing that competitive spirit that had gained her recognition on Rodeo Drive. She was in control again, her eyes sharp, her face determined. Her bids went into the millions with a calculated risk that shocked Pierre and amused Drew.

Even when she took the bid on the van Gogh and also on a Rubens and a Cellini sculpture for her clients back home, she seemed lost in her art world. Not until a seascape by a lesser-known artist went on the block did she seem aware of Drew again. It was a striking painting, the artist's sensitivity coming out in a rich blend of color and bold lines. "Do you like that one, Drew?"

"Powerful."

"Don't tease me."

"I'm not. I really like it."

As she bid on it, Robyn said, "Mom, that's not on your list."

A smile formed at the corner of Miriam's mouth. "It is now. Your father likes it."

When the auction ended, Miriam whispered to Robyn, "I'll be awhile with the shipping arrangements. So be a dear and take the seascape back to the hotel for me. Drew and I'll come later."

Outside, Pierre's frustration mounted as he tried to fit the painting into his car. "This isn't even safe—trying to transport this painting to Geneva. Why didn't your mother ship it to Beverly Hills with the rest of her purchases?"

"The painting isn't for her customers. This one's for Dad."

Pierre frowned. "This masterpiece is worth a mint."

"So Mother's opinion of Dad is rising."

"It'll be out of place in your Dad's dismal flat."

"I think it will perk it up."

"You're pushing too hard. You'll only get hurt trying to be a matchmaker. Drew is going to start running the other way."

"Well, he didn't fuss when Mom ordered a new lamp for him and a throw rug for the hearth. I think he was rather flattered."

"And once Drew gets a blazing fire going, the hot cinders will burn holes in it."

"You're an old grump this afternoon. Even a new rug with holes in it will remind him of Mother. So stop fussing."

"I don't like sharing you with others."

"What are you going to do when we have children?"

"That will be different." He slammed the lid closed and grinned. "Let's get back to the hotel. At least we have a few hours before the opera."

"We're having dinner with the folks."

"No, we're not. I'll leave a message at the desk for them. We'll have dinner in our room—just the two of us."

All the way to the hotel, he alternated between whistling and grinning. "If your parents get back together, we won't have to chaperone them again. We could go on our own holidays."

"Oh, Pierre, you know you've had a good time."

"Much better than I expected. Your folks have been civil."

"They're in love."

"That's what you call it?"

"That's what I'd like to call it."

As he pulled in front of the hotel, two bellhops rushed toward the curb. "Want to trust them with the painting, Robyn?"

"This goes straight to the hotel vault until we leave Vienna."

"Can you manage it?" Pierre asked as he handed it to her. He looked worried now, hesitant, as though he shouldn't leave her walking around with an uninsured painting. He nodded toward a stranger watching them intently. "Will you be all right?"

"I'm fine, Pierre. He's probably a guest at the hotel. He's just watching us because we look so ridiculous arguing about this picture. You park the car, and I'll put this under lock and key."

He surprised her with a kiss. "I want him to know you're mine."

"That man over there? I'll tell him in case he asks."

She smiled sweetly at Pierre and then managed another smile for the bellhops as she struck out for the door without them.

The attractive man—and he was striking, thirtyish—stepped forward politely and opened the door for her. She couldn't help noticing his strong physique; he was muscular and well built with broad shoulders and dark, curly hair. His sport shirt lay open at the neck, his skin bronzed by birth and by the sun. She blushed thinking, *Don't follow me. Pierre won't like it.*

But he did follow her inside. She glanced up at him again, touched by his sad, unsmiling eyes and the gold Star of David that hung on a thick chain around his neck. He gave her a quizzical nod, then turned, and went straight to the reception desk. When she looked up again, the stranger was speaking hurriedly with the concierge and pointing her way as he did so.

❂❂❂

When he reached the State Opera House, Peter felt stretched to the limits in his rented tuxedo, and he was annoyed by his failure to locate the Gregorys. He had left his watch post just long enough to place an international call to his wife to explain his unexpected delay in getting home. "Days, weeks maybe," he had told her.

"Is that so different?" she had asked.

The call went into overtime as he tried to dry Sara's tears long distance—and to defend his unexpected business trip into Austria. The bitter taste of homesickness and the constant risk of never making it back to Sara and the children dug at the pit of his stomach. He despaired at the possibility of never seeing Sara again, never holding her in his arms. And he hated missing his son's bar mitzvah. *Odd*, he thought now. *The more Jewish I become, the more alive I feel toward the living Christ.*

"Can't you fly home with the Ulemans?" she had begged.

No, he couldn't leave now. Perspiring as the call ended, he'd gone immediately to the reception desk. "I'm trying to reach Drew Gregory," he said.

The concierge beamed—with a distinctive nod toward the clock. "The Gregorys left for the opera a half hour ago."

Had Peter been on the phone that long with Sara? "Then I need a ticket for the opera."

The animated smile again, this time restrained. "Tickets are sold out for premiere showings well in advance." A troubled gaze took in Peter's sport shirt and jeans. "Black-tie is *de rigueur*."

Compulsory. Peter ran both hands through his hair. "There must be some way to obtain a ticket. A scalper perhaps?"

"At the State Opera House?"

The polite rebuke angered Peter. "Where can I get a tux?"

The rented suit, it appeared, was easier to obtain than an opera ticket at a bargain price. Peter tried a number of people on their way inside, a steady stream of couples in formal attire, the women in breathtaking gowns. Finally, an enterprising young man agreed that he could wait until another night to hear the stirring music of the Vienna Philharmonic Orchestra. But seconds ticked away as the man held out for a better price.

In spite of the added delay, Peter placed another call to Israel to reassure Sara that he loved her. When she heard the orchestra music, she said, "I thought you were working, Benjamin."

"I am, Sara. I'm looking for a friend here at the opera."

"You'll be careful?"

"Yes. For you."

Twenty minutes later Peter made his way into the magnificent hall and discovered that he had bought standing space only. He tugged at the sleeve of his tux, a fraction too short for his lanky arms, and leaned into the railing in front of him. The second call to Sara had muted his fury, and the splendor of the Austrian symphony orchestra resounding through the auditorium mellowed him. He didn't know whether he was listening to Mozart or Strauss, Schonberg or Schubert, but the music was stirring, comforting.

At intermission he worked his way through the milling crowd searching for the Gregorys, an impossible task he admitted to himself unless he recognized Drew Gregory's daughter. He tried to remember the face of the young woman at the hotel door, an oversized seascape in her hands. Her eyes had been clearly blue, the hair an auburn red, her voice musical as she thanked him for opening the door. With a quick stop at the reception desk, he had her name as well—Robyn Courtland, Drew Gregory's daughter.

In his haste, Peter bumped the arm of a stranger. The scowl belonged to a woman with dark hair and eyes. "Excuse me," he said.

At the sound of his voice, another young woman looked up. He would have kept on moving except for the eyes. There was recognition in them as she smiled up at him. Brilliant blue eyes and that same auburn hair. He did a quick appraisal with his father's eye for style. She looked stunning in her jade shantung evening dress—the kind Sara would love—off the shoulders, sleeveless, a narrow gold band at her neckline. "The lady with the painting," he said lightly.

"Hello there. I see you like the opera, too."

Smiling, Peter lifted her hand to his lips and brushed it with a kiss. "All Vienna loves an opera."

"You're Viennese?"

"Just visiting as you are." He kept the same lightness to his voice. "You're Drew Gregory's daughter. I'm Peter Kermer."

"You know my father?"

"I've been looking for him."

"He's here tonight. Over there—with Mother and my husband."

Drew Gregory turned as they approached, a tall, striking man with streaks of silver through his hair. Mrs. Gregory was more beautiful than the daughter—gorgeous actually in her black sheath dress with a diamond choker at her slender neck.

"Dad," Robyn said, "this gentleman's been looking for you."

Peter sensed immediate caution in Gregory's guarded handclasp. "I'm Peter Kermer, Mr. Gregory."

"What can I do for you, Kermer?"

He returned the bluntness to save time as the guests began filing back into the hall. "You're to call Troy Carwell in Paris."

Robyn's smile vanished. Gregory's wife pulled nervously at a teardrop earring. The son-in-law put a protective arm around each woman. Only Gregory's expression stayed placid, his voice monotone as he asked, "And how would you know that, Mr. Kermer?"

"Carwell asked me to locate you."

Again Peter tugged at his sleeve, wishing that he had taken Jacob Uleman's advice. *Don't get involved, Peter.*

Quietly, Gregory said, "Mr. Kermer, tell Carwell I'll check back with him after my vacation."

"He was a bit more anxious than that, Gregory."

Gregory maintained his remarkable calm as he turned to his ex-wife. The look that he gave her seemed to say, *You've never looked more lovely.* He smiled as he touched her hand. "Miriam, just say the word, and we'll go on with the rest of our trip."

Tears brimmed in her enormous eyes.

Only a few stragglers remained in the lobby. Peter didn't like what he was doing to this family. As Benjamin Bernstein, Sara's husband, he wanted to tear Troy Carwell's request into shreds, walk back to his budget standing space in the opera hall, and recapture the peace he had felt there.

"Herr Kermer," Miriam said, "I'm going back to the concert. Would you be so kind as to show Drew to the nearest telephone?"

Peter lifted Miriam's hand to his lips. "I'd be happy to."

As the others left, Gregory asked, "Who are you, Kermer?"

*Good question,* Peter thought. *I'm not certain who Kermer really was, but he was too young to die. Right now I'm just a CIA errand boy running with the wrong I.D. papers. But I'm glad that we part company here.* He gambled that Kermer had liked opera and said, "I'm an opera fan like yourself, Gregory."

"Do you know what Carwell's call is all about?"

"No, I don't." And he was glad to be ignorant this time.

He tried to recall Austrian courtesy and found himself doing a quick click of the heels and then was not certain he had made the right move. "Good luck to you, Gregory."

🕸🕸🕸

Drew reached Carwell at the Hotel de Crillon in Paris located only steps from the American embassy. "Gregory here," he said.

"So Kermer found you?"

"Isn't that what you intended?"

Carwell's hesitant drawl came over the wire, "That's what we wanted, but we weren't sure about Kermer."

Out of the corner of his eye, Drew watched Kermer disappear into the great auditorium. He blinked against the brilliant glow from the chandeliers. Kermer, he decided, looked harmless enough. "Apparently, he's okay. He told me to call you."

"Langley's order. Sorry about the vacation, but we've got some information that should interest you. We think an old KGB colonel may be rising from the ashes."

Drew's temple pulsated. "You've found Nicholas Trotsky?"

For the next twenty-five minutes they argued strategy in

pursuing him. Last sighted: Brunnerwald. Time element: urgent. Drew's replacement: none. Drew's retirement: deferred.

The intermission was long past when Drew slipped into his seat beside Miriam. He reached out and squeezed her hand. She pulled away as he leaned toward her and put her finger to his lips. "Don't, Drew. Don't say anything. It's okay. Let's just enjoy our final evening together."

# Chapter 4

The Gregorys stepped from the State Opera House into a balmy, star-studded night. Even at this midnight hour, the Viennese were crowding into coffeehouses and pastry emporiums and some into the casino as though the evening had just begun. At the Karntner Strasse intersection, Miriam took Drew's arm as they strolled toward the hotel. Surprised, he put his broad hand around her gloved fingers and squeezed them.

"Are you hungry?" he asked glancing her way.

"No—just tired."

Her face was a shadowed image in the street lights, but he didn't need brilliant lamps to unveil her beauty. He'd spent the last three weeks memorizing each delicate feature, eager to build into his lifetime of remembering how lovely she was. He would need these memories in Brunnerwald. Dark-lashed eyes, well-set and enormous. Soft, curving lips. Her finely sculpted bone structure. And smooth, ivory skin that glowed like a Rembrandt painting.

Nothing seemed to mar her loveliness except that precise half-smile that first rose like a barrier between them in those early years of marriage, Miriam's way of warding off the pain each time he went away. And now he was leaving her again, an unforgivable act. They walked in step, hips touching, arms linked. But he couldn't read her thoughts nor be certain that this togetherness was not her dramatic effort to comfort Robyn.

"I thought you would tell me not to leave," he said.

"And start that old feud between us?"

"I would have welcomed it this time. I want to be with you."

"Aren't you in enough trouble with the Agency, Drew?" Her words drifted. "If you refuse to obey this order—"

"I have nothing to lose."

"Your name. Your honor."

She was right as she had always been. It was the loss of face with the Agency that had left him despondent. Did the Company think he had reveled in exposing Porter Deven's treason? Miriam's arm tightened against his, her gentle touch reassuring him that she was standing with him.

"Drew, do you think Troy Carwell is giving you a chance to step back into their good graces?"

"Carwell couldn't care less what happens to me. To him I'm nothing but the sum of what the men are saying about me."

"Just do your best."

"I've always done my best, Miriam."

"I realize that now," she said softly.

"But by going away, I'm losing everything I really want."

"You'll still have Robyn," she whispered. "And we'll keep in touch, Drew. We'll still be friends."

Drew wanted more than friendship. He focused his attention on Robyn and Pierre strolling ahead of them arm in arm, their heads touching. "I've ruined all your plans."

"We've had some wonderful days, Drew."

"No regrets?"

She didn't answer. The hum of voices around them and their own footsteps broke the stillness. Finally, as they neared their hotel, she asked, "Drew, how did Peter Kermer find you?"

"I don't know."

"It's as though the Agency knows your every move."

"It seems that way." He squeezed her fingers again. "Vic Wilson is the only one who knew we were coming to Vienna."

"It's not like Vic to give your plans away."

"I know, Miriam." He didn't tell her that he had called Vic

from the Opera House. Instead, he turned and studied her lovely face once more. She met his gaze, her eyes dark in the evening shadows. "You're beautiful, *liebling*," he said.

She laughed. "You can't see my wrinkles in the dark."

"I don't even see them in the daylight."

"Can you tell me anything about your trip, Drew?"

"You know that I can't. It's that old code of silence."

She rested her head on his shoulder. "I've always hated that."

They drew apart as they walked through the half-empty hotel lobby to the staircase. "May I see you to your room, *liebling?*"

"I know my way. Let's just say goodbye here."

He swallowed. "I wish it could have been different, Miriam."

She peeled off one glove and touched his cheek with her soft fingers. "We had three weeks—much longer than I thought it would last. Promise me you'll come back safely."

"I'll call you as soon as I get back to London."

Her hand was on the banister now. "In a week?"

"A week. A month. I never know how long I'll be gone."

"I'll be flying to California before you get back. Robyn will keep me up on how you are and what you're doing."

Drew watched her go up the stairs—slowly, gracefully, her long, black gown swishing at her slender ankles. He stood there long after she disappeared as though he could will her back. As he turned, he tore off his bow tie and shoved it into his pocket.

The shops in the lobby were all closed. Even the bar was closing, but he dragged in and asked, "Can I still get a cup of coffee? Black and scalding."

The bartender shrugged impatiently. "We're closed."

But instead of rinsing the coffeepot, he slid an empty cup across the counter and filled it with the end of the day's supply.

Drew took it gratefully and sipped.

"Problems?"

"My holiday is ending. That's all."

"We've got company," the bartender said.

Drew glanced up as Robyn took the stool beside him, her eyelids red and swollen. She had slipped out of her jade evening dress and looked blanched and childlike in Pierre's bulky white sweater. It hung loosely over her narrow hips, almost down to the knees in her patched jeans.

"I thought you went to bed, Princess."

She ran her hand through her sleep-tangled hair, tousling it even more. "I couldn't sleep. Not after Pierre and I argued about your leaving. So I went to Mother's room, and all she did was cry. That's when I really got mad."

Tears splashed down her cheeks. "Then I tried your room."

"No one's home there," he teased gently.

"Why, Dad? Things were going so well for you and Mom. Why are you packing up and running off?"

"I'm sorry, Princess."

"Is that all you ever say?"

"I have a job to do."

"Must you always choose Company loyalty over honor?"

"That's not fair, Robyn."

"That's what Pierre says—that I'm being unfair to you."

"Don't tell me Pierre's rooting for me this time."

"He says you wouldn't leave unless it was important."

"And you don't believe him?" He took her elbow. "Come on, Princess, let's find a spot in the lobby and talk."

They spent half the night there arguing back and forth, Drew's excuses empty and useless as he fiercely defended his decision to leave Vienna. Finally, he said, "Robyn, I'm backed against the wall. I want to leave the Agency with my head up."

"They're just using you. You're a scapegoat for them."

Sharply he said, "Princess, don't make me feel any worse. Is failure what your God wants for me? The bottom of the barrel. Disgrace at the end of a long career."

Her Gregory jaw jutted out. "Dad, all God wants is for one stubborn man to follow Him."

"I'll keep that in mind. But after the Porter Deven affair—"

She softened even more. "Oh, Dad, I got you into that."

"Because you asked my help for a friend. No. Sooner or later we would have known the truth about Porter."

"Then you don't blame me?"

For a minute he couldn't answer her. He'd spent the last several weeks with the European Division against him and Langley blocking his retirement. "Sweetheart, I—I never blamed you."

"I thought you were going to retire."

"Soon. I promise." He stood. "We've got to get some sleep, Princess. Someday I'll explain."

"Will you be safe?"

He had almost lost his life the last time he faced Nicholas Trotsky. "I'll be all right," he said.

They mounted the stairs together and paused in front of Robyn's suite. "Dad, if you're blacklisted with the Company, why is Troy Carwell sending you on this assignment?"

"I'll know soon enough." He leaned down and kissed the top of her head. "I'll call you when I get back."

"But we'll see you in the morning."

"Afraid not. I'm catching a 6 A.M. train."

"I know. But Pierre insists that we drive you to the station."

🏺🏺🏺

Every muscle in Drew's body ached as they stood at the train terminal. He'd had little time for sleep and barely enough time to pack, shower, and slip into clean slacks and a powder blue polo shirt before meeting his family for the ride to the station.

He gave Miriam a sleepy smile. Except for the dark circles that crested under her eyes, she looked stunning in a slim Italian creation, an Austrian cashmere wrapped around her shoulders. Her gaze flicked past Robyn and Pierre toward the streamlined train that waited to whisk Drew away.

"Maybe your train will be late," she said.

"Wishful thinking will do us little good, Miriam. Austrian trains are notoriously swift, clean, and on schedule."

She nodded, allowing her focus to settle on the three-generation family standing beside them; the buxom, gray-haired grandmother clutched a bouquet of spring flowers in her hands.

"You forgot my flowers," Miriam teased.

Drew looked around, trying in vain to spot a flower vendor on the platform, yet knowing that even roses would be meaningless now. "Miriam, I'm sorry," he said.

"You've perfected that speech."

"I mean it."

She twisted the jeweled watch on her narrow wrist. "Yes, you've always meant it," she said softly.

As more porters shoved past them with luggage carts, Drew glanced around and was startled to see Peter Kermer pushing his own luggage trolley. Their eyes met across the station platform, Kermer's sad eyes narrowing as he recognized Drew.

"What's wrong, Dad?" Robyn asked.

He wanted to say, *Troy Carwell has sent a watchdog to make certain I reach Innsbruck.* But he didn't want to worry the family any more. "I hate goodbyes," he answered.

"Odd," Miriam told him. "You've perfected them, too."

To keep from snapping back, Drew searched the crowd in vain for Kermer's broad shoulders and curly, dark head, but Kermer had merged with the crowd and disappeared.

*Einsteigen, bitte.* All aboard. The garbled announcement boomed overhead in German, English, and French. The squawking boarding call broke up the family gatherings around them, filling the air with, *"Bis bald.* Goodbye. *Auf Wiedersehen. Gute Reise!"*

Drew leaned down. "I love you, Miriam." She stiffened as he kissed her cheek, the bond that had been growing between them threatened.

He turned to Robyn and knuckled her chin, not daring to risk a hug that would bring more tears to those puffy eyes. Grabbing his luggage, he hurried off refusing to face the rebuff in Pierre's eyes another second.

"Dad."

Robyn's voice. He turned, his arms too full to embrace her.

"I'm frightened. I don't want you to go."

"I'll be all right, Princess. Be back before you know it."

"But if something goes wrong—"

He saw fear in her eyes. "Nothing's going to go wrong."

"That's what you said when we left for Austria."

"It worked. We've had a marvelous time."

"Until last night at the opera. The whole thing is my fault."

"You didn't know what Peter Kermer wanted."

"I didn't even know who he was."

"I'll be back. I promise."

Drew pushed toward the train, his progress slowed by the grandmother with the flowers shuffling ahead of him. He'd gained another five yards when he heard Pierre's footsteps pounding over the platform behind them. Pierre jerked the heaviest suitcase from Drew's hand. "Let me help you," he said.

His glance was curt. "Drew, I know you're in a bind, but why didn't you wait until the trip was over? I hate to see Robyn and Miriam so disappointed. If something happens to you this time out, Robyn won't forgive me for letting you go. She's afraid the Company has set you up."

"Pierre, I have a job to do."

"I've got that one figured out. There's an article in the morning paper about a Nicholas Trotsky resurfacing in Austria—in the village of Brunnerwald. It aired on BBC last night, too."

"Perkins or Spincrest," Drew said angrily. "Who else would have leaked that to the news media? Don't let the girls hear it."

"I won't. But I want answers. They're putting this Trotsky in the same category as Carlos the Jackal—the terrorist linked with the Munich massacre and the hijacking of an Air France."

"That's not Trotsky's style. I doubt the two ever met. Trotsky liked to work alone. . . . Don't get involved, Pierre."

Pierre kept pushing. "Carlos was the son of a Venezuelan Communist, a privileged rich kid who turned terrorist, his actions mostly linked to the Middle East. So who is this Nicholas Trotsky? Drew, I can read between the lines. You're involved somehow."

Tight-lipped, Drew said, "He's a former KGB agent."

"Where's Brunnerwald, Drew?"

"A couple of hours from Innsbruck."

"Miriam thinks you're heading for Paris."

"She'll worry less that way."

With growing impatience, the conductor waved Drew toward the boarding steps. Pierre stayed on Drew's heels. "Answers first, Drew. This Nicholas Trotsky—any relation to the notorious Leon Trotsky?"

"No. Same last name. No relation, but they were both revolutionaries. And until that phone call at the opera house, I thought they were both dead."

Pierre carried the luggage on board and swung it into the storage rack with minimal effort. Then he faced Drew, his honest features quizzical. "If Trotsky is as dangerous as Carlos, why are they sending you in alone?"

"The only thing that links Carlos and Trotsky is the fact that they both dropped out of sight for years. There are only four of us who would recognize Trotsky. Bill Perry and Lou Garver are dead, thanks to Trotsky, and Jay Friberger was incapacitated with a stroke. According to Langley, I'm it."

"If he's in hiding, Trotsky won't welcome your arrival."

Drew leaned his briefcase against the cushion. "Pierre, you need to get off the train. *Now*. Once it gets started, it hits 186 miles an hour. And that's when Robyn will never forgive *me*."

Pierre shouted above the hissing sounds of a train in motion. "If we don't hear from you in a week or two, I'll call Vic Wilson. And then I'm heading to Brunnerwald. You can count on it."

Pierre bounded down the platform steps and pivoted around as the conductor signaled departure.

"Persuade Miriam to stay in Europe, Pierre."

"Impossible. We're driving back to Geneva in the morning. Robyn will fly over to London and see Miriam off at Heathrow. That's Miriam's revised schedule."

The train jolted forward, the wheels grating against the tracks. "Take care of them, Pierre."

"Take care of yourself."

Back at his compartment, Drew groaned when he saw the elderly woman sitting in the seat beside his, the floral bouquet still clutched in her hands. She smiled over the tops of her glasses—her stunted legs swinging an inch from the floor, her fat folds caught in a permanent accordion squeeze.

As he straddled past her, her comical blue hat dipped to the left. Stubby fingers reached up to grasp it.

"Sorry," he said, dropping into the window seat.

She leaned across him and waved. "That's my family."

*Yes*, he remembered. *Three generations of them.*

"They always see me off," she prattled on.

"How nice."

She took no warning from his moroseness.

"I'm Frau Mayer. I'm seventy-four," she announced. Drew had guessed her older by at least three years.

"I'm a housekeeper for a small parish in the mountains. Well, usually just in the summer, but I'm going early this year. My priest is ill. He had to let me go when I turned seventy, and then Father thought up this part-time job. It makes me feel worthwhile again."

"That's nice, Frau Mayer," he said absently.

"It's a good job." He heard the catch in her voice as she added, "It's not the money. It's just being useful again. My children want me to sit home and be a grandmother, but sitting and rocking isn't half as cheering as being useful." She sighed, and the fat pads did a double roll. "But my children worry about me—being up in the mountains for the summer at my age."

Her years weren't that many more than his own. "What's wrong with your age?" he asked.

"I get short of breath. But there's a doctor up there."

Frau Mayer rearranged her bouquet, happily picking at the stems, and then she shoved the flowers toward Drew's nose, smiling up at him. "This is my favorite time of the year in the mountains. They're alive with flowers now—gentianella and Alpine pansies, and before I leave the blue thistle and edelweiss will be in bloom."

Gently, he pushed the flowers away from his face. For a

few seconds he welcomed the steady sound of the wheels gliding across the tracks. Then his traveling companion spoke again. "Was that your family back there at the station?"

"Yes, my wife and daughter. And Robyn's husband."

"No grandchildren?"

"Not yet."

"I have seven, and it's marvelous."

Drew closed his eyes, trying to blot out her chatter. The thought of seven grandchildren overwhelmed him. He was just getting used to being a dad again.

ಅಅಅ

Robyn and Miriam moved closer to the train, close enough to see Drew take his seat beside the elderly woman. They waved, and then before he even had time to press his face against the window pane, the train picked up speed, making the passengers a river of blurred faces. As the train wound its way around the bend and slipped from view, Miriam tugged her soft cashmere sweater tightly around her shoulders.

"Are you all right, Mother?" Robyn asked.

"Yes, of course."

"You're not mad at Dad?"

"Your father has to do what he thinks is right. He gave me my choice, you know." She seemed surprised, delighted. "He never did that before. This time I had merely to say the word, and he wouldn't have called Carwell in Paris."

"Isn't that what you wanted?"

Miriam's response came in a whisper. "I couldn't ask Drew to make a sacrifice like that. The Company is his whole life."

"But they've turned against him."

"All the more reason for him to go back. When he retires, he wants to go out with his head up."

"That's what Dad said." She felt a catch in her throat and swallowed hard. "Pierre said you're going home—that you won't go on with our trip."

"We're all tired now, Robyn. I want a few days in London if you'll go with me. I have a painting to deliver."

"The seascape from Dorotheum's?"

"Yes. It'll look nice in your father's living room."

"And after that?"

"I have a plane to catch."

"You hate flying."

"I'll try not to think about that. I just have to get back to Beverly Hills. I've an art gallery to run. Remember?"

"We'll have a gallery at the von Tonner mansion soon," Pierre said as he joined them. "You could run that one for us."

"That wouldn't be fair to Floy. She's working long hours while I'm gone. When I called her from the room this morning, I told her I'd be home in a few days."

The frown lines at the corner of Pierre's mouth deepened. "Did you tell Floy about Drew leaving?"

"She guessed something was wrong."

"But you said you weren't mad at Dad."

"I'm not angry with him, Robyn. Not this time. I'm afraid I'm still in love with your father."

"Then stay in Europe and marry him," Robyn urged.

Miriam squeezed Robyn's hand and offered a hollow chuckle. "Darling, I said I was in love with him. I didn't say I could live with him."

"Won't you wait until he gets back—just to make sure?"

"Robyn, he didn't ask me to wait."

# Chapter 5

Nicholas smiled as he watched Consetta Schrott kneading bread, the tip of her wide nose and hands covered with flour. Her disappointment seemed evident as she folded the dough over and punched it severely with the heel of her palm. He slid the silver bowl closer to her, and she filled it and knuckled the dough once more before setting it near the stove.

"Father Caridini, you can't leave yet. Preben won't like it," she said. "He'll think I sent you away."

"Preben knows I have to get back to Sulzbach."

"But you didn't tell him goodbye."

"Then tell him for me. Better yet, come up for mass on Sunday. You never come anymore. Your grandparents miss you."

"They should be here living with us. Preben says they're getting too old for another winter in the mountains."

Nicholas laughed. "Your grandfather is as strong as a mountain goat. And I couldn't spend the winter there myself without Ilse. Your grandmama keeps me in *knodel* and *backhendl*."

Consetta wiped her hands on her apron, sucking at her lower lip. Like her grandmother, she was plain and large-boned, tall and solidly built. Locks of soft chestnut hair cascaded over her forehead. She blew at it, then brushed more furiously at the unruly strands with the back of her hand.

To Nicholas, Consetta's easy smile and honest, deep-set eyes offset her plainness.

"What if something happens to my grandparents?" she asked. "What if Erika finds them dead some morning?"

"Erika is a brave girl."

"She's only twelve, Father Caridini. She's too young to be taking care of them."

Again he chuckled, trying to picture Erika taking care of Ilse and Rheinhold Schmid, as hard-working and independent as anyone he knew. "I'll keep my eye on them for you."

"For how long? You're ill yourself."

"Who told you that?"

"No one has to tell me. Look at you. You're getting thinner every day. You've barely eaten anything these last few days."

"I'll do better in the mountains."

"What will they do when you're gone?" she asked.

"Your grandparents?"

"Everyone. They love you up there. Do they know you're ill?"

He saw no point in pretending with Consetta. "Johann Heppner knows. My dear Consetta—we've been friends for a long time."

She nodded. "Eleven years. Ever since my grandparents took me in. You were there then. I don't remember the other Father Caridini—just you. Grandmama always said you were brothers."

*You are my brother.* Jacques Caridini's own words.

"Yes," Nicholas said guardedly.

"I don't believe that anymore."

He stiffened. "Why not, Consetta?"

"You loaned me books to read—from Father Jacques's library."

"And you always returned them."

"I kept one."

Confession? A sin of omission? Was she trying to clear her conscience because he was dying? "I never kept track."

"It was a book about Sicily."

His brows knit. "I didn't realize it was missing."

"I found important papers in it. Father Jacques's baptism

and confirmation records when he was a boy." Her words tumbled out and merged. "He was an Italian, Father Nicholas. You call yourself Austrian. You couldn't possibly have been brothers."

Nicholas sat calmly studying her. Consetta had dreamed of the day when she could leave Sulzbach behind. Move away. Make a living. Be somebody. He had seen her through so many dreams and had been pleased when she had married Preben—the handsome, ambitious Preben. Twelve years older. Heir to the family cheese factory and owner of two *zimmer freis* in Brunnerwald, yet determined to force progress on Sulzbach.

Consetta waited for his answer.

"Jacques was many years older than I am. Years apart like you and Erika. Were you two born in the same place, my child?"

"No," she whispered. "But we are both Austrians—like you claim to be. And I'm no longer a child. I'm twenty-three now."

He could tell by her expression that she no longer trusted him. Yet it was impossible for her to know that he was Russian-born. "Consetta, I am sorry if I have disappointed you."

"It's all right. You had your reasons for lying. And you have been so good to my grandparents."

"Did you find anything else in that book?"

"Just dates. And names. The Sulzbach Avalanche for one."

"He would have remembered that date without writing it down."

"Father Jacques listed the names of those who died in the avalanche. And the names of those who were hurt."

"Was my name there?"

Consetta laid out the pans for the bread, avoiding his eyes. "Your first name was there."

"Jacques saved my life," he said quietly. "Perhaps that was why it was so easy for me to call him my brother. Consetta, look at me." She turned, and he said, "If I promise you that I will right the wrong before I die, will you trust me?"

"It doesn't matter. I just wanted you to know—"

"Does Preben know?"

"No one knows."

Nicholas pushed back his chair and stood, his annoyance controlled. In the old life—the person he once was—he would have acted swiftly, preventing Consetta from telling anyone about him. Surprisingly, none of the old fury touched him now. Consetta had been part of his parish, one of his favorite people in the village. He admired the straightforward woman she had become, but now more than ever he had to return to Sulzbach and tidy up the trail he had left. "It's time for me to go," he said.

"You mustn't leave. I haven't baked the bread yet, and Preben wants you to wait until morning when grandfather brings the milk wagon down. You can ride back to Sulzbach that way."

"And let your grandfather walk?"

"Preben wants you here when we tell him that we can't buy his milk much longer. It's better to buy from the villages that pipe it down the hillside."

"But, Consetta, Rheinhold has no other way to make a living."

She scoffed. "A living? My husband pays him far more than it's worth. Preben insists that my grandparents must give up their old ways and come down to Brunnerwald to live with us."

Nicholas dragged himself across the room to the window. The clouds hung low over the peaks, threatening another spring storm. "They'll never give up the mountain, my child."

"It's their independence they won't give up."

He turned and gave her a ghost of a smile. "I must go. Will you ever forgive me for calling Father Jacques my brother?"

She flew to him, wrapping her chubby arms around his neck. "I don't want anything to happen to you or to my grandparents. Life can be so cruel. So unreal."

"Nothing will happen to us," he promised. "Only good."

As he stepped out on the porch, she handed him a walking stick and said, "Father Caridini, when the time comes, do you want to be buried beside your—your brother?"

He fought the sudden tears burning behind his eyelids. "I can think of nothing I would appreciate more."

🌹🌹🌹

Drew Gregory needed to stand and stretch. He hadn't seen Peter Kermer since the train left Vienna, and with Frau Mayer's constant prattle, there had been no time to search for him. Forcing himself to be polite, he turned to Frau Mayer and said, "I'm going to the dining car. Won't you join me?"

She shook her head. "I'll eat in Innsbruck."

She would be transferring trains in Salzburg as he was. "It'll be a long day. You might as well have breakfast with me."

He offered his hand, and she was finally on her feet walking slowly in front of him. Her gait proved unsteady in the swaying train, her orientation uncertain through the darkened tunnels. Drew took a firm hold on her elbow and waited until they were back into the brilliant sun. He smiled—grateful that fear had silenced her long enough to reach the dining tables.

She let him order for both of them, and they settled into a companionable silence as they ate. But afterward she was embarrassed when he insisted on paying the bill. While they made their way back to their compartment, he looked for Peter Kermer again.

For the next hour, Frau Mayer slept, her head bobbing to the side and those short legs pointing toes down. As the train sped toward the Salzburg station, he took down his own luggage, found a porter, and made arrangements for Frau Mayer's safe transfer on board the late morning train for Innsbruck.

Drew had thirty minutes between trains and had no intention of missing his connection. He'd worked out the schedule to the second—catch the late morning train out of Salzburg with arrival in Innsbruck by early afternoon and then hop the first commuter train to Brunnerwald. With a final nod toward Frau Mayer, he tipped the porter liberally.

With the added prospect of meeting Vic Wilson in

Salzburg—if a plane flight permitted—Drew made his way toward the end of the car. At the far end, he heard phrases in Russian coming from the compartment on his right. He slowed his pace as he passed the open door and was startled to see three men in a heated exchange, Peter Kermer among them.

❂❂❂

Vic's eagle eye spotted Drew as he stepped from the train. "Over here, old buddy," Vic called. "I told you I was coming."

Drew grinned at the cocky swagger. "I'm glad you made it. I thought you were joking when you suggested meeting me."

"No, and I wasn't joking about going with you."

"Forget that. Just enjoy your leave."

"I'm bored. I've got time on my hands."

*Too much time to think about your bleak future.* A lump the size of a golf ball rose in Drew's throat. He ran his fingers through his dark hair with its sparse gray strands. "I hate what's happening to you, Vic."

"It's not your fault, Drew. You cautioned me against dating every girl in town and out of town. But like I told you, I've been straight." He wiped his mouth with the back of his hand. "But I'm still HIV positive."

"How are you feeling, Vic?"

The cockiness washed from Vic's face. "Good actually. It's Brianna I'm worried about. My cousin doesn't think it's fair, me being sick. But Nicole comes over and spends the weekends with us."

"Nicole knows then?"

"I wanted to be up front with her. We take in dinner and a play—or a game of tennis—nothing else. Don't look at me that way, Drew. I wish things could have been different, but Brianna and Nicole know that someday this HIV bit will zap me."

"Maybe the medical world will find a cure for AIDS before that."

"Not in time for me, Drew. So let me go with you."

"You'd be on your own going into Brunnerwald. I'd never get Carwell's sanction."

"I'm in anyway. The story about Nicholas Trotsky made it into the London papers this morning."

"Yes, my son-in-law told me. Where's the leak coming from?"

"Out of London, no doubt. Maybe Dudley Perkins over at MI5. Or Lyle Spincrest. Little Lord Fauntleroy is an ambitious fellow. He's heading to the top, so everyone please step aside."

"He's not a bad sort, Vic, and great at tennis. But if he's feeding information to the media, it won't sit well with Carwell."

"Nor with Trotsky if he read the morning news. You might as well run an ad in the paper yourself: 'Attention, Nicholas Trotsky. Your old adversary is on his way.'"

Drew flashed a wry grin and then turned his attention to the stocky porter guiding Frau Mayer through the depot.

"Friend of yours?" Vic asked.

"My traveling companion from Vienna."

"She looks harmless."

"In a noisy sort of way." Drew did another visual sweep of the depot, searching among the passengers for Kermer and his friends. "Vic, what do you know about Peter Kermer?" he asked as they made their way to an empty bench.

"Brad O'Malloy recruited him a few years ago. Around the time you almost bit the dust in Croatia."

"Then he's Croatian?"

"Yes, but his grandparents were Russian. Kind of a runt of a guy. Five feet, seven. About my age. Mid-thirties. Average looks."

Drew frowned. The man at the opera house was tall, eye-level with him, a handsome man with sad, unsmiling eyes.

"O'Malloy convinced Kermer to let the Russians recruit him. He's been passing trade secrets to us ever since."

"Anything of value?"

"Porter was on deck then. He didn't think much of anything Kermer passed our way. Disinformation, he called it."

Gregory crossed his lanky legs, his expression thoughtful.

"The way things turned out, Porter may have suppressed vital information to protect his own ties with Moscow."

"If Moscow knows he's running double, then Kermer's in serious trouble. If we don't take steps to protect him, he's a dead man."

Drew considered the Kermer who could identify him. "Vic, the man I met at the opera and aboard the train doesn't fit your description. The real Kermer may already be dead."

Vic's pupils widened. "An imposter?"

"Possibly. He should be called back to Paris and checked out."

"You'd have to sell Troy Carwell on that one, Drew."

"I can't sell Carwell on anything. He's bent on sending me to Brunnerwald. I'm the only one who will recognize Trotsky."

"And if he survived, Trotsky will recognize you."

"For months I dreamed about dragging Trotsky from a plane. Last night for the first time in years that nightmare came back. We had him on board a plane. I know it. He was my prisoner. That's the way it was in my dream. The triumph of capturing Trotsky."

"You had a concussion, Gregory. Memory plays funny games."

Drew rubbed the tense muscles in the back of his neck. "My plane smashed into those mountains. Lou Garver was sitting behind me and someone beside me—Trotsky, I think—with his hands secured in front of him so he could keep pressure on his belly wound."

"He was hurt?"

Gregory puzzled it out, pausing long enough to sort through his memory chronologically—trying to separate reality from the recurring nightmare. "I think Trotsky had gunshot wounds."

"You shot him?"

"I don't know. Maybe Garver did. We began to climb without difficulty. I remember thinking how beautiful it was soaring above those majestic walls of granite with the peaks above the tree line all covered with snow.

Again he massaged his neck. "In the Alps they seem to have cables coming out of nowhere. Ski lifts or avalanche launchers and military installations where the militia can hide a whole division inside a cavern. One of those cables caught the tip of my right wing. We began to lose altitude."

He stood as the train arrived. "Somehow I managed to gain enough power to swoop above a small Alpine village before we veered across a flat cliff and slammed into the mountainside."

"You're lucky you got out."

"The deep snow drifts must have cushioned the crash. My head throbbed, but I'm certain I dragged someone from the plane. It had to be Trotsky. Garver died on impact. When I crawled back to the plane to get Garver's body out, the front end exploded. An Austrian found me. I still remember his eyes, the kindest ones I've ever seen. The dream always ends there. I woke up days later in the village rectory."

"Maybe the priest rescued you."

"It could have been him. Jacques Caridini had gentle blue eyes." Drew turned and faced Vic. "I thought the throbbing pain and noise in my head would never go away. Funny thing, I don't even remember the Sulzbach Avalanche the night of the crash."

"Did the accident jar the snow loose?"

"The slide started higher up. A heavy snowstorm that night caused the top layer to slip. What was left of the airplane went in the avalanche. They never found Lou Garver's body. Nor Trotsky."

"Drew, why is one man still so important to the Agency?"

"I've been mulling that over. Trotsky's important to me. But why this renewed interest in Paris and Langley? That got me to thinking about a small uprising in Russia around the time Nicholas disappeared. Yes . . . there was one. Langley classified it. Think about it, Vic. Why would Langley mark that top secret?"

"You think Trotsky was part of a splinter group?"

"Carwell should know. He served as a case officer in Moscow around then. Check with him."

Wilson's jaw locked off center. "I'm not on good terms with Carwell. He's harder to peel than a sour lemon. He knows we're friends, Drew. That blacklists me."

"Then try Brad O'Malloy. Paris first, okay? And, Vic, can you recommend a charming *zimmer frei* in Brunnerwald? Say, one with blue or green shutters on a cobblestone street."

"That describes a hundred or more of them."

"A cobblestone street limits it to the older part of town."

"And who fed you that line?" Vic scoffed.

"Carwell's Russian agent—via Carwell. Turns out a woman spotted Trotsky in a park in Innsbruck and followed him to the *gasthof* in Brunnerwald. Trotsky's reappearance sent shock waves through Moscow. That should tell us something."

"Doesn't explain why the woman couldn't distinguish between blue and green shutters or read the street signs."

"Maybe it's self-preservation, Vic. Or she's color blind."

"If you need me, fax me word at the embassy in Paris. Just say, 'Skiing looks good here.' I'll be there on the next plane." Vic cocked his head. "Check at the Schrott Cheese Factory when you get to Brunnerwald. Or maybe it's a bakery. Can't remember, but the Schrotts have a *zimmer frei* or two of their own. Brianna and Nicole stayed in one of them when they went skiing last winter."

"Then it's bound to be clean and fair-priced."

Vic grinned. "Leave your address with the Schrotts. Then I can find your blue-shuttered *gasthof* when I get to Brunnerwald."

"Schrott bakery or cheese factory. I'll do that, Vic."

# Chapter 6

**M**arta Zubkov's phone call to Dimitri stirred a rippling effect all the way to Moscow. For days she fought the dryness in her mouth, the stickiness in the palms of her hands. Her new mocha dress gave her no pleasure now. It lay boxed beneath her narrow bed in the *pension* in Innsbruck, the joy of its beauty gone.

Each time the phone rang, Marta shrank back, afraid that Dimitri would be on the other end with new instructions, his voice scathing, accusing. She consoled herself that he merely mouthed the rumblings from Moscow. Surely Dimitri believed her. Yet fear gripped her afresh as she rode the funicular rail up the mountainside to Hungerburg. What if she had been mistaken? What if the man in the park only looked like Nicholas?

Werner Vronin would be the first to accuse her of mental incompetence. For months he had tried to bring her into disfavor with Dimitri, calmly suggesting that she be recalled to Moscow. The funicular rose to its dizzying heights on the left bank of the River Inn, allowing Marta one of those majestic views of the Tyrolean Alps that she loved. But this time she shuddered at the cavernous drop to the valley below.

From the Hungerburg Station she took the downhill walk to the Alpenzoo and in perfect German asked the gatekeeper for directions to the bobcat habitat. She wondered as she smiled at him if he could be Dimitri Aleynik in disguise.

None of the others had arrived. Or was she even now being watched through Yuri Ryskov's miniscope? Or was she an open target for an assassin's bullet—Vronin's bullet? And what of Peter Kermer, the unknown Croatian? Would he meet them here as scheduled?

Kermer intrigued her, but so did Dimitri. There had always been a dead-drop in every major city in Austria, a place for Marta to leave a message or pick up one from Dimitri. In the beginning, he had told her, he lingered in the baroque gardens in front of the Schonbrunn Palace in Vienna and at the fortress in Salzburg just watching her. Her favorite dead-drop had been the altar in Linz at the Church of the Minor Friars. It was her way of lashing back at Nicholas who had bragged of his mother's desire for him—the priesthood. How blind the woman must have been. Yet Marta had found Nicholas as warm and tender a man as she had ever known. Kermer and Dimitri could never compare to him.

She stared at the bobcat prancing wildly in its rocked-in cage. This time Marta's order had come straight from Moscow. A new dead-drop had been selected—the bobcat rockery at the Alpenzoo. She felt caged like the animal, an endangered species.

"Fraulein Zubkov?"

She recognized his voice, the deep baritone quality to it. She was certain of it—her KGB controller, her Kremlin contact, she had always called him.

*Comrade.* The word reached the tip of her tongue. She locked it there, saying in surprise, "You must be Dimitri?"

He nodded, surprising her even more. "Yes, I am Dimitri Aleynik. It was necessary for me to come in person," he said.

"All the way from Moscow?" she asked in Russian.

Dimitri touched her lips gently. "So we meet at last."

He seemed younger than she had expected. For the position he held, he had to be thirty-nine or forty, a wholesome-looking man with a straightforward gaze, a carefully trimmed moustache, and thick, dark hair that squared around his ears. His eyes shone a bold blue. His expression came across pleasant, not cold and sharp as his voice often sounded in their phone contacts. The sleeves of his trench coat hung too long, the wide waist belted tightly as though the coat were borrowed.

He led her to a bench and unraveled the pages of the *International Herald Tribune.* The pages crackled as they sat on them. "The others will be here shortly," he said.

"They'd better hurry. The zoo closes in less than an hour. We'll have to catch the last funicular down."

"No hurry," he said. "They'll be here in time."

Panic gripped her again. *In time for what?* she wondered.

"Marta, are you certain you saw Nicholas here in Innsbruck?"

"Yes. In the park, like I told you on the phone."

"I'm certain the man looked like Nicholas. Otherwise you would not have broken code and called me." He smiled, patronizing her, but reprimand crept into his voice. "If he's alive, then he must have gone over to the other side."

Her throat muscles spasmed. "Nicholas wouldn't do that."

"There was no disguise?"

She thought of the priestly garment. "No," she snapped.

A corner of his mouth curled upward. "What was he wearing?"

Marta tried to remember the phone call. Had she already told Dimitri? "A plain suit," she whispered. "A black one."

"I thought Nicholas liked bright colors."

She blinked against the memory of the stiff Roman collar against his neck. "A white shirt. No tie. And—red socks." She remembered the socks clearly—and how ill he had looked.

"It's been fifteen years since you saw him."

"I'd know that smile anywhere."

"We want him back in Moscow."

A certain death sentence for Nicholas. She nodded. "Yes, of course." Again she bit off the word *comrade.*

"You're the only one who can identify Nicholas."

"I thought you knew him, Dimitri."

"Personally? No. It was my father and Nicholas who were friends. But I know Trotsky's file better than anyone. He

was a brilliant man, Marta. Handpicked by the upper eche-
lons of the KGB. Thanks to my father, Nicholas rose quickly
in our ranks."

She heard envy in Dimitri's voice. He didn't have to
remind her of Nicholas's achievements. Nicholas had
belonged to the Communist Youth League from early boyhood. Had taken an accelerated study program at the language institute at Moscow University. Ties with the secret
service had followed, and then the unexpected move that
sent him off to seminary to study for the priesthood.
Nicholas often called it his perfect cover.

The twisted smile touched Dimitri's lips again. "Your
eyes betray you, Marta. You knew Colonel Trotsky well, but
did you know that he went from the sacred halls of the seminary back to the assassination squad?"

Cold chills raised the fuzz on her arms. "Did he?"

"If he went to the other side, Marta, it would be dangerous for us. You understand that?"

"You want to hunt him down, don't you, Dimitri?"

"Why else would I have worked with you all these years?"

"Why else?" she agreed. The reality of his words gripped
her as she met his hard gaze. "You arranged all of this—my
life here in Austria? My assignments?"

He nodded.

She had made her headquarters in Austria for a number
of years, ever since Nicholas's disappearance. She kept a
rented *pension* not far from the pastel houses that lined
the quai on the Left Bank. "Always stay close enough to
major transportation for an emergency exit," Dimitri had
warned her.

"You arranged my exodus from East Germany?"

"It saved your life. I've always said you knew where he
was."

"No," she protested. "I didn't know."

He considered that. "Perhaps."

She saw it clearly now. Dimitri had brought her here to
Innsbruck, the place Nicholas had loved. "I've been a good
agent," she murmured.

"Yes, an obedient one. You never questioned this location?"

No, she had been grateful for it. Even sentimental. Nicholas had loved Innsbruck and had always promised to bring her here.

"Didn't you expect to find Nicholas here one day?"

*Yes*, she thought. *I did at first.* But she had finally resigned herself to his death. "You've used me, Dimitri," she said. "Just to trap Nicholas Trotsky."

"You've had a good life," Aleynik reminded her as if that settled everything.

"Bring Nicholas in, and you're assured of promotion, Marta."

She knew he was lying—felt it in the deep recesses of her mind. She had been kept alive, used, always with the hope that she would one day lead them to Nicholas.

Dimitri drew her back with another question. "You followed him to Brunnerwald? You're certain that's the name of the town?"

"Yes, he went to one of the *gasthofs* there."

"Then you will start there."

"Nicholas would recognize me."

"Then why didn't he know you in the park?"

She had asked that same question over and over. He was ill. That was it. But she held back. If she told Dimitri everything, her career would be over. Dimitri would have no need for her. It would be a short flight back to Moscow. A permanent one.

"Werner and Yuri will go with you," he said.

"And Peter Kermer?"

Dimitri picked up on her concern. "You question Peter Kermer?"

"He's new to me."

"To all of us. But the records show him as a trusted agent. Boris Ivanski recommended him. Kermer will go with you."

"Yes, of course. But why are we all needed?"

"Nicholas never worked alone. If he has lined himself up with the Americans or Brits or French, we will want to know before we take him to Moscow."

"I'm to bring him back here to you in Innsbruck? Alive?"
"Isn't that what you want, Marta?"
She matched his coldness. "He betrayed all of us."
"Particularly you, Marta."

❦❦❦

Peter Kermer sat on a bench on a rocky ledge above Marta and her companion. Were they waiting for him? Did they know that the real Peter Kermer had died?

He rubbed his brow, tense now with a raging headache. Before catching the Hungerburg Cable, he had posted cards to Sara and the children so they would know he had made it to Innsbruck. Funny cards to the boys, his love for them carved into each word. A serious one to Sara: "Austrian business trip extended. If I'm late getting home, Jacob and Hannah will have my excuses. Forgive my lateness. Accept my love."

If he failed to return home, Sara would read between the lines. She would be brave enough to go on without him, smart enough to contact Israeli Intelligence with the postal cards from the Alpenzoo. They would begin their search for him there. Slowly, he ran his fingers along the gold chain around his neck and touched the Star of David. It served as his constant reminder of his Jewishness, oddly enough, always reminding him of the Messiah he had come to love. Among his own people, it was part of his being wise as a serpent, harmless as a dove.

Peter lifted his binoculars and studied Marta's troubled profile as she faced the man who had met her. Something of the cunning she displayed in the Serbian stronghold had weakened. Or was this man her Russian contact, the man that Peter must identify for Israeli Intelligence? Dimitri. But would Marta's KGB controller meet her in the open like this?

Peter had formed a sketchy picture of him, minimal at best, from Marta's phone call. Young. Powerful. Cruel. Marta's superior, the one giving the orders. Marta both feared and admired him. Peter had delayed too long—concerned that Dimitri would know the real Peter Kermer—and so he had not allowed himself enough time to approach the bobcat rockery from the northerly direction as he had been instructed to do.

All Peter dared do was depend on his camera and the wide-zoom lens. He snapped most of a roll of film, catching the barely discernible facial changes as Dimitri spoke to Marta. Dimitri was at least six inches taller than Marta, his dark trench coat hiding his build and weight. A breeze blew against Dimitri, but his hair stayed in place, disciplined and unmoving like the man himself.

He watched Dimitri bare his wrist to glance at his watch.

The sun cast its late afternoon shadows across the slopes, the approach of early evening stirring a breeze that chilled Peter's body. Still he sat there, moodily watching nature play its tricks against the mountain peaks and scattered patches of snow—not wanting to risk that face-to-face encounter with Dimitri. The crowds at the zoo had thinned as people made their way toward the funicular even now.

Peter took the unfinished roll of film, shoved it in the mailer addressed to Sara, and sealed it. He'd have to depend on the lab for blowups and a profile analysis of the man he had just photographed. Peter dropped a second roll of film into the camera and snapped six pictures in the fading light. He would have to ditch his binoculars, but he refused to leave Sara's camera behind; he'd have to convince the others that he was a photo buff with pictures for his kids in mind.

He slung the camera over his shoulder before cutting out toward the main gate. Checking Sara's address once again, he dropped the mailer into the postal slot. A security box as far as Peter was concerned. Then he backtracked past the bears and the birds, coming in from a northerly approach toward Marta.

The man in the blue trench coat had disappeared, but Werner Vronin and Yuri Ryskov sat on either side of Marta. Peter had traveled with them both from Eisenstadt. The mistrust in Vronin's eyes was as evident now as it had been then. The man had an unfriendly face, an iron will, and an

intense envy of Marta's leadership. His felt hat tipped over
one brow added to his defiant image. Yuri, the younger of
the two, wore a heavy jacket, his left hand shoved in the
pocket as Peter approached. Though solidly built, Yuri
could do with a sun lamp or a day on the beach to brighten
his pallid skin and chalk-white narrow lips.

"You're late," Marta said. "Dimitri couldn't wait."

He met her angry gaze and pointed to his camera. "I'm
sorry, Marta. I was getting pictures for the children."

"Every time I tell you to be somewhere, you're late. So
give me your camera."

"But—"

"Now."

He swung it off his shoulder and handed it to her. "Save
the film for me, Marta. I took a couple of pictures of the
bears. My sons—"

"Forget your sons."

*How?* Peter wondered. His family consumed his thoughts.
The rush of blood to his face would be hidden by his
bronzed skin, but he wasn't certain he hid the anger in his
eyes. He started to sit down beside Yuri.

"We're leaving, Peter," Marta said.

"Good idea. The zoo closes in twenty minutes."

Impatiently, she said, "We're leaving Innsbruck."

"Dimitri's orders?"

Her pencil-thin brows touched. "You question him?"

"Not to his face," Peter admitted.

He had admitted too much. He saw it in Marta's expression, doubt about him clouding her face. She covered her
uncertainty by hastily mapping out plans that would take
them to Brunnerwald.

"Where's that?" Peter asked.

"A Tyrolean village," Yuri said. "A few hours from here."

*A thousand miles away as far as Sara would know.*

Werner flicked the brim of his hat back. "Marta has an
old score to settle with Nicholas Trotsky. Ever hear of him?"

Peter rubbed his forehead groping for a proper answer.

"Colonel Trotsky," Marta said. "But never mind. It's best
that none of you have met Nicholas. I'll fill you in."

Peter crouched down beside her, his gaze meeting hers once more. "Is this what Dimitri wants?"

More uncertainty filled her hazel eyes. *I don't measure up,* he thought. *But I owe her one. Or does she credit me with bringing us safely out of Serbian territory? Where were Vronin and Yuri then?* "And once we find Trotsky, Marta?" he asked. "What then?"

"One of us will escort him back to Moscow."

"What about you, Kermer?" Vronin suggested with a chortle. "You might enjoy seeing our country."

*They know,* Peter thought, *that I'm not the real Peter Kermer. I'm not fooling any of them.* But he smiled and said, "I'll toss you for the privilege, Vronin."

# Chapter 7

Dusk had settled by the time Marta reached the *pension* where she kept a tiny room on the second floor. She inched her way across the yard to the window box and deftly fingered beneath the geraniums.

Dimitri Aleynik stepped from the shadows and dangled her key in his hand. "Is this what you're looking for?" he asked.

"Dimitri! What are you doing here? I thought—"

"That I had gone back to Moscow?"

She nodded.

"No, I won't leave Innsbruck until Trotsky is found. I want to take back a positive report to Moscow."

He offered a controlled smile that stretched his smooth skin even tighter across his bony cheeks. She grabbed for the key. He pulled back, laughing at her. In that moment she utterly loathed him, detested his power over her.

"I've been waiting for you, Marta. I don't like waiting."

"I walked along the river for a while. I'm sorry."

"Alone?"

"Of course."

"Problems, Marta?"

*You ask that?* she thought. *After this afternoon? After the plans to zero in on Nicholas Trotsky.* "I think more clearly when I'm walking along the River Inn. I leave tomorrow, you know."

"You seem quite happy here."

"Yes."

In the old days Austria had given her access into many Eastern Bloc countries. She still considered Innsbruck her crossroads, her escape route over highways and mountain passes into Italy or Germany and landlocked Switzerland. Yet she thought of her *pension* as coming home; she savored this touch of freedom, always knowing that one false move and all that was Marta Zubkov would be taken from her.

"Marta, we must talk some more."

"Not here. It isn't safe."

"Then in your room." He twirled the key. "Shall we go?"

She went reluctantly, her feet dragging to the second floor. What if he saw the new clothes and questioned her about them? No. She remembered she had left them hidden under the bed.

Dimitri unlocked the door and barged in first as though he fully expected to find someone else there. He switched on the light and shrugged, his disappointment well hidden.

The room was plain, almost empty of personal possessions or any identifying features. Her eyes went at once to the drab dresser and the lovely music box that sat there.

Dimitri had seen it, too. He walked over and lifted the lid. Like a Pandora's box, it exploded with memories. Nicholas had given it to her. And now she wished that she had thrown it away—that she had blotted out every reminder of him.

Dimitri bent and sniffed the sweet, spicy scent of myrrh as sounds of an Austrian waltz permeated the room. Still he held the lid, turning it in his narrow hand with meticulous care. "An eagle with red and gold feathers?" he said curiously.

"No, Dimitri. It's the phoenix."

His blue eyes glinted hard like steel. "An odd name," he said, his voice biting. "Did you buy this?"

"No, a friend—"

She regretted the admission and saw in his expression that he had already guessed that Nicholas had given it to her. He clamped the lid in place, shutting off the music of Strauss.

"Trotsky liked classical music, didn't he?"

She staved off the truth, saying, "I—I think so."

"Nothing definite? You were his mistress for all that time, yet you know so little about him."

With fresh, stabbing pain, she felt the shame of those stolen moments with Nicholas and the false promise that he would marry her when he got back. "We were just friends, Dimitri."

"I can imagine. Nicholas was quite the charmer."

"But you said you didn't know him."

"I know everything about him."

*And everything about me.*

He stared at her, his gaze going slowly back to the music box. "Did Nicholas ever talk to you about the phoenix?"

"I don't remember. No, wait. He said it was from mythology. Greek or Arabian." She sounded confused even to herself. "No, Egyptian. Nicholas said the bird built its own funeral pyre."

"And was consumed in the fire?" Dimitri asked.

"Yes, something like that. It used to sadden me when he talked about death. I'd change the subject." *And take his hand. Or kiss his neck. Or beg him just to hold me.*

Dimitri went on musing, his eyes searching hers now, his deep baritone voice hypnotic. "The phoenix is a symbol of death and resurrection. Did you know that, Marta?"

"That's a foolish myth, Dimitri. It's impossible for the bird to rise from the ashes." But Nicholas had believed in the phoenix. More than once he had quoted Milton: "And though her body dies, her fame survives."

Dimitri did not take his eyes from Marta. Defensively, she said, "The phoenix is a bird of poetry, of hope and beginning again, but it's not a religious bird, Dimitri."

A thin smile played at his mouth. "Perhaps your Nicholas is like the phoenix. Perhaps he's ready to rise from the ashes."

"You're frightening me, Dimitri."

"Nicholas was the frightening one. He was a revolutionary, Marta, determined to effect change. He wanted to overthrow the existing government—take control himself—and crush any thought of freedom or attempt at Western democracy. Yes, my dear Marta," Dimitri said, "Nicholas wanted to take over, to have a Soviet Union of his own making."

"You're wrong, Dimitri. He was a committed Communist. Loyal. Devoted. He did everything they wanted him to do."

"Yes, *everything*, and yet I think of him as nothing but a political assassin. He was one of the KGB's elite, trained at the best schools, but he was nothing but a cold-blooded assassin."

She bit her lower lip. "You're lying, Dimitri."

"No, my dear Marta. Didn't you ever wonder where he went on all those special assignments? Didn't you ever question him?"

Question Nicholas? No, she had adored him. She had feared for him, too. Sometimes when he came back from those assignments, he seemed troubled. Marta would cradle his head in her arms and smooth his brow until he slept.

"There's no place to run," he had told her weeks before he went away. "I have locked myself into a world where there is no place to hide."

Lightly she had challenged, "Where would you go, Nicholas, if you really wanted to disappear?"

He ran his fingers gently down her cheek. "To Innsbruck. Back to the mountains. And I would take you with me, Marta. But first I must find the American agent Crisscross and destroy him. Only then could we be truly happy."

A cold, uneasy tingling ran the length of her spine as she remembered that last long walk in the woods with Nicholas. "Marta," he had said, "it is not safe for me to take you with me, but at dawn you must always listen for the sweet music of the phoenix bird. Then you will know that I am always there." Had he been trying to warn her that he must sacrifice himself? Burn himself out rather than be recalled to Moscow?

She met Dimitri's gaze once more. Except for the harshness in his eyes, Dimitri Aleynik was a plain man with a nondescript expression. He could easily fade into a crowd and go unnoticed, drawing little attention to himself.

"Marta, you should walk by the River Inn again this

evening to clear your thinking. For when you reach Brunnerwald, you must find out whether Nicholas went over to the other side."

She protested, "No, he loved our country."

Dimitri gripped her shoulder. "He loved power. Think carefully, Marta. What else did he tell you about the phoenix?"

"Nothing. Nothing that I remember."

He relinquished his grip. "Perhaps you are right," he said. "If he had gone over to the Americans, they would have boasted of it long before now. But many countries would have granted Nicholas asylum in exchange for all the intelligence data stored in his mind."

"You never thought he was dead, did you, Dimitri?"

"In an Austrian avalanche? No. He may have started those rumors himself. Werner Vronin thinks you are still in love with Nicholas—that you've been protecting him all these years."

"I told you, Dimitri, we were just friends."

He smiled at her vehement denial. "Then why would a friend want to betray him?"

"Dimitri, I thought you'd be pleased that I spotted Nicholas."

"Yes, but Werner is worried about you. As I am. Werner thinks we should send someone else to Brunnerwald."

Her anger took a new twist. Dimitri and Werner were in this together. The tiny room closed in on her. Had Dimitri come with the message that she was being recalled to Moscow? She remembered the hollow look in Nicholas's eyes when he had feared the same thing.

No, she had to be wrong. Dimitri needed her to identify Nicholas. That bought her a safety margin. But after that, he would no longer need her. Why else had Dimitri openly revealed himself. Her Kremlin contact had a face now. A complete name. Dimitri could never let her live long with that revelation.

"Have you no answer, Marta? Wouldn't you like me to replace you? There's no need for you to track Nicholas down."

"No, let me have my vengeance."

He nodded. "All right then. I'll wait here in Innsbruck for you in your *pension* perhaps. You have a radio transmitter, the privacy I need. Yes, I'll wait here for word on Nicholas, and when you find him, I want to see him before he goes back to Moscow."

His pause loomed threatening. "Marta, you're certain that Nicholas said nothing else about the phoenix? Nothing about his plans when he walked through the Brandenburg Gate that last time?"

"He didn't know it would be his last time," she shouted.

To offset the fury in her voice, she forced a smile. "Forgive me, Dimitri. I am so tired. This business about Nicholas is painful."

"But you have always been disciplined, Marta. You've never raised your voice to me—"

*I never dared. Whatever your true rank and position is in the old party, you're my superior, my contact.*

"You will never speak to me in that manner again."

"No, Comrade." The word was out, the one they no longer used.

He took the music box in his hand again. As he lifted the lid, the "Blue Danube Waltz" drifted lazily through the room. "Why did Nicholas give you this present?" he asked.

*To remember him by,* Nicholas had said. "He gave me many presents."

"But you only kept this one?"

Surely he knew. The others had been confiscated, her room searched thoroughly after Nicholas's disappearance. Only the music box had been safe, forgotten in the cabin where they had stayed the night before he vanished. As soon as she dared, she had gone back there and rescued it. She fixed her attention on the bird—its wings spread wide, its gold and red feathers gleaming in the light of the room.

The waltz played on. Dimitri frowned and shook the ceramic figure. He had heard it, she was certain, the subtle change in the song where the notes seemed to hesitate and turn sour. He shook it again. "What's wrong with this?" he demanded.

"I've worn it out playing it."

A menacing grimace masked his face. Then with a devilish smile he let the music box slip from his hands and crash to the floor, the ceramic figure shattering, the music silenced forever.

Marta dropped to her hands and knees, fighting the tears that burned behind her eyelids. Their heads bumped as Dimitri grappled for the metal container that held the music tape. He shoved it into his pocket. She clutched broken chips of the bird in her hands and cried out, "Why, Dimitri? Why?"

"The music played off-key, my dear Marta. That was not like Nicholas. His world was a perfect one. Surely he's betrayed us."

Marta huddled on the floor, her eyes downcast. All she could see as Dimitri left was the bottom of his trench coat flapping against his trousers and the shiny, polished shoes.

Marta reached toward a table leg and pulled herself upright, her fingers still clutching parts of the shattered phoenix bird. She opened the palm of her hand and stared at the droplets of blood forming on the surface, framing her broken world in red.

She took five wobbly steps and leaned against the closed door, listening intently to Dimitri's footsteps in the stairwell. Slowly the sound faded. He was gone, but he had taken her room key with him. Marta felt exposed, vulnerable, as though her heart and this small room had lain naked under Dimitri's scrutiny.

Marta turned and faced her room once more, blindly seeing nothing except the broken pieces of the music box that still lay on the floor. She tore the scarf from the dresser and bent down to brush the chips of the phoenix bird into the cloth. Her tears were unrestrained as she tucked the scented bundle into the corner of her dresser drawer.

Suddenly her room was no longer a refuge. She felt trapped within its walls, convinced that Dimitri and the hierarchy in Moscow could anticipate her every move, envision her every secret.

In the past when Nicholas was her life, she had been shy and reticent, uncertain except in his presence. After he disappeared, her strength and confidence came slowly. When Marta finally relinquished him to death, she aligned herself wholeheartedly to his cause. Communism became everything, her devotion unquestionable. She rose in the ranks, respected and capable, yet ruthless and reckless in her abandonment.

No, Dimitri could not question her loyalty, but she realized now that he had used her to mark the path toward Nicholas. She stared in the tiny mirror. The femininity and beauty that she had felt in the fashion boutique just days ago was gone. The face that stared back at her now looked distraught, dejected, her dark eyes sorrowful, their golden glow dead.

Had Nicholas ever intended to come back for her? No, even her beloved Nicholas had betrayed her. She loathed him for his rejection, and yet could she really destroy the only man she had ever loved?

Marta slammed the dresser drawer closed. A week ago she had wanted nothing but vengeance against Nicholas Trotsky. Now she wanted only the refuge he had found. In her twisted thoughts she wanted no harm to come his way. And yet she had set the wheels of destiny in motion—the chain reaction set against herself as well. Nicholas seemed destined for execution on his return to Moscow, a traitor in the eyes of his own people.

Her own safety seemed strangely linked with his. There was only one way—if someone else found Nicholas first. Or what if she went to him and begged asylum within the walls of his parish?

Marta dressed in her best clothes—the new mocha brown dress and wide-brimmed hat, carefully applying bright red lipstick that matched her ruby earrings. She picked up the satchel filled with clothes for her journey, and then she walked out into the night, leaving the *pension* for what she knew would be the last time.

It was four-thirty as she paced along the banks of the River Inn and watched the cloak of night turn to the fiery streaks of dawn. She listened, but she did not hear the sweet music of the phoenix. Still she walked, the breeze from off the river dampening her hair. Her tears spent, she centered her tormented thoughts on escape. Was there no one to help her? No place to hide?

Once she led Werner and Dimitri to Nicholas, she would be recalled to Moscow. No one would believe that she had "discovered" Nicholas Trotsky on the streets of Innsbruck. No, they already condemned her for always having known his whereabouts. Marta struggled to keep her exhausted body moving. As the shadowed waters lapped against the shoreline, the River Inn seemed momentarily inviting.

No. Not that. She would not give in to Dimitri Aleynik.

Nicholas's punishment belonged to her. His betrayal of the party meant nothing to her. It was his desertion, his leaving her behind, that she could not forgive. Hating Nicholas. Loving him. Could she trust herself to face him, or would her emotions crumble when she saw him again?

She needed an ally, someone who could reach Nicholas first and warn him that KGB agents were searching for him. What she wanted was an American or some other foreign country to take Nicholas prisoner. To fall into the hands of the enemy was a fate that Nicholas had abhorred, a disgrace even greater than being exiled to Siberia. His final defeat in the face of an enemy would be all the vengeance she needed. Sweet revenge against Nicholas. A counterblow against Dimitri.

She considered the man in Mitterand's cabinet or Peter Kermer with the Star of David hanging around his neck. Kermer would be going into Brunnerwald with her, but was he really one of them? No, she still believed him an imposter, someone playing both sides. Would he consider helping her, or should she turn once more to the staid Englishman in London?

Yes, Dudley Perkins would help her if she convinced him that the Americans were involved—that the Americans would beat him to Brunnerwald. Her whole body flushed at the thought of MI5 rallying to her cause. Marta would phone Perkins on the direct line to his private office. That gangly, beady-eyed man with the leathery skin repulsed her. But she needed him. Marta would not beg. No, she knew Dudley well enough to know that his intense competition with the Americans would drive him to Brunnerwald in search of Nicholas Trotsky.

She walked to the river's edge, stooped down and splashed her flushed face with the cold water. Drops from the River Inn splashed on her mocha brown dress, but she didn't care. Her mind had cleared; her sense of control had crept back once again.

# Chapter 8

In London Lyle Spincrest spent an irritating morning on an exhausting art safari with Dudley Perkins's wife. Usually he enjoyed currying her favor, but playing escort this morning had forced him to cancel a date with an actress who, though gifted in tennis and dancing, would have proved dimwitted in a dusty gallery.

Molly Perkins knew the art world and visited the Wallace Collection and the Tate Gallery on a regular basis. In her quiet, unassuming way she never bored Lyle nor pounded his ears with senseless chatter. And yet today she had chatted incessantly.

Now to annoy him even more, she had insisted on browsing through a little-known museum not far from the Ritz. "It's a craggy hole in the wall with charming paintings," she said. "You'll enjoy it, Lyle."

He didn't. Once he caught sight of the crowded aisles, his mood darkened. "None of these will make it to Sotheby's auction."

"True," she agreed.

She wandered alone to the next aisle as he stood glaring down at a painting of an eighteenth-century nude that stirred nothing in him this morning but disfavor. He moved on, his hands clasped behind him, the small of his back aching from inactivity, his thoughts on the date with the actress that had been blown completely. They had planned a fast game of tennis and then the opera or a concert on

Fleet Street in the evening. Even a dignified afternoon tea with a pretty girl beside him would be better than to be saddled all morning in the company of Mrs. Perkins—as gracious as she was.

When he looked across the aisle at her, Molly met his gaze, her eyes unsmiling. "You're bored, Lyle. I never noticed that in you before. You're usually most companionable."

His neck burned. "I'm tired," he said lamely. "Why don't I hail a cabbie?"

"No, dear. We're having tea at the Ritz. Dudley reserved a table for us in the Palm Court."

"He's joining us?"

"He'll be there, but not with us."

"Dudley's not having tea with Marta Zubkov again?"

The name had slipped out uninvited. Molly's glossy lips parted slightly as she whispered, "Don't judge Dudley so harshly."

Lyle appraised her as they took their seats at the Ritz. She was tall, giving an even more angular look to her narrow face. He tried to peg her at sixty-three, then more charitably at fifty-nine. Her hair had grayed, leaving a lovely silver sheen to her short, stylish cut.

Gracefully she allowed the waiter to seat her. Peeling off her gloves, she reached out to take the menu.

"Order something for us, Lyle," she said. Her voice so alive in the art gallery had wearied.

Without checking the menu, he ordered tea and scones, a light salad, and a thin cucumber sandwich for Molly. As the waiter left, Lyle pushed his glasses into place and smiled. "Are you ready to tell me why I'm here?"

She unfolded her napkin. "Let's wait until our food comes."

Lyle killed time by glancing around the brightly lighted room styled in Rococo splendor. Shiny bronze statues along the wall. Verdant palm plants by the pillars. An attentive waiter at the small, round table beside them. And Molly— she was making their time together unbearable. As soon as he could be shunt of her, he'd head for the Sherlock Holmes Pub and drown out the mistakes of this day. With any luck at all, he'd run into Miles Grover, the eccentric intelligence officer from Dudley's office—a pathetic man with bony knees and a thick, gray moustache that sopped up half his beer. Even that would give Lyle a laugh and an escape from this boredom.

It struck him as Molly sat so quietly, so uncommunicative, that her features were plain, and yet she was elegantly turned out in her Laura Ashley outfit. Teal looked good on her, bringing out the azure blue of her eyes.

Actually, he liked her—always had—because in spite of the plainness, she proved intellectually challenging, well-read, well-bred. And she was independently wealthy. Given these advantages, he took pleasure in cultivating her friendship. But he felt uneasy in this forced silence.

He moved his arms as the waiter laid out the table. Then Lyle poured from the shimmering teapot, his hand embarrassingly unsteady. "You said Dudley was coming. I haven't seen him since Saturday."

A faint smile drew attention to the dark circles beneath her long-lashed eyes. "My husband's been good to you," she said.

"I know."

"You're in line for a good position."

He knew the promotion he coveted. "Yes, I guess I am."

"Without Dudley you would never have moved up so quickly."

Where was she heading? "Yes—I guess you're right."

"Then why are you accusing him of—of an affair."

Lyle put the cup down without spilling a drop and swallowed the bite of scone melting in his mouth. "I never—"

"Not in those exact words." She glanced away, and then those sad eyes were back on him. "My husband and I have been married almost thirty-eight years."

"That's a long time."

"Yes. His work and his family are everything to him."

"I thought you were worried about his late nights."

"Dudley will never stray far from me." Her ringed hands rested on the table. "I provide a most comfortable home for him."

He risked it. "And you don't worry about Marta Zubkov?"

"I don't ask questions. He has nothing but the good of this country in mind. If having dinner with Miss Zubkov is important to him, then I have to trust that it is for the good of the country."

"She's a Russian. I'm sure of it."

"Dudley would agree with you. That makes her useful to him."

"Then he's playing with fire, Mrs. Perkins."

"I think he's trying to keep the fire from destroying those things he believes in. His family. His country."

"He's a lucky man to have you," he told her.

"I'm the lucky one. My personal wealth never seemed to mean anything to Dudley. He wanted me for myself—even when my father, Lord Gilmore, threatened to cut off my inheritance."

The faint smile broadened. "Dudley is not an attractive man to others," she said simply.

*No. Scrawny and ugly,* Lyle thought. *With pachydermal skin and lanky limbs and a bony face.* For the moment he couldn't get past the features of the man, back to his strengths and intellectual poise. Dudley was brilliant. Skillful. And—as Molly Perkins was pointing out—kindly and loving.

"Lyle, I've spent many nights alone, but I learned a long time ago that Dudley's job is important to him."

"More important than you?"

"It grew increasingly so after we lost our son. Joel would have been close to your age, Lyle. But he was killed in the Falkland Islands."

"I'm sorry." Genuinely sorry. Again Lyle grabbed at memory. The Falklands—an isolated hump of land that lay off the coast of Argentina; a thick fog shrouded its lethal coastline. The islands were made up of hidden inlets and barren rocks that bulged from the south Atlantic Ocean—a trillion miles away from England. Lyle shrugged and said, "I never understood why we fought so hard for those barren rocks."

A flicker of amusement crossed her face. "Come now,

Lyle. Where are your loyalties? Argentina invaded British territory. We had to gain that land back to preserve our honor."

"But a lot of men lost their lives there."

"How well I know."

"Was your son a Royal Marine?"

"A pilot. When Argentina invaded the Islands, Joel rallied, eager to go and defend them. We glued ourselves to the news every day. The *HMS Ardent* went down first, and then other ships were damaged and sunk. By June Joel was dead. Very much dead."

"What a waste."

Her eyes flashed, the amusement of moments ago gone. "Dudley keeps reminding me that young Argentines died too. All for places I never heard about before. Goose Green and the San Carlos Bridgehead. The bloody disaster at Mount Kent. Teal Inlet."

Her elbows rested on the white linen cloth, her quivering chin supported by slender hands. "Joel's wing commander came to us afterwards with glowing accounts of the heroism of his men. It didn't change anything for me. Joel was still dead."

The stillness in the Ritz had become more suffocating than the dusty museum. Lyle swallowed to ease the dryness in his throat. He could offer Molly Perkins no words of comfort.

"After the war in the Falklands, Dudley poured himself into his work. Oh, he'd always put in an honest, full day, ten hours or more. But with Joel gone, he had nothing left but work."

"He had you."

"He takes me for granted—like the sun coming up or going down. Dudley knows I'll always be there." There was a sharp trill in her voice as she said, "After Joel's death Dudley buried himself at the office. Then you came along and reminded him of Joel."

"Me?" He couldn't live up to Joel Perkins. Couldn't fulfill a dead man's shattered dreams or his parents' expectations.

"Dudley has high hopes for you, Lyle. You're industrious.

That's why he had me spend so much time with you. He respects my opinion."

Lyle licked his dry lips, the taste growing more bitter in his mouth. The bombshell was coming. Dismissal? No, Dudley Perkins always tended to hiring and firing himself.

"Somehow I'm not certain that you have my son's strength of character. You're too ambitious and cunning, Lyle, but Dudley doesn't see that yet. Try as I may, I cannot picture you rallying to defend your country in a crisis like the Falkland Islands."

Lyle knew she was right. Defending his position at MI5 was challenging enough. "I have no desire to defend some little-known British protectorate," he said.

"Lyle."

He forced himself to look at the disappointment in her eyes. "We won't be going to the museums together anymore. Nor for tea. And unless Dudley insists, you won't be invited to our home again."

"You've written me off. Has your husband?"

"Dudley still misses Joel intensely. And so he sees potential in you—as the son he lost. I won't tell him that trusting you is more dangerous than his dining with Marta Zubkov."

Molly seemed suddenly absorbed in her salad, arranging and rearranging it on the china. Nothing reached her mouth. Finally she said, "You pry too much. Better if you had just talked openly with Dudley." Her voice dropped to a whisper when she said, "You will return Dudley's file to where it belongs, won't you, Lyle?"

"Yes," he said miserably.

He grabbed another scone and consumed it in three swallows. Any dream he had of becoming the director at MI5 was dying here at the Ritz—being smashed by Dudley Perkins's wife.

"I tried to tell Dudley that you were nothing like our son. He still can't see it."

"Am I to lose my job?"

"That's not the way Dudley works. He'll give you another chance. Why, I don't know. But that's the way he is." She looked up, and there was not a flicker of recognition in her gaze as Dudley Perkins was led to a nearby table.

"Didn't your husband see you?" Lyle asked.

"Yes," she said quietly. "He always reserves me a table when he's having tea or dinner with a stranger."

"There's no one with him."

"There will be in a moment."

They waited, Lyle half expecting Marta Zubkov to slip into the spot across from Perkins, but a tall, young man took the seat.

"Who is that?" Lyle asked.

"Uriah Kendall's grandson."

"Ian Kendall, the cyclist?"

"Yes. Dudley is sending him to Austria, I believe."

"He won't go."

"Then you will go in his place."

*To hunt down Nicholas Trotsky.* Lyle recoiled at the thought.

"Molly—Mrs. Perkins, your husband can't send me to Austria. That's MI6 jurisdiction."

"Dudley thinks that Nicholas Trotsky is a threat to England's internal security."

"Will he bluff his way with counterintelligence?"

"If that's what you call it. He'll be quite discreet if he investigates the situation."

Lyle knew that Molly was the one bluffing. Dudley Perkins did not take company secrets home.

She was pulling her gloves on now with precise, graceful motions. "I'm going to leave you—no, don't get up. You're to stay until Dudley leaves. Then you are to follow Ian. Check out what he does and if possible make certain he takes the train to Brunnerwald."

She paused long enough to pat Lyle's shoulder. "At first I liked you, Lyle, because my husband was so fond of you. But I never quite trusted you in the way my husband does. You're too ambitious, too greedy. You're no match for Joel. But perhaps someday—perhaps you will change. I want that for you."

Lyle sat brooding as she walked away, his thoughts on the

cross files that he had been researching. Rebellions world-wide, particularly in Russia. Codes with no grip on any-thing yet with Nicholas Trotsky's name attached. Assassins. Assassinations.

On Saturday he had gleaned one or two words from Trotsky's folder in that brief encounter in Dudley's office. "Agent-in-place" with a bold question mark behind it in Dudley's red-inked scrawl. And "Phoenix-40" with a triple row of red question marks. Nothing more. Nothing else to go on. Still Lyle had mulled them over and in utter exas-peration had shoved the cross references on birds and code names back into the file cabinet.

And then he had taken Dudley's personnel folder.

Lyle cursed that ill-fated moment, that forbidden curios-ity. He knew now that what he had found had been planted, left there by Dudley to incriminate him. With Dudley Perkins against him, Lyle had sealed his own fate, ruined his chances for promotion. His slim hope for survival at MI5 was still the same—bring about Dudley's downfall. He would prevent him from tracking down Nicholas Trotsky, leaving that triumph to the Americans. Once Lyle left the Ritz, he would make his way to the nearest public phone, dial BBC, and leak more disinformation to them.

From where he sat, Lyle had a good view of Dudley Perkins's stoic profile. His expression gave nothing away, but the tweed vest that blended so neatly with his well-tailored suit shouted exclusive buying from Savile Row. Lyle ached for a well-padded bank account of his own that would allow him to buy his suits from the prestige clothiers on Savile Row. But he longed even more for that day when he would be shed of this humbling need for Dudley and Molly Perkins.

Lyle scowled as Dudley caught the attention of the waiter and ordered. Then Perkins glanced at Ian. Kendall's emphatic no resounded across the room to Lyle's table. Kendall was either not hungry or totally irritated with Perkins—and even more defiant as the eyes of the guests around him turned his way. Kendall had to be in his early twenties, an attractive young man with sandy red hair and intense blue eyes. He tore off his denim jacket and dropped it on the floor, again defiant of his elegant surroundings. Then he grabbed his goblet and drank the ice water straight down.

Ignoring Molly Perkins's instructions, Lyle stood and sauntered past their table, stopped abruptly, and turned back. "Dudley," he exclaimed. "How nice to see you."

Dudley's eyes gave nothing away, no warning glance that Lyle had just stepped out of line. Politely Perkins introduced the men. Lyle reached across the empty water goblet and shook hands. Kendall's grip was strong, his gaze curious.

"I work for Mr. Perkins," Lyle volunteered.

"Forced recruitment?" Ian asked.

Lyle had no background reference. He'd only met Uriah once, and he couldn't drum up a family resemblance in the handsome face of Uriah Kendall's grandson nor in the freckled skin and muscular body. Lyle pulled out a chair and took a seat beside Ian. "Do you mind?" he challenged Perkins. "I'm not interrupting?"

Kendall grinned. "I thought you were here on cue—just to persuade me to do what Perkins wants."

"I wanted to meet you. Your grandfather speaks highly of you."

"Yes, he's proud of me."

"No wonder. You did well in last year's Tour de France."

"Until stage fifteen."

"That wasn't your fault. Another cyclist caused the crash."

"It was a good chance to bow out. I was wearing thin."

"What're your chances this year?"

"I'm going for the yellow jersey." His enthusiasm died as he looked at Perkins. "If your boss here doesn't ruin it for me."

Dudley leaned forward, his gangly hands folded in front of him. "You'd be back in time. In a week, ten days at most."

"You told my sponsor five days."

"Give or take a few."

Lyle remembered no evidence of friendship between Dudley Perkins and Uriah Kendall, only a glaring hostility.

Why, then, did Perkins seem so confident that Ian would do what he wanted?

Forced to acknowledge Lyle, Dudley said, "I think you know that Gainsborough Steel is sponsoring Ian's team. Jon Gainsborough and I are old friends. So it's all set for Ian to go."

"I can't sacrifice a week of practice just before a race."

"The mountains behind Brunnerwald are steep—good for building endurance. Jon agreed to send three of your teammates with you. More natural that way."

"A good cover. Isn't that what you call it, Mr. Perkins?"

"All you have to do is keep me informed on Drew Gregory."

Lyle's jaw dropped an inch. *Gregory. Not Nicholas Trotsky?*

"I've already told you, Mr. Perkins, I don't know Gregory. I haven't seen him since I was a little kid."

Lyle kept thinking, *You're risking this kid's safety with a lie, not even warning him about Nicholas Trotsky.*

"Kendall, your beloved grandmother died ten years ago. It would be a shame if we had to review that tragedy publicly."

Kendall sprang to his feet, leaned across the table, and twisted Perkins's tie. "You leave my grandmother out of this. Just send some Brits over there to do your dirty work."

Dudley loosened Ian's grip. Smoothing his tie, he stared coldly at Uriah's grandson. "We do not want to alarm Mr. Gregory. He will be in Brunnerwald to meet someone— someone that even your grandfather would gladly see in captivity. I'm telling you, Ian, we need that information. A lot is at stake—"

"Yes, my place in the Tour de France, for one."

Dudley smiled. "I would think your grandmother's reputation would be even more important."

Ian grabbed his denim jacket and stalked off without another word. Spincrest pushed back his chair to follow, but Dudley's iron grasp held him back. "Let him go. He'll do what I ask."

"Why? He doesn't even know what's going on."

"I briefed him a bit before you came."

"About Nicholas Trotsky? If you didn't, the kid is definitely risking his life."

The iron grip twisted on Lyle's wrist. "Perhaps. But I can't send anyone in from MI5. Not yet. Not openly."

"Why not?"

"That's what Marta Zubkov expects me to do." He released his grip and finger-brushed his thinning hair. "When the time is ripe, Lyle, I'll notify MI6. Until then, we'll keep this an internal matter. Zubkov contacted *me*."

"Why?"

"There must be a connection between Zubkov and Trotsky."

"They're both Russians."

"It's more than that. She wants to protect him. And she wants to use me to outsmart her own people. Once the rumor of Nicholas's survival reaches other intelligence agencies, all of Europe will be interested. We all agree on one thing—we hated Nicholas Trotsky. I'm not certain that Brunnerwald is prepared for a sudden influx of intelligence agencies searching for him."

He paid his bill and walked beside Lyle out of the Ritz. On the sidewalk, he faced Spincrest again. "I want you to check into the Weinhof Hotel in Brunnerwald. I don't want you to do anything, not even if you see Gregory. If things explode, as they might well do if Nicholas Trotsky is alive, then I'll send in reinforcements. Kendall will report to you."

"Ian Kendall will never go to Brunnerwald for you. He intends to race in the Tour de France. Nothing will stop him."

"Protecting his grandmother's memory will."

"Mrs. Kendall was just a writer, a novelist."

"In my opinion she was also a spy."

# Chapter 9

Drew leaned against the cushioned seat as the train picked up speed, whisking him over the shiny steel rails at 186 miles an hour to Innsbruck. He had eluded Frau Mayer and was enjoying the anonymity of sharing his compartment with a man and a woman, British he was certain, who seemed to consider privacy more important than idle chatter. He didn't care who these strangers were or where they were going as long as they kept to themselves, allowing him to wallow in his own dark thoughts.

Vic's parting words haunted him. *You're not running out on me, are you, Drew? It isn't this virus thing, is it?*

This virus thing that could one day be full-blown AIDS. In a way Vic was right. Drew found it difficult to face Wilson lately, seeing him as a dying man. He had answered emphatically, "Never. We'll go right on working together."

Drew wanted to add, *I don't run out on dying men. I stuck with Jacques Marseilles and Lou Garver. Remember?*

Vic's gaze remained uncertain. "I just had to ask."

"You know me better than that, Vic. I'm not someone who drops a friendship because of an illness." But Vic hadn't known that, and Drew—for all his desire to convince him—still had doubts himself.

As the train roared through one of the long, dark tunnels, Gregory pressed his thumb and forefinger against his closed eyelids, trying to ease the pressure building there.

Thinking of Vic these days gave him a throbbing headache. He worried about Vic's girlfriends in every city, wondering whether there had been a mad race for blood tests. But how could Vic warn them? He wouldn't even remember some of them. The thought infuriated Drew. Only three names stood out with Vic—the two ex-wives who had divorced him and his cousin's best friend Nicole.

Drew felt like the proverbial kettle calling the pot black. He decided to give a whopping sum to AIDS research—to soothe his own distress at a friend's illness and with the hope that science would come up with a cure in time for Vic.

An aching void boiled inside of him, an internal emptiness. Never before had Drew felt so thrust against the wall, incapable of solving his own problems. This time he had hit rock bottom. Drew hadn't expected it to be this way at the end of his career. No farewell speeches. No warm handshakes. No lasting friendships left. He'd been blacklisted, rejected by the Agency for exposing Porter Deven as a traitor. For the men it remained unthinkable that Porter could ever have sold out his country. To them, Drew had broken the code of silence and wiped out Porter's career.

Even Drew's request for retirement was grinding slowly through the wheels of bureaucracy. He suspected a deliberate delay at Chad Kaminsky's desk in Langley, possibly even from Troy Carwell in Paris. They would do everything to keep Drew from writing an exposé of his years with the Agency.

How little they knew him. All Gregory wanted to do was clear his desk, turn over the remaining files, and walk away. But did he? Drew was a Company man, integrity carved into his life from childhood. He'd given the Agency the best years of his life, a costly commitment with a wasted marriage. The ache inside of him turned physical now with a longing for Miriam. But once again Drew had chosen an Agency assignment over her.

No, this time Miriam had insisted that he go.

His daughter's words came thundering back: *All God wants is for one stubborn man to follow Him.* He tried to shake off the conviction, tried to convince himself again that commitment to the Agency and God were incompatible. Now he had neither one.

He felt purposeless, slammed completely into the concrete wall, his marriage really over, his career coming to a screeching halt. But dared he risk ignoring God any longer? Could Robyn be right—God was just waiting for one stubborn man to follow Him?

He opened his eyes and looked at the woman across from him. Her gaze was sympathetic. Before she could speak, he turned toward the lovely hillsides outside the train window. The trip from Salzburg to Tyrol country was one of his favorites, the most scenic ride in all of Austria as far as Drew was concerned. He was encircled with the magnificent Alps—and in awe of the people who lived on them. In the distance stood a lone cabin tucked into a mountain crevice and just beyond that an Alpine village clinging to the steep mountainside. A village like Sulzbach.

He soaked up the beauty as the train snaked its way around the bends of the mountain and began to climb even higher. Wooded slopes and fertile valleys. The inaccessible peaks veiled in layers of mist. Gorges and canyons and limestone cliffs. Dark forests of conifers, their limbs still heavy with snow, and Alpine meadows on the lower slopes with grazing cattle. Alpine pansies and gentianellas already dotted these hillsides. Even the vibrant blue thistle and clumps of edelweiss would be in bloom in a few weeks. Far below, a network of waterways filled with snow-cold water had begun to widen the lakes and mountain streams, sending the streams dashing and foaming over rocky beds to merge with the River Inn as it ran its course toward Innsbruck.

The climb had been gradual, but now from high atop the narrow viaduct, the world dropped off on Drew's right into a narrow canyon edged with sheer limestone cliffs. At this elevation snow still covered the forests and the train trestles, and snowdrifts wrapped around the weather-beaten hamlets. It seemed like winter on one slope, spring budding on another. The mountain peaks always wore their snow bonnets, but as Drew looked down into the deep canyons and valleys, he saw that spring had budded on the lower slopes with only patches of snow on the timbered houses.

Drew loved this time of year between seasons when winter struggled to let go of its bitter cold and the wild Alpine flowers began to set the country ablaze with color. Winters were bleak to Drew, spring renewing. It was a brilliant time of year when skiers became hikers, and the packed snows of winter melted and overflowed into mammoth water-falls—their waters streaked with rainbows as they plunged into the gorges below.

"It's lovely, isn't it?" the woman asked softly.

Feeling a bit more charitable, he smiled at her. "Indescribable."

She shifted, trying to ease the pressure of her husband's head slumped against her shoulder. "We'll be staying in the city for a while," she said. "Living with my son and daughter."

"How nice."

"For us, yes. For the children, no." She nodded at her sleeping husband. "We'd be a burden if we stayed too long. And you? Will you be staying with friends in Innsbruck?"

"Not this time," he told her. "I'm looking for someone."

"For a friend?" she asked.

Drew scowled, annoyed by her curious, faded blue eyes. He stood and took his briefcase from the rack, determined to busy himself and ward off more questions. She sighed as he spread out his map and began scanning the Tyrol country for Brunnerwald.

"Are you going far?" she persisted.

*Far enough,* he thought. "An hour or so from Innsbruck."

His words had been sharp, nettled. He could feel her withdraw, shy and offended by his curtness. He pulled back into his own moroseness, suddenly reminded of how often he had been irked by Miriam's questions about the Agency and his mother's constant prying into his travels. Smitten at the reminder, he felt sorry for this woman, easily his mother's age, traveling with a sleeping husband—perhaps a sick one—and cut off even from talking to Drew.

He lowered the map and looked at her again. A weary face

but pleasant. An apprehensive woman not accustomed to travel. Politely, he asked, "Could I get you something? Something to eat? Drink?"

"Don't bother," she said. "I want my husband to rest."

Gregory was not an unfriendly man. He could be quite sociable when the situation demanded. But when traveling, he preferred to be left alone, particularly on days like this when he was mapping out his strategy for Brunnerwald. But now, not ninety minutes from Innsbruck, his planning had been crushed by memories. All he could do as he stared back down at the map was to remember.

Miriam and his mother.

Innsbruck and Brunnerwald.

Sulzbach and Nicholas Ivan Trotsky.

Trotsky loved skiing, and Brunnerwald was a ski resort that had grown popular with the Europeans. Sulzbach, the place of the salty brook, where Drew had last seen Nicholas, lay within journeying distance from Brunnerwald. And now Nicholas had risen from the ashes there. The irony of it made Drew laugh. Why had he never considered that Nicholas Trotsky could take refuge in Brunnerwald?

Drew flattened the map with his hand and allowed his finger to trace imaginary lines north of Brunnerwald, lingering briefly over each name. Sulzbach was not on the map, but he knew vaguely in his mind that it was possible to reach the village on foot.

He could taste the victory of cornering Trotsky once again. Trotsky had been Drew's thorn in the flesh, the reminder that he had been outwitted. Outmaneuvered. Hornswoggled to the nth degree by the elusive Trotsky. Gregory's case histories had not always succeeded, but only two festered in his mind, putrefying, rotting there—abscesses that wouldn't heal, decaying and decomposing. Two men. Porter Deven—once a friend and colleague—and in the end uncovered as a double agent. And Nicholas Trotsky—always the enemy—a man so savage and ruthless that as far as Drew was concerned, even God Himself—if God existed—could not, would not change Nicholas Trotsky.

Nicholas Trotsky the assassin, gunning down political figures like Klaus Zimmerman in the Olympic Village in Innsbruck. Trotsky the KGB liquidator, the silencer, the executioner who had been on every intelligence file in Europe. Drew found it difficult to accept that Trotsky was simply doing his job in blind obedience to a cause that Drew despised—a marksman taking down his enemy with laser-point accuracy and then calmly walking away in the crowd.

For what? Position? Promotion? Or had that lone assassin been part of a greater plan, a Soviet military coup that would rise from the ashes and return Russia to the iron captivity of the old days?

Vic and Drew had killed men in the line of duty. But Nicholas Trotsky had been a professional killer, almost claiming the British prime minister as one of his victims; and it was still believed that Trotsky had been in on the assassination plot to remove the American president on one of his foreign visits to Geneva.

Drew's vengeance was lower on the political scale; Trotsky had killed one of Drew's best friends—Berl Campione, one of the Company men that Drew had most admired. Berl's widow still lived alone in the Puget Sound area. His kids had grown up and gone off to college. But Berl was still dead.

Drew had taken on Berl Campione's cause and commitment to take Trotsky alive. He had come close at the Olympic Games in Innsbruck when he discovered Nicholas on the bobsled team from East Germany. But while Drew worked his way through red tape and bureaucracy, Klaus Zimmerman had been assassinated, and Trotsky had slipped safely across the border. Zimmerman was another personal score for Drew to settle; Drew had respected the West German political figure whom Trotsky had toppled in the line of duty.

Settling the score goaded Gregory. He sensed its jolting intensity, the darkness of retaliation, as tenebrous and gloomy as the winding mountain tunnel just ahead.

Drew folded the map, creasing the folds with precision as he mulled over Troy Carwell's refusal to send updated records on Trotsky. Carwell, safe in his office in Paris, wanted nothing incriminating in Drew's possession if something went wrong. No link to Langley nor to the Agency in Paris. But Vic Wilson had stopped by Drew's flat in London and hand-carried Drew's own file on Nicholas to Salzburg. Vic Wilson. Carwell. Trotsky. And Miriam. Drew's thoughts seemed trapped in a blender, whirling around, spinning uncontrollably, the disconnect button jammed.

He returned the map to his briefcase and took out Nicholas Trotsky's file, his dislike of Nicholas intensifying as he ran his hand over the manila folder. Trotsky alive. Porter dead. His anger with Porter for dying merged with his fury at Trotsky for surviving. He knew as he sat there, gliding over the steel rails toward Innsbruck, that Porter and Trotsky had been committed to the same cause, both controlled by the KGB. A woman had caused Porter's downfall. But what about Trotsky?

As the train broke out of the darkness of the rock-hewn tunnel, he blinked against the flashes of sunlight streaking through the train window. His traveling companion watched him open the folder, that hint of curiosity lighting her eyes again.

He nodded brusquely and then stared down at the fragmented record of Trotsky's life: An older brother born in Nazi-occupied Belarus. Nicholas born near there four years later, but reared near the Baltic Sea, the surviving son of a peasant woman. His father Valentin, a Russian soldier, had survived the siege of Leningrad only to die in poor health six years later. Valentin remained a committed Communist; Nicholas's mother a committed Catholic—the one similarity between Nicholas and Drew.

From boyhood Nicholas had leaned toward Communist ideology under the tutorship of an uncle in military intelligence. He was rewarded with ski and hunting trips. Early KGB links began with membership in the Communist Youth League, followed eventually with acceptance at the oriental language school in Moscow University. Drew had penciled a notation at this point: "undergraduates from language institute often tapped for work with KGB."

Nicholas had taken an accelerated three-year course. His

assignments as an interpreter in Turkey, Iran, and France followed. Beside Trotsky's membership in a trade delegation, Drew had made a pencil notation: "organization linked to KGB."

While still in his twenties, Nicholas was expelled from Iran for spreading communistic propaganda. He returned to Russia to train as an assassin under the guise of law school. The severance of his relationship with his mother occurred at the same time, her religious convictions the issue. And then a three-year period unaccounted for before Trotsky reappeared on the scene, his name clearly linked with numerous political assassinations.

Drew's fingers drummed on the file top. After that three-year absence, Nicholas had risen from the ashes. Had he spent those three years in disfavor? No, Trotsky was too committed a Communist to be disciplined by isolation. Or had Trotsky gone underground, planning a takeover that after all these years would finally be put into action?

"You look so troubled," the woman said.

"Do I?" he asked. "I'm just trying to get some work done."

She withdrew into her cocoon again, embarrassed.

He closed the folder and slipped it back into his briefcase, his eyes still on her. She had once been a beautiful woman, her delicate features aged but still attractive. Odd. In Trotsky's file, only one beautiful woman had been linked to him—Marta Zubkov, reportedly young and desirable. Drew had never been able to trace anyone with that name. Had she been a romantic interlude for Trotsky—one that would have caused him to drop from circulation for fifteen years or even for that three-year gap in Trotsky's file? A woman? Impossible. No, Nicholas was incapable of loving anyone.

Gregory knew now with hindsight why Porter Deven had mocked him more than once, "You'll never take Nicholas Trotsky alive. He's too clever for you, Drew."

Had Porter known Trotsky personally? It seemed likely now.

But Porter had been wrong. Just weeks before the Agency closed the file on Trotsky—after endless futile leads and dead ends—Drew's long search had ended in a face-to-face encounter with Trotsky at a ski resort. On a tip from Paris, Drew had reversed his flight pattern and retraced the miles to Austria, landing his small aircraft at the ski resort high above Brunnerwald.

Drew clearly remembered the occasion. Trotsky's skis were lined up on the rack outside the lodge, his ski parka and goggles dumped on the chair beside him. Trotsky sat facing the fireside, peering over a frosty beer mug as the flames crept around the logs.

Drew had strolled boldly over. "Nicholas Trotsky," he said.

Nicholas made no attempt to reach for his parka as he faced Drew, nor did he spill one drop of beer from the stein in his hand. The ornate beauty of the beer mug clashed with the cold steel of Trotsky's eyes. It looked as if his face had been sculpted from Austrian limestone or from a lifeless clay stein. Yet it was a handsome face with firmly defined features. Nicholas matched Drew's own six-feet-two, a solidly built man and a muscular handful to commandeer into the plane.

Yes, he had captured Nicholas Trotsky just outside the ski lodge in a rapid exchange of gunfire. Drew was not fighting an unfinished nightmare, not this time. He was wide awake, sitting on a train en route to Innsbruck, remembering something that had actually happened.

# Chapter 10

There were several things that Drew could not recall about that first trip to Sulzbach, large blocks of memory loss between the plane going down and his awakening on a narrow cot, tended by a priest. A whole time period veiled like the mountain peaks shrouded in the thick morning mists. Large segments that he could not piece together even in the nightmare that had been submerged in his subconscious for the better part of a dozen years—until Vienna. Until last night when he had tossed and turned for a couple of hours and dreamed again.

His gut feeling had always been that Nicholas Trotsky had escaped. And when the Agency closed the file, listing Trotsky as dead in the Sulzbach Avalanche, Drew only half believed it possible. And now this.

Trotsky was reportedly alive, rising from the ashes in the area where he had disappeared—like the ancient legend of the phoenix bird rising full-wing to threaten Drew again. To carry him back to a failed mission, best forgotten. To force him to admit that he had been outwitted, outmaneuvered, hornswoggled to the nth degree as he had always been when he challenged Nicholas Trotsky. Drew retraced those days in his mind, allowing himself to reflect on the dust-covered happenings, desperately trying to discover where he had gone wrong.

What Drew remembered of that first trip to Sulzbach was the sudden, unexpected drop in altitude, the wild vibration at the controls, the alarms going off in the cockpit, the panel lights all flashing red simultaneously. Only seconds in time, but he heard Trotsky swearing in German in the seat beside him and Lou Garver pleading for mercy from a Higher Power.

Drew struggled to regain control, but the plane continued to shudder, bouncing like a rubber ball in the wind that swept up through the canyon. Below them lay a small Alpine village—three children standing in the snow, eyes shaded with gloved hands, watching the plane dipping, falling, plunging.

Drew managed to swoop over the village across a narrow ravine almost to the safety of an emergency landing when the wing dipped precariously. Sweat formed on his brow as the fuselage ripped apart and one wing fragmented into metal strips that spread across the snowdrifts. The aircraft charged on pell-mell, the windshield shattering as they slammed into a snowbank.

Drew's head lurched forward, colliding with the navigation panel. The force jerked him back and slammed him forward a second time. As his neck snapped in a whiplash, pain shot through his body. Trotsky was still swearing, Lou silent.

It hurt like thunder to breathe as he turned to look at Lou. Garver lay like a rag doll against the broken seat. The winter sun pouring through the split section of the fuselage sent an eerie pink streak across Lou's lifeless face.

Drew crawled through a hole in the fuselage and dropped to the snow. He smelled the fuel—saw it dripping. Drops of his own blood tracked with him as he circled the plane, each step grueling as he made his way to Trotsky.

Nicholas dangled from the passenger side, his face toward the ground. He was hurt badly. Drew tugged at Trotsky's body, each effort sending another sharp pain through Drew's head. As he dragged Trotsky to safety, snow flurries patted Gregory's face, gently at first, and then the larger flakes and the brisk mountain air chafed his skin. He staggered under Trotsky's weight—fell once, twice.

Trotsky moaned, his back twisted. Drew fell beside him a third time, gasping. He was aware of unrelenting pain pounding in his head as he turned and crawled back toward the aircraft. One eye was half-closed, snow and blood blinding him. Still he saw the Pilatus balancing close to the limestone cliff, a blurred monster with one wing severed and the flaps gone. The contents of Lou's briefcase flitted like toy planes dipping and rising with each gust of wind.

Lou was dead, but Drew had to get him out, had to pull him from the plane before it burst into flames. He dug into the snow with his bare hands, inching painfully toward Garver. From high up on the mountain the earth rumbled. Mammoth stones raced down the mountainside. Drew shielded his head as they flipped over the broken wing and tumbled into the narrow gorge.

"I'm coming, Garver." His words slurred. "You're dead, old buddy. But I'm coming. I'll get you out."

The smell of fuel grew stronger as he neared the plane. And then the front end exploded, the nose of the plane turning into a spontaneous fireball. "Dear God," Drew cried out. "Not Garver. Please, not Garver."

Gregory tried to flip backwards, but he had only enough time to bury his face as the fire skimmed across the top layer of snow. It twisted along a rocky path—singeing the back of Drew's hand as it brushed nearby. Moments after the intense heat moved away, he struggled to his feet, took five faltering steps, and then the piercing pain came again. He fell facedown motionless.

He had not seen the skiers coming toward them, but he heard the muffled sound of a cry, as in a tunnel. Hollow. Distant. "It's too late for this one," a man said. "He's dead."

*Dead? Me?* Drew tried to turn his head, to lift his chin from the bitter cold of the snow, but his words were lost on the wings of the Alpine wind. He drifted in and out until a hobnailed boot prodded him, and then the sound of another voice—deep and kindly. "No, this man's alive."

Drew felt the strength of those hands turning his numb,

bruised body and wrapping him in a coarse wool blanket. From out of the shadowed valley of dying, of drifting into numbness, he forced his one good eye open and focused on the kindest eyes he had ever seen. Drew tried to tell the man about Trotsky, tried to tug on the sleeve of the man's mountain jacket, but the words strangled in his throat as another piercing pain—more severe than all the others—crushed his temples.

Moving swiftly, even smiling, the man tore off his own woolly, ear-flapped hat and scrunched it down over Drew's frostbitten ears. Even through one eye, Drew could see the man's snow-white hair whipping in the Alpine wind, the large ears turning a nippy red, his thick, straggly brows caked with snow.

Gently, the man placed Drew's burned hand beneath the blanket. Above them the mountain rumbled again. Drew tensed.

"Don't worry," the man said, his voice full of confidence and hope. "I'm Jacques Caridini. You'll be all right now."

Drew felt himself floating, drifting into unconsciousness, and he welcomed the glad relief of oblivion.

Days later Drew awakened, his thoughts befuddled, his one eye still sticky but fluttering at half-mast. He lay on a narrow bed in a sterile, well-scrubbed room smelling of soap and cleanser and incense. As he gazed down at his inert body, he discovered he was wearing someone else's pajamas, his own clothes noticeably missing from the room.

Tossing the blanket back, he attempted to sit up, but the sound in his head thundered like a waterfall cascading off the highest peak. Slowly he settled back against the hard pillow, moving only his eyes to take in his surroundings. The furnishings were simple, yet the table and dresser had been skillfully carved. The timbered walls were painted white, unadorned except for a lone crucifix hanging on the wall at the foot of his bed.

The room of his boyhood? No. His mother's room? No,

again. Her room had been full of ruffles and lace and the smell of French perfumes, not cleansing soaps. A hospital? Yes, this had to be a hospital. He tried to remember, then fought remembering.

The plane out of control . . . the crash . . . the rumbling in the mountain. Hobnailed boots prodding him. A coarse wool blanket scratching his skin. Oblivion. He allowed his eyes to track the room again, carefully turning his head this time, and his gaze drifted back to the crucifix. Symbolism. The bruised body of Christ on a cross. Yes, that was what he had learned as an altar boy a hundred years ago. No, not quite that many.

Gregory held up his hands, one bandaged. The effort proved exhausting. *I'm alive.* The pain in his head convinced him. What he didn't want to remember came again. He was alive, but Lou Garver was dead. Drew had crashed the plane, veering across the sheer cliff, killing his friend. Utter stillness gripped him except for the sound of his own breathing. Wherever he was, he was alone—as alone as Garver in the plane.

Gregory tried to escape back into sleep, but the faint sound of a cow bell came into the room, growing louder as he listened. In spite of the pain, Drew forced himself to sit up; his back muscles screamed as he limped toward the two small windows—as sparkling clean as the rest of the room.

As he pushed the window open, the blue shutter squeaked as though he were harbored in a room rarely used. There was a nip to the air as he glanced around, but it made him feel vital, alive. *I'm alive, but Garver is dead.*

The cow bell tinkled again, bringing a smile to Drew's face. From where he leaned, he could count five cows and twenty sturdy, chalet-like homes, snow melting from their steep roofs. *Perhaps this is the Alpine village I swooped over just before the accident.* A brook ran between the homes—a stream that would become like a small river when the snows of winter melted in the spring. He shivered as the mountain air blew against him; still he lingered, his eye on the ski cables that rose from below the village to the distant, snowbound peaks.

He could see now that his room was attached to a white-steepled church with a cross on top and a walled-in cemetery behind it. The idea of taking refuge within the walls of a sanctuary half amused him, half terrorized him.

"*Guten tag.*"

The greeting came from behind him.

Drew turned cautiously, the throbbing sensation in his head controlling his speed. The voice belonged to a man wearing a gray turtleneck sweater beneath his priestly garb. It was a strong, rugged face that had weathered the storm and broke easily into an optimistic smile. A salt-and-pepper moustache matched the gray of the sweater, but the straggly brows were black and curly at the ends.

"Do I pass inspection, Mr. Gregory?"

The priest spoke in German, but Drew had enough presence of mind, enough self-preservation to respond in English.

Obligingly the priest switched to Drew's native language. "You wish to speak in English?" he asked. "Then we will do so. But your German is excellent, especially when I change your dressings. And now you must get back into bed before you take pneumonia."

The intense blue eyes were kindly, sympathetic. The blurred image of a man dragging him to safety came back. The kindest eyes he had ever seen. "You saved my life?"

"Yes, perhaps I did, Mr. Gregory."

Drew touched his head.

"A severe concussion, but you'll recover. And your hand— a superficial burn. You've lost the top layer of skin on your shoulder and buttocks—painful but not fatal." The smile stayed optimistic. "You worried us for a while. At first you had difficulty breathing. We thought your lung had collapsed. But you'll make it."

*But I could have died out there in the snow. Frozen to death. Would surely have done so without this man.* "Where am I, sir?"

"In the village of Sulzbach—the place of the salty brook."

"In Austria?"

"Of course. Is there any other place so beautiful?"

"And you, sir. Who are you?"

THE TWELFTH ROSE OF SPRING

"Jacques Caridini, the priest of Sulzbach."

"Does anyone else live in the rectory?"

"Just my housekeeper and myself. But I sent her down to Brunnerwald. It'll be quiet here, restful for you."

"I'm grateful to you, Father Caridini, but I must leave."

Drew swayed unsteadily, his headache growing to explosive proportions as the priest guided him back to the bed. "Rest a few more days, my son," he said. "You don't have the strength to walk down to the nearest town. Not yet."

Drew was sweating as his head hit the pillow. "I—"

"You've been unconscious for days," Caridini said quietly. "You didn't even awaken when the avalanche hit."

"An avalanche?"

"The night of the plane crash."

Alarmed, Drew asked, "Did the accident cause it?"

"No. One of those late spring storms piled snow upon snow until a bottom layer broke loose." He shrugged, his smile vanishing. "It brought a deadly river of ice blocks tumbling toward our village. It took everything in its path."

"I never heard a thing."

"You were in a deep sleep, too sick to move."

"And you stayed here with me? What about the others?"

"The homes near the gorge were swept away, several of my friends with them. But we're strong here. We'll survive."

Drew felt groggy as though he were drifting. "And my plane?"

"Swept away in the avalanche. Your friend with it."

He tried to remember how many people had been in the plane, but the count slipped away. "There was someone else. I'm certain I pulled someone from the plane." Trotsky. But he couldn't tell the priest the man's name. He couldn't even be certain that his words had been audible. But still he asked, "What happened to your God, Father Caridini, when the avalanche started?"

"Son, the storms are part of His storehouse."

Four days later as the priest dressed his wounds, Drew said, "I've got to get my friend out of the plane before I leave."

"Your friend is gone," Caridini reminded him.

"I know. He died on impact. But I can't leave him here."

Father Caridini scrutinized his bandaging and then walked to the window to empty the wash basin on the ground outside. Then he took up his watch at Drew's bedside once more. "I'll be saying mass within the hour. We'll pray for your friend."

"It's too late to pray for Garver."

"But not too late to pray for his family or for you."

Savagely Drew asked, "And will you pray for the injured villagers that you carried down the mountain?" Trotsky? Had Trotsky been taken to Brunnerwald, too? "Were there any strangers among the injured?"

Drew winced as Caridini removed the bandage from his hand exposing the nerve endings to the air. "No, Mr. Gregory. That would only invite the Brunnerwald authorities to comb our village for answers. We wouldn't want that, would we?"

Drew glanced toward the mountain peaks again, his thoughts on Trotsky. "Could anyone have survived alone in the storm?"

"Not the night of the avalanche."

"Father Caridini, there were two passengers in my plane. One was a Russian." *An enemy agent.* "You didn't save his life, too?"

"We're a peaceful people here, Mr. Gregory. We rescue all strangers. Skiers. Hikers. Plane victims—"

"He's a dangerous man."

"Son, I know no enemies. To me all men are the same— all in need of the peace of God."

"When the snows melt, will they search for him?"

"Perhaps. But when the weather improves, the *polizei* will come up from Brunnerwald and inquire about the accident."

"I must leave before then."

"No one will search the rectory for strangers."

Plural. More than one. Could Trotsky be somewhere in this rectory? Drew pushed himself to a sitting position, allowing the faintness to resolve before asking, "Are we alone here?"

"I told you. I sent my housekeeper down to Brunnerwald."

*So she wouldn't know I'm here. Wouldn't know about Trotsky.*

"She helped take the injured down, Mr. Gregory."

Drew shook his head. "You live up here with the risk of an avalanche. What brought you to these mountains, Father Caridini?"

"The bishop. I'd pastored in the towns for ten years, but I was still trying to find my niche. I found it here by the salty brook thirty years ago. I've been here ever since. And you, my son. What brought you to our mountains?"

"I was on a mission of my own. But now it's time for me to leave," Drew insisted.

"You're still too weak to travel alone, Herr Gregory."

"I'm much better. I can move quite well now."

Caridini nodded to the clean pile of clothes that he had placed on the dresser top. "Clean and mended," he said.

When Caridini returned from saying mass, Drew was dressed and ready to leave. He had already made a hasty search of the rectory looking for Trotsky, checking each room except for the priest's personal chamber. They were empty. But the question lingered in Drew's mind. What had happened to Trotsky?

Father Caridini and Drew walked from the church rectory to the top of the hill together.

"I'm sending the wood carver's son with you." Caridini nodded toward a broad-shouldered young man in shiny boots and lederhosen. "Hans will take you to the clinic, Herr Gregory."

"No clinic," Drew told him. "An airport or a train station."

Caridini nodded to the boy. "As he wishes, Hans."

The priest stood quietly for a moment, his thick hand to his mouth. Then he gripped Drew's shoulders and smiled, his eyes a brilliant blue. "Go then, my son, and God go with you."

🌀🌀🌀

The train slid into Innsbruck's main railway station right on time, the iron wheels braking against the rails, the Goldenes Dachl and the majestic mountain peaks both glowing in welcome. Drew stood, emptied the rack above him, and then offered his hands to his traveling companions, getting them both safely to their feet. But when Drew smiled at them, he was still reflecting on Father Caridini, the man who had saved his life in the village of Sulzbach, the place of the salty brook.

*God go with you.*

The priest's words were as loud and clear in Gregory's mind as they had been fifteen years ago in that mountain village. *But if you could see me now, Jacques Caridini, you would know that God did not go with me.*

# Chapter 11

Peter Kermer sat in the easy chair in the hotel room, avoiding the empty spot at the table where the others huddled over a map of Brunnerwald. He hated to sit any closer, hated the stale smell of cigarettes that clung to Werner Vronin's clothes and the fetid smell of garlic and onions whenever Yuri Ryskov opened his mouth. But Yuri's colorless face looked like a man who was ill, an untreated diabetic perhaps.

How, Peter wondered, did Marta take the closeness? He tried to read her expression, to glimpse behind the hard, tight eyes. Something was wrong. Their mission to Brunnerwald was in danger or perhaps in question. Or was she avoiding him? Did she know that he was an imposter? He pressed his broad hand to his chest and flattened the Star of David that hung beneath his buttoned shirt.

"No, Vronin," Marta said. "You will listen to me. Dimitri put me in charge."

"Not for long," Vronin challenged. "One mistake. One of your emotional blunders, and I take over. Dimitri's orders."

She accepted his words without arguing, her gaze turning from the map to Peter, imploring his help. Her usual steely glint had softened—just for an instant—as though she had seen in Peter an ally, a friend. The thought that he would betray her in the end troubled him. She was a pretty woman, but the hardness around her well-shaped mouth had deepened since their arrival in Brunnerwald.

As she turned back and glared at Vronin, the hardness was there again.

Marta was, Kermer decided, a victim of birth. Given another country, another philosophy to live by, she would have been different—carefree and happy—not cooped up in a hotel room planning the strategy that would most likely condemn Nicholas Trotsky to death. If Marta had been born in America or Israel, she might have married and settled down to raising a family.

Now as she spoke of Trotsky, her eyes seemed grieved, pained at the job at hand. "May I remind you, Werner, I will recognize Nicholas. You will need me to find him."

Vronin's lips seemed to suck in, narrowing in size, his angry rebuttal tabled for the moment.

"Won't you join us, Peter?" she said, her voice more an invitation than an order.

"Must I?"

"I'd prefer it."

He went reluctantly, choosing the smell of cigarettes over garlic as he took the chair between Marta and Vronin.

"We won't have long," she said. "Dimitri is impatient already. He wants Trotsky."

"Yesterday?" Peter asked.

"Or as soon after that as possible."

"It would be sooner," Vronin said, "if you would simply take us to the house where you saw him. Marta, if you don't give us the address, I will take this town apart block by block until I find Trotsky myself."

"We want to find Nicholas," she said coldly, "not warn those who know him best that we are looking for him. Besides, I told you I can't remember the street address or even the exact house."

"I don't believe you."

Peter glanced at Marta again, feeling a sense of pity for her—a concern such as he felt for Sara when she was troubled. Yuri seemed the least interested of all of them, half-dozing in his chair. Yet Kermer was confident that Yuri would pull his weight and responsibility once Trotsky was found.

"You are slipping, Marta," Vronin said. "You're making poor decisions these days. I don't like you and Kermer taking lodging together. Dimitri won't like it."

The accusation stung, but Marta made no effort to defend it. "What hotel Peter and I stay in is my business, Vronin."

*Hotel?* Peter thought. *Then Vronin doesn't know that we've taken rooms at a local* gasthof? He sat tongue-in-cheek, waiting for the next verbal blow.

"It's best this way. If anything—anything," she emphasized, "goes wrong, at least they won't take all four of us at one time."

"And where are you staying, Marta?"

"Across town. We'll keep in touch."

"I can follow you when you leave us."

"But you won't, Vronin. You like to play it safe."

Suddenly Yuri rallied in his chair, all sleep gone from his eyes. "They're not at a hotel, Vronin. They left there for a *gasthof* in the Old Town." He snickered. "I know. I followed them."

Vronin's contempt for Marta blackened his gaze. "Good, Yuri." He shoved back his chair. "Then we'll scour that block door by door until we find him."

"Werner, just hear her out," Peter suggested. "You know that Dimitri approved her plans."

"Politeness will get us nowhere. Just tell me the name of the *gasthof* owner, Marta, and I will get the answers from him."

"No violence, Werner."

"You're a fool, Marta."

Kermer leaned between them. "We must find Nicholas quickly and quietly, but we don't want to leave a trail of blood behind us. And we can't afford to fight among ourselves."

Vronin soured even more, his eyes challenging. "Neither will branching out to separate hotels help us find him."

Ignoring Vronin's rage, Marta said, "Nicholas loved skiing almost more than life itself. That gives us a reason to be in town."

"For a ski trip?" Yuri asked, interested at last.

"We're going to go to every major place in town looking for our missing friend." She had their complete attention now, even Vronin's. "We'll tell people that he came to Brunnerwald two or three weeks ago for a ski trip. We haven't heard from him since."

*It might work,* Peter thought.

Vronin's lip curled. "Do that and we alert those who know him."

"We're not going from *gasthof* to *gasthof.* Just to restaurants and business places." Marta placed several black-and-white photos on the table. "Dimitri had some age-progressions made. This," she said handing them a photo of a handsome man in uniform, "was how Nicholas looked when I first met him."

As the photograph reached Peter, he studied it: a strong muscular man, good-looking in spite of his serious, unsmiling face. *Like mine,* Peter thought. *Unsmiling.*

"Hair?" Peter asked.

"Dark and thick," Marta told him.

"Is it still dark and thick?" Vronin asked. "Or balding?"

Peter saw the muscles in her neck twitch as she said, "I didn't notice. It all happened so fast. He got up from the park bench and was gone—"

"And yet you knew it was him?"

"Yes, Vronin. I'm certain of it."

Watching her, Peter was convinced that she wanted to lie and was afraid to do so. Something had happened since the moment she had discovered Trotsky. Whatever vengeance had goaded her when she called Dimitri had turned to fear, fear that was barely hidden. "What about Trotsky's eyes?" Peter asked gently.

"Blue." Her voice fell to a whisper. "An intense blue like a bright summer sky. Once he looked at you, you never forgot the color of his eyes."

Marta gave herself away, revealed more than she had intended. Peter heard the wistfulness in her words. Her eyes sought his again. He gave her a trace of a smile. She was his enemy, and yet he felt the urge to protect her. *Someday,* Sara had told him, *you will reach out to help the wrong person, and I'll lose you—or you'll lose your life.*

"Odd," Vronin said. "I met him once in Moscow. I don't remember the color of his eyes."

"You don't even remember the color of mine, Werner, and we've been working together for some years now." She passed the second photo, the one that showed age-progression in the lines around Trotsky's mouth and eyes. A mature appearance, the face still cold and unsmiling, the eyes intense, and the thick hair more silvery than dark.

As Peter looked at the picture, he knew at the gut level that Nicholas Trotsky did not look like this photo. Marta had given her stamp of approval to it, had agreed with Dimitri that it was a good likeness of Nicholas, but what had she omitted? And while he pondered on this, Marta passed a flyer to each one of them—a clear image of Nicholas Trotsky in ski pants and a parka, a pair of Volkl skis upright in his hands.

Marta pointed to the map again. "We're going to comb this town. Beginning with the shopping areas. And we're going to tell the people who live here that we are afraid that something has happened to our friend."

"What if Trotsky gets wind of it and runs?" Kermer asked.

"Not Nicholas. He never ran from a challenge. He loved pursuing people, backing them into a corner. If he hears about our searching for him, he'll stand his ground and fight."

*Someone will get killed,* Peter thought. *Nicholas or you, Marta.* Peter saw in her face the same possibility as though she were clinging to that hope. Whoever he was, whatever he had been to Marta, she had no intention of taking him back to Dimitri.

She pushed the map toward Vronin. "I've marked off the streets for you and Yuri. Kermer will go with me."

"Oh. And where might that be?"

"We'll take the cable up to the ski lodge and start there. We'll meet back here this evening—after dark. And Vronin—" The hatred in her eyes matched his. "See if you can show a little compassion. Remember we're looking for a lost friend."

"And will our friend have a name?" he asked wryly.

"Nicholas. Nicholas Trotsky."

"You're a fool," Vronin told her again.

"That's his name."

"You'll have every policeman in town coming to us."

"Good, Vronin. Then they can help us. If we play our part well, we will simply be searching for a lost friend."

"And if we find him?"

"We'll get word to Dimitri."

*Will you?* Peter wondered. *Or what plan do you really have in that pretty, little head of yours?*

The rest of her instructions were precise, scheduled. She had grown even more tired as they sat there. Peter stood abruptly. "Marta, we should be going. It's getting late. There'll be long lines at the ski lift."

She gave him a grateful smile. "This evening then," she said. With a glance at her watch she added, "Good. There's still time to call Dimitri before the *postamt* closes for the lunch hour."

If the announcement annoyed Vronin, he gave no indication. He remained in his chair staring across the table at Yuri.

Peter slung his knapsack across his back and guided Marta out of the room, through the hotel lobby, and out into the street. "The *postamt* is three blocks over," he told her.

"Go on. I'll find it and meet you back at the *gasthof*."

"I thought we were taking the ski cable."

"We are, but I want to slip into something more comfortable. But first I'm going to the *postamt* and place an international call to Dimitri."

*She's really going to call him.* Kermer kept his grip on her elbow steering her away from the post office. "We still have time. We'll go down by the river and then cut back through a side street."

"Why all the maneuvering, Kermer?"

"Yuri is following us. No—don't turn around. We can lose him. Besides, I have to buy some stamps." *What I really have to do,* he thought, shifting the weight of his backpack, *is send*

*my gift to Sara—to let her know where I am. To let her know*
*where to start searching if I don't get home.*

"Yuri knows where we're going."

"He's more interested in what we are up to. I'm going to
take your arm and draw you toward me. No, Marta. You're
safe. I mean nothing by it."

She shuddered beneath his grip.

"It's all right, Marta. Right now I'm just protecting you."

"Why would you do that, Herr Kermer?"

"Why wouldn't I?" he countered.

Drew Gregory had arrived in Brunnerwald late the
evening before and had crashed in the first hotel he came
to, registering for two nights in the event that anyone
showed interest in his activities. He had been asleep five seconds after dropping his luggage on the floor and kicking his
shoes off.

With nine good hours of sleep behind him, he showered
and dressed, penned a quick note to Miriam, and left the
hotel with two major goals in mind: a trip to the post office
and a contact at the Schrott Cheese Factory a ways from the
town center. He had checked that one out on arrival at the
train station in Brunnerwald and had the layout of the town
fixed in his mind as he hit the streets after breakfast.

Brunnerwald was laid out like a Y, with a small shopping
center at the cross point and one branch stretching south to
the railway station. The Schrott Cheese Factory was somewhere in this direction. Drew could catch a bus or taxi or
even a horse-drawn carriage—blanket provided—but he
could walk back to the railway station in twenty or twenty-
five minutes. If the Schrotts' place of business was there,
he'd find it.

Old Town lay to the west, built in close proximity to the
River Brunner with an unobscured view of the Tyrolean
Alps, its quaintness found in cobblestone streets and the
old-fashioned hospitality of well-established *gasthofs*. The
rapidly growing tourist section was on the east and boasted

one of the largest sports chalets in Austria—with more modern hotel accommodations and extravagant shops still popping up around it. Two buildings towered above the rest—the clock tower and the steepled church with the stained-glass windows. The newest ski lift was situated on the right tip of the Y, its cables riding high above the gentle, verdant slopes that rose toward the rugged, snow-capped peaks.

Nicholas Trotsky had been an excellent skier. Reasonable then, Drew decided, if Nicholas had spent the last fifteen years hiding out near the Brunnerwald Ski Run. *And if you're here, I will find you.*

Bent on posting his letter to Miriam, Gregory covered the remaining distance to the post office like a marathoner. He barreled into the building barely aware of the faces around him and was standing impatiently in line, fifth from the counter, when he realized that the man being waited on was Peter Kermer. Drew's reaction was swift. As Kermer turned to leave, Drew bent to tie a shoe, avoiding a face-to-face encounter.

*Okay, Carwell,* Gregory thought angrily, *what's Peter Kermer doing in Brunnerwald?*

Marta Zubkov knew that an international phone call from Brunnerwald would have to be made from the *post-amt,* but she had not expected Peter Kermer to accompany her there. She hesitated at the corner by the newsstand, groping for an excuse. He solved the problem for her. "Marta, we've lost Yuri. I think I'll run some errands— maybe buy another present for my boys. I'll meet you back at the *gasthof.* You'll be all right?"

She nodded gratefully and watched him walk away.

Ten minutes later as she stood at the phone dialing Dudley Perkins in London—and getting nothing but a busy signal—she saw Peter enter the post office. He hesitated when he noticed her, then waved good-naturedly, and made his way to the counter. She kept her eye on him as he reached into his knapsack and pulled out a parcel for mailing.

*And what are you up to, my friend?* she wondered.

The same uneasiness that had nudged her in Zagreb crept back. She had questioned his true identity then. She questioned it again now. But she had needed him then to slip safely into Austria. She needed him now as a safeguard against Vronin. But Marta had to know who Peter was—where his parcel was going.

She redialed the London number.

But as Peter left the post office and melted into the crowd, she dropped the phone and dashed through the *postamt* up to the clerk who had waited on him. She pushed her way ahead of the man at the front of the line with a quick, "Excuse me."

She had the clerk's attention. "I'm sorry," Marta told her, "but my husband just mailed a parcel home to our family." She hesitated, allowing her words to smother her embarrassment. "Fraulein, I must check the address."

"This is most unusual, Frau—"

"Frau Kermer. Peter gave you the wrong address. The family moved only recently, and, oh, he sent me back to correct his mistake. You've got to help me."

Again the clerk said, "We can't do anything—" But there was sympathy in her eyes.

"Oh, but you must," Marta told her. "Peter will be angry if I go back and tell him I couldn't correct his error."

The postal clerk relented. "The name again, please?"

"Peter Kermer. I'm Marta—Kermer." She hesitated, thinking about the Star of David she had seen around his neck. "Our package is going to Israel."

The clerk picked up Kermer's parcel and eyed the address label curiously. "Your hotel, please, Frau Kermer?"

"The Gasthof Schrott—in the Old Town."

The clerk tilted the parcel toward Marta. She read the addressee: "Bernstein. Mrs. Sara Bernstein." But Marta couldn't read the street address clearly. Marta reached out and tore off the label. "Peter did use the wrong address," she said.

Her relieved expression turned to a smile. "Should I just cross out my husband's mistake and correct it?" she asked.

"It's going international, so just make a new one."

Marta left the package with the clerk and stepped aside to fill in the form. Carefully, she copied the exact name and address and tucked Kermer's original label into her pocket.

◉◉◉

Drew Gregory had just reached the front of the line and was handing Miriam's letter to the clerk when the stranger pushed ahead of him. Now as she departed, he finally had the clerk's attention again. "You were weighing my letter to America," he said quietly.

"Yes. Yes." The clerk was still flustered and apologetic, far from professional. "I'm sorry for the interruption. It's these tourists. Is there anything else?" she asked nervously.

"Just stamps for my wife's letter."

Once more the pushy customer brushed Drew aside. "There," she told the clerk. "The correct address—that should reach the family."

She turned and walked smartly from the room.

*Like someone anxious to be gone,* Drew thought. But he could see from the corner of his eye that she was waiting at the bus stop.

"I'm sorry again," the clerk said. She was really rattled this time. She glanced anxiously at Kermer's parcel. "I'm certain it's the same address. I should never have helped that woman."

"Mrs. Kermer was insistent," Drew offered.

"Yes, she pushed you aside twice."

"She didn't tamper with the parcel," he reminded her. "So there's no real harm done, not if the address is the same."

Relief filled her voice. "Maybe she was just a jealous wife."

"Or a jealous lover."

The Austrian looked shocked as she hastily dumped Kermer's package onto the outgoing conveyor. But not before Drew had memorized the name of the recipient. Sara Bernstein. There hadn't been enough time to read the street or zip code upside down, but Gregory did know that Peter Kermer's package would soon be winging its way to Tel Aviv.

He'd put in a call to Carwell and start the ball rolling. At least they had a contact point for the man calling himself Peter Kermer, but what about Kermer's wife? His wife? Not likely.

Outside Drew could hear the bus roaring to the curb. He slapped money on top of Miriam's letter, more than ample for the stamps to Beverly Hills, and took off sprinting.

"You forgot your change," the clerk called after him.

He shoved through the glass door and ran toward the curb in time to watch the bus pull away. Frau Kermer had taken a window seat, her face expressionless when she saw him.

# Chapter 12

Going at a brisk clip, Drew reached the Schrott place of business fifteen minutes after leaving the *post-amt*. An impressive hand-carved shingle swung above the double doors:

THE SCHROTTS
CHEESE AT ITS BEST SINCE 1865

A family affair—three or four generations' worth, he decided. He crossed quickly to the right-hand side of the street and went inside. Displays of cheese lined one wall, each one sealed in a bright red protective coating. Gift baskets were artistically arranged with a sign behind the cash register that announced the Schrotts' willingness to mail anywhere in the world. At a hefty price, of course. To get beyond the tourist counters, he'd have to show an interest in the products.

Drew couldn't recall Miriam's tastes. She was weight-conscious, always had been. But her employee Floy Belmont, chunky and bosomed, would no doubt have a liking for cheese. He selected one that included a smoked sausage and three types of Emmental cheese and then made his way to a table to fill in the mailing instructions. As he did so, he glanced around. The front of the store had crowded with a dozen or more shoppers, but behind the swinging doors the factory opened into a large work area with shiny steel vats and a tiled floor.

He considered various strategies and settled on bringing up his boyhood on a dairy farm. If anything would get him beyond the swinging doors, that would. He chose the pretty, young sales girl wearing a white starched apron and a blue dirndl dress. She looked innocent and talkative, her face flushed and happy.

"I own a dairy farm in New York," he volunteered.

Interest sparked in her eyes. "Do you make cheese?"

"No," he said. "We sell our milk." And for a moment he stepped back in time, remembering those days in coveralls and knee-high rubber boots when he had been his father's shadow. His nostrils twitched at the thought of the barn, and then he smiled—not at the smells or hard work of farming—but at the remembrance of those days when he had walked beside the towering Wallace Gregory and longed to be like him.

As Drew finished his transaction, he asked, "Is Herr Schrott in this morning?"

"Which one? My father or my grandfather or my uncle?"

He decided on the grandfather. She disappeared behind the swinging doors with a curtsy and returned with an older man with hair the color of his long, white apron. His skin was spotted and aged, the face weather-beaten like Wallace Gregory's, and the smile warm and friendly as Wallace's had been.

"I'm Ulrich Schrott," he said wiping his hands on the apron. "My granddaughter tells me you're a dairy farmer."

Drew had trapped himself in a lie. Apologetically, he said, "I'm retired from farming. A young couple work the farm for me."

"I'd like that, too," Ulrich admitted. "But my sons are not as interested in cheese-making as I am. They want an easier life. Twelve- and thirteen-hour days are too much for them, especially for Preben." Ulrich shrugged unhappily. "It's been in the family since 1865. Makes me sad to think of it dying out when I do."

"We had a thousand head of cattle at our peak. We still have a good dairy business going—with your same long hours."

"Come," he invited. "Let me show you the work area."

The fermented odor was stronger as Drew stepped through the swinging doors. Ulrich led him over the tiled floors to one of the steel vats where the curds bubbled across the surface. They paused to watch an employee grip a metal pulley and hoist the curd-filled cheesecloth from the vat.

"Michel is a good worker," Ulrich said. "We're trying to convince him to stay on when he finishes his apprenticeship. He doesn't mind getting up at five in the mornings and working until seven at night. Michel is here for both milk deliveries, gallons and gallons of it." His sharp eyes glowed. "Ninety percent of the milk goes into the cheese-making process."

"Do you have your own cows?" Drew asked.

"Actually thirty farmers in this district pay me to turn their milk into cheese. We share the profits. I own the process." Sadly he added, "And they own me."

Drew went leisurely through the cellars with Ulrich where the cheese was cured and fermented and finally to the wooden shelves where large blocks of cheese ripened in their salt pans.

He thanked Ulrich profusely for the tour and then said, "Your family's been in this area for a long time. You must be familiar with all the neighboring villages."

"Name them, and I've been there." Ulrich patted his right hip. "I can't do as much hiking or skiing anymore, but I know these mountains as well as anyone."

"I was in one of those villages once," Drew said. "Dozen years or more ago. Beautiful scenery. Always vowed I'd go back. But I waited so long. I'm not sure where the place is."

He decided not to rush the truth or be too informed. "A place called Sultsen . . . Sulzfeld . . . Sangwedel . . . no, Salt something."

Ulrich smiled. "Sulzbach, the place of the salty brook."

"That's it. How do I get back there?"

"My son could tell you that. His wife came from there."

Drew noticed the younger man now—a well-groomed man in his early thirties with Ulrich's profile, one of the sons who wanted no permanent association with cheese-making.

"Preben, come meet Herr Gregory. He owns a dairy farm in New York State."

"Your father's been showing me around."

"So I see. But what is a dairy farmer doing in Brunnerwald?"

"Farmers like to vacation, too. And ski."

"You're here to ski then?" Preben was coldly curious.

"If the weather holds."

"The weather is not a problem, Herr Gregory. We have snow up to six and seven months every year. And if the snow thaws before you leave Brunnerwald, there are always the glaciers. We ski those even during the summer."

"Preben should know," his father said. "His *gasthofs* stay filled with skiers all year long. And before he married, he spent his time on the slopes as a ski instructor."

For an instant Ulrich's voice filled with pride. Then he shrugged. "If I had put my cheese factory on top of the mountain, he might have had more time for us."

"Father," Preben said coldly, "the factory was here when you were born. It'll be here when my sons are born."

Ulrich sighed. "So it was—for four generations. Five when Preben and Consetta get around to having a child."

Preben's face relaxed into a smile. "Someday, Father. Not yet. My wife is just beginning to enjoy her freedom."

"Freedom?" Drew asked.

"Yes, as my father told you, Consetta comes from Sulzbach."

"Perhaps she would be willing to show me the way there."

"Why Sulzbach, Herr Gregory?"

"I met a priest there on my last visit."

Preben's brief warmth faded. "It's a small village with no room for tourists. Let me help you choose a more modern village to visit with better accommodations."

"Ulrich tells me you own some guest houses in Brunnerwald."

"Two in the Old Town."

*Blue shutters and cobblestone streets.* "Typically Austrian?"

Ulrich answered, "The best. Nothing but the best for my son. You should be staying with him. Where are you staying?"

"At Hotel Kellerhof."

"Nice," Ulrich said, "but expensive."

"So I'm finding out."

"Preben, do you have a place for this gentleman?"

Gregory was certain that Preben did not share his father's interest, but with Austrian pride, the younger man said, "We'd be happy to have you as our guest."

"I've paid through tonight at Kellerhof. What about tomorrow?"

Preben nodded and pulled a card from his pocket. "Take a taxi to here. Check-in time at eleven. But, Herr Gregory, my wife is shy about her village background. You'll understand, won't you, and not force her to talk about Sulzbach?"

Drew caught the surprise in Ulrich's face, the tightened lips. *I'll be on my best behavior,* Drew thought, *especially when you're around.*

🌺🌺🌺

When Drew got back to the *postamt,* he discovered that it had closed at seven. He didn't dare wait until morning to fax word to Vic; he'd have to risk calling directly from his hotel room.

He reached Vic shortly after eight, saying, "Vic, old buddy, *skiing is good here.*"

Vic's piercing whistle followed. "I'll catch the next plane."

"Wait. Give it a day or two more in Paris. See if Langley nibbles and see what Carwell really expects out of my trip here."

"I've checked it out with Brad O'Malloy. They really believe your old friend is in the area. And they want you to find him before London does."

"Perkins?"

"Sounds that way. Rumor has it he's really interested."

"Why all this concern to find someone who's been dead

on the vine for fifteen years?" Drew asked. "Unless he's part of the PHOENIX PLAN."

"You won't let go of that one, will you?"

"Keep digging."

"It's just an old legend, Drew. I can do more good by joining you. O'Malloy is tossing me out of his apartment by tomorrow night. He's not anxious for Carwell to know I'm here."

"He'll keep you on when you tell him Peter Kermer's in town. So tell Carwell to call off his shadows. I don't like it."

"Kermer can't be there. They found him in Zagreb—dead. The Agency claimed his body. Shipped him to Austria—what was left of him—for an autopsy."

"You're certain?" Drew thought of the woman at the post office, the self-proclaimed Mrs. Kermer. "Was Kermer married?"

"They whisked his young widow and infant daughter into a Croatian community in Burgenland. She'll be safe with them."

"There's no way she could be here—where I am?"

"Impossible. She's staying out of sight. Refused to talk to anyone from the Company. Says they killed her husband."

"Nonsense."

"That's the way she sees it. What's up, Drew?"

"That gentleman from the opera—the passenger on the train from Vienna—is here in town with a woman who calls herself his wife. An attractive woman—say, fortyish."

"The lady in Burgenland is in her twenties—too frightened to travel alone. She's not the type to do vengeance for her husband's death. She'll just spend the next ten years weeping about it."

"Do you think Carwell put a tag on me?"

"Didn't ask him."

"See what you can find out about the real Kermer."

"That's a big order."

"Start with the Russian file. Just get me some more solid answers before you pack your bags for your ski trip here."

"But you said the skiing is already good."

"So's the cheese. Sent Miriam some directly from the factory."

"Worth the visit?"

"The samples were good. The owner friendly. Can't say as much for his oldest son. Preben took an immediate dislike to me."

"Any word on the *gasthof* with blue shutters?"

"I pounded the pavements all afternoon for that one. Must be a hundred blue-shuttered, blue-shingled places."

"Don't forget the cobblestone street."

"I didn't. But old man Schrott likes to sell cheese and send customers to the family-owned *gasthofs*. The oldest son owns two of them. I'll be checking into one of them tomorrow."

"Everything else in good order?"

"Things weren't right when I got back to the hotel."

"Visitors?"

"I'd say so. Oh, the room looked like it did when I left it this morning. Even my luggage was right where I put it. But when I opened my suitcase, I realized someone had been nosing around."

"Not your old sock routine?"

"I always pack seven pairs flat in the bottom of the case."

"I don't like what you're about to tell me, Drew."

"My guest made two rows out of them, piled on top of one another. Nothing missing. He just miscalculated."

"Kermer?"

"That was my first thought. But when I stopped by the concierge's desk to ask for my messages, he told me I'd had a visitor—a Britisher with thick glasses. If London is interested in Trotsky, then Perkins may have sent his right-hand boy."

"Lyle Spincrest? You're friends. Tennis buddies. Why would he inspect your luggage?"

"I'll ask him if he comes back."

"Well, Drew, don't wipe the guy posing as Kermer off your list. If he followed you to Brunnerwald, he'd be bold enough to check out your room."

👁👁👁

Preben's *gasthof* was a charming Tyrolean-style chalet with a steep roof and blue-framed windows that had lace curtains hanging in them. A porch extended over the storage bins, and the rustic balconies were bright with red geraniums. Gasthof Schrott was painted in bold letters across the top of the building, and a hand-carved shingle out front announced the same ownership.

Drew pressed the bell and then rang it a second and a third time before the door finally opened. A schoolgirl with solemn, dark eyes and a narrow face looked up at him. She brushed back the loose strands of flaxen hair that almost hid her frown. "Herr Gregory?" she asked.

She could hardly be Preben's wife, but he smiled and said, "Is Herr Schrott in, Fraulein?"

"He's in the kitchen with Consetta."

"They're expecting me."

"I know," she said softly, stepping back and allowing him to enter. "I'm Erika. You'll be on the third floor."

His guard stiffened. He liked the ground floor—easy entry, easy exit. "There's nothing on the first floor?"

She shook her head. "The place is full. Preben insisted that my sister find room for you."

Consetta's sister. *Also from the village of Sulzbach?* he wondered. He hesitated at the foot of the steep stairs. "I'd like to settle the account with your sister."

"You can register later. Preben trusts you."

She was too anxious. Something was wrong. He made his way down the hall to the kitchen, pushing his way in ahead of Erika.

Preben Schrott looked up startled. He reached out at once and placed his arm protectively around his wife. Consetta was younger than Preben, chubby, round-cheeked, and nicely dressed except for the blood stains down the front of her blouse. She looked as though a fist or the butt of a revolver had been slammed against her cheek.

Her eyes as they met Drew's were full of fear. Full of pain.

"Consetta Schrott?" he asked.

She nodded. "Herr Gregory, Erika was to take you to your room. We told her—"

"I know. But—what happened to you?"

He wanted to plow into Preben, to mar his face as Consetta's had been marred. But the hard man he had met yesterday had nothing but tenderness for Consetta.

"You need a doctor, Frau Schrott," Drew said.

"No, I'll be all right." Her words squeezed through the tightly swollen lips.

"Dr. Heppner was already here," Erika told him.

Drew looked to Consetta for confirmation. She nodded again.

"Erika, you must leave. You're already late getting back to school. Your teacher will be fretting. Now go."

"I'm not going, Consetta. You need me."

Consetta reached out and cupped her sister's chin. "Dr. Heppner will be back. He'll stitch my lip. I'll be all right."

"I'll come back after school."

"No. I don't want you on the trails after dark."

"Do as your sister tells you," Preben said. "Take your skis with you. I'll ask Dr. Heppner to wait until school is out. Then you can go up the mountain together."

"I'll be all right. Preben is here now." She touched her bruised face. "And, Erika, not a word of this to Grandmama when you get home. Nor Grandpa."

As Erika left, Preben gently led his wife to a chair, his steadying hand on her arm. Her color had paled even more, her torn mouth seeping a crusty red.

"What happened?" Drew asked again.

"A thief. Consetta caught him—"

"No, Preben," she said. "A thief steals things. The men who came to our house meant only harm. They would have killed you if you had been here."

"They weren't looking for me," he reminded her angrily.

Drew's stomach muscles tightened. "Were they looking for one of your guests?" he asked.

Preben didn't even glance Drew's way. "No, a former guest."

Consetta tried to smile up at him. "I don't want our guests to see me like this. I'm so glad they're still out skiing and shopping," she told him. "They won't be back until dinner."

"You're in no condition to cook, Frau Schrott."

She looked at Drew gratefully. "Everything's ready—it's mostly serving. Preben can do that. But you'll be on your own tomorrow. I'll be gone for the day," she said apologetically.

Preben crouched down beside her. "You mustn't go up the mountain, Consetta. Not until I can go with you."

"I have to go," she whispered. "I must warn him."

"Consetta, Dr. Heppner can take a message for us."

"No. We will tell no one. Now, please, Preben, show Herr Gregory to his room." She faced Drew, her right eye rapidly swelling. "I'm sure there will be no more trouble."

"Don't worry about me, Frau Schrott. I'm an expert at taking care of myself—and finding my way around new places. Third floor, right? Erika told me. I'll just find my own way up. Which room?"

The swollen lips tried to smile. "It's the only room up there, Herr Gregory. Erika stays there when she's with us. Every other bed is full. Will there be anything else?"

He didn't like the timing, but he risked it. "I knew a man who used to visit Brunnerwald from time to time. Trotsky stayed here in the Old Town." Drew threw out the name without batting an eye. "For all I know, he may have been on your guest list."

"We have many guests, Herr Gregory. From many countries."

"I suppose you do, Preben." Drew kept the description of Nicholas general. Around fifty. Tall. Well-built. Dark hair. Blue eyes. Complimentary words about Trotsky's good looks. Daring comments on him being an expert skier and hunter. Drew even slipped in, "He lived behind the Berlin Wall for a while. An East Berliner. But he left there even before the wall went down."

*Fifteen years ago,* he thought bitterly.

But Drew enjoyed baiting Preben with words about

Trotsky. Nothing threatening. Everything casual. The description of a man who might be living out his life in Sulzbach or Brunnerwald.

Consetta lifted the corner of her apron and pressed it against her swollen lip, her pupils wide with fear.

Preben brushed Drew's words aside. "Many people stay here. But do you recall anyone by the name of Trotsky, Consetta?"

She shook her head, avoiding Drew's eyes now.

"Tomorrow you can look through our guest register," Preben offered coldly. "You might find your friend's name."

"I'd like that." He turned and took Consetta's hands in his. "I trust you will feel better in the morning. Get some rest now."

Drew didn't wait for her answer but made his way back to the stairs, hoisted his luggage on his shoulder, and began the steep trek upstairs. Midway he turned back and saw Preben leading Consetta into another room. As they slipped inside, the door closed quietly behind them, but not before Drew saw a man with glasses stand up to greet them. *The doctor? You've been here all along, and I was not to see you.*

👁👁👁

Drew's quarters were in the back of the chalet, a crowded little room under the eaves that offered an unobstructed view of the mountains. The melodious sound of Alpine horns and the tinkling cow bells could be heard in the distance. Above the grazing area, the slopes rose gently toward the rugged peaks—mountains filled, he knew, with Alpine villages.

What if Nicholas were no longer hiding in Brunnerwald? Where would he go? Back to the village where memory had taken Drew a dozen times or more in the last few days. He grabbed his map from his briefcase and tried to locate Sulzbach again, fixed as it was in his mind. He knew the village had clung to the steep mountainside like a valley nestled between two mountain ranges.

Through his open window, Drew heard voices on the balcony below his. He stepped to the window, his attention drawn to Preben Schrott and his friend. "We can't send for the *polizei,* Johann. I have to consider Consetta. She's terrified." Schrott's voice tightened. "She won't tell me who they were—what they wanted."

"Does she know?"

There was a decided pause. Finally Preben said, "She may be trying to protect her grandparents, but they have no enemies. And it's not like Consetta to hide something from me."

"But the two of you do argue about her grandparents?"

"Yes, they fight progress in the village. Rheinhold is so content with the old ways. Keeping a handful of cows and dragging himself down here everyday with milk we can't even use. I can't cover for him forever, and he can't take many more winters on the mountain. They're getting too old to be alone, Johann."

"They have Erika. And Rheinhold's a good man, Preben. As long as he can live out his life by the church, he'll stay in Sulzbach."

"Consetta insists that she will go up there tomorrow."

"And I insist that she stay here and rest. Now I must go and meet Erika. But first, tell me. What do you think of the American guest? Was he involved in the attack on your wife?"

"Herr Gregory? No. I don't like him, but he was genuinely concerned about Consetta. But he's curious, too. I don't like that."

"Could he be working with the men who beat her?"

"I don't know. But I think they're looking for the same person."

Their voices died away. The accusation lingered—was Kermer or MI5 involved? No, Lyle Spincrest would not beat Consetta. But what about Kermer? Drew stepped back into his room for his binoculars. For several minutes he gazed over the sun-filled hills. The ruby lens filtered out the afternoon glare as he tracked the run-out zone of the Sulzbach Avalanche. He allowed his eyes to follow the barren, treeless path up to where the avalanche had first begun. Sulzbach lay somewhere to the left of that ugly, gutted gully, but for some reason Preben and Consetta Schrott did not want him climbing up the narrow trails to Sulzbach.

# Chapter 13

In the darkness just before dawn Nicholas Caridini lay quietly on his narrow iron bed, his body stiff and unyielding from the dampness. He still felt the exhaustion of Wednesday's climb and the gnawing physical pain that had forced him to pause every few yards. But the nearer he had come to the village, the more exhilarated he felt. Home to his mountain.

In spite of the morning chill, the back of his neck and spine tingled with sweat. The relentless ache in his abdomen was there, but it was not the pain that had awakened him. No, some distant noise like the groaning of the mountain had shattered his sleep, a sleep that was feeble at best these days. His fogged mind grasped it as the thunderous rumble that could send a violent avalanche tumbling down on Sulzbach again.

From his window he saw that another late snowstorm had layered its wet crystal flurries on top of an already over-burdened hillside. Even in the darkness he could see that his window ledge and the branches of the tree were weighed down with a new coating of snow. A blanket of white had buried the budding spring flowers.

Now when he should feel the warmth of spring, now when the snows on the lower slopes should be melting and the waterfalls rippling over the higher cliffs, a new storm over Sulzbach seemed ominous. He listened for the warning sounds of a breakaway on the mountain—a crack of thunder or the roaring swoosh of the unstable white dragon glissading over the packed winter snows, threatening a massive slide along the rubbled path of the old avalanche. The old avalanche of Sulzbach had come blasting down the mountain hours after the plane crash had dumped Nicholas near the village.

In those early years in Sulzbach, the failed coup in Russia and the memories of the plane crash and the avalanche seemed to come as one. The memories always merged: the PHOENIX PLAN in ashes, a death warrant if he went back to Moscow, the threat of captivity under the Americans, a plane tumbling from the sky, paralysis. Then—here in Sulzbach—came the chance to start life over with only thoughts of Marta Zubkov blurring his beginning again.

It all stole back from the past to haunt him now. He felt the plane spiraling from the sky and splintering across the cliff, the screech of metal and tearing fuselage roaring in his ears. Death and stillness. The American agent Crisscross dragged him from the plane. Each movement sent an excruciating fire along Nicholas's spine. Fifteen years of memories repressed and now remembered.

❂❂❂

The American agent lay unconscious in the snowbank. Colonel Trotsky stole the man's automatic and then crawled to the shelter of an overhanging cliff, an agonizing thirty minutes of pain. He inched deeper into the rocky cave and then lay motionless in his parka, his abdomen riddled with gunshot.

From his shelter he could see the narrow ravine between the slopes. Above that lay the PC-6, twisted and leveled on the mountainside. In his mind Nicholas was certain that he had been in that plane—a prisoner restrained in the co-pilot seat. How he got out alive, he didn't know, but he did remember the sudden downdraft, the American losing control, the altimeter spinning toward zero. The nose dive leveled out just before crashing, the belly of the plane splitting open as it slammed across the cliff.

All morning the sun warmed the snow-laden hills, yet he would welcome death, the pain in his gut and back were so intense. He half feared, half wanted a search and rescue patrol to find him.

He slipped in and out of consciousness, realizing as night fell that the American was gone, that his own bloody trail had been hidden by fresh snow. At midnight a blizzard howled as it dumped thirty inches of snow, its crystals unable to stick to the whitened slopes. Nicholas shook as a whumphing roar rumbled underground. The mountain seemed to crack and explode above him as a slab of snow broke loose and began its destructive journey over the mountainside. It careened down the narrow gully, spreading its path a mile wide as rock and timber crashed down the mountain.

A rush of wind roared past Trotsky. Trees uprooted like broken sticks. Chunks of rock, twisting like tumbleweed, somersaulted. The avalanche picked up speed, shooting by his cave at seventy miles an hour. The edge of the slide rode toboggan-fashion over his rocky rooftop. Then stillness, deathly stillness as the rumbling mountain calmed. He fought for air and spewed snow from his mouth.

Fear and shock. Pain and blackness.

Nicholas awakened again in the cold predawn hours, his head pillowed on a snowbank. The bleeding in his belly had stopped. Death had eluded him. A mile-wide gully had been stripped bare of rocks and trees, leaving behind a stretch of blackness where the avalanche had tracked its way to the run-out zone. He searched for the plane. It was gone, swept off the cliff and splintered into fragments like a broken toy. As far as he knew, the American agent Crisscross, his arch nemesis, had been swept away in the avalanche.

With his watch cracked and broken, time swept away, too. Hours? Days? He could not be certain. Finally a priest came cautiously around the cliff, a long, thin metal rod in his hand, a transceiver pinned securely to his hooded jacket, a backpack and shovel slung over one shoulder, a dog at his side.

Gently, the priest prodded the path ahead of him. The

dog raced ahead, then stopped, sniffing as she hovered above a glove—Nicholas's glove lying surprisingly on the surface of the snow. The priest dug frantically with his shovel as the dog loped on toward the rocks.

"I'm over here," Nicholas called faintly in Russian.

His rescuer turned, smiled, and dropped on one knee as he reached Nicholas. "My friend," he said, "I'm Father Jacques. Jacques Caridini. We've been hunting for you. Thank God, you are safe. You'll be all right now. Good girl," he said to the dog.

The next morning Nicholas awakened in the parish rectory in an antiseptic room filled with religious icons on the walls. The same priest stood at the foot of his bed. Another man—his features blurred—bent over Nicholas probing his wound. Gruffly, he instructed the priest in Nicholas's care.

"If I could just get him to the clinic, I could x-ray his back. I'm certain he's fractured a vertebra or two."

"You really trust that battery-run machine of yours?"

"It's better than no picture at all."

"Couldn't the ski patrol carry him down to Brunnerwald?"

"No," Nicholas whispered. "Don't move me."

"But what about his belly wound?" Father Caridini asked.

"He needs surgery. But he's too weak to carry down the mountain. I know a good surgeon in Innsbruck—but this man would die before we could even get him to Brunnerwald."

"Then I will take care of him myself."

"Is that wise, Father Jacques? You told me he was carrying a gun when you found him, not skis. He may be wanted by the *polizei*."

"Perhaps," the priest agreed.

Nicholas tried to focus his eyes, but the belly pain was excruciating. As he drifted in and out of a dazed slumber, he heard the stranger say, "He must have been in that plane."

"Perhaps," the priest said softly. "But it doesn't matter now. The plane was destroyed in the avalanche."

"And any other passengers with it." The man's voice sounded farther away as though he had reached the door.

"We must notify Brunnerwald as soon as we pick our way out of this storm."

"No," Caridini cautioned. "He's a guest in my home. My brother."

"Have your own way, Caridini, but I think you're making a mistake. Those are gunshot wounds. You should have left him on the mountain. You're risking your own safety. Tell me, Father, does anyone know he's here?"

"My other guest? No. And Frau Mayer is in Brunnerwald."

Angrily, the other man said, "Take care of him then. My concern must be for the people of this village. We have several seriously injured. My responsibility is to them."

The door clicked, leaving Nicholas alone with the priest. And not even caring, Nicholas slept—a troubled sleep. Each time he closed his eyes he saw the avalanche again. Trees toppling in front of him. Ice chunks as hard as concrete spinning through the air. Blinding shafts of snow hurtling past his cave. A plane in shattered pieces twirling, gusting with the violent winds and falling, carrying, he was certain, Drew Gregory with it.

🌹🌹🌹

Fifteen years gone and yet, oddly enough, even now he still pitied the American agent for dying in such a violent way. Lately when he closed his eyes, he still heard the screams of the dying. The villagers perhaps or his own screams. Or were they the haunting cries of Drew Gregory? Nicholas had forgotten the images over the years. They had been repressed, buried in the recesses of his mind, shelved like the person he once was. Now they rose from the ashes of his past and struck again.

His brows arched as he heard the sudden sound of voices in the rectory kitchen. He turned carefully, swung his lanky legs over the side of his bed, and propelled himself upright. The first streaks of dawn had broken through the mist.

Still he listened for the rumble in the mountain.

Again there was silence until the muffled voices of Erika Schmid and Josef Petzold erupted into an argument. They must have awakened at the crack of dawn as he had and were already at their chores. Since he had taken over the parish, the Schmids and the Petzolds always vied to help him—to fetch food or stack his wood for the winter. Josef served as an altar boy now, and Erika had already received her first Communion.

"I can start the fire, Josef," Erika insisted.

"Stoking the fire is man's work."

Nicholas heard the lad stomp his booted feet on the kitchen floor, half in fury. Then came the grating, scraping sounds as the stove was set with wood chips and sticks of timber.

As Nicholas reached for his robe and shuffled toward the washroom in fleece-lined slippers, he was keenly aware that he possessed so much—the Petzolds and Schmids so little. Unlike so many in the village who were limited to a Saturday bath, Nicholas had a generator that allowed him warm water, if not hot, for a daily shower, and his chemical toilet kept him from a brisk walk to the outhouse. He showered and dressed hurriedly, choosing the thick gray sweater that fitted loosely under his clerical garb.

When he reached the kitchen, Erika was alone, her shabby coat and scarf and mittens piled neatly by the door. She looked anxiously his way, almost filling the kitchen with her shyness.

"*Guten Morgen,* Father," she said softly.

"Good morning, Erika."

She was a sweet child with a solemn face, much like her older sister Consetta. But Erika's mouth was wider, her hair parted unevenly in the middle; strands of it fell over one eye. At twelve, almost thirteen, she was quick and efficient, eager to please. "Josef is gone?" he asked.

"His mother promised to bake you some bread this morning. Josef will bring it on his way to school."

The dark Russian rye bread that Nicholas loved, that Olga Petzold had perfected at her village bakery.

"Grandmama says you are not well."

"I'm better, Erika," he said, not wanting to trouble her.

"You're not dying?"

"Someday," he said amiably.

She giggled. "That's what Grandpa says." More seriously she added, "I've made buckwheat porridge and brought you some warm milk for your coffee." She nodded timidly toward the pail on the counter. "Grandmama insisted that I bring some."

He felt humbled by their concern. Milk was their livelihood, most of it sold in Brunnerwald to the cheese factory. Even a small pail was a sacrifice. Nicholas nodded gratefully and filled his cup. She seemed happy as he took a sip, but the thick, creamy mixture stuck in his throat, nauseating him. Hunger never seemed to come anymore. Food no longer appealed to him.

Under her watchful eye, he sat down at the place she had carefully set for him and forced a spoonful of lumpy gruel into his mouth. He barely ate, smiling apologetically her way. "I'll wait until the bread comes," he said, knowing that she would be on her way down the mountain to Brunnerwald by then.

He took a quick swallow of coffee to hide his emotion as he studied her childlike smile, her innocence. And yet Erika was growing up without a childhood. He wondered whether she ever had a toy except the two or three that her grandfather had whittled for her—or the harmonica that Nicholas had given her at Christmas. She showed no bitterness at the hard life that was hers here in the mountains. Too much responsibility helping her grandparents. Too many hours going to and from school. Even now she was standing by his side serving him—filling his cup with more black and bitter coffee.

If the heavy spring storm kept up—if the snow held—she could ski partway down the mountain, saving energy and time from the two-hour walk down to school in Brunnerwald. *Or maybe,* he thought hopefully, *she can hitch a wagon ride with her grandfather.* "Will Rheinhold take you to school this morning?" he asked.

She giggled. "In the milk wagon? Oh, no, Father Caridini. Grandpa went up the mountain with Dr. Heppner this morning. They're afraid of another avalanche."

That's what had awakened him—the explosive boom of the avalauncher blasting one of the snowy slopes and triggering a small slide. The Alpine howitzer, Nicholas called it.

Erika's rich, dark eyes met his. "Are you afraid, Father Caridini?" she asked.

"Of an avalanche starting? I think about it sometimes."

"I'm afraid," she said softly. "Grandfather says last week's warm weather started the spring thaw, and now with the temperature dropping again—"

Her words trailed. She glanced out the window and up the mountainside. "Grandmama doesn't like him to go up there anymore. She says the younger men should go."

"I should have gone for him."

"But you've been ill."

His body was reminder enough. "Someone should have gone in your grandfather's place."

She smiled. "Don't let Grandpa hear you say that. He's good with explosives. That's why the doctor let him go up the mountain this morning to help blow away the new snow."

*If they don't blow away the whole mountain,* Nicholas thought gloomily. But he knew it was one way to prevent an avalanche. "Will they be checking the snow fences?" he asked.

She nodded but lingered by the door, hesitant to leave him. "Is something wrong, my child?" he asked.

"I promised not to tell Grandmama, but you should know."

"Know what, Erika?"

"It's Consetta. She was beaten yesterday."

His hands actually shook. "Did one of the guests hurt her?"

"No. Strangers. I think it was something to do with Grandpa. Or with you."

"With me?" he asked.

"She wanted to come up the mountain today to warn someone, but Dr. Heppner forbade it."

"Warn me about what, Erika?"

"She wouldn't tell us. But the men who hurt Consetta were looking for someone. Grandpa goes down to Brunnerwald almost everyday, so it must be you she wants to warn."

A faint sense of alarm played tricks with his thoughts. "Does Consetta think the strangers were looking for me, Erika?"

She shrugged. "Consetta didn't say. I'll ask her today."

"What you better do," he said, "is run along, or you will be late for school."

"I'll come back tomorrow, Father Caridini."

"Don't forget, Frau Mayer will be back soon."

Erika scanned the half-filled porridge bowl. "You're not pleased with my cooking?"

"It's fine," he said hastily.

He would have to persuade Frau Mayer to let the girl help with the wash and the sweeping. The Schmids needed the few extra schillings each week. "Would you be able to help?" he asked.

The girl nodded. "But when the weather grows warmer, I will be helping Herr Burger's wife."

"The wood carver's wife?"

"They're fixing their place up for summer tourists."

"I warned Herr Burger about that. Tourists threaten our privacy." *And my security.* But Senn Burger was right. The people of Sulzbach were struggling for survival, their economy at its lowest ebb. He controlled his voice. "And does your Grandmama plan to turn her home into an inn as well?"

"No. She's afraid it would displease you. But she says Herr Burger thinks you keep the village from growing."

"Do I?" he asked.

"I don't know. But Grandmama tells Consetta that's why Herr Burger doesn't go to church anymore." Erika grabbed her coat and scarf. "I must go, Father Caridini."

The warmth of the kitchen chilled for the moment as Erika opened the door. He watched her go slipping and sliding on the trail down toward Brunnerwald, her skis over her shoulder.

*Strange,* he thought as she disappeared from view. *In neither life have I had room for a child of my own.*

In the old life as a KGB officer, he had never chosen to marry. But he had loved. Not many women, but one—and she so much younger than himself. Nicholas rarely allowed himself to think of Marta and never spoke her name aloud. But if he had ever been a father, he would have wanted it to be her child.

But in this life—this life that he had chosen for himself, this life of deception that had fallen so innocently into his hands—there still was no place for a child of his own.

Johann Heppner, Sulzbach's only doctor, trudged steadily up the mountainside toward the snow fence, his German shepherd heeling him. Johann had a craggy face, the sides of his jaw and chin covered with a frostbitten, short-cropped beard. The hairy chin and moustache almost hid his narrow lips. A thick wool cap stretched over his wide forehead and reached down to the sparse brows, hiding the fuzz of thinning hair that clung to the back of his head. The thick bifocals that pinched the middle of his nose had fogged with the weather, blurring Johann's vision.

Again this morning when he washed and dressed, he had scrutinized the tiny red veins that covered his nose and cheeks, the early signs, he knew, of a well-drenched liver. Still he drank, wines mostly, even with breakfast. Oddly enough, his hands remained steady, capable. *Capable of what?* he wondered now. To play chess with the priest and to scratch his dog's ears.

"Come on, Girl," he called. "There's a day's work ahead."

As he waited for the dog, he whipped out his transceiver and listened in vain for Rheinhold Schmid's transmittal signal. He'd left the old man turning back on the lower slope, too winded to push on. But Rheinhold would make it back to the village safely. He knew every turn on this mountain, every risky crevice.

Johann scrunched down and scratched the dog's erect black ear. "Well, let's go on, Girl," he said, "and blast that mountain before this snow catches us with an avalanche."

The German shepherd nuzzled his gloved hand, then raced ahead at a loping gait to roll on the ground. She stood again, her dark coat shiny from the snow bath, and shook the flurries on Johann when he reached her. The dog was Heppner's life, his constant companion. Johann kept a warm rug in the clinic and another by his bedside for Girl. They seemed inseparable and never more so than when they were on a rescue patrol in search of lost skiers.

Today the dog was also his comfort as they climbed higher. Johann had almost memorized the medical report from Deiter Eschert written on hospital letterhead. The proper terminology and the diagnosis and terminal prognosis were all carefully recorded as though Nicholas were a number, not a fellow traveler.

*Odd*, Johann thought now. We have nothing in common except the chessboard. But it was more than that. They'd had fourteen years of arguments, of solving the world's problems over the chessboard, of caring about the people of Sulzbach. Fourteen years of watching a friendship rise from their differences. As far as Johann was concerned, Nicholas's God was a cloak of darkness, a shelter from his past—whatever that past had been. For Johann, God did not exist. And soon . . .

As the thought struck him, his throat tightened. Soon his friend Nicholas would cease to exist. The dog nuzzled closer, her cold nose pressed against his gloved fingertips. "Nicholas is dying, Girl," he told the dog. "And I'm going to miss him."

They had reached the steel-reinforced tower where one of the avalaunchers was permanently installed. It stood near the sheer cliff where the American's plane had crashed so many years ago. And suddenly Johann was crying, the tears freezing on his cheeks as he stood there.

Moments later he fired the avalauncher, sending another round of explosives up the mountainside into the starting zone of the old avalanche. The blast shook the fresh-fallen snow, its rumble reverberating down through the valley as a controlled block of ice tumbled gently toward the snow fence.

"That one's for you, Nicholas," he said. "That one's for you."

# Chapter 14

Drew slept soundly in the privacy of the third floor and awakened ready to tackle the day except for an irritated left eye. Ever since his assignment to the embassy in London, he had worn contact lenses. But this morning he was forced to give his eyes a rest and go back to the horn-rimmed glasses he always carried with him for an emergency. He stooped down to Erika's pint-sized mirror and scowled as he battled the cowlick in his hair. He gave it an extra dash of hair cream and then adjusted the glasses, barely recognizing himself on the final scrutiny.

The silver strands at his temples and the horn-rims seemed to age him, something he didn't need nor want. But they added a touch of dignity too, giving him the studious look of a history professor—a casual, relaxed prof in a blue turtleneck sweater. All he needed was a smoking jacket and a pipe dangling from the corner of his mouth. But Drew didn't smoke. Never had. Never would. Prof. Gregory! He chuckled. The impression in the mirror was a realistic one. British history had become Drew's passion, and for the moment researching the Battle of Britain or the Falkland War had more appeal than going downstairs to study the *gasthof* registry.

He tried to reason why he would even want to scan a boring registry and knew it went back to Vic Wilson at the train station in Salzburg. Vic rarely dropped an idea without having some hidden purpose. Vic's cousin had no doubt stayed here with the Schrotts last winter—in this charming guest house that would easily appeal to Brianna. But Drew was convinced it went beyond that. He dropped to the edge of the bed and did a spit polish on his shoes, buffing them with a handkerchief; the more he polished, the more he wondered why Vic had directed him here.

Vic had an uncanny ability to lift facts from the surface of a conversation. He'd lasted at his Moscow assignment for three months—banned from there by the station-chief—but he had been there long enough to make friends. And though he didn't get on at all with Carwell in Paris, he had over the years maintained a bartering exchange of information with Brad O'Malloy. Knowing Vic, Drew thought his friend had probably been in touch with Moscow and O'Malloy gleaning facts that would shorten the search for Nicholas Trotsky.

Drew tied his shoes, stowed the stained handkerchief on the dresser, and decided to follow up on Vic's only lead—the contact with the Schrott family. In a tourist town this size, Drew didn't have any other starting point than the rumor that Nicholas Ivan Trotsky had resurfaced in Brunnerwald. Langley believed it. Carwell had acted on it. Dudley Perkins in London was interested. As Drew locked his door, he wondered how many other intelligence agencies were moving in. And where were the Russians? They'd never let Trotsky slip into someone else's hands.

Other than the muffled sound of voices behind one of the doors on the second floor, the house seemed deathly still. Drew concluded that some of the guests were already up and gone on their all-day outings, and others were still snuggled under their eiderdowns, trying to offset the exhaustion of being on vacation. The last six steps creaked as he descended, a sound he didn't remember from the night before. He prowled cautiously down the hallway, but the Schrotts were nowhere to be found.

Mornings without coffee aggravated Drew, but his mood brightened considerably as he reached the dining room. Consetta had laid out a continental breakfast for her guests, a help-yourself, come-when-you-can meal. Juices and canned pears, a pitcher of warm milk and sugar cubes, croissants and a variety of hard breads, and packets of butter and jams artistically arranged. The aroma of coffee came from the side counter, and Drew made it in two quick strides. He was eagerly pouring his first cup when he saw the note propped against a book with "Herr Gregory" printed boldly on it. Tucking the *gasthof* registry under his arm, he balanced the coffee cup and a plate of food and headed toward a single table, safeguarding himself against others joining him.

Two hours later he was still doing a detailed check of the registry. Trotsky's visit to Old Town had occurred within the last ten days—to a blue-shuttered *gasthof* on a cobblestone street. Like a hundred other homes in Brunnerwald, the Schrotts' guest house had blue shutters. It even stood on an old stone street, but this didn't guarantee that Nicholas Trotsky had ever registered here. Drew had nailed down two things for certain: Consetta had a close relationship with Sulzbach, and Preben had an intense dislike of Drew's presence.

Drew narrowed his search down to the last three months and went through the names again, eliminating the couples and families. It left him with three names, one as American as Smith or Jones and one who used the European seven. None of the three were currently registered. But what if Nicholas had not been a paying guest but a family friend? Consetta Schrott had taken a beating, and now she wanted to risk even more—to go up the mountain and warn someone. Did she want to protect her grandfather as Preben had suggested? Or protect a friend? Drew chuckled wryly to himself. He wanted easy answers, and he wanted more than anything to follow his intuition and hike the trails to Sulzbach.

He looked up as a woman entered the room. She was attractive, fortyish. Mrs. Kermer! Their eyes met. Not even a flicker of recognition showed in her enormous, dark eyes, but surely shock was visible in his own. He was thankful for the horn-rimmed glasses, thankful that she had simply shoved him out of the way at the post office without looking directly at him.

She drank down a glass of juice as she stood at the table and then snatched up a croissant roll. Her gaze strayed his way again. In German she asked, "How does one register at this *gasthof?*"

"You'd have to check with Frau Schrott at the desk," he said.

"She's apparently not on duty."

He reflected on Consetta's bruised and swollen face and knew that it would be even more discolored this morning. "Frau Schrott wasn't well last evening."

He kept his chin tucked down as he peered at her over the spectacles. Last night he had suspected Kermer and his friends of attacking Consetta. The disquieting, prickling thought remained. "She was injured," he volunteered.

Something in the woman's expression gave her away. Her facial mask slipped—and returned. Her voice lowered. "What happened?"

"Two assailants entered the kitchen and gave her a severe beating."

"Robbery? Oh, then it isn't even safe here."

"Nothing is missing," he said.

The wide, dark eyes filled with uncertainty. "Is she all right—this Frau Schrott?"

"She was in much pain last evening."

The croissant fell to the floor. She turned and fled. Drew followed her to the living room and watched through the lace curtains as she ran down the steps and hurried across the street.

۞ ۞ ۞

Peter Kermer steadied Marta as she reached him. "Are you all right, Marta?" he asked.

She regained her breath. "Yes, I just called on an old friend."

"Did you?" he asked. "Was he there?"

"No, but Yuri and Vronin must still be following us.

Vronin made good his threat. I think he and Yuri really did go door to door in this neighborhood."

"Are you surprised?" Peter brushed a strand of copper hair from her cheek, feeling once again the need to protect Marta Zubkov from danger as he would protect Sara with his life.

"They didn't find him, but they know," she whispered.

"Know what?" he asked gently. But he knew without her telling him that she had last seen Nicholas Trotsky going into that house. Why else would Marta have chosen rooms on this street? "Is that where you saw Trotsky the other day?"

"Does it matter?"

"It does if you don't want him to be found."

She glared up at him. "Isn't that why we're here?"

"Is it?"

"Kermer, I must talk to Nicholas first—before we take him back to Innsbruck. Once Dimitri Aleynik takes over, I will never know the truth. Please, help me, Peter."

"I don't want a long stay in Siberia, Marta."

"Who are you?" she cried. "Who are you?"

"A friend. Perhaps your only friend right now. If Nicholas is really alive, someone might find him before we do."

She nodded wearily. "Someone has already been to the *gasthof*—asking questions. Demanding answers. It had to be Yuri and Vronin."

"You're certain it was them?"

She shook her head. "No, but the owner's wife, Frau Schrott, was beaten yesterday. Vronin is so adept at torture. Maybe he did find Nicholas there. Vronin would never tell us."

Kermer guided her into a small cafe and ordered coffee. "If Vronin found Nicholas, he would not have beaten the woman. He wanted answers—"

"But what if she told him?" Coffee splashed from her cup as she set it down. "Kermer, you're not running out on me. I need you." Her long-lashed eyes turned hard. She patted her purse. "I'll kill you if necessary."

"Then I'd be of no use to you."

He pitied her. She was a woman accustomed to pitting her wits against others, of using anyone to reach her goal— of living without emotion. Peter had no doubt that until this assignment, Marta had been a loyal Communist—still was—and in the end against all her inner drives, she would take Nicholas back to Innsbruck.

Before that, he had to stop her. "I'm staying," he said. "But not because you've threatened me. I want Nicholas, too. Alive."

"I don't understand you, Kermer. In the beginning you didn't even know who Nicholas was."

"I do now." He was still sweating over the one call he had placed to Israeli Intelligence, a call severed when Marta walked into his room unannounced. Dimitri and Marta were committed to finding Nicholas. Whatever Nicholas represented to them, he was an equal threat to Kermer. Israel could not risk the old guard taking over Russia again—could not risk that great country to the north swooping down through Turkey and Syria and marching against the Holy Land. "We're not the only ones looking for Nicholas, Marta," he said.

"You know about Dudley Perkins?"

*MI5?* "No," he admitted. But he did know about the Americans. And the only way he could reach Nicholas Trotsky in time was to work with her.

Once again the sense of betrayal saddened him. This woman knew nothing of the coming Messiah, nothing of the peace that he and Sara had discovered a few short years ago. The Star of David dug into his chest, reminding him that he had come to know the living Christ. But he could not mention the truth as he knew it. He dared not let Marta know his true identity—or even mention his faith—until he took Nicholas Trotsky captive.

"Marta, do you think Nicholas is still in Brunnerwald?"

"Not if he saw any of the flyers we've been putting up."

"You wanted to warn him, didn't you?"

"I needed time. What else could I do? The Yeltsin government wouldn't welcome Nicholas back to Moscow."

"No, I suppose it wouldn't. I'm not certain that Yuri and

Vronin want to take Nicholas that far, or even to Innsbruck." He smiled. "I'm not even certain that it's what you want."

Marta's harsh expression went passive, but the tips of her ears turned scarlet. Kermer was convinced that she had followed Trotsky from Innsbruck to Brunnerwald. In this, she had been truthful. But Trotsky had only passed through this town en route to somewhere. But where? It was unlikely that Marta knew, but he pressed her for answers.

"Marta, I think you know Trotsky well—his habits, his likes and dislikes." As her ears turned a deeper hue, he asked, "Where would Nicholas go if he left Brunnerwald?"

She wrapped both hands around the cup as though holding on to something gave her stability. "He loved Innsbruck."

"What was it about Innsbruck that he liked?"

"The mountains," she whispered. "He loved the mountains and skiing." Her gaze wandered from Kermer to the Tyrolean Alps beyond the cafe window. "We'll never find him. Nicholas always said that he could drop off the world from the mountain peaks."

"Did you believe him?"

"Not when he said it. I do now. He's gone, isn't he?"

"And what happens to you if you don't find him?"

"You should know that, Peter. It would be my life for his."

For an instant Marta's face blurred, and he saw Sara. The ache inside of him to go home to Sara and his sons was overpowering. "Marta, when this is over, perhaps I could take you home with me."

She looked shocked.

"It's not what you think," he assured her. "It's just that you would be safe with my wife and family."

Her knuckles blanched against the purse. "Who are you?"

"Right now I'm the only friend you have."

Marta didn't hear him. She was looking around. "Peter, I left my camera back there in the dining room at the *gasthof.*"

"Wait here." Peter didn't give her time to protest. He was on his feet. "I'll go back and get it. No one will recognize me."

The bell rang as he opened the door and stepped into the empty room at the Schrotts' *gasthof*. He paused at the desk and out of curiosity ran his finger down the guest registry, looking in vain for Nicholas's name. His eyes widened as he read the last notation: "Drew Gregory."

So Drew Gregory had already traced Nicholas Trotsky to the Schrott *gasthof*, perhaps even to his present location. Kermer had waited too long to line himself up with the American, but if Drew Gregory left Brunnerwald, Kermer and Marta would follow him.

❈❈❈

Drew Gregory had not waited for Preben Schrott to come back for the promised trip to the ski lodge. He took off a few moments after breakfast and headed on foot for the ski lift. En route he stopped off at a cubbyhole book stall that boasted new and used editions and trail maps of the mountains.

He picked up an outdated mystery by Dick Francis, one of the few English editions on the shelves and then turned to the cluttered rows of maps. He had selected several and was narrowing it down to the trails along the old avalanche when he heard a young Britisher saying, "This one will do us, Ian. They look like good biking trails."

The exasperated answer was clearly American. "I told you, Chris, we've got to stick with Brunnerwald a couple more days."

An Italian expletive followed, and then in English the third voice snapped, "Ian, you stick with your little needle in the haystack. Alekos and Chris and I are heading up the mountain."

"Orlando's right," Chris answered. "We're leaving."

"Give it a few more days. Let the snows melt some more."

"Ian, the trails are fine," Orlando argued. "I've checked. We won't be ready for the race riding the streets of Brunnerwald. Just find your friend and let's get out of here."

"I told you, it's my grandfather's friend."

"Then just leave a message for him at his hotel."

"Chris, I don't know where he's staying."

"Great." And another Italian phrase poured from Orlando's mouth. "Why don't you just find this Gregory and join us later?"

Drew turned slowly. An aisle separated him from the four young men in red and blue riding shirts with the word *Gainsborough* down the side. The Italian had sunglasses on and a day's stubble of beard. Two of the men wore goggles, their biking helmets still on their heads. Drew figured that the lad on the right was Alekos; he had a strong Grecian profile, skin bronzed by birth, and eyes so dark they were almost black.

That left two to choose from. Drew waited for them to speak again so he could pinpoint the American, but it only took a second. Ian had caught Drew's eye.

Surprise whipped across the American's face. Given any other situation and Drew would have been struck by the wholesome quality of the boy's features. He was fair-skinned and attractive, his eyes a more probing blue than Robyn's.

Ian wet his lips, spun around, and stalked from the store.

"Hey, Kendall," Orlando called after him, "do we want the maps, or don't we?"

"We don't need them for a few days," Ian called back.

Orlando shrugged, his palms extended. He grinned over at Drew. "Americans! That one is so explosive. But—we like him."

He adjusted his glasses, grinned again, and took off after his three friends.

*Ian Kendall.* Uriah's grandson here in Brunnerwald? Drew hadn't seen Ian for more than a dozen years. He'd been a boy then, a scrawny eleven-year-old. Drew couldn't be certain that the young man was even related to Uriah. But the name kicked in again—Ian Kendall. The pieces didn't fit together smoothly—not unless Uriah had been in touch with Pierre or Vic Wilson. They were the ones who knew about Brunnerwald, not Robyn and Miriam.

Drew lingered over the maps for another five minutes, giving Ian Kendall time to slip back into the store on his own. He gave up at last, made his purchase, and struck out again for the ski lift.

Drew was three or four blocks from the store when a pack of bikers steamrolled past him. They rode bent forward, the muscles in their arms and legs shining with sweat. He recognized the three in Gainsborough jerseys, but another group bearing other colors had joined them. The back rider turned up the tempo and launched an attack, chasing wildly and skillfully toward the front of the pack. Drew half turned expecting the fourth rider in the red and blue jersey to come riding along when someone yelled, "Look out."

The warning came too late.

The fourth biker in a Gainsborough jersey was pedaling furiously, his face obscured by the thick goggles and biker's helmet. He bounced his bike onto the sidewalk and swerved directly toward Drew. Drew's trousers and trench coat took the blow, tearing at the seams as Drew fell.

For an instant the driver swayed, fought to regain his balance, and then rode pell-mell at the back of the line.

A stranger helped Drew to his feet. "That biker deliberately turned into you. Should I call the *polizei?*"

"No," Drew said, dusting himself off. "I know who it was. When I catch up to him, I'll give him the tanning he deserves."

"That's not too popular these days," the man warned.

"I'll keep that in mind," Drew promised.

🟤🟤🟤

With his clothes torn and his temper at the boiling point, Drew grabbed a taxi and headed back to the guest house. In the privacy of Preben Schrott's office, he placed a call to London.

"Perkins, this is Drew Gregory from the American embassy."

A decided pause was swallowed up with, "Oh, yes. We met over the Breckenridge affair."

"Right. And now I need your expertise again."

The suggestion fell on deaf ears.

"Perkins, I said I need your help."

"Quite all right." His voice came across the line with its distinct upper-crust Kent accent. "I heard you, Gregory."

"I'm trying to get in touch with the CEO at Gainsborough."

"Jon Gainsborough at Gainsborough Steel?"

"Yes. The steel magnate."

"And how can Jon be of service to you, Gregory?"

"He can take some disciplinary action on his bicycling team."

"Bicycling team? Is Jon into cycling?"

"No games, Perkins. Gainsborough is big news in the London press. It would take all but a blind man to miss it. He's boasting possession of the yellow jersey this July."

"Ah. The Tour de France team. Why didn't you say so? Jon does expect his team to win this year."

"One of his chaps tried to run me off the road an hour ago."

"An accident, of course." Worry had crept into Perkins's voice.

"Of course not. The young man deliberately swerved into me. If I hadn't moved, he would have broken my leg—or skinned my thigh at best. I should have separated him from his bike. Permanently."

"It's quite unlikely that Jon has any cyclists in your area."

Gregory smiled. Now he was getting somewhere. He hadn't even told Perkins where he was calling from. "From my vantage point—four of them. I couldn't see his face—not with those goggles and helmet, but fortunately for me, he rode with Gainsborough's logo."

"Say, old chap, if you need Jon, call him direct."

"I don't have the number that goes straight to his desk. And I'm not in the mood for arguing my way through a long line of polite secretaries. You're good friends. You call him for me."

"And what am I to tell him, Gregory?"

"Just have him warn them off. If he doesn't, I'll go through the local *polizei*. By the way, you didn't ask me where I am."

"Didn't you say Brunnerwald?"

"I didn't say anywhere."

Perkins was not easily rattled, but Drew heard him suck in his wind—heard that gangly fist slam into the desk. While Perkins gathered his wits, Drew pressed further. "I understand Lyle Spincrest is in town, too. If you sent him into my hotel suite uninvited, you'd best call him off as well."

"Spincrest," he sputtered, "is on holiday. Ah—skiing, I believe. Yes, that's it. A ski trip."

This time he allowed Perkins to save face. Spincrest, as Drew knew, never did anything that risked his physical safety. He was swift on the tennis courts, but beyond that, Spincrest was a spectator at most sports and an avid attender at concerts and stage plays. And he was well acquainted with art museums, anything that would take him up the social ladder. But skiing? No. Lyle wouldn't even have the courage to ride an open-air ski lift.

"Skiing in Brunnerwald?" Drew asked.

"Yes. Yes. I do believe he is. If he checks in, I'll have him get in touch with you. Where did you say you're staying?"

*I didn't. And I won't.* But he relented. If Perkins was taking the search for Nicholas Trotsky seriously, then he already knew where Drew was staying. Consetta's bruised face flashed in his mind again. Some of the boys at MI5 might play rough, but not Perkins. MI5 didn't usually cross international boundaries. That was MI6's jurisdiction. So Perkins was moving in unofficially. A searched suitcase was one thing, a physical attack another.

"Well," Perkins asked, "where can Lyle reach you?"

"The Gasthof Schrott in Old Town. Don't have the number handy."

"Lyle can read."

"Dudley, we'd do better working together on this."

"On what?" Perkins asked innocently.

"The Trotsky business."

"I'll have Spincrest call you."

*I bet you will.*

As he disengaged the call, Drew smiled to himself and formed a mental picture of Perkins drumming his fingers on the desktop. Perkins was a good man, given to traditional ways and satisfied with his spartan office, surviving instead, Drew was confident, on his wife's inheritance. Dudley had come up by the bootstraps, overcoming a childhood battle with stuttering and rising rapidly to his present position—an intellectual and successful man who had never overcome the loss of his only son. In this, Drew pitied him. He neither liked nor disliked Perkins, but he had an innate mistrust of him, born, he was sure from Uriah Kendall's unspoken fears. Drew had Uriah's curiosity now. Drew couldn't understand Perkins's interest in the Trotsky search unless it was a personal one or the sheer desire to beat his American counterparts at the game.

But Drew had accomplished two things in his phone call: Spincrest would surely get in touch with him, and one of London's wealthiest men would be contacting his cycling team in Brunnerwald with the threat of disciplinary action or a warning that would send them pedaling out of town.

۞ ۞ ۞

Dudley Perkins drummed his fingernails on the desk for five minutes. Finally, he reached for the phone and placed a call to Lyle Spincrest's hotel in Brunnerwald.

"You're overstepping your authority again, Lyle," he told him. "What got into you, searching Drew Gregory's hotel room?"

"I didn't. I don't even know where he's staying."

"The concierge told Gregory you were looking for him."

"Sorry. I didn't think you'd approve. I haven't seen much of Gregory since the Breckenridge affair. Your orders. I thought a cup of coffee together outside of London wouldn't hurt."

"Did you plan to warn him about Gainsborough's cycling team?"

"No. Not a word about them. But Gregory wasn't in. I left a message at the desk for him. Contacting him was better than running into him accidentally."

"I suppose you're right. And you didn't go to his room?"

"No."

"Are you keeping in touch with Ian Kendall, Lyle?"

"Yes, and he's not cooperative. You'd better call him off."

"Can't. Gregory thinks I'm on to the Trotsky search."

"We are."

"It's up to Ian and his friends. But I want you to contact Gregory and have that cup of coffee."

"I checked with the Kellerhof today. Gregory checked out."

"He's at the Gasthof Schrott in Old Town."

"And what am I to tell him?"

"What were you going to tell him a couple of days ago?"

Lyle's silence was convicting.

"Lyle, you're to convince Gregory that you're there on a ski vacation."

"He knows I don't ski."

"You're about to start. I'm good for whatever it costs. Just put it on your expense account. But I want you up that mountain this afternoon signing up for beginning classes."

"No."

"When your nose is sunburned and you have a few good bruises to prove your efforts, then call Gregory. Tonight preferably. Ask him to ski with you tomorrow. Maybe give you a few good pointers."

"I can't. Heights scare me. I'd break my neck coming down that slope. I'll go up to the lodge with him. Nothing more."

"Losing your job should scare you even more. Now get in touch with Ian Kendall and tell him I've already pulled his grandmother's file. It's cooperate with me or take the consequences."

# Chapter 15

Vic Wilson entered the American embassy through the side entry with a flick of his identity tag and a friendly wave to an old friend. He made his way straight to Brad O'Malloy's cubicle and met his first obstacle. She was an American, blonde and pretty with long, dark lashes and a stunning outfit that had come from one of the boutique racks just off the Champs-Elysees.

He tweaked her cheek. "You're looking lovely this morning, Christabelle. Why don't you have lunch with me over at the Amitie?"

"And what's in it for you?" she asked.

"Good companionship. Besides, you can't afford three meals a day, not when you're wearing your paycheck."

She didn't even blush. "Sorry, I'm lunching with Mr. O'Malloy."

He thought of the golden arches on the main avenue. "Brad can only afford hamburgers."

"True. But he'll be here next week. And the week after that. And we like to talk about back home, Colorado in particular."

Christabelle smothered her hint of homesickness as she answered the phone, her voice pleasant and professional, Colorado an ocean away from her.

Vic nodded toward the closed office. "Is O'Malloy in?"

She cupped the mouthpiece. "He's with the boss."

"Carwell?"

She was obviously on hold. "Yes, Brad's on the carpet again."

"Let me guess. No tie or dress shirt."

She took down a number and disconnected. "The tie this time. Mr. O'Malloy will never learn."

"I like his independence."

"You would. Carwell doesn't. You're just like O'Malloy. They might as well throw out the procedure book when you two walk in."

"Did they?" he asked, loosening the top button of his polo shirt. "I'll just wait for O'Malloy inside."

"No, he doesn't like his office disturbed."

Vic leaned down and kissed the top of her head. "Brad is expecting me," he said, tapping his briefcase. "I brought some work to do. And how about lunch with me some other time?"

He kicked open the door and shut it before she could block his way. Glancing around at the disorder, he chuckled. Aloud he said, "And Carwell's worried about you not wearing a tie."

Troy Carwell kept his office polished and shipshape, in an elegant style that matched the ambassador's quarters. But Brad O'Malloy hid any elegance with a clutter, his room as relaxed as his personality. Vic made a beeline for the chair, swiveled a time or two and then placed his lanky legs on the crowded desk top. Brad would attribute the heel smudges to coffee spills or his own blunders. But O'Malloy was a good man; he'd be around doing service for the Company long after Vic bit the dust.

Vic stretched his body, hands behind his neck, moodily facing the solitude as the international fax beeped and clicked into play. He cocked his head, intrigued as the message rolled into view: "PHOENIX PLAN aborted June 13, 1980, following execution of General Boris Jankowski and Colonel Vasily Kavin."

He swung his legs off the desk and scanned the next paragraph. Five more names, none that Vic recognized, executed in those first six weeks. Seven more men from the

KGB and military stripped of their power and rank and exiled to labor camps in Siberia.

The fax stopped clicking. Vic examined the rest of the two-page report—a list of KGB officers who had been destined for recall to Moscow with Nicholas Trotsky's name at the top. Men who were still wanted. *The Phoenix Plan*— Drew had been on to something bigger than either one of them had even imagined.

Wilson was so engrossed that he didn't hear O'Malloy come in or even sense his presence until Brad's voice boomed out with an expletive. As O'Malloy tore the fax from the machine, he thundered, "What are you doing, Wilson?"

They faced each other. "Who's your contact, O'Malloy? This kind of info should go straight to Carwell."

"It's no longer classified."

"I bet it is now."

"Get out."

"Not until you tell me why you're nosing around at this level. Don't you like the way things are going in Brunnerwald?"

"I don't like Gregory."

"You did until Porter's death."

"I don't like him. But I don't like the risk he's taking either. Going in alone uninformed."

"Trotsky's not the only one hiding out there. Right?"

"You read the report."

"I scanned it. Come on. Gregory's my friend."

Brad dropped to the edge of the desk and sat there rereading the fax. "I think this PHOENIX PLAN went underground. It was only aborted in the eighties until they could regroup."

"Fifteen years is a long time."

"Men like Trotsky don't count time by years. They calculate their steps carefully—the ultimate takeover primary. A planned overthrow like this in Moscow now would put us right back into a cold war with Russia."

"That serious?" Vic asked. "How involved is Trotsky?"

"He may have instigated the rebellion. That puts him in

from the planning stages. I've got that much straight from Carwell. I just told Troy we couldn't let Gregory go after Trotsky alone."

"And what did Carwell say?"

"He reminded me that he is the station-chief. And he told me to go put my tie on. That man is driving me crazy."

"I'm joining Gregory in Brunnerwald. Keep us informed, Brad."

"I can't take that risk."

"But will you?"

"Carwell's calling the shots, and he says Gregory is the only one who will recognize Nicholas Trotsky. If we can get Trotsky—"

"Before he gets Gregory. You can't let him go on alone."

Brad wet his lips. "If we charge into Brunnerwald like the Light Brigade, every intelligence community in Europe will be tailing us. We'd lose Trotsky. If we get him, we may be able to stop the PHOENIX PLAN from reorganizing."

"Save the world, eh? And forget Gregory." Vic stood. "Sorry, I don't agree with you." He took out a card and wrote down an address. "If you change your mind, get in touch with me here. I'll be out of your apartment by the time you get home tonight."

"Good," Brad told him. "I like the privacy."

"Say, Brad, can I have a copy of that fax?"

"Get out."

He gave O'Malloy a cocky salute. "Never mind. I've got the highlights memorized."

O'Malloy seemed determined to have the last word. "When you see Gregory, remind him that Zach Deven is still gunning for him."

"Tell Porter Deven's brother to take a rowboat to Baltimore and cool down. Porter's downfall was his own doing, not Drew's."

As he left O'Malloy, Vic considered barging into Carwell's office, but he changed his mind when Christabelle smiled at him. He winked back. "Sweetheart, we'll have to cancel our lunch date."

She shook her head. "What date?"

"The one I was trying to talk you into. I'll catch you on my next trip to Paris."

"You're leaving? How nice!"

"Be out of here before you lock up your desk this evening. So keep O'Malloy happy while I'm gone," he said.

Vic winked, more cockily this time, and left the embassy by the front entry. He struck out from the Avenue Gabriel toward the Amitie for something to eat. And then he'd pack it in and kiss Paris goodbye. Right now the action lay in Brunnerwald.

🜚🜚🜚

In Beverly Hills Miriam Gregory looked up from Drew's letter as Floy Belmont stepped into the glass-encased office at the art gallery. "What's wrong, Miriam?" Floy asked as she sat down. "You've been so unhappy since you came back from Europe."

"Does it show that much?"

"More each day. It isn't Robyn, is it? She's not regretting her marriage?"

Miriam felt the trace of a smile form on her lips. "No, Robyn and Pierre were meant to be together."

"Like you and Drew?"

"Oh, Floy, that was so long ago." She ran her hand over Drew's letter. "The trip to Austria was all wrong. It just stirred up old memories and longings for both of us."

"All wrong? That's not what you said on the telephone."

Dear Floy. Plump, pleasant, and bosomed—those wide, blue eyes inviting trust. Floy's snow-white hair made it seem like more than six years between them. "I guess I did call you from Vienna."

"Twice. Once to tell me you'd be delayed getting home a week or two. Two days later to tell me you were flying home at once. What happened, Miriam?"

"Drew had a job to do."

"Just like that?"

"It was always just like that."

"Miriam, why don't you let go of the past?"

"Because the past is never faraway. Drew's career with the CIA always came between us."

Miriam watched Floy's wrinkles crisscross from a smile to a frown, the jolly face deadly serious now. She tried to remember when the employer-employee tie fell by the wayside and friendship took over. Floy was so much like Olivia Kendall, open and honest, caring and comforting, a tower of strength.

"Then he isn't an attaché at the London embassy?" Floy asked. "Why the pretense, the charade, even with me, Miriam?"

"To protect Robyn. I thought it was safer for her to tell her friends that her father was with the diplomatic service."

"As adventuresome as Robyn is, she would have liked the CIA better. So why lie to her all these years?" Floy asked gently.

"It really wasn't a lie. Drew does work for the government. And he did register as an embassy employee in foreign countries."

"Was he an intelligence officer when you met him?"

"I thought he was joking, and it didn't matter. He was so attractive, Floy. I think I fell madly in love with him the moment I first saw him at the art museum."

"He can be charming," Floy agreed. "About flattered me to death at Robyn's wedding. And I loved it. Reminded me of Frank—"

"Drew wanted you on his side so you'd persuade me to marry him again. Oh, Floy, I'm scared. I'm still in love with him."

"Is that so bad?"

"Before I ever married him, Olivia Kendall warned me that Drew's career would come between us."

"And did you believe her?"

"No, I was certain that Drew and I could make it. But it was a lie from the beginning. He promised me Paris for a honeymoon." Tears balanced on her long lashes and blotched the desktop as they fell. "Even Paris was a lie. Drew was working a case, tying up loose ends. I spent most of the time alone at the hotel waiting for him, wondering what had happened to him."

"The Drew I met seems so thoughtful."

"It's me, I guess. Drew is compassionate and tender, but I think of the Agency as a band of men more loyal than intelligent. It puzzles me why so many liars and cheaters are attracted to the Company—men who like the secretive lifestyle, the adventure and travel and the girl in every port—even risk-taking and killing. But Drew is not like that. He's a Gregory—honest and hardworking, patriotic and politically oriented, a man of integrity. I used to tell him that he was the noble type—committed to driving communism from our borders and smashing the Iron Curtain by himself."

"But you never liked his job?"

"From the beginning, we had our separate worlds. I loved art. Drew called it my lifeless still life. I could rarely drag him inside an art museum. Yet with me he was charming, Floy. Stoic, yes, but something about his closed mannerisms drew me to him."

Floy's eyes never left her. Miriam felt the crimson flush begin in her body and rise to her cheeks. "Drew never wanted the divorce," she admitted. "He was devoted to me. Sometimes life seemed like a perpetual honeymoon. I'd be so angry when he was away, and then he'd wire roses or be home again, and everything seemed all right."

"But it wasn't," Floy said. "You left him."

"We made a go of it for eleven years. I went with him to Frankfurt, Germany, for two years and to Libya for three. I hated it there. I was always nervous about Drew working undercover. Every time he went to the airport, I'd fall apart."

The gallery chimes rang, but they sat still, allowing Floy's daughter to meet the customer. "Like the other CIA wives, I was alone 50 percent of the time, so I refused to have Robyn born in Frankfurt. In the end Drew took a leave and came home with me. As thrilled as he was with the baby, it didn't change his loyalty to the Company. We were back in Europe a month later."

"Did he ever tell you much about his work?"

"We fought about it constantly. My never knowing. His code of silence. And then I quit asking for Robyn's sake. I didn't want anything to happen to her; I was foolish enough to think that if I didn't know, Drew would be safer, too." She put Drew's letter into the envelope. "Frankfurt is a pleasant memory, but Libya frightened me. There were so many bomb scares and such bitter isolation."

"And no art museums?"

"Not where we were. We wives stuck together, ignoring rumors of marital infidelity, feigning surprise with each new divorce, keeping a stiff upper lip at each sudden death in the line of duty."

Floy reached across the desk with her smile. "The thought of going back to Europe to live again frightens you, doesn't it?"

Crimson flushed Miriam's cheeks again. "It's the same problem," she said softly. "Robyn is still her daddy's girl. I was starting to feel left out—until our trip to Austria. That's when I realized that Drew and Robyn both want me there. Even my son-in-law does."

Miriam glanced at the customers browsing in the gallery. "I thought all of this would be fulfilling. The gallery. My art work. But lately I keep wondering if I really gave our marriage a chance."

She forced herself to face Floy. "Robyn turned five when we were stationed in Libya. That meant sending her to a U.S. army post or government-run school. I didn't want that for her. In spite of Drew's pleadings, I shut my ears to the threats behind the Iron Curtain and the nobility of preserving our country's position overseas. I finally decided to go home and be an American and take Robyn with me."

"And Drew didn't stop you?"

"Drew was on a special mission and didn't know I was gone until he got back to Libya. He thought he had good news for me—a chance to move to Italy for two years where I'd have my fill of museums. I refused. I'd had my fill of Company living."

She opened her desk drawer and slipped Drew's letter into her purse, trying desperately to shut him away. "We gave life together one more go around when Drew took an assignment at Langley. But he'd fly out of there and be gone for weeks and months at a time."

Floy waited in silence, the questions in her eyes unspoken. Finally she asked, "Miriam, with Drew so near retirement, what now? Is there any chance that you two can get back together?"

"On the trip to Austria, I felt like that young woman back at The Metropolitan Museum of Art seeing Drew for the first time and being drawn to him. And then—" She lifted her hands and inspected her polished nails. "The Agency needed him."

"And you didn't try to stop Drew from going?"

"Floy, I insisted that he go. It's been rough for Drew since the Breckenridge affair and Porter Deven's suicide. I couldn't let Drew come to the end of a long career defeated. When he leaves them—and if he comes back to me—I want him to do so with his head up. The Gregorys are a proud lot. Yet that's the Drew I know and love."

Sighing, she added, "If I marry Drew again, he'd want to split his time between upstate New York and Europe. Now that he's found Robyn, he wants to be near her. That's what I want—to be near Robyn and Pierre. But I'm more practical. The kids need to be alone, and they don't need Drew and me bickering near them. I'll just spend my vacations in Europe. Maybe in time they'll agree to spend Christmas here."

Miriam sounded lost and nostalgic to herself. She examined her slender, groomed hands again. "Life in upstate New York is out. I'd never make a farmer's wife. Drew loves the farm—he's always wanted to go back there."

"I thought he was putting the farm up for sale."

"I encouraged him to wait. The property is a good investment. And it's really home to Drew. He has a young couple there serving as caretakers. They love the place."

Floy seemed to stare right through her, jolting Miriam's guard. "Have you ever considered compromising about the farm? What about vacations? Couldn't you even do that?"

"I'm a city girl at heart, Floy. I'd be going against my own dreams like I did when we first married. But the truth is, it's a beautiful place. Drew loves the winters, the isolation and beauty of it. The last time I visited my mother-in-law it was fall. Autumn there is gorgeous, alive with vivid colors. I wouldn't mind vacationing there once in a while."

She began to laugh, a rippling sound so much like Robyn's. "But what am I talking about, Floy? This is my life. I've worked so hard to build this art gallery. It's me. I did it on my own. I can't leave it all for the uncertainty of marriage."

"Or won't?"

"I don't want to fail at marriage again."

"One can't put a price tag on this gallery of yours, Miriam, but if this magnificence were all mine, I would throw it all away for just another week or month with my Frank."

Floy's wistfulness blew across the desk to Miriam. "Your Frank was a special man."

"So is Drew. Why don't you let someone oversee the gallery for you and fly back to Geneva? You could be there when Drew arrives, talk it out—see whether you have a future together."

"You're the only one I'd trust with the gallery, Floy."

"No, I'm too old to fret about sales, but my daughter and son-in-law would be interested. Let them manage the place for you. You could fly back to Los Angeles every month to see how things are going."

Miriam let go of her half smile and chuckled. "You know how I hate flying."

"Then use the phone and the fax machine."

"Floy, we're a couple of old fools. Drew hasn't even asked me to marry him lately—let alone to move to Europe."

"And if he does?"

"He's the only one I've ever loved, but right now we're good friends again. I wouldn't want marriage to destroy that."

"Have you forgotten how good it is to pillow your head beside the one you love? I still wake up in the middle of the night and cry when I reach out to Frank's empty side of the bed."

"But, Floy, you had a good marriage."

"Forty years. It had its ups and downs, Miriam. But it's lonely being a widow, waking up each morning and missing Frank more. You and Drew have wasted so many years, dear friend. Don't let the rest of them slip away into regrets."

Floy stood and came around the shiny mahogany desk. "If he's worth fighting for, Miriam, don't let him go." She gave Miriam a quick hug. "Now go on and powder your face. We have some Rembrandts to sell so you can afford a new trousseau."

"You're getting ahead of yourself, Floy," Miriam warned.

"Humph! I don't think so. I rather think Drew Gregory doesn't plan to let you get away a second time. And if he does, then he's a bigger fool than I thought."

# Chapter 16

Drew was drinking coffee in the Schrott kitchen when Erika burst through the door. She slid to a stop when she saw him and said shyly, "*Guten Tag,* Herr Gregory."

"Erika, isn't it?"

She nodded as she glanced around. "Where is Consetta?"

"I was going to ask you the same thing. Perhaps she went up the mountain today."

"Preben told her not to go."

"And does she always do what Preben says?"

"I think so."

Drew tried to see the similarity between the sisters and saw differences instead. Erika's gangly, all-too-thin body; her older sister's chubbiness. Consetta's lovely chestnut hair; Erika's straggly, blonde strands. Consetta's large-boned features; Erika's narrow, serious face. He glanced around the well-furnished kitchen and tried to imagine Erika's more simple way of life.

"Are you alone?" she asked.

"Some of the guests have gone to their rooms."

Drew felt drawn to Erika—to the smile that was bewitching and bashful at the same moment, to the adult worry lines puckering her youthful face. She tucked her chin in, her anxious, dark eyes searching his. "The men didn't come back, did they?"

"The ones who hurt your sister? No, I don't think so. I'm sure she's with Preben."

Erika surprised him when she dropped her coat on the floor and went to the simmering coffeepot to pour herself a cup. As she sat down across from him, she said, "I left school early just to see her. And now I'll have to go back to Sulzbach without knowing if she's all right."

"I'm sure she's better." Quietly he asked, "Erika, would you be staying here if I weren't using your room?"

"I only stay when the weather is bad. My Grandmama needs me."

"It's a long walk alone."

"Josef is supposed to wait for me." A faint shade of pink touched her cheeks.

"Is he somebody special?"

"Grandmama thinks so, but I don't like him." Her cheeks denied it. "Josef likes to go off without me. I don't care," she said stoutly. "I didn't want him to come here and see Consetta's face. Not when I promised not to tell anyone." Her gaze locked with Drew's. "But I told Father Caridini," she admitted.

Drew started at the name, a pleasant memory pricking him. "Father Caridini—so he's still the priest in your village?"

"He's been there as long as I can remember."

"And how many years is that?" he teased.

"Eleven. He knows everybody in Sulzbach. Everybody loves him except," she said matter-of-factly, "Preben and Herr Burger."

"Reprobates?" he asked.

She scowled at the word.

"Not part of Father Caridini's parish," he explained.

"Preben never was. And Herr Burger won't attend anymore. He's mad at Father Caridini for wanting Sulzbach to stay the same."

"And what's Preben's excuse?"

"He's only been to church a few times, once for his wedding. And that made him mad. They'd already had a civil wedding here in Brunnerwald. Preben said that was good enough."

"I see. And your grandmother didn't like that?"

"Neither did Consetta. So Father Caridini married them again."

*A double bind,* Drew thought, *for a man like Preben.*

"I'd like to talk to your priest, Erika."

"He was here last week."

"Here at the *gasthof?*"

"Yes. He stayed for several days."

Father Caridini's name had not been in the *gasthof* registry. Drew was certain of that. "Does he stay here often?" he asked.

"Whenever he comes down to Brunnerwald. He uses my room."

Drew remembered the honest face of the priest, his love for the people of Sulzbach. If anyone would remember Nicholas Trotsky, it would be Father Caridini. Drew pushed his cup aside and pulled a trail map from his pocket. "Where would I stay if I went up to your village with you?"

"Next month you could stay with Frau Burger."

"But what about this month? Today? Tomorrow?"

She considered and said, "You couldn't stay with Dr. Heppner. He'd have room in the clinic, but he doesn't like you."

"He doesn't even know me."

She shrugged at that. "That's what he said. But Grandmama says he's just grumpy because he drinks."

"Does he?"

"Everyday and he plays chess with Father Caridini every night." She giggled. "The doctor doesn't believe in God, but they're still the best of friends."

*Yes*, Drew thought. *Father Caridini was like that. Kind and friendly to his people. Kind and caring to a stranger.* "What if I came up to Sulzbach tomorrow? Could you find me a place to stay?"

She pushed the hair from her face, and Drew realized now that the dark eyes were closely set, the frown lines narrowing her features even more, aging her.

"Preben would send you to the pretty gingerbread houses on the far side of the village." He heard disapproval in her voice. "They rent rooms to skiers and hikers. The families are nice, but Grandmama says they are outsiders— that they don't know the old ways. That's important to us."

Drew's fatherly tug toward Erika came afresh. She was not some prattling child, but a twelve-year-old with adult worries—voicing them aloud as she tried to grope with them. Watching her, he thought, *You should welcome the excitement of change in the village, but your loyalty to your grandmother is pulling you in two directions.*

Gently he asked, "Erika, where would you like me to stay?"

"The Petzolds have room, but you'd be staying with Josef."

Drew could tell by her frown that Josef's place was off limits as far as she was concerned. "Or maybe Frau Katwyler would have a place for you."

She leaned across the table. "I'll ask her. You'd have to pay her," she said earnestly. "She's very poor. And you mustn't tell Preben that I helped you. He doesn't want you in Sulzbach."

"Then it will be our secret." He pocketed the map. "It's settled then. Tomorrow first thing I'll rent boots and a backpack—"

"Preben can rent you those."

"Well! He's an ambitious young man."

She agreed, saying, "He likes to make money."

There was no envy evident in her voice. She seemed to accept Preben for who he was—an heir to the cheese factory, an owner of a *gasthof* or two, the renter of hiking equipment. "Yes, he's an enterprising young man," Drew said.

Her shy smile broadened. "Preben and Herr Burger are the ones who want to turn Sulzbach into a tourist town."

"Is that what you want, Erika?"

"I don't think my grandparents do. But Preben says my grandfather could work in Herr Burger's wood carving shop, and then he wouldn't have to come down to Brunnerwald every day with the milk."

"And your grandma?"

"She's getting old, but she still remembers how to make good strudel, and Josef's mother promises to sell it in her bakery."

She had gone to the stove for more coffee, and he sensed a confidence in that awkward gait, a sensitivity for other people. Erika's hand was steady as she poured it into their cups. "Herr Gregory, why do you want to come to my village?"

"To eat your grandma's strudel."

She laughed. "You can get strudel in Brunnerwald."

"But she's not in Brunnerwald. Besides, I want to talk to your priest. He befriended me a long time ago."

The wide eyes went even bigger. "You know him?"

"You mustn't tell him I'm coming. I want to surprise him." *And thank him for saving my life. And find out what lies between here and the village that Preben Schrott wants to keep from me.*

He glanced outside and didn't like the lowered position of the sun. "Why don't I go to a hotel tonight and let you use your room? Then we can hike up to Sulzbach together in the morning."

"Oh, no. Preben's father insisted you stay here."

"Because I own a farm in upstate New York?"

Her head bobbed. "That's so far away. I'll never get there." She swallowed her wistfulness with her coffee. "Preben set the room aside for me. I don't have a room to myself in the mountains."

*And only a cracker box here,* Drew thought. But it revealed the kinder side of Preben. Or was it the business side? Drew could not be certain. "Erika, are Preben and Father Caridini good friends now?"

"They like each other, but Preben is going behind Father Caridini's back to open up Sulzbach to tourists."

"Would it be so much different?" Drew asked. "You've had hikers and skiers passing near your village for years."

"And they depend on Dr. Heppner's ski patrol to rescue them. If Dr. Heppner knew what Preben and Herr Burger plan, he'd move away, and we wouldn't have a clinic in our village."

Again the worry lines knit her brows. "Father Caridini would be lost without Dr. Heppner. But maybe it doesn't matter anymore. Grandmama says he's dying."

Before Drew could ask who was ill, Preben and Consetta came from the hallway into the kitchen. Consetta's face looked even more bruised and swollen, her upper lip puffed abnormally.

"Erika," she cried out, "what are you doing here? It'll be dark before you get up the mountain."

"I'll hurry. But I had to see you."

Erika stumbled out of her chair and ran to her sister. Chubby arms encircled her. "I'm all right, little one. Now you must go. And not a word to Grandmama. I'll be up to see her when I'm better."

Preben stood morosely in the doorway. "You worry too much, Erika. Now run along. Where's Josef?"

"He went on without me."

Preben's scowl deepened. "Then I must go with you."

"No. I'll run all the way."

Drew had kicked back his chair. "I'll walk her partway," he offered. He grabbed up his wool jacket and followed Erika from the *gasthof*.

She sprinted into the wind like a mountain goat, edging the main road for three blocks. Just past Erika's school, they turned right at one of the smaller hotels, and Drew spotted the path doing a loopy-loo up the verdant knolls.

"I'll be all right, Herr Gregory. I know my way from here."

He glanced up the mountainside where the land seemed to be divided into rolling hills, the homes more scattered on the higher slopes. "I'll go with you to the fifth knoll," he said.

She shrugged and bounded ahead of him.

For all of his hiking skills, he felt slightly winded as they climbed higher. As they reached the tree line, she stopped. "Go back," she said. "But tomorrow come this way. You'll go straight to Sulzbach if you do."

She smiled. "My grandfather will come to meet me

before I get there. He always does if I'm not home by milking time."

"I'll see you tomorrow then," Drew said. "But, Erika, how will I find Frau Katwyler's place?"

"Just ask anyone. They'll tell you." She peeked around his shoulder. "Do you know those men?" she asked.

Two strangers were within shouting distance. "Go on," Drew told her. "I'll intercept them."

Gregory watched her disappear in the trees, and then he turned to face the strangers. "*Guten Abend,*" Drew said. "It's rather late to be hiking. It'll be dark soon."

"I see the girl is going on," the older man said.

"She knows these mountains." He put a hedge of safety around Erika saying, "Her grandfather will be meeting her."

"My friend Yuri and I plan to do some hiking."

"There are plenty of trails to follow," Drew told them. "But you'd do better with a guide."

"He's right, Vronin."

The man called Vronin shrugged. "It is getting darker."

Drew took one final glance. The sun had slipped behind the mountains, leaving the higher peaks shrouded in shadows. The green knolls blended as one now, their verdant greens grayed by the semidarkness. Lights appeared in the chalet windows. Drew turned and followed the men back toward Brunnerwald. Even though he was slipping over the rocky trail, he made no attempt to reach the town before the encroaching darkness. He ambled along, giving Erika ample time to reach her grandfather. Twenty minutes later he waved at the strangers and turned toward the Schrott *gasthof.*

⚭⚭⚭

The fireplace in the rectory at the Saint Francis Chapel in Sulzbach crackled and popped with a blazing fire. A chessboard lay between the parish priest and the village doctor. Both of them were tall and lanky-legged, intelligent men capable of deep concentration, yet they were content and companionable as they studied the black and white squares on their nightly battlefield.

Nicholas Caridini watched with amusement as Johann Heppner stroked his beard and focused on the next play. "I almost had you that time, Johann," Nicholas said.

He looked up as Frau Mayer shuffled into the room and placed a glass of wine in front of the doctor and a piping hot cup of tea by his hand. "Will that be all, Father Caridini?" she asked.

"Anything else for you, Johann? We still have some of Frau Schmid's strudel in the kitchen."

"Then bring on the strudel," Johann said.

Frau Mayer was breathing heavily when she returned and placed the plate near the doctor. "If it's all right, I'll retire now."

Johann reached for her hand. "Frau Mayer, slow down," he said. "You're short of breath."

"Just a bit, Doctor," she said, patting her chest.

"I'd like to see you in my clinic in the morning."

"I was fine until I came up the mountain this time. I think it's the cold air."

"It's the altitude," Johann said as she left them.

"She knows that. I'll make certain she sees you tomorrow."

"And what about you, Nicholas? How are you feeling?"

"The pain is worse at night, but Frau Mayer is determined that I eat her soups and *wiener schnitzel* and grow stronger. What do *you* think, Doctor?"

Johann recovered quickly and said, "If she goes easy on the red peppers, the *letscho* would be good."

Nicholas chuckled. "My housekeeper knows that's your favorite stew, Johann. She'll be making some soon."

"Have you told her?"

"About my cancer? No, but she knows I'm ill."

"You'd both breathe better down in Brunnerwald."

"We're both happier here. This is Frau Mayer's last summer in the mountains. Maybe that's why she came up early. But if she must go back home now, I'll let it be her decision."

"Or mine," the doctor said. "Does she even suspect that this could be your last summer in the mountains, too?"

"But it won't be, Johann." Nicholas reflected on the cemetery behind the parish and on the poorly marked grave of the first Father Caridini. "Like Jacques, I plan to stay here forever," Nicholas said.

Johann peered over the top of his thick glasses. "I promised Dr. Eschert I'd keep an eye on you."

"Am I wasting away in your eyes, Doctor?"

"Don't joke, Nicholas."

Johann pushed back his chair and went for a decanter of wine from the cupboard. He poured a glass and took it straight down.

"Keep drinking like that, Johann, and you'll pound the nails in your own coffin." As Heppner made a move on the chessboard, Nicholas said, "And don't worry about me, Johann. I have ample medicine. Plenty of painkillers and pills for nausea."

"Are you taking them?"

"Only when the pain is severe."

"That's not the way Eschert prescribed them."

"No, but there are things I must do, best not done when I'm drowsy. I'm concerned about the Schmids—making sure they will be cared for. But I seem to be losing Erika. She's avoiding me now that Frau Mayer is back."

"She's working for Senn Burger's wife for a few days. They have four guests in their home, just in from Brunnerwald."

"Tourists?"

"They're not ordinary tourists. Three men and a woman all traveling lightly and poorly equipped for the mountains. But I did see one camera and a pair of laser binoculars."

"Bird-watchers?"

"Hardly. They're more like people-watchers."

Nicholas stiffened as Erika's words came back to him. *Consetta was beaten yesterday. . . . I think it was something to do with Grandfather or with you. . . . Consetta wanted to warn you.*

The prickling sensation in Nicholas's back was not pain. For the first time in many years, he tasted fear. Dry heaves rose in his throat, and he doubled over as a spasm ripped across his belly. He leaned away from the chessboard, retching.

Heppner grabbed his arm. "Let's get you to bed."

"No, I don't sleep well when I get there." The first wave of fear settled. "I'm all right now. Let's get on with our game."

"It's something I said, isn't it?"

"It doesn't matter, Johann." He lifted one of his men, a pawn in his hand and set it down again. "I intend to beat you at this game, so let me rest a few minutes. Go on about the guests in town. It'll give me time to catch my breath."

Johann's voice flattened as he said, "Zita Burger cut her thumb, so I dropped by to dress the wound. She's upset about her guests coming off season. That bothers me, too, Nicholas. We've had a hard winter with spring struggling to get here. Two weeks from now in the splendor of May would be a good time to visit Sulzbach."

He seemed to move his man without even thinking. "They are not a pleasant lot, Nicholas. Not one word about places to see or places to go. Nothing about how to get to the ski lodge from here."

"Almost impossible from here," Nicholas reminded him.

"At least they could have asked. Mostly they wanted to know about the number of homes in town and the number of people."

"Are they looking for someone?"

Johann eyed him curiously. "I've been mulling that over all afternoon. Seems to me they came here on the heels of the American over at Helene Katwyler's place."

"Frau Katwyler has a guest, too?"

"Yes, Nicholas. Five strangers descending on Sulzbach in less than six hours. To me that means nothing but trouble."

"We're the only ones who want to keep Sulzbach to ourselves."

"The council met at the Schrott Cheese Factory yesterday to vote me out of office."

"And who will be mayor then?"

"Senn Burger is Preben Schrott's choice."

"Johann, he's not even a member of the Sulzbach council."

"Preben is in on all their meetings now. They depend on his financial backing. He's got good ideas, you know."

"Ones that will make Sulzbach a main thoroughfare between Brunnerwald and the mountain."

"It'll be good for the economy." Johann lit his pipe. "They even plan a smaller ski lodge just above Sulzbach."

"That's risky. Too close to the old avalanche."

"But good skiing. That's what matters to Preben. We've known these changes were coming, Nicholas. Let the council have the town and see what they can do. You may have to go to a third mass on Sunday morning."

"I barely make it through the second one now."

"Perhaps you should ask for your replacement soon."

"Is that coming from you, Johann? I thought you'd be glad to see the doors of St. Francis close forever."

"Don't joke, Nicholas. Preben's community plans are centered around the church. He says it makes a nice image for the tourists. By August Sulzbach will have a new face and a new mayor."

Nicholas reflected on Johann's words. "I'll be gone by then."

"You're running away after all?"

Nicholas stared at the flickering flames. "No, Johann. I'm dying. So you'll have to find a new chess player."

"But he won't be my friend as you have been. Funny thing, you have never pressed me to be part of your parish."

"In a way you are. Who knows me better than you do, Johann?"

"I know about your heart and lungs—"

"And even my soul, the dark inner me." In the light of the fire he could see the tears behind Johann's glasses. And the thought that he had deceived even this, the closest of friends—perhaps his only real friend in his whole lifetime—overwhelmed him. "There are things we must discuss, Johann. I'll need your help to get my house in order."

"Later, Nicholas. There's still time."

"Is that the doctor speaking—or the friend?"

"Both. Because if you're going to discuss the settling of accounts, I can't help you. I wouldn't know the first thing—"

"Johann, I have a letter that I want you to deliver."

"Let Rheinhold Schmid mail it for you in the morning."

"It must be hand-delivered." Nicholas choked on his words. "I have heard many confessions in my time. Now I must write my own."

"To the bishop in Innsbruck?" Heppner asked.

"No."

"To the archbishop in Vienna?"

A softer, "No."

"Good grief, man, not to the Vatican?"

"No, my friend," Nicholas said as he limped to the fire-place. "To my people here in Sulzbach."

As he sat down again, the roaring fire snapped and crack-led with a new log, the flames lighting both of their faces and adding warmth to his own body.

"A farewell letter?" Heppner asked.

"I told you—it's a confession. Johann, will you deliver my letter when the time comes?" He nodded toward the desk in the corner. "I'll put it there in the drawer. My people may not want me on the mountain when they know the truth. Perhaps it would be best if it were read from the chapel before my burial."

"You expect me to enter your chapel to read a letter?"

Nicholas laughed wryly. "The rectory and chapel are attached, so in a way you enter it every evening."

"For a game of chess."

Caridini fought the tightness in his chest. "Johann, I think our long chats have gone deeper than that."

Heppner relit his pipe and leaned forward facing the chessboard. "Old friend," he said to Nicholas, "I believe it's your move."

"It has always been my move, Johann."

In one final calculated step, the priest picked up the black knight and moved it. He felt the smile curling at his mouth, the triumph of winning, the cunning of blocking Johann's king. "There's no way out for you, Johann."

As suddenly Nicholas's smile faded. There was no way out for himself. "Checkmate, my friend," he said.

# Chapter 17

Nicholas stood at the rectory door smiling at the weather. Sulzbach had crawled out of its snowbound winter for the second time this season with spring flowers struggling to pop up on the hillsides. A permanent covering of deep snow lay on the higher mountains, but here in the village the snows had begun to melt in the last three days with only patches left on the bakery roof and Schmid's old barn. Even the widow Katwyler had placed her handwoven cloths on the frosty ground to bleach in the sun.

Although another late spring storm seemed unlikely, Frau Mayer bustled to the open door and shoved a scarf and gloves into Nicholas's hands. "Take these, Father Caridini."

"It's spring. It's much warmer today." But he took them to pocket later on and smiled at her.

"Do you have everything—the wafers, the cup."

"Everything," he said.

"Don't forget Frau Helmut. She wants Communion."

"She's on my list."

He had forgotten Frau Mayer's motherly ways. They always got lost in his memory during the winter when he made his own schedule and quite successfully accomplished the daily routine. He couldn't decide whether she was fretting over his illness or regretting her own last summer on the mountain. But he was glad to have her back. The cluttered kitchen had been tidied, the furniture polished to a shine, the curtains freshly washed and hanging in the windows again.

She seemed much like his own mother—stocky and short, with an honest face and work-worn hands, always smelling of soap suds and cleansers, never of perfume. He added to his growing list a bottle of French perfume for Frau Mayer, his farewell gift to her.

After several revisions, his written confession lay locked in his desk drawer, the first six attempts in ashes in the fireplace. He prayed that Frau Mayer would be gone by then and never hear it read to the people of Sulzbach.

He smiled down at her. "I miss you when you're not here."

She blinked back tears, embarrassed, pleased. "Go on. And don't tire yourself. I told Frau Petzold not to give you any sweet breads today. I'll have stew and tea for you when you get back."

Nicholas nodded. "And I'll try to eat some to please you."

She pressed a walking stick into his hand. "Remember to take your time, Father Caridini, and rest at Frau Schmid's."

He leaned down and kissed her on the cheek. She pulled back in surprise, her eyelashes wet with tears.

As he heard the door close softly behind him, he set out for Frau Katwyler's first, invigorated with the mountain air on his face. He never ceased to marvel at the beauty of Sulzbach or the gracious warmth of its people. As he walked along, the thought of being cut off from this life that he loved—when he was still too young to leave it—pained him almost as fiercely as the physical pain he was enduring.

When he reached Frau Katwyler's cottage, she came out to meet him. She was traditional in her ways, always wearing a large, dark skirt and starched apron and today one of her new hand-embroidered blouses with its laced-up bodice stretched over her ample bosom. Her swollen feet were squeezed into buckled suede pumps, and the familiar gold cross lay tight against her neck.

"*Guten Morgen*, Father," she called happily. "I have a guest. My first one—he's from America. Such a nice man. Imagine me with a little *gasthof* of my own—"

He stopped her fast flow of speech. "He came alone?"

"Oh, yes. He was here once before—before the avalanche."

She seemed suddenly lost in memory, as though she had drifted back to the disaster that had claimed her husband. Encircling her cold hands in his, Nicholas brought her back. "Does your guest know you've given up your only bedroom?"

"I am quite comfortable in the kitchen," she said softly. "I like having guests. But, Father Nicholas, you still can't accept the changes swooping down on us?"

"They'll be good for you," he said.

Nicholas knew that Preben's plans for expanding Sulzbach would help Frau Katwyler. But had Consetta been part of Preben's plan? No, for all of Preben's heavy-handed ways, he loved Consetta. In time her constant devotion might mellow Preben and turn him from the almighty schilling to the almighty God.

"You must have Senn Burger add another room someday."

"Yes, one with a bathroom. My guest didn't seem surprised about the outhouse. But, oh, Father Caridini, what will I tell him about Saturday's bath? We'll have to use the same bath water, and he'll hate my old metal tub. He's kind of—tall, like you."

He squeezed her hands and slowed her down again. "Now, Frau Katwyler, only the children use the same bath water. Just heat some kettles on that old woodstove of yours and give him some privacy. If he's been here before, he knows."

*And if he's been here before, who is he?* He glanced behind her. Sensing his question, she said, "He left early to catch the sunrise. These Americans and their cameras."

*And their curiosity,* he thought. "I must meet him."

"Come tomorrow and have coffee and strudel with us."

He gave Frau Katwyler a quick blessing and made his way to the other houses in the village, carefully avoiding the Burgers' place with its four guests. An hour later Nicholas decided to bypass the Schmids', too, and stop there on his way back to the rectory.

He feared that his belly pain would prevent him from reaching the Helmut house on the far side of the village. He struggled on a few yards to the sheltered wayside shrine with its bronzed statue of Mary holding the Christ child. There were two of them in Sulzbach, one on the trail coming up from Brunnerwald and this one that nestled into the cliff, intended as a place of prayer for the weary wayfarer, but used solely now by the people of Sulzbach as a rest stop. He dropped on the tiny, warped bench and caught his breath.

Nothing comforted him more than to watch the thawing snows cascading down into spectacular waterfalls. The force of melting ice would soon turn the salty brook of Sulzbach into a summer river that coursed along the edge of town and pushed its way down toward the valley.

From here he had a good view of the older farm homes in Sulzbach, land that had been held by its owners for generations. Rheinhold Schmid's home was one of the oldest, founded two hundred years ago when the first villagers claimed this part of the mountain as their own. Schmid had lost part of the land in the avalanche. Now the property was only half what it had once been—twelve hectares of stony ground tilled for generations, but Rheinhold would never leave this mountain. He had clung tenaciously to the old sheds, turning them into living quarters with the barn still attached—the place for the animals more important than his own needs. These days the Schmid farm seemed more and more in a state of disrepair, but the tractor that Preben had purchased gleamed in the sun.

The thought of strangers invading this peaceful village infuriated Nicholas. Frightened him. He stood and stared at the bronzed statue, offering a quick prayer before setting out for the Helmuts' charming gingerbread house. As Nicholas trudged along, a cheerful voice called, "Good morning, Father."

Four young bikers in riding helmets and goggles had ridden up behind him, the face of the man nearest him wreathed in smiles.

"I'm Orlando. Nice scenery you've got here—just like home."

"Italy?" Nicholas guessed.

"That's me. Italian all the way—and my cosmopolitan teammates. We're planning to race in the Tour de France come July."

"You won't find good riding trails up here."

"I know. We bounced over the rocks all the way from Brunnerwald. A couple of kids pointed us in this direction."

*Erika and Josef*, he thought, with Josef awed by the mountain bikes and the men who rode them.

Orlando kept grinning, but the friendliness in his voice cooled as he jerked his thumb toward the fair-skinned rider. "Ian here just had to come up to Sulzbach to see his father's friend."

Ian whipped off his helmet, making a tousled mess of his reddish blond hair. His features were striking, the bone structure strong and well-molded. It was a handsome face, yet the lips were turned down, arrogant and sullen at the moment. "You talk too much, Orlando," Ian said, his accent clearly American.

Nicholas grabbed the opportunity to be friendly. "I'm Father Caridini. Why not join me for mass on Sunday?"

"Count me out," Ian said.

Orlando shrugged. "Say, *Pfarrer*, can you suggest a place to stay with cheap beds and good food?"

"With the four of you, you'd have to go over to one of the newer chalets. I'm going that way to see one of my parishioners."

"Then we'll ride along with you." Orlando waved his friends on and then propelled himself beside Nicholas with one foot turning dirt on the ground and the other jammed on the pedal.

"Ian never said who his father's friend was, Orlando."

"We don't know either. We've stuck with Ian this far, but not much longer. Alekos wired home for some money just before we left Brunnerwald—enough to get Chris and him and me back to London. If Ian wants to stay on by himself, that's his problem."

"You're not running out on him?"

"Priester, the whole team has been counting on him. He's been our best chance for winning." He gave an extra thrust of his foot against the gravel. "Now Ian's forgotten about the race. His pacing is off. His concentration gone. He'll ruin it for the rest of us."

"Maybe he just had a bad day."

"A bad week, you mean." He grinned as though he had latched on to a million-dollar idea. "Father Caridini, why don't you talk to Ian? Maybe he'd open up to you and tell you what's wrong."

Nicholas stumbled and gripped the bike handle to break his fall. He liked this boy's simplistic way of solving problems—and liked the gigantic grin spreading from ear to ear. "Orlando," he reminded him, "Ian doesn't go to church."

"Does he have to go to church just to talk to you?"

"Why, no. Of course not."

As they followed the trail, they caught glimpses of the river. "Father, the lady in the bakery said you call that the salty brook."

"That's what Sulzbach means. Did she tell you our legend?"

"Couldn't get Ian to stay long enough to be polite."

Nicholas had a captive audience as he said, "It goes back a long way. One of the first villagers—so the legend goes— was angry at her husband for going fishing when he should have been farming."

"Sounds like more fun to me."

"Yes, but he wanted to fish for a mermaid so his life would be happier. When his wife got wind of that, she poured sacks of salt into the river. It killed off all the fish. But the farmer got the best of his wife. He gave up fishing for his mermaid and began hiking in the mountains. He's frozen up there—said to be one of those higher peaks with a mountain nymph beside him."

As Nicholas pointed skyward, Orlando's gaze turned with him. "Now as legend has it, the old farmer blows the wintery winds down on his wife to remind her that he hated farming."

"Guess it worked. Your farms seem to be dying out."

"Now the wives of Sulzbach don't nose into their husbands' pleasure. They fear the consequences." He heard his voice turn hard as it had once been. He must not allow these strangers in Sulzbach to delve deeper into the secrets of his village.

"Something wrong, Father Caridini?" Orlando asked.

Nicholas stopped to catch his breath, the memory of his past life taking a stranglehold on him. He wondered whether he had the strength to push ahead and reach Karl Helmut's chalet.

"You all right, *Pfarrer?*"

"Just tired. I've been making my rounds all morning."

Nicholas dragged on, finally reaching a row of new chalets and choosing the picturesque wood structure with a painted facade and a steep snow roof. "I'll find a place for you to stay here. And then—then I'll give Communion to the grandmother in the house."

"Maybe I could take it with her," Orlando suggested.

"She'd like that, my son."

🦉🦉🦉

Just before eleven Drew Gregory took the trail that led high above Sulzbach along the path of the old avalanche, hunting in vain for the crash site. He had not thought of Lou Garver as intensely for a long time and realized now that he had always carried a measure of guilt over Lou's death. Death at least had been swift. Yet it seemed a lonely, rugged place to die.

He balanced on the edge of a cliff, his face to the winds that swept down from the higher peaks. The trees were covered with snow, the peaks dressed as always in a dazzling white. He managed a quick farewell to Garver, the one he had failed to say fifteen years ago. Drew summed it up with a promise to find Trotsky and take him in this time. His imagination ran wild; for an instant he thought he heard Garver's rich chuckle in the whistling wind.

At last he looked down on Sulzbach. The avalanche disaster had changed the boundary lines for the village. He knew that some of the people had packed up and moved down to Brunnerwald. Many had simply moved away from the path of the avalanche—away from that barren stretch of land where the top soil had eroded and the trees no longer grew.

Before part of the mountain tumbled down on them, the village had consisted of thirty homes. From where he stood, there was still a nucleus of the old chalets surrounding the Saint Francis Chapel, with a new row of gingerbread chalets far to the west.

Glancing at his watch, he knew he had to head back toward Sulzbach. He'd been up since sunrise, wandering around the village waiting for the right moment to visit Father Caridini. The right moment, according to Frau Katwyler, would be around one in the afternoon. "After he visits the shut-ins and elderly parishioners, he has a little nap," she had said. "About one will be a good time for you to go."

It was one straight up as Drew reached the rectory. He rapped the brass knocker twice and adjusted his tie as he figured out what he would say. But what words do you use with a man who saved your life—a man who might not remember you?

He was prepared for that and planned to ease slowly into a conversation before he asked Father Caridini about Nicholas Trotsky. The priest would be in his late seventies by now or older. He might not remember Drew or the plane crash, but he would surely recall the disastrous avalanche that brought a mighty section of the mountain thundering down toward the village. Drew didn't remember the avalanche himself. He had lain in a small room in this rectory in a semiconscious state as the world collapsed around him.

He tried the knocker again, a bit more impatiently this time. With another tug at his tie, he smiled broadly as he heard the latch turn and the door opening. His smile changed to a silly grin as he looked down on the shocked expression on Frau Mayer's face.

"Herr Gregory!" she said.

She seemed even shorter standing up, her roly-poly middle covered with a massive apron. "Frau Mayer," he said. "I didn't expect you. Not here in Sulzbach."

"I looked for you on the train to Innsbruck," she said.

He could hardly tell her he had avoided her. "I guess we were in different compartments."

"Different compartments indeed. And what are you doing here?"

"I came to see Father Caridini."

"Come in. Come in. I'll tell him you're here."

The sweet smells of baking came from the kitchen, but she led him beyond that into the sitting room on the left side of the rectory, a comfortable room with a stone fireplace. He ambled past the wide desk in the corner and a bookshelf laden with theology books, finally choosing to stand with his back to the fire. The warmth felt good as he surveyed the rest of the room, his curiosity aroused at the unfinished game of chess before him, the huge cushioned chairs on either side of the table. So this was where the priest and the village doctor spent their evenings together.

And now he had his second shock as the priest came into the room, a much younger man than he had expected, with a halting gait as though walking pained him. Drew had the uncanny feeling that a stick figure walked beneath the flowing robe. His face was drawn, the puffiness of illness beneath his eyes.

"Mr. Gregory," the priest said, "you asked to see me."

"Yes, but I was expecting Father Caridini."

"I am Father Caridini."

The voice was pleasant but not as deep as Father Caridini's had been. "You're not the person I remembered," Drew said.

"I can imagine, Mr. Gregory."

"It's been a long time," Drew admitted. "But I really came here to thank the priest for saving my life." He looked around as though he expected the real Caridini to walk through the door.

"Mr. Gregory, I'm the only priest in Sulzbach."

Gregory tried to regain his composure, to keep his voice normal. "I was injured in a plane crash around the time of the Sulzbach Avalanche. Were you here then?"

"Yes, I lived through it."

"Then we both did. Look, Father Caridini, I'm sorry. You just aren't the person I was looking for. I'm disappointed."

"How can I help you then? You certainly didn't come all the way to Sulzbach just to see someone who doesn't exist."

"Oh, but he did."

"The bishop from Innsbruck came to help us at the time of the avalanche. Perhaps he's the one you remember."

"He was a big man, the strong, outdoor type, but gentle." He sketched the picture in his mind and added, "Snow-white hair and a peppered moustache. Big ears and hands. A kind, smiling man."

"You might describe the bishop that way." The priest pointed to one of the easy chairs and kept the chessboard distance between them. "Do you play chess, Mr. Gregory?"

"Not often."

"Often enough to suggest a good play when the game resumes?"

"Would that be fair?"

"Is life fair? Besides it would depend on whether you favored the white king or the black one."

"Which side of the board are you playing, Father Caridini?"

"The black one this time."

"Then you don't want my suggestion."

"Perhaps Dr. Heppner would."

Drew felt rattled, a hideous nudging inside, as though this priest were mocking him without a smile. The priest's eyes looked wide and sickly as they out-stared Drew. Unshaven hairs dotted his chin and upper lip, black like Nicholas's hair had been. This was not the priest he was looking for—no. But as incredible as it seemed, he knew this man. An outrageous, irrational possibility. Nicholas Trotsky had been a cold and unfeeling man, but this priest—as sick as he was—had a softness around his mouth and eyes.

Father Caridini reached up and tugged on a velvet cord.

The effort seemed to exhaust him. "If you are through studying me, Mr. Gregory, I'll ask Frau Mayer to bring us some tea and strudel." His smile seemed shaky, pain-ridden. "She tells me you've met."

"Yes, on the trip from Vienna."

"And why would you leave such a lovely city for the mountain?"

"I remembered that the view was awesome here."

"We're in agreement on that, Mr. Gregory. No one who has ever been here could forget it. But you came here alone with no other purpose than to see—this priest who saved your life?"

"I came for a vacation," he said. *And I came for Nicholas Trotsky. But I can't tell you that, not when I think I've come face to face with him.* The thought was preposterous.

The Nicholas Trotsky in the Agency file was a handsome man with thick, dark hair and a strong, muscular body. But the file couldn't record the sound of Trotsky's voice. In Drew's one encounter, Nicholas had spoken only briefly, lapsing into total silence once they had commandeered him into the plane.

This priest was at least thirty pounds lighter than Trotsky. But he was obviously a sick man, his ashen color overlaid with a jaundiced yellow. Father Caridini's hair was thin and gray, barely more than a light fuzz, as though it had only recently grown back in again. It was not thin from balding, but more like a sudden loss, through chemother-apy perhaps. Yes, he looked like a man who could be riddled with cancer. Somehow it seemed an unfair match. What challenge was there to capturing a dying man?

If this was Colonel Trotsky, the odds were against him ris-ing from the ashes to leadership in the Phoenix rebellion. Yet in this brief exchange, he knew that Caridini's mind was still sharp enough to mastermind and direct the plan from his death bed.

But Drew couldn't be certain. He couldn't even take the man, not without more proof, not without Vic there. And he had delayed Vic's arrival himself. Wilson would go to Brunnerwald, and only if he went to the Schrott Cheese

Factory or the *gasthof* would he find Drew's messages. He had left one at each place.

Vic's arrival was crucial, but it was at least two or three days away, ample time for Nicholas Trotsky to find the strength to disappear again—if this was indeed Colonel Trotsky.

Drew went for a second cup of tea and a third sliver of strudel, anything to keep himself here for a few moments longer.

He tried talking about world politics.

Father Caridini showed no interest.

He baited the priest with comments on the new Russia, the leadership of Yeltsin, changes for the better in that vast land. Caridini smiled. "Our world is small here. News filters in, but not as often as we would like. Tell me, Mr. Gregory, have you no family?"

"One daughter."

"No wife?"

"We're divorced." Drew determined to stick to the facts, to tell only what might be in Trotsky's own file on him.

"What line of work are you in?" the priest asked.

*You're as cagey as ever, Nicholas,* Drew thought. *And you know who I am. But can you play your hand?* He laughed and was grateful that it sounded normal. "I'm about to retire," he said.

Drew was so intent on his own mental gymnastics that Father Caridini had to repeat himself. "Are you a Catholic, Mr. Gregory?"

"A cradle Catholic. It never went much beyond that."

"Do you plan to stay in our village long?"

"A few days—unless the weather gets better."

"I apologize for the lateness of spring. But it's here. In the air. In the flowers. In the waterfalls. Give us a few more days, and even the weather will improve. Right now one of the warmest places in Sulzbach is the church. Perhaps you can come to mass in the morning."

"I might do that."

"And afterward have a meal with us. Frau Mayer is making some *wiener schnitzel* for the doctor and some *leber-*

*knodelsuppe* for me. It'll give you a pleasant memory of Austria when you go home."

Drew stood. *I think you are baiting me, Nicholas Trotsky. But I will be here. And I'll sleep with one eye open tonight.* "Thank you. Until tomorrow then," he said.

Drew left the priest sitting in his chair, staring at the chessboard. Contemplating his next move?

# Chapter 18

Saturday came with an Alpine burst of glory—an azure sky, woolly white clouds, and the breaking sun scattering the mists at the high peaks and making mauve trails on the mountains. It was the kind of artist's haven that Miriam would love. Drew could picture her gliding up the hills and picking a bunch of Alpine pansies and gentianellas. *Miriam.* He had promised her he would close out this case in a hurry and get back to London safely.

The problem at hand crowded thoughts of Miriam from his mind. Far to his right, a barren run from the old avalanche left a wide trail for masses of earth to rush down the slopes. In spite of the brilliance that surrounded him, without warning a rumbling crack of thunder beneath the mountain could start another avalanche that would bury the village beneath tons of rock and packed snow.

Yesterday he had muddied the waters and kicked the top layer of Sulzbach, setting it on a course of destruction. He had tracked Nicholas Trotsky to the run-out zone, and he couldn't do a thing—not without proof, not without Vic Wilson on hand to help him.

Sounds from the kitchen brought him back. He gave the widow Katwyler an added ten minutes to dress and hide her bedroll behind the woodstove, and then he went out to greet her. Helene Katwyler was all smiles, bubbly and chatty. She had set him a place at the table, and at the smell of *schwarzer*, he took it gladly.

This morning she offered him more than a roll and coffee. "I've made you a fork breakfast," she said proudly. It was all there—bacon and cheese and *gugelhupf*, an unsweetened raisin cake that Frau Katwyler would normally serve in the late afternoon. Rolls and honey and marmalade were there too, but he held her hand back when she offered to pour hot grease over his bowl of buckwheat meal. He tolerated warm milk fresh from the barn and the dry cake, but he wasn't Austrian enough to take grease on his cereal.

He hurried through his meal, not wanting to keep her from the wooden loom by the window where she wove her clever designs with a mixture of cotton, linen, and wool. "You make lovely cloth," he said. "I'd like to buy something for my wife."

She beamed. "When the summer tourists come, Frau Burger tells me they will want to buy, too. It is happy work," she said. "We used to work the land like everyone else—taking care of the cattle and cutting the hay, and then the avalanche came."

As he downed his second cup of *schwarzer*, she talked of the years when her husband was alive and took the cattle up to the *alm* to graze in the summer months and of the garland celebration when he brought the cattle back down in September.

"And then we face the harsh Alpine winters," she said, "when we're snowed in. But we keep busy repairing our tools and weaving and rescuing lost skiers and feeding them dry meats and cheeses."

"And there's always the church," he said.

Again she beamed. "We're the only parish on this part of the mountain. People come from other villages to hear Father Caridini."

The image of the man who had saved his life came flashing back. The priest with the snow-white hair and the kindly cerulean eyes no longer lived in the rectory of Sulzbach. As Frau Katwyler rambled on, Drew's gaze drifted back to those sheer cliffs high above Sulzbach. Somewhere up there he had crashed the plane, and as surely as he sat in the widow Katwyler's kitchen, he remembered Nicholas Trotsky crying out in pain as he dragged him to safety. Trotsky had been injured badly, perhaps enough to give him a halting gait, but how had he limped into the role of a priest?

Turning back to face Frau Katwyler, he said, "I guess the priest has been in Sulzbach a long time?"

"Long before the avalanche."

"I thought I met him once before—a kindly man with blue eyes. But I guess my memory played tricks with me."

Frau Katwyler chuckled. "There were two priests, you know. Brothers. Jacques and Nicholas."

*He knew, but he asked anyway.*"Which one is here now?"

"Father Nicholas. He took over when his brother died."

Drew shuddered. Nicholas Trotsky would have felt no qualms about removing the only man who might identify him. Had he taken him down with an assassin's bullet? But to take on the role of a priest. Drew felt a fresh loathing for Trotsky. A steep, narrow trail lay between Sulzbach and Brunnerwald, the only exodus from this mountain, and a village of people lay between Drew and the village priest. He had to wait for Vic's arrival—a day or two at least—and then they would confront Nicholas Trotsky together.

As he left Frau Katwyler's, he crossed the street and made his way through the Saint Francis Cemetery. A stone wall surrounded the yard, and trees shaded Father Jacques's grave. *Jacques and Nicholas, brothers.* How had Trotsky worked that one? Was the dual priesthood the secret that Consetta and Preben wanted to preserve?

Drew would need friends in this village if he intended to walk down the mountain with their priest. Olga Petzold's bakery was the local gathering place where people dropped in for the best of Austrian coffees and a variety of breads and sweet rolls, and while they sipped coffee, cup after cup, they chatted.

Inside the store, the smell of fresh baking grew stronger. Olga Petzold smiled pleasantly when she saw him. Behind her, round loaves of bread filled the shelves. She held another in her hands and placed it on the scale. In the back room Drew saw Josef giving a halfhearted thrust of the broom across the floor.

Three round tables were crowded with customers, the four young cyclists from Brunnerwald huddled at one of them. Drew avoided eye contact with Orlando, but not before Alekos glared angrily at him. Drew stood his ground glancing around casually and stifled his surprise when the customer at the counter turned.

"Kermer!" Drew exclaimed. "What are you doing up here?"

Kermer brushed Drew's greeting aside, grabbed his unwrapped loaf of bread, and stalked from the bakery.

Quietly Drew said, "Frau Petzold, somehow I don't think the people of Sulzbach want outsiders here."

She lowered her voice to match his. "Oh, he's not one of us, Herr Gregory. He's one of the four guests staying over at the wood carver's place. Five, if you count that young cyclist who spends so much time with them. That one," she added as Alekos sauntered out.

"Alekos. He's training for the Tour de France."

"Up here?"

He smiled at that. From the store window, they watched Alekos walk his bike toward the Burgers' shop. She shook her head. "See that. They come in here and pretend they don't know each other, but we're not blind in this village. Frau Burger says something is going on, and that young man will get himself in trouble."

"They're just tourists, aren't they?"

"Frau Burger doesn't think so. She says her guests are not at all friendly. She wishes they'd go back to Brunnerwald."

*But they won't,* Drew thought. *They followed me here.*

۞ ۞ ۞

Sunday began with a round ball of fire cresting the peaks, its rays shining through the stained-glass window in the front of the church. Nicholas stopped at the end of the passageway to adjust his chasuble over the alb. He pressed the narrow stole to his lips—as Jacques had done before him—and placed it around his neck. As he walked across the front of the church and stood in front of the altar, he felt the warmth of the sun on his back and smiled down at Josef, the altar boy of Sulzbach.

Without thinking, he winked down at the boy, and Josef winked back. *Odd,* Nicholas thought, *you may remember me for that in the days ahead. And for little else.*

Nicholas began reading, and the congregation gave back their soft responses. He looked at the familiar faces and saw strangers among them. Some guests from the neighboring villages. Two of the young cyclists—Alekos and Orlando. And the woman near them, her face partially hidden by a scarf, her eyes riveted on Nicholas. Surely he had seen those eyes before—and looked deeply into them often. He breathed out the word, "Marta."

His legs felt like jelly, but he remained stoic, his solemn expression unchanged. Twice his voice faltered as he leaned into the lectern and hurried through the mass, not missing a word. Twice Josef looked quizzically at him. Candles flickered. The sun kept pouring through the windows. The woman's lips did not move during the Eucharist, but her eyes stayed fixed on Nicholas. At last he turned and knelt before the altar, and only then could he avoid that unflinching gaze. At the last prayer he led his parishioners to the door and greeted them as they left.

Orlando passed him with a grin, Alekos with a frown. As the woman hurried by, their eyes met briefly. She pulled her scarf off and her glowing brown hair fell freely. Marta was here in Sulzbach, but how had she escaped from East Berlin? In the maze of shaking other hands, he remembered that the Berlin Wall had been torn down long ago. In its place stood an invisible barrier between Marta Zubkov and Nicholas Trotsky, between the stranger in the village and the priest of Sulzbach. She knew him, and she would betray him.

Peter Kermer waited at the bottom of the church steps. He took Marta's arm and steadied her. "You're taking too many risks."

She dug her nails into his wrist. "What do you want?"

"We're being watched. I'm trying to save your life. They know, Marta. Yuri and Vronin know that you're hiding things from them. Vronin sent word to Dimitri yesterday."

Her body tensed. "Who are you, Kermer? Who are you really?"

"Peter Kermer," he said quietly. "Your only friend."

"Liar. I don't know who you are, but you certainly are not Kermer. I've known that since the day we met."

"Strange," he said, his voice remarkably calm. "You trusted me to get you safely into Austria."

🌀🌀🌀

Nicholas went back to the quiet sanctity of the rectory and took refuge in the fire room, his thoughts on the young Marta and his brash promises to her. He had deceived more than the village of Sulzbach, more than himself. He knelt, prayed, confessed again his guilt and deception. As he made the sign of the cross, tears welled in his eyes. "Lord, I have sinned against Marta—against You."

When he stood, he found Johann Heppner sitting by the chessboard. "The American will come back when you're feeling better."

"I'd forgotten my lunch invitation to Gregory."

"Apparently he didn't. But sit down. Enjoy the fire."

As they faced each other, Nicholas said, "Johann, my health is failing rapidly. It's time for me to leave the village."

"But you planned to stay here. You can't forsake your parish, Nicholas. You only have a little while left to serve your people."

"It's better for them if I go."

"Will your replacement come before you leave?"

"There won't be a replacement, Johann. I didn't notify the bishop in Innsbruck. There would be too many questions."

Johann sipped his glass of wine. "There's not much more I can do except to deliver the letter for you. What about that letter, Nicholas? Have you written it yet?"

Nicholas felt more like Father Caridini, the priest, than like Nicholas Trotsky, the spy, the KGB agent. His smile came slowly, tugging at his dry skin. "You'll find my confession in the drawer."

"Should I know what it's about?"

"Something I could not tell the people all these years I've been with them. But perhaps you already know the contents, Johann."

"Perhaps."

"You saved my life fifteen years ago."

"I thought Jacques Caridini did that."

"But you were there. You've kept my secret all these years."

"Grudgingly—until we became friends. After that your past didn't matter to me. I just wish I could give you back your health."

"You've tried."

"I could send you back to Deiter Eschert. You might do better in the city—maybe even Rome. Don't they take care of their own?"

Nicholas stifled a cough. "No more medical advice, Johann. You've done your best. It is medicine that has its limitations on this worn-out body of mine."

Johann studied the priest. "Nor can medicine heal your troubled spirit, Father Caridini."

# Chapter 19

Except for the chair by the window, Nicholas Caridini's room looked exactly as Father Jacques had left it, spartan and puritanical, with its single bed, narrow chest of drawers, and the small altar where Jacques had prayed—the soft leather cushion still bearing the imprint of his knees. In the old life Nicholas would have scoffed at living in such barrenness. But over the years it had become a refuge, his private, sheltered world.

Fifteen years ago when he had first awakened in this room, he had faced the icons on the wall, the crucifix at the foot of the bed. He would have torn them from the walls and burned them, but he was trapped in a crude back brace that immobilized him. The pain in his back had been excruciating, his belly hot and throbbing. From a makeshift I.V. stand hung the infusion tubes attached to his arm. His feet felt cold, and then he realized that he had no feeling in them at all. He drifted—and then fought his way back from grogginess at the sound of voices.

A priest stood at the foot of the bed, arms folded, his chin cupped in one broad hand. The other man bent over Nicholas, giving a sharp command as he probed Trotsky's wound. "Don't move."

Nicholas had cried out in agony and groped futilely for his gun.

The same sharp voice said, "Your weapon is gone."

Alarm jabbed at Trotsky's fog. *I'm stripped of everything.*

*My clothes. My weapon. No, not my gun, the American's. The microfilms are gone, too.* He blinked and tried to focus. As in a telescopic lens, the priest's face faded, returned. Receded and came back. Black, bushy brows. Deep-set, reflective eyes. A guileless face with large features, the kind of person you might trust if you trusted anyone. Even in his feverish state, Nicholas could see that everything about the priest seemed big—a wide forehead, a large nose, powerfully built shoulders. He stood tall in a long black robe, those thick hands clasped, his white hair unruly, and yet everything about him seemed kind and gentle.

The brace held Nicholas's body rigid. He scanned the room with his eyes, his search ending as he spotted his watch and the sealed envelope with the microfilms. One third of the PHOENIX PLAN lay on the bedside table, and he couldn't move his hands to reach it.

The harsh voice again, "This man would die before we could get him down to Brunnerwald and on to a hospital in Innsbruck."

*I won't die,* Nicholas thought. *I'm part of the Phoenix-40. One of the top three. We have a plan for world conquest. At thirty-six, I'm powerful. Nothing can stop me.* And with cold reality creeping into his fogged mind, *I'm thirty-six, almost thirty-seven, and I'm paralyzed on some Austrian mountain.*

Drifting. Fighting back to a level of consciousness. And drifting again. Each time he came back, his focus seemed stronger, the pain more unbearable. It came back then—the threat in Moscow with Jankowski and Kavin executed and a price on his own head, the escape to the Austrian ski lodge, and the American agent finding him.

"My stomach," he said in Russian.

"Bullet wounds." Still Nicholas could not see the man's face, and even when the man turned to the priest, Trotsky saw only his back. In a hushed exchange with the priest, the doctor said, "This patient won't survive. And if he does, he may not walk again. The odds are stacked against him."

"God isn't." That had to be the priest.

"You're taking chances, Jacques, caring for this man. He needs surgery. His back is fractured, and one of those bullets may be lodged near his spine." He placed a sterile abdominal pad over Nicholas's stomach. "This wound is infected, Father Jacques. He needs more medical help than either of us can give him."

"I know." The priest's tone was deep and kindly. "But surgery would not make this man whole."

"No sermons, Jacques. You're harboring a Russian."

"It wasn't a Russian plane."

"My duty lies outside the church, Jacques. I will notify the *polizei* in Brunnerwald as soon as this storm abates."

"No, he wouldn't have a chance in Brunnerwald. I will care for him myself as I would any guest in my home." And then with deep sympathy, "How are the others?"

"We lost Herr Katwyler. And at least five others. Only your God knows how many strangers were swept away, too."

The avalanche. Nicholas had survived an avalanche.

"At least three homes, Father Caridini, and a large part of Rheinhold Schmid's farm. And the plane."

The man's angry voice seemed directed at him—as though he had deliberately crashed in the village, as though he, Nicholas Trotsky, had set the mountain tumbling down on the village.

"Most of the wounded are down the mountain now, except this one." The biting tongue bit harder. "I've given him something for pain, Jacques."

A shot that Nicholas didn't even feel.

"Then he'll rest for a while. I'll go to Frau Katwyler then." The priest had called the man by name as he left the room. Nicholas had never wanted to remember, and yet he had always known that it was Johann Heppner. But why then had Johann allowed him to live out this farce for so long?

🌑🌑🌑

Father Jacques was a legend in Sulzbach, turning down the offers to more thriving parishes and choosing rather to live out his life on this mountain. He proved a positive man with a quick, easy chuckle that endeared him to his people.

But in the beginning Nicholas had hated him—the priest who would not let him die.

The priest who called him "brother."

Day after day, week after week, the priest forced him to do exercises, forced Nicholas's numb limbs to function. He suffered the humiliation of Frau Schmid or Frau Mayer bathing and spoon-feeding him, and months later Caridini pressured him to stand and walk, compelled him to live when he wanted to die.

After those first few steps, he had screamed out, "Get out."

"I can't, Nicholas. This is my home, my parish."

"Then why do you stay in this isolated village?"

Father Jacques sat on Nicholas's bed. "I stay because I found myself here. I had visions of grandeur, Nicholas." The bluest of eyes turned merry. "I wanted to be a bishop. And one day to be appointed to the College of Cardinals."

He patted Nicholas's arm. "My mentor sent me here to test my faith—to see if it were real. Since I have been here, I have wanted nothing more than to shepherd these people."

Nicholas's faith had never been tested. He stayed in Sulzbach because there was no parish for him except this one of his own making.

Back then, Jacques's jovial laugh had filled the room. "I understand you, my friend. I was an ambitious man, too, ready to leave my stamp on society." He seemed amused at what he had once been. "My goal was to pastor the largest cathedral in the world and to bypass the little places. What a wise mentor I had."

Nicholas shot a furtive glance toward the bedside table.

"It's there—in the drawer," Jacques said. "Untouched. Your ambitions are there, whatever goals of glory you have, Nicholas. I won't touch them. You alone will decide what to do with them." His face turned suddenly serious. "But, my son, those ambitions of yours brought you to this mountain. Were they worth it, Nicholas?"

Sometimes when he stood by the window as he was doing now, he could still hear the priest saying, "You're safe here, my son."

Safe in the shelter of the church. Now his safety was in

jeopardy, the mountain he loved turning into a prison. Marta had forced him to remember the old life, the days before Sulzbach.

For fourteen years this had been his own place, and suddenly it was Jacques's room again. Jacques's parish and people. His clothes tailored to fit Nicholas. His books. Jacques's life that he was living. Only the chair by the window really belonged to him. At Jacques's orders, it had been hand-crafted in the Burgers' wood shop; Frau Schmid and Frau Mayer had cushioned it with hand-sewn pillows. Five months after the injury, they had placed him in that chair.

But even that had not satisfied Jacques.

Nicholas had entered this village as a stranger, carried on a makeshift stretcher straight to the priest's sleeping quarters, arriving at a time when the village was struggling to survive a devastating avalanche. The villagers had grown accustomed to Father Jacques taking in strangers and wayfarers, the ill traveler and the traveling priests, the lost mountain climber or skier. As with every stranger at his door, Father Caridini had been content to know Nicholas's name, nothing more. He simply saw Nicholas as a man in need, a stranger that he called "my brother."

Word spread quickly through Frau Mayer and Frau Schmid that the sick man at the rectory was Father Jacques's brother. Frau Katwyler spread the rumors further. "He's a priest, too," she had said. "Another priest from Innsbruck. I'm certain of it. He came here to be with his brother—to get well."

The villagers cheered each phase of his recovery, taking, he was certain, some of the credit because of their prayers. When he finally walked again, there was nowhere to go. He dared not risk climbing the slopes or trust himself to go down the mountain. Instead, he sat for hours in the gardens regaining his strength, sometimes listening to the music from the church, and always planning for the day when the PHOENIX PLAN would rise from the ashes, and he would be strong enough to go back to Russia and find that nucleus of the Phoenix-40 who had survived.

During that year of recovery, he found nothing to study

except the theological books that lined Jacques's book-shelves. Nicholas devoured them and debated their contents over the chess games. Now and then he thought of his three years at seminary, but more often he thought of his aging mother in the homeland, a rosary in her wrinkled hands, a prayer on her lips for her wayward son. He resented that as much as he did the candles lit for him in the Saint Francis Chapel.

And daily in those first months he thought of the lovely Marta behind the Berlin Wall. In time, Marta and his mother would think him dead. And Marta—perhaps would forget him.

On the anniversary date of the avalanche, Father Jacques suffered a massive heart attack. Nicholas grabbed the robe of the priest and dragged himself out into the village for help. In the excitement, someone asked Nicholas, "What is your name, Father?"

Nicholas remembered the words of the priest who always said, "Nicholas, you are my brother. Someday you will realize that."

He answered, "I'm Father Caridini's brother. Nicholas Caridini."

Nicholas assured the people that he would notify the new bishop in Innsbruck and those in Rome about Jacques's death. Yes, he would ask the bishop for the privilege of staying on to be the pastor in Sulzbach. No, he had never had a parish of his own. He had been too ill. The people there in Sulzbach would have to help him. The next day, with a cocky air of confidence, he conducted the burial services for his "brother." Nicholas had ventured out into the village in the robes of the priest. He still wore them.

How easy it had been. He—Nicholas Trotsky, waiting for the right moment to lead the Phoenix rebellion, well-educated, a learned man himself—stepping into a strange new role, a role the KGB had once planned for him to fill.

The real Father Caridini had been a meticulous note keeper, all his sermons and theological notes kept in detail. Soon Nicholas was mimicking Jacques's ways, using his old homily notes—changing a word here and there. But something happened to Trotsky as he played out his clever, deceptive role at Sulzbach. He began to study the life of Christ for himself. Nicholas was not certain when he quit pretending and the passion to be a priest took over. At first it seemed merely a game, a protective cover as he waited to lead the Phoenix-40. And then in his own mind and commitment, he became what he pretended to be. Now it was his life.

🔥🔥🔥

In the semidarkness of midnight, Peter Kermer glanced around the sleeping village before he walked in through the unlocked doors of the Saint Francis Chapel. He eased the doors closed, not even allowing them to creak, and then stepped into the vestibule, adjusting his eyes to the blinking red light of an icon and to dozens of flickering candles near the altar. He stood stock-still, listening intently for the footsteps of Yuri and Vronin to come up the church steps behind him. Nothing.

He wiped his chin and brought his hand away dry, dry like his mouth. As the pounding of his heart eased, he could see that Saint Francis had been patterned like a small cathedral, designed in the shape of a cross and facing east. Rows of pews lined either side of the single aisle in the nave, and on both sides of the room stained-glass clerestory windows were set high above the Stations of the Cross. On the far end of the apse hung a massive carving of the Anointed One. His Messiah. His Christ.

The sanctity of the room drew Peter forward. He stepped around the holy water font and made his way down the aisle to the altar. Two transepts formed the arms of the cross, but he thrust himself beyond the crossing and dropped on his knees at the altar railing and buried his head in his arms.

"Sara, Sara," he cried. He reached up to the chain around his neck and wrapped his hand around the Star of David—his link to Sara, her gift to him. The plans they had dreamed together might die for him here on this mountain slope in

Austria. He had overstepped his safety margin and rushed ahead without waiting for reinforcements. He could go to the American and offer his allegiance, but it might compromise Gregory's purposes here.

Behind him he heard the doors open and someone coming into the vestibule. Yuri or Vronin or both, he knew. Still he stayed on his knees. If they planned to shoot him, let them put a bullet to the back of his skull. He would die on his knees praying for Sara and the boys. His prayers were short-lived, bouncing in his mind and heart, his longing for his family stronger than he'd ever known.

The Star of David was drenched in a sweaty palm. He wrapped both hands around it and tried to lift his soundless prayer again. "Oh, God, I want to die as Ben Bernstein, not as Peter Kermer."

He began to sing, to chant one of the Hebrew psalms of David that Jacob Uleman had taught him as a boy. The mournful lament broke the stillness in the room; truth as he knew it now and the old traditions of his boyhood merged. Somehow the two lifted him back from despair to hope. To Christ the Messiah.

Without warning the doors of the church closed again. Peter saw the hem of the clerical robe before he heard the priest say, "Can I help you? I'm Father Caridini."

Peter stumbled to his feet. "Yes, I know. I'm Peter Kermer, one of Herr Burger's guests. Are we alone now?"

Nicholas nodded. "Whoever was in the vestibule left. One of your friends perhaps? I did not recognize him."

"I came in here to be alone."

Nicholas smiled. "And I came over to lock the doors. The village is already asleep."

"I couldn't sleep. I was thinking about my family. I promised my oldest son that I'd be home for his—for his celebration."

The Star of David lay exposed. Nicholas touched it. "Your son's bar mitzvah?" he asked.

"Yes. Benjy's. We're Messianic Jews."

"Yes. One does not usually sing in Hebrew in this setting."

"Yet Saint Francis is comforting somehow."

"I would think your family would be in Odessa or Moscow."

"No—Jerusalem. Tel Aviv actually."

"But your friends are Russian?"

Peter's dry mouth felt like cotton candy. "Yes."

"And you are traveling as one of them?"

In the empty church Peter faced the priest. "Yes. I need your help, Father Caridini. I'm being watched every waking hour. If I can't trust a priest to send a message for me, where can I turn?"

"A message to someone in particular?"

"To Ben Bernstein's wife, for one—"

In the vestibule the doorknob turned again. Peter tensed. "I'll bring a message back tomorrow. Can you get it down the mountain for me?"

"I could send it with Josef or Erika."

"Lock the door, Father Caridini, as soon as I leave."

Kermer left the church and stayed well in the darkness. Before he could even cross the street, he heard the faint steps of someone stalking him. To protect Marta, he turned away from the Burgers' house and walked higher up the mountain, planning to double back as soon as it was safe.

Still someone pursued him. One moment it sounded like steady steps behind him, the next as though someone were dragging in a halting gait, struggling to keep up. The pursuer lost distance one moment, came within an arm's length the next.

The higher Peter climbed, the more unsure he became on the unmarked trail. He decided to take cover among the trees and wait it out until dawn. Someone ducked in and out of the trees behind him. In the shadowed midnight hour, he saw the clerical robe.

The priest walked by, his breathing sounding labored as he climbed higher. Kermer stayed motionless until he heard the footsteps again. Marta had deceived them all. It was not Vronin or Yuri tracking him. No, Nicholas Trotsky, the priest of Sulzbach, was hunting him down.

# Chapter 20

Nicholas finally slept in the wee, small hours, the darkness of the night brighter than the blackness of his soul. He tossed and turned, his body wet with his own perspiration. At dawn he awakened to the sweet sound of a bird, its music announcing that springtime had come to stay—no more late storms.

He had made it to the beginning of a new season. Something of the triumph of seeing the mountains bud with Alpine flowers and the winter snows thawing at last pleased him. The sweet music persisted, arousing him completely.

Nicholas padded barefoot to the window, searching for the lilting feathered friend that had awakened him. Nothing. Had he been dreaming? No, the music seemed to be playing in his mind, tugging at memories, taking him back to East Germany. Suddenly the blackness was there again tormenting him.

He hid his face in both hands, refusing to be drawn back, refusing to admit what he had once been. But his past rose out of the ashes, the dying embers burning in his memory. He raced for the shower and stepped inside, allowing the warm water to cascade over him. He wept, praying that the blackness would leave him. "Oh, Father, I have betrayed her. Oh, Father, I have betrayed You . . ."

As he toweled down and dressed, Marta filled his thoughts, along with an ache that was physical. The image of her beauty and softness overpowered him. As he recalled her dark eyes meeting his in the quiet sanctuary, he wept again.

He was certain that Marta was in trouble. It was not chance that had brought her up these mountains. Marta was too clever for that. She had followed him here. But how? Consetta and Preben had warned him that strangers were asking for him. Until last night he had not believed them.

The sound of the music was there again. The mirage that rose from the ashes was of Marta running away from him, her shoulders convulsing. The mental imagery with its flashing lights turned blinding. He must find Marta and beg her forgiveness. But if he did—if the people of Sulzbach discovered who he was—it could destroy their faith. He could not bear to think of hurting Ilse and Rheinhold Schmid, nor shattering Erika's fragile trust, or turning Josef Petzold away from the church forever. Deep inside he knew that those with Marta would stop at nothing to find him, putting the entire village in danger.

In his mind's eye, Nicholas had wanted her to turn around, but he knew he could never look into her eyes. The music pierced his ears. And then he remembered saying to her, "Marta, at dawn you must always listen for the sweet music of the phoenix bird."

In his warped thoughts, the words *celibacy* and *chastity* taunted him. How could he tell her that he had made these vows, made them here in Sulzbach when he took on the role of a priest? No, it was not a role. It had been for years but no longer. This was his parish, his people. He paced through the house, room after room, finally making his way into the kitchen as he tried vainly to throw off his tainted past.

Nicholas stopped, startled. Erika Schmid stood in the middle of the rectory kitchen, her entry so quiet that he had not even heard her come in. She put her finger to her lips.

"Father Caridini, Grandmama wants you to come at once."

"Is she ill?"

Erika shook her head. "No, but hurry."

He grabbed his cassock from the hook and slipped into it as he followed her up the sloping hill toward the Schmids' small home. In the old days—when she was a small child—

Erika had always walked by his side and slipped her hand into his. But now—flowering between childhood and womanhood—she shied away from him, keeping her distance on skinny legs. Her washed-out blonde hair bounced against her narrow shoulders, uneven and styleless like the plain dress that had once belonged to Consetta.

"Hurry," she called back.

As the tightness in his chest increased, he gulped at the mountain air. But he pushed himself, struggling to keep up, and was panting by the time he reached the Schmids' three-room cabin.

Ilse Schmid stood in the courtyard, her wizened, weather-beaten face framed in a black scarf and tight with worry. She leaned on the wooden cane that Rheinhold had made for her, her long skirt and blouse and threadbare sweater black as though she were in perpetual mourning. The hands seemed as gnarled as her face, but those tired, dark eyes brightened when she saw him—brightened in spite of her recent forgetfulness.

"Erika came for me. Are you all right?" he asked taking one work-worn hand gently in his.

"Better than you," she said, listening to his breathing. "The years are still kind to me." She pulled her hand free and wrapped a protective arm around Erika, the girl's youthful face as concerned as Ilse's.

Nicholas looked around. "Herr Schmid—he's well?"

"Rheinhold's already down the mountain to Brunnerwald with the milk, but we saved a pitcher for you."

"You're very good to me, Frau Schmid."

The Schmids had become two of his dearest friends, accepting him in their simplicity and in their poverty still meeting his physical needs. He dared not tell her that milk no longer settled in his stomach, that in swallowing it, he choked excessively. Yet morning after morning, as faithful as dawn, Rheinhold trudged past the rectory, his trustworthy bay Noriker pulling the sturdy milk cart down to the cheese factory in Brunnerwald. Each morning as the wagon wheels creaked by, Erika would slip from the cart and appear at Nicholas's door with a pitcher brimful of milk for him. This morning in her haste she had forgotten it.

He smiled to himself. The old woman would tell him what she wanted in good time in her slow, deliberate manner. He tried to match her patience, tried to hide the pain he was feeling from her. He said, "Someday we can be like our neighboring villages and have a pipe system that will carry the milk down the mountain to Brunnerwald. It will be easier on Rheinhold."

She nodded. "Then the evening milking would not be wasted."

"But you sell to the bakery and to neighbors."

"Herr Burger says the pipe system would be more economical for all of us—that Sulzbach must not remain trapped in the old ways."

"I'm afraid he's right," Nicholas said.

Her gnarled hand tightened on the cane. "But that means we must open our village to tourists like the Burgers have already done." She shook her head sadly. "They have guests now."

"I know. Four of them." *Three men and Marta.*

"And Olga Petzold is housing a few boys."

"And Frau Helene," Erika reminded her.

"Oh, yes, dear Frau Katwyler, the lady with the loom. She took in the American. Can't talk about anything else. Says he's a nice man, but why would a man come here alone, Father Caridini?"

"He knew Father Jacques—came back to see him."

Ilse's voice begged for understanding as she said, "My Rheinhold fears change. He says no good can come of all these strangers in the village. But we are growing old, and what will my Erika do when we can no longer send milk to Brunnerwald?"

"I'll always be here to take care of you, Grandmama."

Frau Schmid chuckled as she touched Erika's trembling chin. "You will be like Consetta and fall in love and go away. With Josef Petzold maybe," she teased.

Erika buried her face in Ilse's sweater. "No, never."

Nicholas would be gone before progress came to

Sulzbach. He had fought change. Like Rheinhold he feared it, feared strangers discovering who he was. His guilt nagged at him as he looked impatiently at Ilse. She had lived a hard life in these mountains, facing cold winters and the threat of an avalanche when the snows thawed. The Schmids had eked out their living on the land by long hours and hard work. Ilse's coarse skin was so wrinkled that any former beauty was lost in the creases. Long beyond the year when she should have been resting, she had taken on the care of two orphaned grandchildren and reared them.

Isle's words drew him back. "Rheinhold thinks that God has been good to us—that we are fortunate that the Schrott Cheese Factory still purchases our milk. But Senn Burger insists that Sulzbach will not survive with the old ways."

She brushed at her faded clothes and shrugged. "What could Rheinhold and I offer to tourists? Our house is too small for them, and we are just farmers."

"Grandpa is still a good wood carver," Erika defended.

"What would I do? My old legs are too tired to dance for them, and my memory, Father Caridini, is getting worse. I would go out to my garden and forget to make breakfast for my guests."

Her memory lapsed even now. Still he waited, wondering why Erika had brought him to Ilse in such haste. *Communion! Ilse wanted Communion,* he decided. She had missed evening vespers. But he had left the Eucharist elements at the rectory. "Frau Schmid," he said apologetically, "I forgot—"

She shifted her weight to the other hip, her arm still lovingly around Erika. "It's nothing you forgot," she said. "I'm the one forgetting. I do have a guest. It's someone—"

A sour taste rose in his mouth.

Ilse lifted her cane and pointed toward the door. "Inside, Father Caridini. The woman is waiting in there."

His jaw felt wired, his feet like lead, his heart stony. She knew. The Schmids knew. "Is it Marta Zubkov?" he asked.

"I don't know her name. She's been staying at the Burgers'. But she didn't go back there last night. She's frightened."

"Of Senn Burger?"

"Oh, my, no. Of her traveling companions, I think. I didn't know who else to send for—except you, Father Caridini. She's so distraught I thought—"

"Did you tell her you were sending for me?"

"She fought that at first—said she had no time for a man of the cloth. But I persuaded her that you are a man of prayer, that you could help." Her eyes grew tender. "She is so troubled."

Nicholas started for the door as she said, "Erika and I will take a little walk. Maybe we'll meet Rheinhold on his way back."

Marta paced the tiny cabin listening to the muffled sound of Nicholas's familiar deep voice outside and then Ilse Schmid's slow, soft responses. Was he refusing to come in? Or did he even know yet that she waited inside?

The muscles in her neck went rigid; the sense of immediate suffocation grew so intense that she ran to the window and thrust open the green shutters. As she faced the paneless window, the mountain air cooled her hot cheeks. She blinked back the scalding tears, gulped in the sweetness of the air, and then allowed the splendor of the magnificent Alps to calm her. The mountains that Nicholas loved. That she loved.

Here in Sulzbach the mountains seemed more spectacular, deceptively serene. Yet they were majestic and rugged, rising higher, slope after slope, to the peaks shrouded now in mist. Veiled as Nicholas's last fifteen years had been. Or had she misjudged him? Fifteen years? Yes, he could have finished seminary in that time. But could Colonel Trotsky, Communist party member, have changed so drastically?

She heard the latch click and the door swing open as Nicholas entered the spotless room. She dreaded facing him again, wondering how much pretense would follow.

"Marta," he said quietly, "it's Nicholas."

*Not Father Trotsky?* she wondered.

Her arms folded involuntarily across her chest as though she could ward off any pain or lies that he might tell. Marta turned, her graceful body moving in slow motion. She felt weightless, light-headed, frightened. She expected him to be standing with his hands clasped piously in front of him.

She met his gaze. "You're not Father Trotsky?" she asked.

"They call me Father Caridini here in Sulzbach."

"How quaint. A family name?"

"It's a long story," he said.

Nicholas looked different. It wasn't just the vestments he wore. He seemed leaner, his color grayish, the flesh stretching thinly over those prominent cheekbones. His facial muscles twitched as he watched her. Even his eyes seemed darker.

"Your eyes," she said.

"Tinted contact lenses. My eyes are still blue."

A brilliant sapphire blue, she remembered.

"Why, Nicholas?" she asked. "Why did you come here?"

He smiled an uncertain, uneven smile. "I was about to ask you the same thing, Marta. Why did you leave the church on Sunday? I wanted to talk to you—to explain."

Her arms tightened against her breasts. "Were you going to explain this charade?"

"Marta, I don't know what I was going to say. I just wanted to tell you—"

"Why you left me at the Brandenburg Gate. Why you kissed me goodbye and promised to come back for me. Oh, Nicholas, did you know when you left me there that you were going back to the seminary—that you were going to be a holy man?"

Her contempt was contagious. He despised himself at the moment, but he felt anger at her for not understanding. "It's not what you think. I was going after the American Crisscross."

"One more time? And did you find him?"

"He found me."

As he wiped the sweat from his brow, she mellowed. "You're ill, Nicholas," she said in alarm. "Come. Sit down."

With relief he took the chair across the table from her and hid his weak knees beneath the rough-hewn tabletop. "I'm getting better, Marta," he said.

"Frau Schmid told me you are dying."

"And how would she know that?" he asked gently.

"The village doctor told her you have terminal cancer."

"I see."

*Nicholas dying?* She met his gaze again, coldly at first. She knew at once by the look in his eyes that whatever lies he might tell, this information was true. Nicholas Trotsky was dying. She had set out to revenge his betrayal, to destroy him for hurting her, for deserting her. And now death itself was cheating her of taking vengeance on him. It gave her no joy. She forced herself to ask, "Nicholas, are you in pain?"

"Some. More when I lie down. It's harder to breathe then."

"Do you sleep well?"

"Not last night. Not after seeing you."

"I didn't sleep either. Frau Schmid found me wandering in her yard. She took me in and gave me some coffee and hard rolls."

"I'm glad." He reached across the table and touched her icy hand. "Marta, how did you find me?"

"I saw you in a park in Innsbruck two weeks ago."

He blinked, trying to remember the blurred image of a young woman in a wide-brimmed hat and sunglasses. He'd been sitting on the park bench across from her so violently ill that he had considered going back to the hospital. "It had to be the day I left the hospital. I had discharged myself against medical advice. No more chemotherapy. All I could think of was getting back to Sulzbach and putting—" He smiled playfully now. "Putting my house in order."

"You looked so ill that day. I noticed your clerics and Roman collar when you sat down, and then you lifted your face, and I knew it was you. I called your name, but you didn't hear me."

"Perhaps you didn't say it aloud."

"I guess not. All I could think was *Nicholas is alive. Nicholas is a priest.*"

His hand went involuntarily to his vestment. "This is not pretense, Marta."

Her scornful laughter filled the room. "You expect me to believe that? I know better."

"My mother always wanted me to be a priest."

"And does that make it so?"

"I'm sorry, Marta."

"No," she said emphatically. "It is I who am sorry that I ever saw you again."

❀❀❀

Nicholas felt the spasm welling up in his chest and tried to stop it. It erupted uninvited, filling his handkerchief with blood-tinged sputum, leaving him spent and exhausted—and diminished, less than a man in her sight. A weakling—a dying man. But he could not die until she knew the truth, until he made his confession to the people of Sulzbach.

The coldness in her expression startled him. He tried to remember the youthful Marta, the sweet Marta giving herself completely because she loved him—setting aside her own dreams so she could be Colonel Trotsky's girl.

Some of the hardness in her face was his own doing, and he felt both shame and remorse at what he had done to her. He tried to remember clearly, but his thoughts were like tangled vines on a winding forest trail. He only remembered that he had truly loved her. Yes, he had loved her. But she would never have been first in his life. His commitment and loyalty was to the Communist party and later to the Phoenix-40 that offered his country a chance for the old way of life.

He had loved Marta as he had once loved his own mother, but the party came first. He had loved them both, but that was in a past life that he could barely remember. He owed Marta the truth—that he had fled East Germany to avoid recall to Russia when two of the Phoenix-40 had been executed for a failed coup. She was too troubled now to tell her that he had been part of that rebellion or to describe how easily he had slipped into the role of a parish priest. How could he break through her anger to tell her that over the years Jacques Caridini's sermon notes had stirred in his heart until the Christ of the sermon notes had become real to him?

Marta slipped from the table and went for two mugs of water from the bucket on the kitchen counter. He smiled gratefully as she took her seat again. "Thank you, Marta."

"You really, truly are dying, aren't you?" The question was accusing, as though he were about to desert her once more.

"In a few weeks perhaps."

"There's nothing the doctors can do?"

"Nothing that I want them to do." He swallowed the water, glad for the coolness on his parched lips.

Outside they could hear Ilse and Erika Schmid returning. "I must go," Marta said.

"But we haven't settled anything."

She shrugged. "There's nothing to settle."

"Oh, Marta, why did you follow me here to Sulzbach?"

"I was listening for the sweet music of the phoenix bird."

This morning's awakening cry pierced his thoughts once more. "Don't, Marta. That was a long time ago."

"But I never forgot." Her mouth twitched, hard and bitter. "I recognized you in Innsbruck, Nicholas. And you looked right at me and never even saw me."

"I'm sorry. Will I see you again?"

"In church? That's not my way, Nicholas." Her chair scratched across the floor as she stood.

"Then come to the rectory. I have a housekeeper. She could fix dinner for us. We could talk again."

"About what—your God?"

"Perhaps I could explain."

"It's too late to explain."

"Then why were you willing to see me?"

"I wanted to warn you. I didn't come to Sulzbach alone."

"I know."

"My friends don't know who you are yet."

As her wide, brown eyes drowned in tears, he reached over and gently touched her hand. "Are you in danger, Marta?"

"I am in love," she said bitterly, "with an old memory."

# Chapter 21

Nicholas needed no reminder that his body had wasted away. He felt it in every move, tasted it in the dryness of his mouth, fought it with each breath he took. Yet he clung to life, not fearful of death, but reluctant to let go of everything, everyone. Heaven lay beyond his last breath, but he struggled against the unfairness of saying goodbye.

Strategy had always been Nicholas's strong point, a skill learned at the chessboard as a boy. Clever moves that took him toward his goals of leadership. But where was strategy now? He could not map out the future. He had none left. No cunning, no tactical move on his part would alter the eternal blueprint, the game plan for his own immortality. Nicholas had accepted the fact that he would not reach his fifty-second birthday, but he would spend it—if one spent birthdays in heaven—with Abraham, Jacob, and Jacques Caridini. Illness had not lessened his mortality or his human feelings; these kept him sad at the thought of saying goodbye.

He did a mental check as he lay on his bed. Tuesday, *four days since the strangers had come to Sulzbach*. For fourteen years he had greeted each day at sunrise, cheerful and expectant. Now the days weighed heavily on him; Marta's presence had robbed him of the peace that he had found here.

Each new thought of her thrust him further into his past.

He had hated his poor beginning and had often turned away embarrassed at his mother's simplicity. In his own way he had loved her. Yet in the end he chose to break that relationship for advancement in the party, her safety guaranteed as he made the choice. It was all that he could give her for her many sacrifices for him.

It took discipline and determination to turn his back on his mother. Yet discipline and determination had taken Nicholas from a poor neighborhood to power and position with the KGB. General Jankowski had picked Nicholas from the ranks for key positions and training at the top schools. The general always took the credit for Colonel Trotsky, but the Phoenix-40 plan was Nicholas's strategy. Yes, Nicholas was the intellectual giant, the mastermind behind the PHOENIX PLAN.

Now only sheer grit and tenacity gave him the strength to stand and edge around the narrow bed on his unsteady legs to the dresser. He pulled open the top drawer and stared down at the bottles of medication. Eschert had promised that for a while pills would ease the pain. He grabbed one of the bottles and flipped open the lid with his thumb, dumping two pills into his palm. They were in his mouth—the water from his bed stand in his other hand—before he spit them out.

His bone-thin body ached. He wanted the awful pain to go away, the terrible nausea to stop for even an hour.

"Nicholas."

He leaned into the bed and looked up at Frau Mayer and Johann Heppner crowding in the doorway. "Are you all right?" Johann asked.

"I'm almost dead, and you ask me that?"

Frau Mayer's hand flew to her mouth as she rushed across the room to him. "Sit down, Father Caridini. Here by the window. I'll get you some food."

"I couldn't eat it. Not this morning."

Johann held Nicholas's eyelids open, and the glare from the penlight set Nicholas's nerves on edge. "Frau Mayer," Johann said, "freshen his bed. We'll let him rest this morning."

"No—"

Johann cut off the protest with a tongue blade pressed against Nicholas's tongue. "I'll treat you here. You're dehydrated, my friend."

"I'm sick," he said.

"I'm going to the clinic for some equipment. That way no one will know I'm treating you. Satisfied?"

"No pain medicine."

"Something light so you can sleep awhile this morning."

"I've got to keep my mind clear. What's wrong with me, Johann?"

"You need fluids. I'll give you an intravenous infusion right here in your room."

"The American is coming for lunch."

"He can come some other time."

"We already sent him away on Sunday. Really, I need to talk to him." *I need to use him. Barter with him.*

They stripped him of his pajama top, and he reared back as Frau Mayer deftly applied a wash cloth to his face and upper torso. "Don't fuss, Father Caridini," she said. "I took care of you when you first came to this village."

"We both did," Heppner said.

Their eyes met. "I thought so, Johann."

"Frau Mayer's a good nurse, Father Caridini. We're here to help you with the unfinished business of dying."

"What?"

Their gaze met again over the tips of Johann's glasses. "We all have things we want to finish," the doctor said. "A lesser man would have been gone months ago, Nicholas. You've got an iron will."

"A less stubborn doctor would have given me permission to die weeks ago and not sent me down to Deiter Eschert in Innsbruck."

"I know." Johann struggled for control as he said, "When you're ready, Nicholas—when the time comes—I'll let you go."

"Even in the middle of a chess game?"

"As long as I'm winning."

"Bury me in my red socks, Johann," he said as they eased

him back against the fresh-smelling linen. He felt childlike and weak, his discipline and stamina shattered.

"Frau Mayer," Johann said, "I'll run the infusion for several hours, but keep your eyes on it."

Nicholas groaned. "It's Johann's way of making me rest."

"Someone has to outwit you. Besides a thousand of dextrose and lactated ringers will give you a burst of energy."

"Just a burst? Not a cure?"

"I wish it could be more, Nicholas. I wish it could be longer. Frau Mayer will take the I.V. out when it's done."

"Oh, no. Not me. I haven't done that for a long time."

"Nothing to it," he reassured her. "Just turn it off, take the needle out, and apply pressure. Otherwise he'll bleed."

"Don't worry, Frau Mayer. I'm already dying."

At the pained look on her face, Nicholas regretted his words. "I'm sorry. You've been so good to me. Did this old rogue convince you to come up to Sulzbach early this year?"

She nodded. "He wanted me to look after you."

"You've done that, and I'm grateful."

As Frau Mayer went to answer the door, Johann helped him into clean pajama bottoms and pulled the eiderdown to his waist.

He looked respectable when Johann's German shepherd nudged her way into the room. Frau Mayer was behind the dog, shaking her head. "Came to the door with the American. What should I tell Mr. Gregory, Father Caridini?"

"He's early."

"Says he needs to talk to you."

Girl's muzzle was on the bed now, the eyes woeful, her cold nose pressed against Nicholas's chalky hand.

"I'll leave the dog with you," Heppner said. "I'll be right back. What should I tell the American on my way out?"

"Send him in."

"It's as I thought. He's past history—a part of your unfinished business of dying. Right?"

"Part of the tidying-up process." *An old score to settle,* he thought. Nicholas could still use his wits—still force this wretched body to work for him a few more days, and he needed the American's cooperation.

"The mass," he said, suddenly remembering.

Heppner glanced back from the doorway. "I'll have Herr Schmid or Petzold do the reading this morning. Might even go over and light a candle for you myself."

"That will be the day. It's too late for candles, Johann. Look at me. But go on. Get your D5LR. Girl will stay with me."

*And hurry,* he thought. *Keep me alive a few more days.* He would welcome the infusion as he must now welcome the American.

☙☙☙

Drew Gregory followed Frau Mayer into the priest's room and stood quietly by Nicholas's bedside until she left the room again. Then he looked down squarely at Trotsky. If anything, the priest looked worse than he had on Saturday. If Vic Wilson didn't hightail it up the mountain in a fat hurry, they would have to piggyback Trotsky down to Brunnerwald—or worse, carry him in a box, one of those caskets made at the wood carver's shop.

"Can I get you anything?" Drew asked.

"Get yourself a chair and pull it over."

At eye level Drew found himself at a loss for words. Vic would look like this one day—emaciated with a yellow hue to his skin. Would Drew be able cope when that happened?

"Gregory, what would you do if a man needed a few days?"

Trotsky at his best—tossing a catch-22, one of those subtle tactics to throw Drew off guard. "Is that what you're asking for?"

"Yes. I'll barter with you, Gregory."

He wanted to say, *No bartering, Colonel Trotsky.* But he didn't have the manpower at his beck and call. And Trotsky was still wearing the robe of a priest. At least it was hanging in his closet in full view.

"I'll protect you, Gregory, if you'll do the same for me."

"For a few days?"

"Yes."

The man was sick but clever. Did he really believe he could rise up from this sickbed and disappear as he had done fifteen years ago—that he could bluff his way with American Intelligence? But why not? He had done it a dozen times or more since Drew opened the file on him.

"You seem speechless this morning, Herr Gregory. I'm offering you the sanctity of this rectory and parish once again. You can have your old room across the hall."

Nicholas's eyes were glazed with illness, yet bright and alert with challenge—a wry smile on his face as he admitted his identity, once again outsmarting Drew.

"Why would I need your protection, Father Caridini?"

"Sulzbach is not a safe place for you. Four cyclists are here—looking for the old friend of Ian Kendall's grandfather."

"And you think I'm the man?"

"I know it. Four others are looking for someone else. Five, if I count you. I could help you find him. But, then, the four at Burgers' place followed you here. Surely you know that?"

*I've already found you, Colonel Trotsky, but I need something more tangible than this elusive conversation, and you know it.* "Are you trying to warn me off?" Drew asked.

"The young Grecian—Alekos Golemis—is forming a strange alliance with the guests at Frau Burger's. It can only bring harm to Alekos and his friends and put you in danger. So I'm asking you, Herr Gregory, for a few more days. We'd make a good team—the priest of Sulzbach and the American agent."

Another admission that only Trotsky could make, an unsavory alliance that could only bring harm to the village. *We'd make an odd team,* Drew thought. *Enemies. Arch rivals.*

Each effort to speak took its toll on Nicholas's labored breathing. "Can I count on you?" he asked.

"You haven't told me why?"

"I promise you answers in a few days. If you took refuge here, we could talk of things that matter. I believe you came to this mountain in search of peace. As I did."

*No, I came in search of Colonel Trotsky.*

Johann scowled as he came back into the room. "I'll have to ask you to leave," he said. "Father Caridini needs to rest."

Drew stood and shoved the chair back by the window.

"Think it over, Gregory." Nicholas's gaze followed Drew as he passed the foot of the bed. "You mentioned a wife and daughter the other day. Where are they?"

*Safely out of your hands.* Yet anyone as clever as Nicholas Trotsky already knew. "My daughter lives in Switzerland with her husband." He hesitated. "My ex-wife is still in the States."

"California, isn't it?"

"Yes. She owns an art gallery in Beverly Hills."

"You're an honest man, Gregory. I like that in a person."

Miriam Gregory reached the turnoff to the family dairy farm in upstate New York early Tuesday morning. She hadn't been back since her mother-in-law's death and feared a touch of gloom at the prospect of seeing the farm again. She dreaded a bout of sneezing from the smell of hay and spring flowers, but as she drove along, she felt fine, alive, not at all sad about returning.

"The weather gods have blessed us with a good day," Mother Gregory had always said. She said it for every season. This morning Miriam agreed with her. It was a glorious May morning, canopied with a powdered blue sky. The fingers of spring had painted the valley in shades of green, and as far as she could see, the slopes were dotted with farms and grazing cattle, the hills freckled with wild flowers. The welcome serenity was set to the music of a gurgling brook and the happy serenade of the long-tailed sparrow balancing on the utility pole. She shared the bubbling mirth of the smartly feathered bobolink that had funneled up from the south at the first burst of spring. No wonder Drew loved this place.

She drove along the white picket fence that outlined the sprawling Gregory property. As she turned in through the iron gate, she tried to spot a purple martin in the multi-chambered birdhouse that Drew had built. Parking, she remembered another of Mother Gregory's happy sayings:

"Spring really comes when the red-breasted robin sings a cheery round as it bounces across my lawn."

Miriam smiled as Loyal Quinwell opened the door—a startled smile, for Miriam had expected a plain, aproned woman. Loyal was fortyish, slender in dark slacks and a colorful sweat top. Her short, curly hair framed a rosy-cheeked grin.

"Mrs. Gregory, we're glad you drove up to see us."

"Drew sent a painting. Perhaps Aaron could carry it in."

"Let me help you. Stan and Aaron are out in the barn."

There was a peppy zing to Loyal's movements, a bounce to her steps as they lifted the painting from the trunk of the rented car and carried it into the house.

"May I?" she asked as she laid it on the table.

"Do," Miriam encouraged.

She tore back the wrappings, her face glowing as she held up one of John Constable's landscapes—a serene country setting with a horse and wagon caught in the stream and a dog on the water's edge. Storm clouds hugged the huge trees and chimneyed house.

"Constable is a British artist," Miriam said. "Drew thought the delicate shades would blend with your Winslow Homer painting."

"This is just right for above the fireplace. But why? Mr. Gregory didn't have to do this."

"Drew wanted to—for all you're doing for his brother Aaron."

Loyal laughed. "I'd better send the picture back. With all the modern equipment, Aaron still has trouble getting the hang of milking." More seriously, she said, "But he's sticking to the rules: church on Sunday and a full day's work with Stan—every day."

"It's working out then?"

"It almost didn't. Work starts around here before sunup. Aaron didn't like that at all and gave us nothing but trouble. Stan finally told him, 'It's up or out.'"

"I hate getting up at five," Aaron said as he came into the kitchen. "But everything else is great, especially Loyal's cooking."

Aaron looked like a stranger in his boots and jeans. His gaunt cheeks had filled in; the arrogant slant of his mouth had softened. But those shifty, dark eyes were wary as he watched her.

She extended both hands. "Aaron, you look wonderful."

"That's my line." He took her hands in his, his once-smooth skin callused. "Loyal tells me you're heading back to Europe?"

"I plan to be in Geneva when Drew gets there."

"Are you getting back together?"

"If he asks me."

"I'd always hoped—"

"Don't, Aaron. Drew was always the only one for me."

Pride kept his head up. "So when do you leave, Miriam?"

"Late tomorrow evening. I want you to go with me."

"Is that Drew's idea?"

"Mine. I'm here on my own. I'm sorry about not inviting you to Robyn's wedding. I just couldn't face you and Drew arguing."

"I thought you crossed me off the list because of the von Tonner paintings."

"That, too. The fraudulent ones."

He licked his thin lips. "Can you ever forgive me?"

The apology from Aaron startled her. Softly she said, "I've already forgiven you. But it won't be settled for you until you go back to Zurich and face the charges."

"Believe me, I was only Ingrid von Tonner's lawyer."

"Aaron, I won't argue that point with you."

"If I go back, I'd end up in jail."

"We won't know that until the inquiry. Robyn and I will be there for you."

"What about Drew?"

"You will have to work that out with your brother. I've asked the airline to hold a reservation for you. It's up to you, Aaron."

She had pushed him too far. He walked doggedly to the stove and poured himself a cup of coffee, sloshing it down with his back still to her. She glanced at Loyal Quinwell.

"Well, Aaron?" Loyal asked. "What do you think about going to Europe with your sister-in-law?"

He shrugged. "Miriam never did like flying alone." He kept his back to her, his voice tight as he asked, "Miriam, can you promise me that my brother will be in Zurich when I get there?"

"I don't know where Drew is. I can only hope and pray that Vic Wilson is with him. It's safer with the two of them."

☙☙☙

The wires had grown hot between Paris and Langley, leaving Troy Carwell and Chad Kaminsky at odds about the next move in Sulzbach. Things were hopping again—the way Vic Wilson liked them. The threat of the Phoenix rebellion had blown wide open with a red alert sounding in more than one intelligence agency. The White House was threatening troop movement if another coup hit Moscow. As a result, Troy Carwell had revised his strategy and sent Brad O'Malloy packing for Brunnerwald—with the promise of more men arriving on Saturday.

Joining up with O'Malloy was to Vic's liking, but meeting Pierre Courtland in Brunnerwald had not been on Vic's agenda. If Drew's son-in-law got in the way, he could stir up trouble all the way to Paris. "Go back to Geneva, Pierre," Vic said as he spread the trail maps on the table.

"No. If you're heading up the mountain, I'm going with you."

"No way," O'Malloy argued. "This is Agency business."

"My father-in-law is *family* business. I either go up there with you, or I go alone."

Reluctantly Vic said, "You're in, but you take orders from us." He thumped the map. "Drew is in Sulzbach. That's where we're heading."

"Nope," said Brad. "No can do. Troy Carwell wants us to check out Innsbruck first."

"That's crazy. We're wasting time. Preben Schrott's wife says there's trouble up on that mountain, and I believe her."

"I still say, no can do." Brad was at his relaxed best—

dressed in a crew-neck sweater with threadbare elbows, baggy jeans, his size ten clodhoppers sprawled on the table. Drooping eyelids shadowed the old twinkle as he ran his hand over a receding hairline. "Wilson, we've got to run with Carwell's orders."

"Carwell isn't here."

"He's sitting tight in Paris keeping in touch with Langley and London. If you hadn't rattled Perkins's cage—"

"O'Malloy, it paid me to fly back to London and confront Perkins. If it hadn't been for Lyle Spincrest fracturing his tibia in these mountains, there would have been no cooperation at all. The Brits are worried about the Phoenix-40 flying under a new cloak."

"Sorry, Vic. Langley has a possible address on the woman who sighted Trotsky in Innsbruck. We've got orders to check that one through." Brad flattened his hand on the table and shoved the maps on the floor. "We're going back to Innsbruck. That's where Trotsky was sighted, and that's where the woman has her *pension*."

"And that still leaves Gregory in the mountains without reinforcements."

"Vic," Pierre offered, "I can go on up to Sulzbach. That way Drew will know you're still coming."

"Tell him by Friday or Saturday. We'll head over to the cheese factory and check with Preben Schrott first. If I have to beat it out of him, I'll find out whether Drew is still up in Sulzbach."

🏺🏺🏺

When they reached the Schrott Cheese Factory, Vic stormed through the swinging doors back into the work room demanding to see Preben. The young man came toward them, his startled expression turning to rage. "Out," he said. "Get out. This is for employees only."

"We're looking for Drew Gregory."

Vic and Preben stalked each other by the gleaming steel vats. "No one here by that name. Out or I call the *polizei*."

"Gregory stayed at your *gasthof*. Where is he?"

They were a strong match, the good-looking Preben as arrogant as Vic. Vic slammed Preben against the massive vat bubbling with curd, bending him backwards until they could both feel the heat rising up from the boiling surface.

"Schrott, Nicholas Trotsky stayed at your place, too. He's from Sulzbach, they tell me."

Preben tried to wrench free. "I know no one by that name. Only the priest from Sulzbach stays with us. But Father Caridini is sick. He may be back in the hospital in Innsbruck even now."

"Then give me the hospital's name and address."

Sweat poured down Preben's angry face. "I'll get it for you."

# Chapter 22

Nicholas awakened from a deep sleep early in the afternoon. The I.V. pole had been removed from the room, and a dried, bloody gauze was taped on his inner arm. He stretched and waited for the burst of energy that Heppner had promised and felt surprisingly well-rested, with only a mild headache pressing at his temples.

The air felt nippy and refreshing, but the rectory was deadly quiet. His mind cleared slowly, lifting from the medicine downer and allowing him to reflect on the evening vespers. He couldn't count on many more opportunities to stand in his small chapel and speak to his people. Time was running out.

Until yesterday he dreaded only the loss of the familiar, of being snatched from his parishioners and never seeing his beloved Alps again. Now something sinister lurked within the perimeters of the village, something stalking him without face or form, some unknown assailants set on returning him to Moscow where devious, dividing cancer cells would stop them from shipping him to Siberia. But Marta's life was threatened more than his own if she persisted in hiding his identity.

He showered and dressed and finally found Frau Mayer in the kitchen tiptoeing around. "Oh, you're up. You're better."

"I'm rested," he said.

"I didn't want to wake you."

"Dr. Heppner forbade it," he teased.

Still she didn't smile. "Frau Mayer, what's wrong?"

"One of the strangers in town went over the cliff higher up on the mountain. They sent for Dr. Heppner."

*Marta!* Nicholas turned toward the door.

"Father Caridini, you mustn't exert yourself."

"I may be needed."

As Nicholas hurried across the street, he saw Johann enter the Petzold bakery. He followed him inside. "What's this I hear about an accident on the mountain?"

"It's true. Peter Kermer is dead. Catholic, wasn't he?"

"He was a Messianic Jew, Johann. He came to the church at midnight. That's when I saw the Star of David around his neck."

Johann slapped a broken chain and the Star of David in his palm. "This must belong to Kermer. It took quite a skirmish at the top of the cliff to rip it from his neck that way."

They slipped outside the bakery and edged along the store front talking in whispers. "Kermer was anxious to get home to his wife and sons in time for the oldest boy's bar mitzvah. Where is he, Johann? I should go to him."

"Kermer's at the bottom of a deep ravine up by the old avalanche. It'll be hours before the patrol can reach him. He's a twisted mess down there." Johann shook his head. "The fool broke the rules of the trail—hiking alone after dark."

"I followed him last night, Johann. But he was alive when I saw him last. Someone else—"

"I believe you. You're too weak to have struggled with anyone up there. But someone will be looking for a scapegoat."

"Kermer's friends may have followed him."

In a rare display of affection, Johann clapped his shoulder. "You're pale, Nicholas. Go back to the rectory and conserve your strength. I'll handle Peter Kermer's friends."

Nicholas's thoughts twisted. *They already know. And one of them pushed him over.* Marta would be in even more danger. From where they stood, Nicholas could see the Burgers' place. "Curb the rumors, Johann. Examine the body first."

Heppner's sharp gaze demanded answers. "Stay out of it. The whole village knows about the accident already."

"Then Kermer's friends do too. Before they can do anything, I must get a message down to Preben in Brunnerwald. Josef can take it for me after you examine Kermer's body."

"Stay out of it, Caridini."

"I can't. Kermer's friends won't notify his family. That leaves it up to me. Preben can contact the embassy in Jerusalem to locate the Ben Bernsteins in Tel Aviv."

"The Ben Bernsteins?"

"That was his real name. There can't be too many Bernsteins working for the Israeli Intelligence."

Johann's eyes bulged. "Kermer?"

"The others don't know. At least they didn't know yesterday. I can't explain everything, Johann. He talked to me as a priest."

"Why all this interest in Kermer, Father Caridini?"

"Coming to Saint Francis Chapel last night cost him his life."

🏵🏵🏵

Nicholas dragged toward the rectory, stopping twice with a coughing spasm. When he reached the cemetery, the gate stood open. He hesitated and then went in and saw Marta wandering among the flat headstones. When she paused by Jacques's grave, he went to her.

"Are you all right, Marta?"

She looked up at him, her dark-lashed eyes smiling as though she were glad to see him. "You startled me, Nicholas. But then you were always one to come in on feathered feet."

He returned her smile, realizing again how lovely she was to look at when the lines around her mouth softened. "Marta, there's a bench over there. Could we sit down? I'm quite tired."

"Just for a few minutes. I'm waiting for Peter Kermer."

*You don't know.* While he tried to form the words to tell

her, she said, "Sulzbach is beautiful. I think you've been happy here."

"I have."

"I should hate you for being happy."

"I hate myself for making you feel that way." He didn't find the courage to ask her about the long years since he had left her behind, yet it was important to him for Marta to understand and forgive him. "Marta, when I came here, I never planned to stay."

"But you never went home."

"I wasn't well enough to walk off this mountain then, and now I don't want to leave it."

"You've forgotten your old loyalties."

"Until you came back."

He stole glances at her, and each time the hurt in her eyes pained him more. She pointed to Jacques's grave. "Who was this man?"

"My brother."

"I didn't know you had a brother."

"I didn't until I met Jacques. I owe my life to him."

"Your new life, Nicholas?" Scorn ate at her words. "You never plan to leave here, do you? Nicholas, have you forgotten who you were? Have you forgotten your country?"

"I would never be well enough to leave now, Marta."

"And you wouldn't want to go—not even to see your mother? Is she still alive, or is she gone now?"

"I don't know."

"You never tried to find out?"

"She was safer not knowing where I was." A taste of homesickness stuck in the roof of his mouth, a bitter longing for the country he would never see again. "Marta, tell me about my country."

"You keep up on the news, don't you? Gorbachev—and Yeltsin's reform. Zhirinovsky. The breakup of the Soviet Union and the battle in Chechnya. The KGB dismantled. The end of the Cold War."

He'd heard of them all, often over a game of chess with Johann. "Is it true—all the street fighting and disorder?"

"It's worse—hopelessness and long bread lines. A growing

rift between the old order and the new. The pains of democracy are awful." He heard the contempt in her voice, saw it as balls of fire in her eyes. "It will take another revolution to stop it, Nicholas. Someone with the courage to take over."

*Don't*, he thought. *Don't involve me. Don't make me think about my country that way, about its need for new leadership.* "The PHOENIX PLAN failed. Half of the Phoenix-40 are dead, dead in the first attempted coup. Austria is my home now, Marta."

She tugged her sweater around her shoulders. "You've changed, Colonel Trotsky. You have forgotten your homeland. But will you let your mother starve to death with the rest of the elderly?"

He winced at the thought of her hungry and malnourished. She had gone through the bitter winter of 1942, a victim of the Nazi siege of Leningrad, her husband in a prison camp. "The last I knew, she was still living with her brother. They would have enough money."

"No, Nicholas. In Moscow a hundred-ruble note is worth little anymore. If your mother is dead, it would be merciful."

"Then why would I want to go home again?"

"My friends will insist on it—as soon as they know who you are. Peter Kermer has guessed. I'm sure of it." She glanced toward the gate. "When he gets here, ask him. But what's keeping him?"

He looked away. The high wall of the cemetery stared back at him. He couldn't find the words to tell her about Kermer. "Marta, what do you know about Kermer?" he asked.

Even her eyes seemed to frown. "We met in Zagreb and crossed the border together."

Sweat soaked the palm of his hand as he linked himself with the past. Old challenges flashed in his mind: the thought of power, of rising on behalf of the old glory days of Russia, of still holding the key to the PHOENIX PLAN rising from the ashes. Plans and strategy. Pitting wit against wit. The threat of Peter Kermer was behind them. Excitement stirred inside of him at the thought of outmaneuvering

Drew Gregory again, and his tone sharpened. "Marta, you thought Peter Kermer was one of us?"

She stared at him. "I'm not sure that I even trust him."

"You don't have to any longer. Peter Kermer isn't coming back. Something happened to him last evening. He's dead."

She didn't move.

"Who are your other friends?" he asked. "Did they mistrust him, too?" As he waited for her to answer, his thoughts raced. If the plan had been to assassinate Nicholas, only one man would have come up the mountain, not a team of four bent on taking him alive. Perhaps he was not destined for Siberia or execution. They wanted the PHOENIX PLAN, and they wanted Colonel Trotsky to lead them again. "Come on, Marta, I can find out soon enough."

"Yuri Ryskov and Werner Vronin. There's a third man waiting in Innsbruck."

"Waiting for you to take me there? They're not Yeltsin's men?"

She didn't have to answer. The PHOENIX PLAN had been set in motion. "I have to know what side your friends are on, otherwise it's not going to work. There's an American agent in Sulzbach; that means a problem for us. Kermer would have stopped us, too." He shocked her even more. "Kermer was an Israeli agent."

Coldly she said, "It doesn't matter. We don't need Peter Kermer. And we can get rid of that American agent. Nothing will stop us."

He picked up the purse that lay between them and opened it. "What, Marta—no Beretta or hidden tape recorder?"

"Give that to me."

He pulled back playfully. "An address book. Is my name still in it? Or have you crossed Colonel Trotsky from your life?"

As she grabbed for the book, a scrap of paper fell from it. He picked it up. *Dudley Perkins. London. Perkins? MI5.* "Marta, what kind of game are you playing?" he asked.

She stood and claimed her purse and the piece of paper. "Come to Moscow with us."

"I'm too sick. But I can organize things from the rectory."

She wavered considering. "No. Give me the PHOENIX PLAN. I'll take it back for you. Yuri and Vronin won't leave without it."

"And you won't live without it."

Her chin jutted out. "You'd be safe that way, Nicholas."

"But you won't. Without me, your assignment here is a failure. The plan failed once, an abortive coup. Men died for nothing."

"You're wrong. Vronin said that some of the Phoenix-40 are still holed up in one of the breakaway regions—just waiting."

"Waiting for the plan to rise from the ashes?"

"My Kremlin contact plans to start a powerful new splinter group. We need you, Nicholas. You could still come with us."

*To the first bend in the trail or the first high cliff?* "No. You need the PHOENIX PLAN, not me."

"Then I'll talk Vronin in to going on without you. You'll be safe here, Nicholas. Vronin says we've devised a perfect plan."

"And the perfect plan didn't include Peter Kermer either?"

"What kind of man are you, Nicholas?" she asked. "You are mocking me when I'm offering you a chance to live."

"Such a guarantee to a dying man." His laughter merged with a choking spell. His lungs felt as if they had collapsed. He bent over trying to ease the pain. When he opened his eyes again, her slender arm rested on his shoulder, but his eyes saw only Jacques Caridini's grave. Jacques's words came back. *My mentor sent me to Sulzbach, Nicholas, to test my faith—to see if it were real.*

In the last few minutes Nicholas had wavered between the old and the new—eager and ready to throw away the peace in Sulzbach for the glory days of Russia. He had graduated from one of the elite Soviet military schools with high honors and recognition and then rose to a top rank and position in the KGB, but he had failed the test of obedience in the village of Sulzbach.

Marta's soft hand slipped over his cheek. "Goodbye," she said.

❁❁❁

Nicholas sat by the fireplace, desolate and alone. For years the choices he made had been between the PHOENIX PLAN and the people of Sulzbach, between Marta and his God. A hundred failures, a myriad of choices. Now Marta offered him her silence—the chance to continue his deception at Sulzbach. But what of Marta's safety. Should he go to Yuri and Vronin and surrender? They would have him out of the village before he could say his next mass. His thoughts darkened. He could lead them to the American Intelligence officer and place Drew Gregory's life in jeopardy, not his own.

To help Marta, Nicholas had to reconsider the PHOENIX PLAN. As he did, the old excitement and power of days gone by energized his weakened body. Russia was still his homeland. He owed her something. He would mastermind the PHOENIX PLAN from the safety of the chapel. In these last days of his life, he would rise from the ashes—he, Nicholas Ivan Trotsky, would go down in the glory pages of Russia. He must not die now. Marta needed him.

Nausea more wretched than the cancer had caused doubled him over. He gripped the desk. Sweat poured from his face. He tried to shut away the image of Christ on the wall, tried to block out the happenings of the moment as he had been trained to do in assassin school. He could at this moment recall many of his victims, recall them as he had done then without emotion.

Frau Mayer slipped into the room and placed a steaming cup of tea beside him. "I didn't want to disturb you, Father Caridini. You looked so troubled. But it's time for evening vespers."

"I'd almost forgotten."

"You won't forget to go to Frau Helmut first thing tomorrow?"

"I go every morning," he reminded her.

"Go earlier this time. Frau Helmut is so afraid of dying."

*Nicholas Trotsky recoiled. Nicholas Caridini understood.* "I'll see to it," he said. "First thing in the morning."

"Oh, thank you, Father Caridini, but don't look so troubled," she said as she left him. "Things will work out. You'll make the right decisions. Your brother Jacques always did."

He cupped his face in his hands and wept and begged for forgiveness. Blindly, he took the letter of confession from his desk and tapped it in the palm of his hand. Yes, he would send it to the bishop of Innsbruck—down the mountain with Rheinhold Schmid in the morning—and even the KGB could do nothing about it.

# Chapter 23

At the close of evening vespers, Nicholas hurried to Ilse Schmid's side. "Frau Schmid, can you take a message to Rheinhold?"

She stared at the note in his hand and then looked up again. Her eyes seemed dull this evening, the old brilliance fading.

"He may be asleep," she said.

"Can you awaken him? It's important, Frau Schmid."

She reminded him of how his mother might look with that gentle, wizened expression, the gaze kindly in spite of the uncertainty. As always, she was dressed in black, a thick scarf hiding her sparse gray hair, a walking stick in her hand, those hands as gnarled and ancient as her wrinkled face. A well-worn rosary bulged in her pocket.

Erika reappeared, anxious as she exclaimed, "Grandmama, we must go now. It's a long walk. Grandfather will worry."

Smiling at them both, Nicholas put the note in Ilse's pocket. "Tell Rheinhold to come by in the morning—before he goes down the mountain. I have something he must take with him."

"It's important," Ilse remembered. "I'll tell him."

Nicholas stood at the door of the chapel and watched them wend their way toward home. Ilse shuffled slowly behind the other parishioners, her black shawl snug around her shoulders, Erika by her side. Would Ilse remember his note to Rheinhold tucked in the pocket of her apron? He could only pray that when she reached for her rosary, she would find it there.

And now he needed to talk to Marta once more to explain how he could get her to safety—that he was making arrangements for Rheinhold Schmid to take her down to Brunnerwald in the milk wagon before Yuri or Vronin had time to miss her.

When Nicholas reached out to shut the church doors, he saw Marta come out of the Petzold bakery. Instead of turning home toward the Burgers' *pension*, she stopped at the curb and seemed to be staring across at the rectory. Did she see him? Did she sense his desperate need to talk to her? As he lifted his hand to wave, she turned onto the same path where Ilse and Erika walked.

He hurried down the steps and across the street, not daring to call her name aloud. Even those few steps winded him, jolting him to an abrupt stop in the middle of the street. Pressing his hand against his chest, he bent forward and sucked in air.

When he looked up again, Marta had slipped into the darkness. He followed, his own steps slowed by the rubbery legs that held him and the lungs that were slowly, steadily giving out.

"It won't be much longer," Johann had told him yesterday at the clinic. "But you could make it easier on yourself if you took your medicine."

"I can't think when I'm groggy."

"Can you think any better when you're in pain?"

Nicholas was grateful that the clinic bell had rung, and Johann's scolding had turned to a warm welcome to the stranger in his waiting room. "Fraulein Zubkov," he said cheerily. "How can I help you?"

She had noticed them both, her surprise at seeing Nicholas evident in the flush of her cheeks. "It's my constant headaches, Dr. Heppner," she said.

"Come along. Let's take a look."

As Johann led her toward his examining room, Nicholas had bowed out politely, acknowledging her with a whispered, "Can you come to dinner at the rectory this evening? We must talk."

She shook her head. "It's safer for you if we don't."

But *her* safety now filled his mind as he followed the trail toward the river. He caught up with her at the fork in the road.

"Marta."

She turned at the sound of his voice. "It's you. I expected Yuri or Vronin."

"Marta, I'm sending you away."

"It's too late, Nicholas."

"No. I've worked it out. Preben Schrott will help you once you get to Brunnerwald. He'll send you on to London for me."

"Nicholas. Nicholas. Since Peter's death, Yuri and Vronin are watching my every move. They follow me everywhere."

"I saw no one on the trail."

"You've forgotten some of the old ways, Nicholas."

"It will work. I'll send you down the mountain tomorrow."

"Nicholas, give me the PHOENIX PLAN. That's all they want."

"Ah, Marta. It is you who has forgotten the old ways. But I will provide the microfilms in exchange for your safety."

She turned and walked away. He hurried ahead of her and stopped, breathing heavily. "Marta, it was always in my heart to go back and find you. But when Jankowski and Kavin were executed, I knew it was only a matter of time until Moscow came for me."

He smiled into the dark. "I went skiing while I waited."

"You promised to take me with you."

"You didn't know about the Phoenix-40. If I crossed the Brandenburg Gate alone, it guaranteed your safety. Even if they interrogated you, how could you confess what you did not know?"

"You could have brought me here with you."

"I didn't know I was coming. And then that plane accident changed my life. I was ill for a long time, Marta, and when I finally walked again, my plan was to find any of the survivors of the PHOENIX PLAN and start over."

"I was never part of that plan, was I?"

His thoughts raced back to the music box. "In time perhaps."

"You were always a master of deception."

He pointed to his clerical robe, but he knew in the darkness that she had not noticed. "This is real," he said. "Oh, not in the beginning. When Father Jacques died so suddenly, falling heir to his job was unbelievably easy. Yes, it was pretense at first—for my own safety. But in time, what I was teaching, what I was reading became life itself to me."

"I do not want to know about your God. I am a Communist, Nicholas, as you are. As you will always be."

"It's dark," he said, and his voice filled with gloom. "Let me walk you back to the village."

"No." She reached up, her hands soft as they cupped his thin cheeks. "Dr. Heppner said that you don't have much longer."

"Why did he tell you that?"

"I demanded it."

"The headaches were just an excuse to talk to him?"

"They've been real enough here in Sulzbach."

He put his own icy hands over hers. He wanted to remember forever that her hands had rested on his cheeks once more.

"Don't, Nicholas." But she was gentle as she pushed him away. "You don't realize, do you? I am the one who turned you in."

"I know. Marta, what happened to the music box I gave you?"

"The phoenix bird?" she asked. "It's gone—shattered."

He saw her bite her lip. "Nicholas, I will persuade Yuri and Vronin that we must go back to Innsbruck—that you are not here." She laughed softly. "It will give you time to find a new parish."

She left him and walked on toward the river, but he made no attempt to follow her.

❦ ❦ ❦

Dimitri Aleynik liked strolling alone. He left Karl Helmut's chalet with the full intention of returning within the hour. Now as he ambled along, he heard voices on the trail ahead. He ducked behind the trees and listened.

It was Marta Zubkov, her soft voice easily recognized. How often he had heard her over the phone—her handler, his agent. She was a pawn in his hands, trained to obey on a minute's notice.

The man with her sounded mellow and muffled. Not Vronin nor Yuri. Where were they? He had insisted that they follow her every move. "Why bother?" Vronin had asked. "Her steps always lead back to Dr. Heppner's clinic."

No, they had to be wrong. Nicholas Trotsky had never trained as a doctor. But . . . Yes, he was clever enough. He had played many roles. Johann Heppner looked strong and muscular, an intelligent man behind the straggly beard and thick lenses—but he had a booming, explosive way of speaking.

The woman sounded persuasive now, and sudden rage grabbed hold of Dimitri. Marta Zubkov had always fascinated him. How often he had waited at the drop zones just to watch her, always longing to know her better. And days ago when he confronted her in her *pension* in Innsbruck, he had wanted her.

A clever, beautiful agent! Yet she had not known her own beauty. Her ignorance in this—her simple, unpretentious ways, her commitment to the party, those mythical Daedalian eyes glowing like a goddess one moment, frighteningly shrewish the next—had made her more appealing. At first Dimitri had been drawn to her silvery voice. Once he had seen her, he could picture her in his mind each time he called: long-lashed eyes smiling, slender fingers cradling the phone, the well-shaped, sensuous lips touching the mouthpiece. She had become his fantasy, his future. Another burst of rage engulfed him as he recalled picking up the music box in her apartment to challenge and test her, and when he let it shatter on the floor, he knew that she had always loved Nicholas Trotsky.

And now for the last two weeks she had deceived them

all, keeping Trotsky's identity well hidden. Letting him walk freely.

In the darkness someone walked away. But it was not Marta. Dimitri would know her shadowy form even here on the trails of Sulzbach. He stepped from the trees and stole to the wayside shrine. Marta had taken refuge on the bench. Alone. Desirable.

"Marta," Dimitri said.

A quartered moon slipped out from the cloud and unveiled the fear in her eyes. "Dimitri, what are you doing here?"

"You asked me that in Innsbruck."

"I'm asking you again. How did you find us?"

"Vronin sent word to me. A few shillings to Josef Petzold, and he was more than willing to send Vronin's message from the *postamt* in Brunnerwald."

The moon left them in darkness again, and he took a flashlight and shone it in her eyes. The long lashes blinked against the brightness as he said, "I sent you here to find Nicholas Trotsky."

"We're still looking."

"Vronin was right. You know. You can't be trusted." As his anger reached its peak, he hit her with the back of his hand.

"Where is he?"

Her head reared back. "Gone," she whispered.

This time he hit her with the flashlight, and she cried out in pain. As he brought it against the side of her face again, the light bulb went out.

She pulled free and ran from him down toward the embankment, stumbling toward the river. He caught her and threw her against the rocks.

His laughter rose above the bubbling water as she crawled away from him. He gave her a yard or two to reach the river and then was upon her again, tightening a wire against her mouth. "Where is he, Marta? Tell me where he is, and I won't hurt you anymore."

He loosened the wire, waiting for her answer. He could feel her blood on his hand as she mumbled, "He'll give you the plan if you go away."

If she had begged, he would have let her go free. The proud Marta Zubkov stayed defiant even as the wire cut into her mouth and tongue.

As Marta's fingers dug at the river's edge, Dimitri heard someone whistling as he buzzed toward them. The person was coming too fast to be walking. *One of the bikers.*

Marta lifted her head and cried out, "Help me. Get Heppner—"

Desperately, Dimitri demanded, "Where is Nicholas, Marta?"

The happy whistle came closer, filling the air.

When Marta still wouldn't answer him, Dimitri tightened the wire against her mouth and thrust her face into the water. She struggled, and suddenly she was still.

Dimitri washed his hands in the icy water and dried them on Marta's dress. When he looked up the embankment, he saw the biker waiting there. He lunged toward him as the bicyclist sped away.

Consetta Schrott heard the barn door creak and waited with heart pounding as the beam of a flashlight made its way toward her. The animals stirred, their tails swishing against the stalls. "Preben," she whispered, "you will have Grandfather out here."

"Hush," he said as he knelt down on their bedroll.

She tensed. He had never spoken so sharply to her. She sat up and glared at him in the moonlight that crept through the high window. He seemed only a form in the darkness. "Preben Schrott, it's past midnight. What have you been doing?"

He clamped his hand over her mouth, and she felt a stickiness against her lips. His fingers tightened, bruising the still painful wounds of a few days ago.

"I'm going to let you go, Consetta, but not a word."

She nodded as she tugged at his damp fingers. "What's on your hands?" she asked softly.

"Mud. I slipped on the trail coming back from Karl Helmut's."

She didn't believe him. "You promised to be back before dark. Why are these meetings lasting so long?"

"Can't you understand? All of this is for you. Sulzbach will be one of the most sought-after holiday places in the world."

"You'll ruin Sulzbach for the people here." She reached up and touched his cheek. "Dear Preben, you are doing all of this for yourself. The *gasthofs*. The ski lodge. You're the one who wants these. Sometimes I think you married me so you could control Sulzbach."

He turned to the wash bowl and pitcher. His hand shook as he filled the bowl and plunged his hands into the water. He washed as though they would never come clean.

She went barefoot over the hay and stood behind him, slipping her arms around his waist. "What's wrong, Preben?"

He trembled, his voice so husky that she feared for him. "I'm going back to Brunnerwald," he said.

"Not in the dark."

"I have to, Consetta. I must go for help." He freed himself from her grip and dried his hands. "I'll make it down. Nothing will happen to me. I must see my cousin."

"You wouldn't go to the *polizei* when I was beaten, and you go to them now?"

"You're still alive," he said miserably. "If I had gone then, maybe—"

It seemed as though her heart stood still, as though it missed not just one beat, but many. "What have you done, Preben?"

"Nothing." His strong fingers touched her lips. "Make some excuse in the morning and come back to Brunnerwald with Erika."

"I'll get dressed and go with you now."

"No. It's safer this way. Senn Burger and I will go together. We'll make it. When your grandmother asks you, tell her I went home right after supper."

"She won't believe me."

"You must make her believe you. No matter what happens, no one is to know I was here. Not the doctor. Not the priest."

"But Herr Helmut?"

"He'll keep quiet when he hears what happened at the river."

Preben leaned down and hugged her so tightly that again her heart missed a beat or two. As he pushed away, she could see the dark stain on his shirt. "You'd better change your shirt," she said. "And your jacket. I'll burn them."

"The jacket won't burn. Hide it."

He was gone before she could dress and flee with him. She watched him slip away, down the straw aisle that separated the stalls. The door creaked once more, and Preben was gone.

The tails of the animals stopped swishing. The moon hid behind a cloud. Blackness encircled the barn. Into the deathly stillness, a frightened voice asked, "Consetta, what has Preben done?"

Consetta ran toward her younger sister. They fell into each other's arms, and she held Erika against her. "Erika, we cannot tell anyone that Preben was here."

"But Father Caridini can help us."

"No," she said fiercely. "No one."

"Is Father Caridini in trouble?"

"Erika, don't say that."

"But you wanted to warn him. What has he done?"

"I don't know. I don't care. It's Preben I'm worried about."

She coaxed Erika to lie down on the bedroll cushioned by a mound of hay. She covered her with Preben's jacket. "We'll hide this in the morning," she whispered.

She found the strength to sing softly, and at last Erika slept. Consetta remained wide-eyed, terrified. At the first streaks of morning light, she picked up Preben's blood-stained shirt and went into the Schmid kitchen to burn it in the old woodstove. As it kindled, her grandfather Rheinhold came in and watched her. He said nothing as the odor of cloth and blood filled the room.

# Chapter 24

D rew came out of a groggy sleep at the persistent tapping at his open window. Fresh air was blowing in, the green shutters squeaking, a frightened voice calling, "Herr Gregory, Herr Gregory."

He stumbled barefoot across the room and stared into the breaking dawn, finally spotting Erika's thin body crouched against the wall of Frau Katwyler's house. "Erika, what are you doing here?"

"I have to talk to you."

At the urgency in her voice, he mellowed. "I'll be right out."

Drew grabbed his shirt and trousers from the bed post and pulled them on. He zipped his jacket on the way outside and was in a lighter mood by the time he reached her, still hunkered down by the wall. He put his hands gently on her bone-thin arms and helped her to her feet. "Now what's this all about?"

"Preben's in trouble," she whispered.

*Cocky, self-serving Preben?* "What kind of trouble, Erika?"

She pointed to the leather jacket hidden behind a bush. Even in the gray of the dawn, Drew saw the blood stains. *Preben's?* "Where is he, Erika? He might be hurt. I have to go to him."

"He went back to Brunnerwald in the dark."

"Alone? That's not safe."

"Consetta burned his shirt this morning. She told me to hide his jacket. Herr Gregory, something awful has happened, or he wouldn't have run away without taking Consetta with him."

He heard loathing in her voice for Preben, anxiety for her sister. Those dark, close-set eyes were wide with fear. If Drew rushed her—demanded answers—she would back away. "Erika, was Preben at the farm with you last evening?"

She shook her head, the straggly strands of ash-blonde hair swiping her cheek. "He didn't leave Herr Helmut's until midnight."

"And when did he get back to the farm?"

"Around then, I guess."

Helmut's place lay in the newer section of town. There was nothing between Helmut's and the isolated Schmid farm except the river and the wayside shrine. No homes and little chance that others would have been out at that hour.

"Erika, did Preben say what frightened him?"

"He just said that no one—absolutely no one—was to know that he went to Herr Helmut's house. Especially Father Caridini."

"Erika, go on to school. I'll take care of everything."

"I won't leave Consetta."

He struggled against the loyalties of Sulzbach. "Then go back to her. I'll try to find out what went on last night."

"You're going to Herr Helmut's?"

"Yes, but I'll stop off at the clinic first."

Erika grabbed Drew's wrist. "Don't tell the doctor. He's friends with Father Caridini."

"I know. But this has nothing to do with friendship. I need Dr. Heppner's help. You have to trust me, Erika. I'm a stranger in Sulzbach, and Dr. Heppner is still your mayor."

He turned her around and began walking with her toward the Petzolds and the Burgers with his arm gently around her shoulders. "I'll tell you what, Erika. We'll stop at the bakery."

Strands of hair swiped her cheek again as she vigorously opposed him. "I don't want to be seen with you."

She sprinted ahead, breaking into a run as she reached the Petzold bakery. He trudged along alone, his stomach growling from hunger, his mouth salivating at the smell of fresh bread.

"Herr Gregory," Olga called. "Come have coffee with me."

He took his coffee and sweet roll standing up. "I'm heading out to the Helmuts', Frau Petzold," he said.

"That's where Josef went. He was due back here long ago. I want him to sweep the shop before he goes to school. But let him out of your sight, and he finds a hundred things to do along the way."

"Most boys are that way," Drew said.

"If you see him, tell him to hurry."

Drew arrived moments later at the clinic and walked in through Johann Heppner's unlocked door. As he wandered inside, the German shepherd snarled but quieted at his master's command.

Johann sat at a table lined with half-empty glasses, but he was sober, clear-eyed, and alert this morning, his greeting cool as he said, "Gregory, is this a medical visit so early in the morning?"

"No, but possibly an emergency. Erika Schmid is worried about her brother-in-law."

"Not uncommon," he answered. "What is it this time?"

"Preben's bloody jacket." Drew thrust it on the table in front of the doctor. "What's your expert opinion? An animal?"

"Not likely." Johann put on his rimless glasses and then studied the jacket over the tops of them. "Maybe Consetta finally put him in his place with a bloody nose."

"Whatever frightened Preben occurred along the route between Herr Helmut's place and the Schmid farm."

"And you want my help?"

"You're still the mayor of Sulzbach, aren't you?"

Johann shoved back his chair. "Come on, Girl," he said to the dog. "Let's go for our walk."

He slipped into his warm jacket and picked up his medical bag and walking stick. As he strolled toward the door, he said, "I was going out to Helmut's place to see the old lady. Father Caridini takes Communion to her every day. I take pills. But Frau Helmut is dying anyway." He glanced over his shoulder. "We'll stop at the Schmids' on the way. Preben will have a simple explanation."

"Preben is in Brunnerwald."

The news displeased Heppner. He barreled ahead on the narrow trail. When they came to the cut-off point to the farm, they found Josef Petzold leaning against a tree vomiting. He was as white as a glacier, his socks and shoes sopping wet.

Behind him they heard the soft, rippling sounds of the salty brook. "I couldn't help her," he cried pointing toward the water.

A woman lay there, facedown, her body half-submerged, the contents of her purse lying on the muddy bank. The dog raced ahead of them down the embankment and plunged into the water. Girl nuzzled the body and then lifted her head into the air and growled pitifully as Drew and Johann dragged the woman from the water and turned her over. Her face was bloody and bloated, her mouth and tongue torn, but she was recognizable.

"That's Marta Zubkov," Drew said.

"First Peter Kermer and now this." Heppner dislodged a scrap of paper from her stiff fingers. "Looks like a name and phone number in London," he said handing it to Drew.

*Dudley Perkins!* The possibility of another Philby in the British ranks sickened Drew. "I'll take care of this," he said.

Heppner didn't seem to care. He peered at Josef over the rim of his glasses. "Get your father, Josef. Tell him there's been an accident. We need a stretcher to take this woman to the clinic."

"Is she—"

"She's dead, Josef."

The boy went up the embankment and ran, tripping and stumbling over his own feet. Heppner went on examining the body, carefully turning the head and pointing out the bruised markings on her neck.

"Apparently her friends play rough."

*Someone played rough,* Drew thought. Preben had been on this trail at midnight, but Marta was not a threat to Preben. No, only Father Caridini had reason to fear her.

As Drew picked up the contents of the purse, Heppner stood. "Tourists," he said in disgust. "This is what Preben and Senn Burger want. What they all want. They'll ruin Sulzbach."

"Do you want me to go for the priest?" Drew asked.

"Why? This woman wasn't Catholic. But it's best if you're not found here. Let me be the one to go by the Schmids' farm. When Consetta learns about this, she'll need something to calm her."

Drew walked away with his hands thrust into his pockets, one fist around Dudley's phone number, his thoughts on Trotsky's violent history. Trotsky was a sick man, too weak in Heppner's eyes to harm anyone. But had Marta stood in the way of the priest of Sulzbach? Or had her friendship with Kermer cost Marta her life?

Drew needed to get inside the rectory. He checked his watch. Nicholas would be making his morning rounds, and, with any luck, Frau Mayer would be out buying vegetables at one of the farms.

He rang just to be certain and heard the doorknob turning. "Oh, Herr Gregory. Father Caridini is not in, and I'm on my way to Frau Petzold's bakery."

He feigned disappointment. What if Nicholas was planning an escape? He had to get inside. "Perhaps I could wait for his return. I was hoping for some of your coffee and strudel."

She frowned. "I guess there's no harm in your coming in. You can wait in by the fire. I'll bring you something to eat." Her voice was still uncertain. "I'm sure Father Caridini won't mind."

He waited until Frau Mayer left the rectory, and then he sprang into action. He needed proof that Caridini and Trotsky were the same man—something more than his gut intuition. He ran his fingers along the shelves of the bookcase—volumes of theology, prayer books, devotional manuals, but no hidden safe. He checked again—nothing outside the religious life. Nothing political or secular. Nothing to read for pure enjoyment except a single book on the art of playing chess.

He eyed the desk and went to it, picking up books and papers on top and scanning them. There wasn't even a hint of clutter. Nicholas was a meticulous man. Drew tried the desk drawers. Locked. He forced them, finally opening the top drawer on the left. Filed neatly toward the back of the drawer was a single envelope marked: "To the people of Sulzbach."

Drew slit the envelope with the letter opener. His caution slipped away as he read the priest's hand-written confession. "I am dying," the letter began.

For a minute Drew considered not intruding into the priest's private world, but inside he knew that this was Nicholas Trotsky's confession. The queasiness in the pit of his stomach dipped to utter disgust, the revulsion so intense that he was only aware of someone entering the room when a gust of wind blew across the floor.

"Herr Gregory, do you always read other people's mail?" Johann Heppner asked from the doorway.

"Only when I'm looking for answers."

"And did you find them?" Heppner asked coldly.

Drew nodded, silenced for the moment.

"When did you first suspect?"

"The day after I arrived in Sulzbach—the day I came here to see Father Caridini."

"And found a stranger in his place?"

"I was puzzled at first," Drew admitted. "Until I talked with Frau Katwyler and visited the cemetery behind the church. I waited too long to take him down the mountain. Two people dead already."

"And you think Nicholas killed them? Look at him, Gregory. There's no strength in him. He's a dying man."

"That's what this letter says, but, Heppner, I'm going to take Nicholas Trotsky down to Brunnerwald and on to Paris. We'll hold him accountable for everything he's done."

"Don't. Nicholas's cancer may have spread to the brain."

"Oh, of course, Dr. Heppner. Give him a medical excuse."

Heppner met Drew's angry gaze. "It's all in Dr. Eschert's report."

"Eschert?"

"Deiter Eschert, Father Caridini's surgeon in Innsbruck. The disease has definitely gone to his bones, and the brain scan showed some questionable markings."

"Does Caridini know this?"

"Eschert spared him that. Nicholas is an intelligent man. The thought of losing control of his mind would have been too devastating—devastating for any of us, Herr Gregory."

"Doctor, how long have you known who he really is?"

"Fifteen years."

Drew parted the curtain and tracked the path of the old avalanche with a quick gaze. "You were his doctor?"

"And yours—immediately following the plane crash. I was washed out as a surgeon in Innsbruck. My drinking had cost me a successful career and my wife. I came back here to drink myself to death, and then I realized that I could use my training here in Sulzbach. You and Nicholas were two of my first successes."

"And Nicholas went right on deceiving the people of Sulzbach with you knowing it all along? You're as guilty as he is."

"Nicholas never knew I was his doctor. I tended him in the first crucial days when his life hung in balance. And for a few more weeks when he barely knew I was there. It didn't take me long to figure he wasn't the kind of person we wanted in Sulzbach. I wanted to turn you both over to the authorities, but you had gone, Gregory. And Jacques Caridini insisted that he would continue to care for the remaining foreigner—and treat Nicholas as a brother."

"And then the whole charade began?"

"It was more than a year before that happened. Nicholas had a severe back fracture. I wasn't sure he would ever walk again. I—I really thought he'd die, and I wanted him to."

"But you stood by when he got rid of the real Father Caridini."

"Is that what you think? No. No. Father Jacques died of a massive heart attack, and Nicholas tried his best to save him. He put on Jacques's clerical robe and ran—well, as best he could with that back of his—for help. In the excitement when the people asked him who he was, he said, "Father Caridini's brother."

The wheels turned for Drew. "That's what Father Jacques called me."

"Yes, but the people misunderstood. They thought that was why Jacques had taken care of Nicholas for such a long time. They thought they really were brothers and that the brothers were both priests. The people begged Nicholas to stay on."

Heppner's face seem caught in a permanent frown. "Your plane crash and the avalanche happened so close together that I was the only one who knew how Nicholas came to the village. Nicholas was clever. He promised the people that he'd take care of all the paperwork surrounding Jacques's death with the archbishop in Vienna. You can guess the rest."

Drew glanced at the dying embers in the fireplace. He was certain that the paperwork had turned to ashes there.

"Nicholas needed a way out, Gregory. I don't think he ever intended to stay here long. The priesthood offered him a good cover. After all, he'd actually been a seminarian once."

*The missing three years in my file,* Drew thought.

"You learn a lot when a man's running a high fever and only semiconscious. I pumped him for answers in those first few days of his delirium." There was no triumph in Johann's voice as he said, "The seminary was part of his Russian training, part of an initial plan to spread their terrorism through the church. Nicholas figured he'd leave Sulzbach as soon as he had the strength to do so."

"And you just stood by and let it all happen?"

Johann smiled. "I began playing chess with him back then, trying to trap him. Over the months I saw him change. I don't remember when he stopped playing the role that made him so fascinating to me as a doctor." Johann rubbed his beard making a crackling sound in the empty room. "He made a marvelous psychiatric study for me. I thought him quite mad. I had no concept of God performing some miracle in Nicholas's life. Then I realized one night over a chess game that we had become friends."

"Johann, you had every opportunity to turn him over to the Austrian *polizei.*"

"For what? I had no proof that he was a Russian agent, and I saw no need to expose him as a fake priest. That was a matter for the church, not my concern. He had no idea that I was aware of his past. His plane had crashed in my village—that was all."

"My single-engine plane."

"What does it matter, Gregory? The avalanche disintegrated it like a toy plane. Nicholas found a new life here. The people of Sulzbach liked him. That was good enough for me. Nicholas deceived them, yes—but he saw to their needs over the years. He visits them, prays for them, takes them Communion."

"Nothing but penitence, day after day, year after year."

"Mr. Gregory, I believe you're a harder man than Nicholas. What's it going to take to soften your heart?" He shrugged. "I didn't have many friends, Gregory. Didn't want them. My grudge was with life. And it was Nicholas, the new Father Caridini, who encouraged me to head up the ski patrol and put my training as a physician back into daily practice."

Johann's eyes smiled. "Nicholas gave me the dog one Christmas. Girl, I call her. And he gave me something else— he gave me back my self-respect. If I turned him in, I'd have no close friend left. No one to squirrel away the nights over a chessboard. Girl and I are going to be lonely when Nicholas dies."

Drew eased into one of the cushioned chairs facing the chessboard. But the game he was playing was with the Austrian standing stonily by the fireplace. "Johann," he said, "I am going to take Nicholas down the mountain with me tomorrow."

"You don't seem to understand, Herr Gregory. The people of Sulzbach will stop you."

"But he's a Russian agent. A sleeper."

"An agent-in-place? Here in Sulzbach? Gregory, do you

think the people would believe you? To them he is their priest. He's been their confidant, their comforter in illness. He's blessed the newborns, buried the dead."

"And played chess with you, Doctor—a clever, crafty game."

"You make it sound like I've been nothing but a pawn in his hands."

"He'll use anyone to reach his goals."

"You've got the wrong man, Gregory. Nicholas doesn't have an unkind fiber in his body. No, you'll never take him away. You'll see. Even Preben Schrott would block your way in Brunnerwald. Preben is politically important there, too. But as overbearing as he is, he won't let you harm Nicholas in any way. Preben respects the friendship between Nicholas and Consetta."

Drew's exasperation mounted. "Dr. Heppner, you've got to help me. Trotsky has been a sleeper in place all along, hiding out here in Sulzbach. He's a dangerous man."

"He's a dying man. He doesn't have the strength to walk down that mountain again."

"Then we'll carry him."

"You're a fool, Gregory. You'd ruin the lives of so many people and rob them of their hope and faith just to capture one man."

"That one man has the power to destroy the fragile peace in Russia."

Heppner roared with laughter. "He could barely play chess last night."

"If you don't believe me, Johann, then ask Father Caridini about the revival of the PHOENIX PLAN. Ask him what it will do to Yeltsin's government and the world if the old guard takes over there."

"You make Father Caridini sound like some merciless revolutionary."

"He was, and as far as I know, still is. Trotsky embraced communism and all that it stood for."

"I think you'd better leave Sulzbach, Gregory. Now."

"Not without Trotsky. You've been worried about the guests at Frau Burger's place, and well might you be. I don't know which side of the PHOENIX PLAN they're on, but they're here to take Trotsky back to Russia. Two of them have died for it already."

Drew saw a flicker of alarm light in the doctor's rugged face. "Next you'll tell me the bikers were planted here, too."

"They were. By British Intelligence." Drew scored a point. "Why do you think there's been this sudden onslaught of tourists in Sulzbach? A dozen intelligence agencies perhaps."

Again Drew scored; Heppner seemed to crumble under the truth. "Doctor, the people of Sulzbach are in danger with this influx of strangers. These men will stop at nothing. Peter Kermer's death should have been your first warning."

"We listed that as an accident."

"Was it? Did Caridini tell you to say that? We can still save face for you, Heppner. I'll take Nicholas quietly. You can tell the people that he had to go back to the hospital. They don't have to know the truth."

He watched Johann wavering. "According to the rumors circulating in the village, Father Caridini was the last one to see Kermer alive, Johann. Kermer was a threat to Nicholas. I think Nicholas pushed him over the cliff."

"You're wrong," Nicholas said coming into the room.

The priest looked even thinner, his color ashen white like his Roman collar. His hands drooped at his sides, a surprisingly strong grip on the Luger in his right hand. Drew had no doubt that in spite of that weakened body, Nicholas Trotsky would still have his assassin's accuracy.

"How long have you known who I was, Gregory?" he asked.

"At first it seemed too impossible to believe."

"That's what's wrong with the Western mind," Trotsky said. "You tend to trust too much. That's how I won with you, Gregory. I could always outwit you because you were bound by integrity."

Johann stared helplessly at his friend. "Say no more, Nicholas. You're still the priest in this village."

"It's over, Johann." He turned back to Drew.

"I even trained for the priesthood. Did Johann tell you that, Gregory? But I only had three years as a seminarian."

"The missing three years."

"The hole in your CIA file, Herr Gregory."

"We knew you would reappear. But why this charade?"

"It was all part of the plan," he said sadly. "We'd take over Russia, and we'd find a foothold in the Vatican."

"Was the Pope your target?"

"Yes, eventually. Until I had trouble at my seminary—questions over my doctrinal beliefs. Or lack of them. Boris Jankowski and Colonel Kavin decided it was safer to call me back to Moscow. And so I resumed my job of taking out some of the top political figures in the world."

Johann stared at his friend. "You killed men for a living?"

Johann's contempt startled Nicholas. His expression caved in, a look of regret and grief taking over. "Since coming to Sulzbach, I have tried not to think of my past—to put Nicholas Trotsky from my life entirely. In these last few years I've learned that one can be forgiven. But you cannot erase the past. And it's too late to tell those men I'm sorry."

Drew steeled himself before he ended up believing Trotsky's sincerity. Nicholas had stooped to a low level as far as Drew was concerned, using the church as a cover and blatantly tampering with people's souls.

Johann tugged at his beard hopelessly. "All these years, Nicholas, I've kept your secret. I saw good in you and now—" Johann couldn't find the words to rebuke his friend. "Gregory tells me you've been an agent-in-place all this time, that you're still working with the Russians. Tell me it's not true."

"Johann, I would be a liar if I told you I had not considered working with them again. After all, the PHOENIX PLAN was my idea from the beginning. But I was not sent here by the KGB. I was not an agent-in-place. Never a Russian sleeper." The corner of his mouth turned up. "Gregory here brought me to Sulzbach. After the accident when I couldn't walk, still I planned to return to my country and lead the rebellion."

"You've used me, used my friendship?"

"No, my friend. I've been content here as the priest of Sulzbach."

"Until Marta Zubkov came?" Heppner asked.

"When I saw Marta, I realized how much communism has destroyed her. I couldn't go back to that, not for all the glory in Russia. Not when I have found God's peace here in this village."

"Nothing could persuade you?" Drew mocked.

"Marta tried, Gregory. And now I must protect her at all costs."

"Nicholas," Drew said, "Marta is dead."

He stared at them. His facial muscles collapsed, and the old Trotsky of moments ago fell like shackles from his wrists. "No. No. No. Not Marta." He staggered across the room toward the door.

"Don't go, Nicholas," Drew told him. "She's not a pretty sight. Or perhaps you didn't notice that in the darkness."

Heppner gripped the priest's arm and eased him into a chair.

"No," Nicholas protested. "Let me go to her."

Johann took the Luger from his hand. "Gregory's right. It's best if you don't go. She was badly beaten."

"You followed her to the river," Drew accused.

"But she was alive when I left her. Marta insisted on sitting at the wayside shrine so she could be alone. I came back to the rectory for my game of chess with Johann."

"And were you on time?" Drew asked.

"He was fifteen minutes late," Heppner said.

In disgust Drew said, "The PHOENIX PLAN was always your dream, wasn't it, Colonel Trotsky?"

"It was a good plan." His eyes glowed. "Don't you understand? It was all for the glory of the Soviet Union."

"With a little bit of glory thrown in for you, too."

"This morning when I went to the chapel, I knew that it was wrong to let the PHOENIX PLAN ever rise from the ashes. I knew I couldn't go back to my old life."

"'Almost thou persuadest me,'" Drew mocked.

"Believe what you want, sir. But I was going to ask Erika's grandfather to take Marta down to Brunnerwald hidden in his milk wagon. That's why I followed her last night—to tell her my new plan. Marta had an important contact in London. I was going to ask Preben to get in touch with him and get Marta to safety."

"Were you planning to go with her?" Johann asked.

"No, as soon as Marta was safe, I was going over to Frau Burger's and identify myself to Vronin and Yuri. I have nothing to lose. I am already dying. I was confident that they'd have me out of Sulzbach and on my way to Moscow before my people knew."

"You don't know your people then," Johann said. "Oh, yes, Rheinhold Schmid would have done what you asked. But he's a wise old man—and your friend besides. He would alert the people. You are still their priest, and they would do anything to protect you."

Tears made rivulets over Nicholas's bristly face. "I want Marta buried in the cemetery, Johann. Will you do that for me?"

"She's not Catholic."

"She was nothing, Johann. Last night I spoke to her again and tried to tell her what I had learned about God here in Sulzbach. She only laughed at me and said, 'You're a Communist, Nicholas, as I am.' And then she left me."

He found the strength to push himself from the chair. "Take me to her, Johann. Take me to Marta."

# Chapter 25

At the gate to the Saint Francis Cemetery, Johann Heppner put a restraining hand on Drew's shoulder. "Have the decency to let Nicholas bury her himself. Give him that much solitude."

"And risk him getting away and warning others?"

"And how do you propose that? He doesn't have the strength to scale that stone wall. Believe me, Gregory, Nicholas has no need to warn them now that Marta Zubkov is dead."

Nicholas walked on, blinded to their presence, a strangely pathetic man in a flowing robe, his hands clasped in front of him, his thumbs lodged on a prayer book. He stopped in the far corner of the cemetery near the freshly dug grave and the shiny mahogany box that Senn Burger had constructed. It was closed, nailed shut on Johann's orders, and carried to the graveyard in Schmid's milk wagon, with few villagers even aware of the tragedy.

They gave Nicholas space to be alone, standing a few feet behind him as he intoned the liturgy—words that Drew had once believed as a boy and Johann had never heeded. Words that Marta had never even heard. A squally gust of wind swept down through the mountain pass, whipping against Nicholas's robe and wrapping the white clerical gown against his spindly legs.

The solemnity touched a kindly cord in Drew. He tried to recall the proud arrogant stance of Colonel Nicholas

Trotsky, the powerful muscles, the rigid expression. Instead, he saw only a lonely priest hunched forward, wisps of his thin, gray hair ruffled by the wind. Nicholas was younger than Drew, but he had aged considerably in illness—and even more in these last few hours in the simple act of grieving—of burying the woman he had once loved. Perhaps still loved.

Father Caridini stood, a man to be pitied—Colonel Trotsky, a man to be dealt with. As Drew struggled with the duty that lay ahead and the reports he would send on to Paris and Langley, the peace that Caridini had found in measure here in Sulzbach eluded him. He had no qualms about stripping Trotsky of his rank and power or even of sending him to death as a spy, but to defrock a priest went against Drew's boyhood teachings.

Johann stirred beside him, looking uncomfortable and out of place at a funeral. Drew knew that Johann Heppner would protect the priest for the sake of an old friendship, for the sake of the people of Sulzbach, in spite of his agnostic principles.

Drew tried to block out the faces of Sulzbach: Frau Katwyler and Olga Petzold, Frau Mayer and Josef. He had to put a distance to his friendship with the Schmid family, especially Erika. If they knew that Nicholas would be defrocked—deprived of the clothes he had no right to wear—they would suffer. And they would point their fingers at Drew Gregory.

Here on this mountaintop he was torn between the code of honor—his commitment to the Agency—and the demand for integrity ingrained in him as a boy. Commotion on the other side of the wall caught his attention. From the corner of his eye he saw Alekos, Ian Kendall's friend, peering over the wall, standing, no doubt, on his bike.

Something soured in Drew's stomach. Alekos had been making friends with the guests at the Burgers' place. The boy was too curious, too aware of what was going on in the village of Sulzbach, and too ignorant to realize that his own life was in danger. Vronin and Yuri would not leave any witnesses behind.

Their gaze held fast, Alekos's dark eyes meeting his. Drew tried to warn him off with a cold stare. Slowly Alekos's bronzed face and long fingers slipped from view.

"Fool kid," Johann whispered.

"Yes, I'll talk to him later." He'd have to contact Ian Kendall and his friends and send them on the race of their life, pedaling at high speed out of Sulzbach back to Brunnerwald and London before something happened to them.

The brief ceremony had come to a close. Suddenly the priest dropped on his knees by the open grave, weeping. Drew and Johann ran to him and put their strong hands beneath his armpits and lifted Nicholas back to his feet. As Johann brushed the smudges of dirt from his tunic, Nicholas's flicker of gratitude evaporated. He pushed them away, the old strength of Colonel Trotsky taking over. "Give me a shovel," he demanded.

Johann nodded to the three men by the fence. "No, Nicholas. Senn Burger and Manfred Petzold will tend to that for you. And Herr Schmid if you'll let him. He feels strong enough."

Another faint smile touched Nicholas's chalk-white lips. "Members of your ski patrol. Yes, thank them for me."

He walked ahead of them toward the rectory, refusing their support. When he reached the gate, he stopped. "I want the person who killed her, Johann."

"We're not certain—"

*Preben?* Drew wondered. *Would Johann mention Preben?*

Nicholas's face seemed rigid and empty, the way Trotsky's had always been, his voice cold and determined as he said, "I'll start with the strangers in the village."

"Leave that to me," Heppner told him.

Nicholas smiled, that crooked twist of his face that would fool his friend, like a final move on the chessboard.

*You know, don't you, Nicholas?* Drew thought. *In that well-disciplined mind of yours, you've narrowed it down to one man, one of three: Yuri, Vronin, or that third man staying at Herr Helmut's chalet. You intend to ferret out Marta's killer. I intend to keep an eye on you until morning.*

Drew touched the prayer book in Nicholas's hand.

"Colonel Trotsky, I'm going to take you back to Brunnerwald in the morning. If you have anything you must do before we leave the village, any farewell words for any of them—"

"Are we going in a single-engine plane this time?" Nicholas asked, amused, scornful.

"On foot."

Johann's fury exploded. "Use your head, Gregory. Nicholas doesn't have the physical strength left to harm anyone. He's dying."

"Yes, I know. You've told me several times already. But for the safety of this village, I'm turning him in. We want to plug the dikes and keep the PHOENIX PLAN from breaking through again and destroying us all."

Johann jabbed Drew. "The people of Sulzbach will stop you from taking him away. We don't give one hoot about your PHOENIX PLAN."

"You will when you find that Father Caridini is running it from the parish. Your lack of interest threatens the free world."

Nicholas lifted a hand, a smooth palm extended toward the doctor. "Gregory is right, Johann. If I go willingly—and take the strangers with me—the people here will be safe."

Johann whipped off his glasses. "And when they find out—when the truth shatters their faith—what then, Father Caridini? You and this American agent will both be gone. You have no right to run off and rob these people of their faith in their God."

An amused twinkle lit the priest's tired eyes. "Johann, perhaps it is your faith that is at risk."

He patted Johann's shoulder, the grip becoming so strong that he seemed to be leaning on his old friend. "Someone will come along to play chess with you, my friend. Now—I must take Herr Gregory's advice. I'll tidy up my affairs. And then," he added sadly, "I will pay my debt to society."

When they reached the rectory door, Frau Mayer stood timidly in front of them, Erika at her side. She touched Nicholas's hand. "Father Caridini," she whispered, "it's Frau Schmid. She's having chest pains—she's asking for you."

"Then I better go to her," Johann offered.

"No, Doctor. Frau Schmid is an old woman. Your medicine won't help her kind of pain. She wants Father Caridini."

Something changed in the priest's face—a warm look of compassion filled his countenance. He ran the back of his hand gently across Erika's cheek. "So the Grandmama is sick?"

Erika could only nod, the weight on her narrow shoulders almost more than she could bear.

"Gentlemen," Nicholas said, "I must go to her."

Drew and Johann stepped aside. "Of course," Drew said.

"She wants Communion, Father," Erika told him shyly. "She didn't get to mass this morning."

*Did anyone?* Drew wondered.

Nicholas went briskly down the walk, his height shortened by those bent shoulders, his cassock swishing around his ankles. His steps slowed by the time he passed the cemetery, but Erika waited for him, and as he reached her, she slipped her hand into his.

Drew zipped up his jacket. "Johann, I intend to move my things over to the rectory. I'll keep watch here tonight."

"Nicholas won't try to escape. Not now. I think he sees surrender as a final act of penitence."

Drew thought of Robyn's theology, of Pierre's strong faith in God. "It's not needed," he said. "As my son-in-law would say, forgiveness is forgiveness."

"But my friend's conscience may not know that, Gregory. No, I assure you, Nicholas Caridini will not try to escape."

*But would Nicholas Trotsky?* "No," he agreed with Johann. "I'm more worried about protecting Nicholas. Someone has already killed two people." *You perhaps, Doctor,* Drew thought. "Whoever it was may strike again. For Nicholas's safety, we'll try to be off by dawn."

"Then I'll come by tonight for a last game of chess." As Johann rubbed his jaw, the freckled fingers locked with his bushy whiskers, and Drew was certain that Johann flicked a tear away.

🔯🔯🔯

Dimitri Aleynik stood boldly in front of the bakery, not even trying to hide his binoculars. In his two days in Sulzbach he had frequently been seen studying the scenery with field glasses. Now he leveled them on a flock of birds scattering from the trees in the cemetery.

He smiled to himself. Someone was burying Marta Zubkov.

"Good morning," Frau Petzold said. "You're quite a bird-watcher, the people say. As the weather warms up a bit more, the village will be full of them. But the barn swallows are back nesting in the barns already."

"I saw one at the Schmids' yesterday."

"Talk to Dr. Heppner. He knows the name for every fine-feathered bird that comes to Sulzbach."

Dimitri could believe that. Heppner's wary gaze didn't miss a thing. He might welcome the birds, but he was cool to strangers invading his village—and well guarded by that snarling German shepherd. The doctor's nightly toddy might relax him, but it didn't dim his curiosity about newcomers in Sulzbach. Fortunately, Dimitri decided, the doctor's love of wine and chess and a nightly whiskey kept him from the wayside shrine last evening.

"Please, have you had your coffee?" Olga Petzold asked.

"What? Oh, yes. *Danke Schön.*" He lifted the binoculars again and focused on the cemetery across the street. "I think there's a funeral going on," he said.

"Impossible. No one has died. Unless—" She looked utterly distressed now. "Unless old Frau Helmut died."

"Someone did," he said calmly. "The wood carver was nailing a coffin together an hour ago."

She rushed in a flurry back into her bakery. He was glad to be shunt of her as he watched the Grecian cyclist stand on the seat of his bike and stare over the cemetery wall.

Satisfied, Dimitri hurried on to the Burgers' place. He brushed Vronin's questions aside and went to the window and lifted his field glasses in time to see Alekos drop from the cemetery wall. Alekos seemed in a rush now as he put on his helmet, hopped on his bike, and pedaled straight toward the Burgers' house.

"Alekos is on his way," Dimitri announced.

"But Marta is not back yet. She's been gone the whole night."

"Forget about Marta. They just lowered her into the sod."

"Dead?" Yuri exclaimed.

"People do die, Yuri. Don't they, Vronin?"

Vronin's eyes narrowed. "Dimitri, what have you done to her?"

"What you refused to do. You took her into your confidence, Vronin, and told her too much about Trotsky and the Phoenix-40."

"She and Kermer asked questions. They guessed mostly."

"That was a foolish alliance. I sent the four of you here to work together—to find Trotsky and to test his loyalties."

"Were they in question?" Vronin asked.

"After fifteen years of silence? Yes. I doubted Moscow's wisdom of having him lead a powerful new splinter group."

"A breakaway from the PHOENIX PLAN?" Yuri asked.

"Something more deadly and venomous. A perfect plan."

As Alekos leaned his bike against a hedge and knocked, Vronin asked, "Why is he helping us? He risks our safety."

"Alekos wants to wear the yellow jersey at the Tour de France. But Kendall is the one expected to win for the Gainsborough team."

"Who cares?" Vronin asked.

"Alekos does. I promised him some contacts in the cycling world in exchange for his cooperation here."

"Bribery will disqualify him, Dimitri."

"There's no money exchanged. Just favors." Dimitri smiled and opened the door. "We've been expecting you, Alekos."

"I can't stay. My friends are asking—"

He yanked Alekos inside and saw the first glimmer of fear in the boy's dark eyes. Alekos was a solidly built, broad-shouldered, young man, his present weight against him winning the yellow jersey. His facial features looked blunt, his lips too thick, his black hair held in place with a sweet-smelling spray.

"What went on over there?" Dimitri asked.

"A funeral." The boy's courage was returning, his arms folded against his thick sweater. "They buried that woman—the one that got killed at the river last night."

"You heard them say that?"

"No. I saw it happen. I was riding in from Schmids' place." He gloated over his knowledge. "Erika wanted to ride my bike, so her grandmother had me stay for supper. It was late when I got away."

"Was the woman at the Schmids'?" Dimitri demanded.

"No. I didn't see her at first. But I saw the priest—I think it was him—kind of shuffling off, and then I heard the woman scream." His voice ebbed. "I couldn't get to her in time."

"Alekos, did the priest kill her?"

The thought shook him into reverse. Fear replaced the budding confidence. "No. Not a priest. It couldn't be him. I heard her scream after he walked away. It had to be someone else."

*Someone else like me,* Dimitri thought.

"But why a hush-hush funeral, Dimitri?" Vronin asked. "These people do things as a community."

"Not this time. Who was at the funeral, Alekos?"

"Father Caridini and the American tourist. Erika's grandpa and a couple of other grave diggers; Herr Burger was one of them."

"That's reasonable. I saw him preparing a coffin earlier."

"And the doctor was there."

"I told you, Dimitri," Vronin said angrily. "That's Trotsky."

"Vronin's right," Yuri agreed. "Marta contacted the doctor several times since we've been here."

"Three times, Yuri."

"And at the rectory once and at the bakery yesterday."

Alekos's voice was brittle as he said, "She was at the doctor's clinic yesterday when I was treated for a saddle rash. The priest was there—said my rash goes with the territory for cyclists. Miss Zubkov arrived as the priest left."

Ryskov hit the palm of his hand with his fist. "The doctor. Like we told you, Dimitri. It's the doctor."

"You fools. Who was there every time Marta saw Heppner?"

Vronin's countenance soured as the truth hit him. "Father Caridini. *Nicholas* Caridini."

"Nicholas *Trotsky*," Dimitri said. "Marta knew all along."

"Mr. Aleynik, I heard the American tell the priest that he's taking him down to Brunnerwald in the morning." Alekos backed to the door. "My friends and I plan to leave Sulzbach, too, so I can't help you anymore."

He slipped through the door before Dimitri could stop him.

Dimitri swore. "I'll be back, Vronin. I'm going to follow Alekos. He's in too deep. You two go on down to Brunnerwald. I want you out of here before Trotsky puts everything together."

"Are we taking him with us?"

"I think Herr Gregory will take care of that for us. And quite nicely with no problem from these people." He tightened the belt of his trench coat.

"Don't we get rid of Gregory? He's American Intelligence."

"No, we'll use him. When he reaches the foot of the mountain tomorrow with Trotsky, you'll be waiting. I don't care what you do with Gregory then, but get Nicholas Trotsky to Marta's *pension* in Innsbruck as quickly as you can. I'll deal with him there."

# Chapter 26

For an hour Drew trekked through the village and then hiked out on the main trail trying to find Kendall and his friends. Now he considered taking the seldom-used avalanche trails, wondering whether the crazy kids had risked riding in a zone where loose gravel and the still-melting snows could plunge them to their deaths. As he struck out for that higher elevation, he heard a familiar voice behind him saying, "Well, Drew. There you are."

When he turned around, he was eye-level with his son-in-law, Pierre Courtland. Pierre eased his backpack to the ground and dropped down on it—his dark hair wind-tossed, his cheeks ruddy from the climb. "You're a hard man to find, Drew," he said.

"I wasn't planning on being found."

"I figured as much, but Vic Wilson put it together for me. He said you crashed a plane on this mountain around the time of the Sulzbach Avalanche. It was the last time you saw Trotsky."

"Wilson talks too much."

Drew brushed off a large rock and sat down beside his son-in-law. "Pierre, is something wrong at home?"

"Robyn and Miriam are fine. But Vic Wilson is worried about you being up here alone. His worry is contagious, so I came to take you home. Your mission here is not my business, but your safety is."

"I still have unfinished business." Solemnly Drew

pointed to the barren ridge to the right of the old avalanche. "That's about where I crashed fifteen years ago."

A sudden wind off the Alps sent shivers down Drew's spine. "It's not your problem, Pierre. You'd better leave now. Night closes in quickly here."

Pierre allowed his sweeping hand to encompass the calm, pristine setting around them. "This tranquility may blow any minute, so I'm not leaving you until Vic Wilson gets here."

"I still say Wilson talks too much. Where is he?"

"He doubled back to Innsbruck with Brad O'Malloy. They plan to talk to Lyle Spincrest. Seems like Spincrest ran into a bit of trouble on the mountain—broke his tibia in a skiing lesson."

"That wouldn't take Vic back to Innsbruck. So what's up?"

"He's been nosing around, flying to Paris and Zurich and back to London doing a little file-searching himself. Then he met me in Brunnerwald, and we had a little run-in at the cheese factory."

"With Preben Schrott?"

"That's his name. Vic got a little overwrought when Schrott wouldn't tell us where you were. So he used a bit of muscle to persuade him. Hanging over a cheese vat loosened Schrott's tongue."

"That's dangerous."

"It paid off." Pierre picked up a stone and tossed it into space. "Vic said to tell you the man you are looking for was hospitalized at Landeskrankenhaus recently. Same place that Spincrest is staying. Vic's checking it out."

They rode an uneasy silence before Pierre said, "Vic wants you to get out of here or stay low until he arrives. He can be here by tomorrow or the day after."

"He'd be the last one to run. Why should I?"

Pierre's frown was disconcerting. "Because the Agency hasn't given you all the facts. Vic says Trotsky is part of the old PHOENIX PLAN, and that's bigger than you trying to take in one man."

"One of Vic's old riddles. Did he say anything else?"

"Said you were an old believer in things rising from the

ashes—an old hand at deadly uprisings. He doesn't seem to trust you to wait for his arrival, and he definitely doesn't trust Troy Carwell in Paris. So what's this Phoenix business?"

Drew breathed in the heady scent of the fresh mountain air, taking in Pierre's same unobscured view of the towering mountain ranges, their grand old peaks cloud-free at the moment. He had to be honest with Pierre or risk a bigger political barrier between them. "It's a plan to return Russia to the iron-handed leadership of men like Khrushchev," he said.

He traced Pierre's thoughtful gaze as it shifted from the terraced hillsides alive with Alpine pansies toward the plunging waterfalls cascading from the higher slopes.

"Drew, is Yeltsin and his government involved?"

"No. In spite of that trouble in the Chechnya region, Yeltsin is for reform and democracy. This PHOENIX PLAN is a splinter group from the old hard-liners."

"With Trotsky right in the middle of it?"

"He was."

"Dead?"

"Dying. I located him the day after I got here."

"You've been here a week and haven't taken him in?"

"No. I had to have proof. What I thought was preposterous, but Trotsky's been hiding behind the garb of a village priest. I couldn't just walk into the parish and say, 'Pardon me, Father Caridini, isn't your name really Colonel Nicholas Trotsky?'"

He risked trusting Pierre more. "I've got opposition. At least three Russian agents and an MI5 lookout. Several other strangers have arrived in the last week. And if I take Trotsky, as I plan to do, I'll have a whole village rising up against me."

"You've had enemies before. I'm a good shot, Drew. Thanks to the Swiss army. Is that manpower enough?"

"It's not just the villagers at risk, Pierre. Uriah Kendall's grandson is in the area with three of his cycling friends. They're building up endurance for the Tour de France, but I don't think Ian's arrival here is coincidental."

"Does he know who you are?"

"He was just a boy when Miriam and I separated. But I'm certain he recognized me in Brunnerwald. He's avoiding me here."

"Does he worry you?"

"I'm keeping my eye on him. We've met at the bakery a couple of times. He's a good cyclist. No wonder Uriah's proud of him."

"Drew, I ran into a young cyclist on my way here. Dark skin, black hair, sullen young man. Acted like he didn't trust me."

"That would be Alekos Golemis. Orlando is cheerful."

"When I asked for directions to Sulzbach, he sent me off on the wrong trail. I had to backtrack for over an hour."

"Deliberately?"

"That's the way I read it. I didn't see anyone else, but he acted like he was avoiding someone." Pierre pointed toward the avalanche trails. "He was heading that way when I last saw him—just above the village."

"Pierre, go back home. The more incoming traffic, the more chance there is that some of the strangers in Sulzbach will smell danger and disappear again."

"Sorry. I'm in the area on a business trip, Drew. I can stretch it a couple more days until Vic joins you."

"I'm leaving here in the morning."

"Then I'll stay over and go back with you." He stood and put on his backpack. "The view is spectacular, isn't it? I grew up with the Alps at my back door—with Germany and Switzerland as my playground. But this view! You should bring Miriam here someday."

"She'd like it," Drew agreed. "But I'll make certain we come in June or July when the weather is warmer and the roses are out."

"Red ones," Pierre teased.

"Any color, as long as Miriam can pick a rose for my lapel." Their bantering over, he asked, "Did Miriam get off safely?"

"Right on schedule. And she's back again. She persuaded your brother to fly back to Zurich to face the charges against him."

Drew felt sick. "Will the charges against Aaron hold?"

"My uncle questions it."

"Is that his opinion or Interpol's?"

"My uncle's. He still says they won't have enough against Aaron with Smith and Ingrid von Tonner both dead and Miriam refusing to testify against him. Aaron vows that he didn't know that Ingrid von Tonner had flooded Miriam's gallery with those fraudulent paintings. Your brother may be telling the truth."

"That isn't one of Aaron's strong points."

"Well, Robyn is salvaging something good out of it all. She's going to pull off one of the best art museums of our time."

"I know and I'm proud of her."

"Me too, Drew. As confused as Baron von Tonner is, Robyn and Felix can sit for hours talking about the portrait paintings of Van Dyck and Van der Weyden or of the work of Rembrandt."

His voice caught for a moment. "Robyn has done so much for Felix. I think he understands that she is planning a Baron von Tonner Museum there at the mansion. And if his dull eyes say anything, they say, 'Yes, Robyn. That's a good plan.'"

Drew massaged his aching temples. "And all I can think of is how Aaron almost destroyed that collection."

"Not by himself."

Drew ignored Pierre's comment. "So what does Aaron get for his part in it? A couple of years in prison?"

"Eighteen months minimal. More if the courts here have their way. And all he ever wanted was to outwit his older brother."

"Half-brother," Drew corrected.

"You never let him forget that, do you?"

Drew broke off a blade of grass. "Big-brother rivalry."

"You're still brothers."

"The old bloodline, eh? I know Miriam wants the Gregory brothers to be friends. She may forgive him. I can't. Aaron even spat on our mother's grave. Wash that one away if you can."

"The sun would have dried that. Think about it, Drew.

You were grown men when she died, but you're still harboring a childhood jealousy."

Drew leaned against the tree and tugged at the memories. "I've never really given him a fair chance, have I?"

"It's not too late."

"Do you know any good lawyers?"

"What Aaron needs is his brother standing with him."

"He's got Miriam. What else does he want?"

"She'll be busy," Pierre said grinning. "She plans to be in Geneva negotiating a big deal with a stubborn man."

"An art dealer at an auction house?"

"No. *You.*"

ᗑᗑᗑ

Rheinhold Schmid trudged down the trail toward them. They watched him come in silence—a man with an old and rugged face, a green felt hat pulled over his gray hair. His skin stretched like leather, worn with age, but he carried himself sturdily. As he reached them, he glanced at Pierre, the tip of his bulbous nose resting on a straggly moustache.

Rheinhold's tweeds looked threadbare but clean; a heavy gold chain with no visible purpose hung from his vest. He kept his eyes on Pierre as he relit his pipe. Like Ilse, he was slow in speaking, testing them with silence.

Sharply, Drew said, "Rheinhold, this is my son-in-law."

Rheinhold nodded, sucked at his pipe again until it drew to his satisfaction. His eyes crossed as he watched puffs of smoke rise from the bowl of his pipe.

"Herr Schmid, you can speak in front of my son-in-law."

"Come then," he said. "Father Caridini sent for you. One of the young bicyclists is dead."

*Not Uriah Kendall's grandson!* "The American?" he asked.

"No, Alekos. The one who gave our Erika a ride on his bike."

Alekos, not Ian. Relief swept over Drew, then shame. The Grecian—solidly built, thick-pursed lips, drooping eyelids—was only twenty-two, a young man with an intense dislike for Drew.

"What happened?" he asked. "An accident?"

More smoke rose lazily from the pipe. "Father Caridini says no. Come, I'll take you to him."

"Have you notified the doctor?"

"Herr Heppner is with Father Caridini."

Drew was on his feet, ready to follow Rheinhold. He turned to Pierre. "Go back, Pierre. I don't want you involved."

The muscles in Pierre's throat twitched. "I already am. I may have been the last one to talk to the young biker."

❧❧❧

Rheinhold Schmid led them to the doctor's clinic a short distance from the rectory. As they entered without knocking, the German shepherd lifted her head and snarled.

"Down, Girl," Rheinhold commanded.

The dog stretched out on the rug again, a low growl rumbling in her throat, but she allowed them to follow Rheinhold into the back room. Alekos Golemis lay on a narrow metal table, his youthful body lifeless, the tan face and thick lips colorless in death.

"Where's Father Caridini?" Drew asked.

Heppner barely looked up. "He's come and gone."

"But he sent for me."

"At my request. Thank you for coming," he said. "The young man's friends insisted that we talk to you."

Ian Kendall stepped from the shadows, visibly shaken. Close up, without the helmet and goggles, he quickly took on the Kendall features—Uriah's cheeks and jawbone, his grandmother Olivia's narrow nose and sensitive mouth. The unruly red hair fell in unmanageable waves much like his grandfather's had once done.

"Mr. Gregory, can you help me, sir?"

*Mr. Gregory? So you acknowledge me now.* "How, son?"

Ian looked grief-stricken, his lean, unsmiling face intense and drawn, his pale blue eyes avoiding his friend's body. "The doctor and the priest think we deliberately hurt Alekos. We weren't even there when it happened. Honest."

"He's right," Pierre said. "When I saw Alekos on the trail, he was alone heading toward a higher elevation."

The doctor chuckled mirthlessly. "And who are you?"

"My son-in-law," Drew said. "He just came up to overnight. He'll be going back in the morning."

"Not until we give the clearance," Heppner warned.

Drew glared at Heppner. "What happened, Johann?"

Heppner ran his fingers gently over the dead boy's neck, carefully outlining the bruises for Drew. "He was strangled. A trachea choke hold would be my guess. Or a thin wire." He pointed his chin at Ian. "He insists that you'll help him."

"If I can. And the dead lad?"

"Leave that to me." He dropped the dirty instruments onto a tray. "What a waste," he said angrily. "He shouldn't even be here. It wasn't our idea to open Sulzbach to tourists. And now, thanks to Preben and Senn Burger, we have murder on our hands."

Heppner taped Alekos's mouth in position and zipped the body bag, anger in every motion. "I head up a rescue patrol. Injured skiers in the winter. Lost hikers in the summer."

"I know," Gregory said.

"It never gets easier. Now Father Caridini suggests that my patrol and I accompany the body down to Brunnerwald."

"And from there?" Drew asked.

"I'll file a report on his death. And for the record, we'll want to know exactly where you were, Gregory."

"He was with me," Pierre said.

Ian's face had turned chalky. Drew gripped his shoulder. "Let's step outside, son. You need some air."

They left Pierre standing in front of Heppner's clinic and walked for several minutes before Drew paused and asked, "Ian, Dudley Perkins sent you here, didn't he? Why?"

Ian swallowed hard. "Yes, he's an old acquaintance of my grandfather's. They worked together a long time ago. Perkins arranged for my friends and me to train near Sulzbach for a while."

"Because I was going to be here?"

Ian looked too scared to bolt. "He didn't give me a choice."

"Kendall, you recognized me in the bookstore in Brunnerwald. I saw it in your eyes. And then you tried to run me down."

"Yes, sir. I thought if I could scare you off—maybe even hurt you a little bit—you'd leave and go back to London."

"And if I left, you'd be free to go?"

"Perkins couldn't hold me to my promise if you weren't here. I wanted to get back to really preparing for the Tour de France. I want to win that for my grandmother." He glanced back toward the clinic. "I never thought Alekos would die."

"It's not your fault, Ian."

"It is." His gaze strayed past the clinic to Herr Burger's place. "I didn't stop him when he got in with those strangers."

"You still haven't told me why you followed me here."

A strand of hair fell over Kendall's brow. "I was to find you and follow you, Mr. Gregory. If I didn't, Perkins would ruin my chances with the Tour de France. And he threatened to run a story against my grandparents in one of the British tabloids on the anniversary date of Grandma's death."

His misery grew as he said, "When you left Sulzbach, I was to let Perkins know. He'd make certain someone met you."

*Someone who would take over Trotsky.*

"Something happened between Perkins and your grandfather, didn't it?" When Ian's jaw tightened, Drew said, "Perkins ruined your grandfather's career with MI5. It was some connection to your grandmother's background, wasn't it? Was she British? Welsh?"

"She was Czechoslovakian."

"I didn't remember that."

"It's not likely my grandfather told you. She worked underground there. It's the best-kept secret of the century." He looked up. "Are you going to turn me over to the *polizei*, sir?"

"Because you tried to run me down in Brunnerwald and

followed me here? No, you're bearing a heavy enough burden."

"I searched your suitcase in your hotel room too. I'm sorry—especially about my friend Alekos. What will I tell my grandfather? What will you tell him when you see him?"

"The only thing I'm going to tell Uriah—if he asks—is that you plan to win the Tour for your grandmother. He'd like that."

"I've messed everything up," Ian said unhappily. "Now Perkins will smear my grandmother's name all over London."

"There's nothing he can say that would hurt Olivia."

"But it's important that nothing mar the family name. Gramps loved my grandmother and sacrificed a great deal for that love."

"And Uriah expects the same of you?"

"I expect it of myself. My grandmother and I were the best of friends, Mr. Gregory. If my grandfather knew that Dudley Perkins called me into the London office, there'd be the devil to pay."

Ian's face twisted. "I came even though I knew that you and Grandpa are good friends."

Drew gripped Ian's shoulder. "I'm sure Uriah will understand."

"But I was wrong to bring my friends with me. I never meant for Alekos to get killed. I don't know what happened."

Drew stopped quizzing the boy and backed off. "Ian, I want you and your friends to leave while you can."

"We can't. Dr. Heppner said there'll be an investigation—that they'll want to question my friends and me. If we run, Mr. Gregory, they'll think we really did murder Alekos."

# Chapter 27

Father Caridini closed the evening vespers and with a lump in his throat watched his small, faithful flock leave the Saint Francis Chapel. Only Rheinhold Schmid looked back, his oldest and dearest friend in the church. Rheinhold seldom came to vespers, the farm duties claiming his time. Even now his wife lay ill at home. Why then had he come this evening? To light a candle and to plead favor and good health for her?

When the chapel emptied, Nicholas made his way to the shiny altar that Senn Burger's grandfather had designed decades ago. Jacques Caridini had called it his treasure chest, for hidden in the hollow of the thick, hand-carved railing lay a small metal vault. Jacques had kept the offering moneys safe there—until the bishop passed through Sulzbach or Jacques himself traveled to Innsbruck.

For fourteen years Nicholas had concealed the secrets of the PHOENIX PLAN within that same railing in the spot where many of his parishioners prayed. Where Nicholas himself prayed. Numerous times he had determined to destroy the microfilms, but they represented the triumph of survival. He had emerged from the plane crash with a broken body and the coded plans in his pocket. The sealed packet had lain by his bed through that long year of recovery, but Father Jacques never touched it, never opened it.

His hand trembled as he took the packet from the vault and slid it up his sleeve. Using the railing for support, he pushed himself up from the altar, left the chapel, and made his way slowly through the sheltered passageway that connected the chapel to the rectory. He would go back to the church later before retiring and turn out the lights and lock the doors for the last time.

Frau Mayer didn't hear him come in, didn't even notice him as he hung up his cassock. He slipped past the kitchen, unable to face the thought of food, and went into the sitting room to stoke the fire. He added some logs and then emptied the contents of the envelope into the flames. As they burned, he sat in his favorite chair watching with an unbelievable sadness as the celluloid snapped and curled and rose in puffs of black smoke up the chimney.

The crackling sounds in the fireplace had often sounded like music to him. He thought of Marta, and his shoulders convulsed. At dawn he would be leaving Sulzbach forever and be dragged away from these mountains that he loved. "At dawn," he had told Marta, "you must always listen for the sweet music of the phoenix bird."

The black smoke filtered away. "The music is gone, Marta," he said aloud. "The phoenix bird cannot rise from the ashes. And the PHOENIX PLAN is dead, disintegrated, a mere legend now. Dear Marta, I have only one thing left to do."

The warmth from the fire did not touch him. Nicholas felt cold inside, his bony legs numb, his fingertips blue, his lungs screaming for air. The physical pain seemed unbearable. Each cough exhausted him. Each minute seemed to stretch forever.

Lifting his hands, he examined the bulging veins. These looked like the hands of a sick man. What had happened to the robust man he had once been? To the stalwart colonel who had once courted Marta? Sulzbach had happened. Christ—a real person, not a statue—had put a gulf between them. He had tried to tell her, but Marta had mocked him. Another deep cough wracked his emaciated body. Johann was right. They would have to carry him down the mountain.

The thought of returning to Moscow in disgrace or standing up to American interrogation with his body already riddled with disease seemed hopeless, the alternatives less than appealing. He would rather die than fall into the hands of the CIA or face the bishop of Innsbruck. He closed his eyes against the images that danced there. Moscow and the glory that had once stirred him. That modest boyhood home near the Baltic Sea; his aging mother, dead perhaps. Marta in East Germany, young and beautiful. Marta meeting his gaze inside the Saint Francis Chapel. Images of Johann tugging at his beard as he beat at a game of chess and the American agent Gregory winning at the contest of will. There was only one way out. The medications had piled up. Painkillers and sleeping pills still in their bottles. Tonight he would swallow all of them. He would do it for his people. No, he would do it for himself.

He closed his eyes tighter, trying to blot out the memory of Father Jacques leaning over his bedside right after the plane crash. *No, Nicholas, I will not give you more medicine. I will not let you take your life—not when you're going to walk again. No, my son, suicide is a mortal sin. . . .*

A mortal sin that would hurt Erika and chase Johann Heppner even further from the church. No, he must not heap that kind of pain on the people of Sulzbach. Nicholas stretched his head back, but pain radiated down his spine, leaving him spent, burned-out, fatigued beyond healing. He gripped the arms of the chair. He had to stay awake until Erika and Josef came back for Frau Mayer.

"Father Caridini, you haven't eaten."

He opened his eyes and smiled up at his housekeeper. "I know, Frau Mayer. I was too tired."

"The children are here."

"I want you to go with them. I promised Ilse Schmid that you would spend the night there. I think she'll be all right, but she needs a good nurse with her."

"What if you take sick during the night, Father Caridini?"

"Herr Gregory and his son-in-law are spending the night here. They'll look after me. If I'm feeling up to it in the morning, we're leaving for Innsbruck."

"Back to the hospital?"

"Do you think I should go there?"

She shied away, trying not to reveal her concern. "You're losing so much weight. And you won't eat."

"It's not your good cooking, Frau Mayer. My stomach—"

"I know," she said.

He didn't have the strength to stand. "Would you stay on a few days and set the rectory in order? I've asked Dr. Heppner to pay you for a full summer and then to get you safely to the train."

"You're not coming back here?"

"I don't think so. And next summer—"

"This is my last summer, Father Caridini. That's why I came in May this year. But, oh, how I will miss this place. And you."

"You mustn't keep the children waiting."

"We're not children," Josef said coming into the room.

She tousled his hair. "I'll get my things, Josef. And, Father Caridini, I'll leave the stew pot on the stove for your guests."

"I'll tell them."

As she left the room, Erika said, "Don't go away, Father Caridini. We need you."

"I'll ask the bishop to send another priest."

"But if *you* go away, Grandmama may not get well again."

Josef interrupted. "What's wrong with Frau Schmid?" he asked. "Today I heard her call you Father Jacques."

Nicholas nodded. "Sometimes as we get older, we mix names up."

Erika squatted down by the arm of his chair. "Consetta says it's more than that."

Nicholas ran the back of his hand gently over her cheek. "Erika, Consetta and Preben want you to live with them. They'll help you take care of your grandparents."

"Grandpa will take care of us—here in Sulzbach."

She was right. Rheinhold would never leave this village, and Erika would stay here with him, growing up without a childhood. He glanced up at Josef. "Josef, did you and Erika do as I asked?"

"Yes, we gave your message to Herr Helmut and Frau Burger."

"Good," he said. "I'm glad they know."

"Frau Burger said you mustn't tell people that you know who killed Fraulein Zubkov. It isn't safe for you. She says the trouble won't stop until the strangers leave town."

"They'll be gone soon," he promised. He jerked as another sharp pain ran down his spine.

"Are you all right? You're breathing funny," Erika said.

"I'll be fine."

She waited until the wheezing eased. "Father Caridini, do you really know who hurt Fraulein Zubkov?"

"Yes, one of the strangers."

He shivered. Josef went at once to lay another log on the fire. "Mother says you should wait until the *polizei* come and not try to figure things out by yourself. Not after Alekos died, too."

"Your mother is a wise woman, Josef. Ah, there you are, Frau Mayer." She looked even stouter in her buttoned coat, a small case in her hand. "The children were growing restless."

"We're not children," Josef reminded him.

They reached the door before Erika ran back to hug him. "Please don't go away, Father Caridini."

He flicked a strand of hair behind her ear. "Let me sleep on it, my child. And as you go out, Erika, leave the door unlocked. Herr Gregory and his son-in-law will be along soon."

🌑🌑🌑

Nicholas studied the unfinished chess game from the night before. It was one of the things he would miss the most, the friendship with Johann, the clever moves that he made.

Outside it was totally dark, and still Drew and Pierre had not come. He worried lest Johann had made good his threat and stirred up the people of Sulzbach. And then he heard footsteps in the passageway. He tensed, ears cocked. Odd that they should approach that way. The creaking stopped. Silence again.

But he knew someone was there. He waited, too ill to stand. "All right," he said. "You can come out now. We're alone."

The man who came into the room was the stranger staying at Herr Helmut's chalet. Calm. Self-assured. Threatening. He wore a belted trench coat, a slender, dark-haired young man who combed the room with his gaze, one hand in his bulging pocket.

"I was half expecting someone else," Nicholas said.

"Yuri or Vronin? I'm Dimitri Aleynik. Givi Aleynik's son."

Nicholas saw the likeness now—a strong bone structure with that long Aleynik nose, the well-placed eyes, the sharp features that refused to smile. "A priest," Dimitri said with scorn. "We find you hiding behind a priest's robe."

The flames leaped at the logs, the glow reflecting on Dimitri. His well-favored, clean-cut look was deceptive. His eyes went from cold to deadly as Nicholas shifted in his chair.

"No need to get up, Comrade Trotsky."

Dimitri came into the room and stood by the fireplace, leaving himself a clear view of the front door, his back turned to the entry hall from the chapel. From his pocket he took his 9mm Makarov and laid it on the mantel, his fingers still touching it.

"Father Caridini, isn't it?" He shook his head, the first hint of a smile on his thin lips. "My father trusted you."

"How is Givi?"

"Dead like my uncle. His friends were executed. Others were sent to Siberia, and still my father trusted you. He said you had to be a sleeper, an agent-in-place somewhere. Even on his deathbed, Givi believed you'd come back and lead the Phoenix rebellion."

"Marta's death cancelled that possibility. Why did you kill her, Dimitri?"

"She wouldn't identify you, Comrade Trotsky. Not back in Innsbruck when I broke her music box. Not last night. No matter how hard I hit her, she didn't betray you, not even when the wire cut into her mouth. She was a fool trying to protect you and more of a fool trying to convince me that you would help us."

"That's what I promised her."

"Marta Zubkov in exchange for the plan. Was that it, Colonel Trotsky? We came here to ask you to lead us against Yeltsin's programs. And you refuse to align yourself with your old comrades?"

"Totalitarian power can't win, Dimitri."

"Align yourself with your God then. No matter. I'll take the microfilms. And I'll do what my father refused to do. The rest of the Phoenix-40 will go on without you, Colonel."

"Dimitri, when you broke Marta's music box, you destroyed the part of the PHOENIX PLAN hidden there." Nicholas struggled against the unrelenting pain and nodded toward the fireplace. "The rest of the microfilms that you want are ashes at your feet, Dimitri."

❦❦❦

As Rheinhold Schmid left the vesper service, he hesitated in the vestibule, looking back once more at Father Caridini. The priest seemed troubled, but he could not help him. A few yards from the chapel he stopped again and leaned against the tree. Whatever was happening to Father Caridini was making Ilse ill. Rheinhold's beloved hard-working, God-fearing wife was growing too old for the mountain. This evening's chest pain had left her inconsolable until he sent for the priest. But as he left Father Nicholas alone with her, Ilse seemed to be comforting the priest.

As Rheinhold stood there, the stranger from Herr Helmut's place stole by, not even noticing him. Schmid had encountered the man on the trail twice and had been forced to step aside so the younger man could pass. His arrogance still annoyed Schmid as he watched the man go covertly up the steps and enter the church.

"Father Nicholas will be the next one," Ilse had warned.

Rheinhold could not risk the priest's safety. He allowed the man ten minutes of privacy within the chapel, and then he went in. Saint Francis was empty. No one in the pews or at the altar. He swung open the confessional—vacant.

Rheinhold was almost running now, swinging his muscled legs over the altar. He raced breathlessly through the apse to the right transept and jerked to a stop at the open door that led to the rectory. The passageway stood empty.

Rheinhold moved as quickly as he could out of the church and across the street to Heppner's empty clinic. Alekos's body bag still lay on the steel table, a cruel reminder that Father Caridini might be the next victim. He lifted a rifle from Johann's cabinet, checked for ammo, and hurried back to the chapel. He arrived in time to stop Drew, Pierre, and Johann from going inside.

"There's trouble," he warned, telling them briefly of the stranger from Helmut's place. "He's not a man to be trusted."

Heppner took charge. "Karl Helmut tells me the man's name is Dimitri Aleynik. An unwelcome guest, I'd say."

"What about Frau Mayer?" Rheinhold asked.

Johann smiled. "She's already on her way to your place for the night—to be with Ilse. And Nicholas is expecting us. We'll go on inside. Rheinhold, can you enter through the chapel?"

Schmid gripped his firearm and filled the chamber as Johann said, "We'll give you a minute to see if the chapel's unlocked."

"No, give me six minutes to position myself." Without another word, he slipped into the darkness. He tested the door, turned, waved, and disappeared. He knew they would not count on the lightning speed with which he would transit the narrow passage. As they opened the front door and stepped stealthily inside, Rheinhold was only steps behind the stranger pointing at the double-action weapon gleaming in his hand.

"*Guten Abend,* Herr Aleynik," Drew said.

Dimitri swung around and fired at Drew, but it was Rheinhold's rifle blast that shattered the silence. Dimitri's bullet reflected off the mantel as his body lifted from the floor and sprawled at Nicholas's feet, a gaping hole in his back.

As Rheinhold cocked the chamber, ready to fire again,

Nicholas looked up, startled, grateful, a coughing spasm ripping through his body. "*Danke,* Rheinhold," he said.

Rheinhold turned to Johann. "Senn Burger and Preben went to Brunnerwald today. They'll bring the *polizei* back up in the morning."

Drew and Pierre knelt beside the body. "Dead," Drew said. "Now what's going to happen to Herr Schmid here?"

Johann winked over the top of his spectacles. "He'll be all right. I'm still mayor here—until Burger takes over. And that," he said half-amused, "was my rifle."

He stepped over Dimitri's body and ran his fingers along the mantel finally spotting the reflected bullet hole. "Self-defense I'd call it. A simple case. Dimitri killed the biker—we stopped him."

"And Marta Zubkov?" Drew asked.

"He killed her, too, and Kermer. All three of them. I'm certain of it."

"Yes," Nicholas said, his voice trailing. "Dimitri bragged about killing all three of them just before you came. Said they got in his way."

"And did he tell you he was hoping that you would take the blame, Nicholas."

The priest nodded.

Johann was decisive. "Leave it to me. When the *polizei* come, we won't mention Marta. We bury our own people, don't we, Nicholas?"

The hollow eyes brimmed with tears.

"Gregory, Brunnerwald won't interfere with the classification of Marta's death as accidental—as long as we file a report later on." Johann glanced around at the others. "We'll leave Aleynik where he fell."

Schmid nodded, toed Dimitri once more, and picked up the hearth rug and dropped it over him.

Johann passed the chessboard and reached out to help Nicholas to his feet. "Well, Father Caridini," he said, "it looks like Somebody is looking after you."

"What about tonight's game of chess, Johann?"

Johann's voice was even as he said, "Another time, Nicholas. Right now you need to get some rest so you'll be strong enough for the trip down the mountain with Gregory."

At the mention of Gregory's name, Nicholas turned again. "Herr Gregory, Frau Mayer left some stew for you and your son-in-law. Just stir the woodstove a bit to warm it up."

"We'll do that, Nicholas."

"And, Gregory, I'll be ready by dawn."

Rheinhold Schmid watched the priest and doctor pacing themselves slowly from the room. His grip tightened on the rifle as he faced Gregory and his son-in-law. "Father Caridini is not strong enough to walk down that mountain."

"I know," Drew said. "But I won't tell your priest that until morning. If I wait until dawn to tell him, it will be like hearing the sweet music of the phoenix bird."

"What?" Schmid roared.

"Apparently it was an old memory that your priest shared with Fraulein Zubkov. Good night, Herr Schmid."

🥨🥨🥨

In Tel Aviv Jacob and Hannah Uleman sat on the hard sofa in the Bernstein living room, their craggy faces twisted with grief, their crooked fingers interlocked. Jacob moaned as though he were at the Wailing Wall weeping for the lost temple, the lost heritage.

But he was weeping for Benjamin. For Peter Kermer. For the only son he had ever known. Handsome, unsmiling Benjamin with the fiery eyes like his grandfather Aaron's.

They heard Sara laughing before the door opened, heard her call out happily to the neighbor, "Benjamin will be home soon. In time for Benjy's bar mitzvah."

*He won't be here then—or ever,* Jacob thought.

Sara still smiled as she came into the room, tall and slim, her face looking as lovely and youthful to Jacob as on the day that she and Benjamin had married.

"Jacob. Hannah. I didn't think you were coming over today."

"Benjy called us."

"Dear Benjy. Just like his father. He told me he would call

you and insist that you come for the day. Where is he?" And then alarm edged her voice. "Jacob, where are the boys?"

He struggled to his feet. "We sent them out to work in the garden until we could talk with you."

Sara's smile crept into despair. The joy left her eyes. The happy crinkle lines slipped down over her cheeks, drawing the curve of her mouth into a downward slant. The parcel in her hands crashed to the floor, the rich aroma of coffee filling the room as the glass shattered. "It's Benjamin, isn't it?" she cried.

Jacob caught her hands. "He's gone, Sara."

"No. It's a lie."

"They were here," Jacob said. "An hour ago."

From the sofa Hannah agreed. "Some men in uniform."

"Only one official in uniform," Jacob corrected. "Our Benjamin—"

"*My* Benjamin. Where is he? I'll go to him."

Jacob's hoary head turned from side to side. "No, no, Sara. Whatever Benjamin was doing in Austria must remain a secret. He would want it that way. He's so much like his grandfather Aaron—"

Sara pulled away from Jacob, her fists tightening. "You're talking about my husband—not some spitting image of his dead grandfather. A war forced Aaron to be a hero. But Benjamin—Benjamin chose that way of life."

"He's at peace, Sara."

She was crying now, her lovely face turning into a waterfall. "He promised to be here for Benjy's bar mitzvah. He—he promised to be here when the Messiah came back."

"Sara," Hannah said softly. "Come here, child."

Sara went and was encircled with Hannah's arms. They rocked together. Wept together. "Cry, child. Just cry."

"Oh, Hannah, we just had postcards from Ben last week."

"It was an accident," Jacob said. "He fell from a cliff."

"You know that's a lie, Jacob."

"For the boys' sake, let it be as the men said—an accident."

Her agonized protest filled the room. "Don't you think I know he's an Israeli agent? Risking his life. For what?"

"For Israel." Hannah hugged her tighter.

Jacob kept rocking on his feet. "Sara," he said miserably, "when we saw Benjamin in Vienna, he told us that if anything happened to him, we were to tell you that he loved you."

"But he won't be coming home. What will I tell the boys?"

Jacob patted her shoulder clumsily. "Tell them that Benjamin is already Home. And, Sara, in the days and years ahead tell them how proud he was of them and how much he loved them. Nothing can change that."

# Chapter 28

At the crack of dawn Drew found his son-in-law wandering through the Saint Francis Cemetery, squinting at the names on the weather-beaten markers. "What's up, Pierre?" he asked.

"I was looking for Miss Zubkov's grave."

"Over there." Drew pointed. "Unmarked."

They walked through the wet dew to the fresh rounded turf. "Eerie feeling," Pierre said, "knowing that her arrival here in Sulzbach changed the lives of the people."

"Mostly it just brought back old memories for Nicholas."

Pierre had reached the far corner sheltered by the largest tree. The ground sloped higher here, offering another spectacular view of the Tyrolean mountains. "Father Caridini," Pierre read.

"There were two priests, Pierre."

"Brothers?"

"In Jacques Caridini's eyes they were brothers."

"Is Jacques the priest who saved your life?"

"And Trotsky's life. In a way, he's the one who changed both of us—Nicholas, it would seem, for the better. If it hadn't been for Jacques here—and my gut intuition—I think I would have let my search for Colonel Trotsky run out in Brunnerwald."

"Not you, Drew. You always track things to the finish. Did Father Jacques know that Nicholas was an espionage agent?"

"It wouldn't have mattered to Father Jacques. He welcomed all men as his brothers."

"That's dangerous."

"Not for Jacques. He was a particularly kind man—I think you would call it something of the eternal in him. Judging men was out of character for him."

"You thought well of him, didn't you, Drew?"

"You don't forget a man when he saves your life."

"Then consider his principles. Wouldn't Jacques allow a dying man to have his last few months with the village people?"

"As a fake priest?"

"No, Drew. As their shepherd. As the man they have come to love. They know nothing of Nicholas's past. Must they know it now? I don't envy you, struggling between duty and an act of kindness."

"Johann told me that the downfall of one man could shatter the faith of the people, so get off my back, Pierre. I already told Herr Schmid that I won't be taking Nicholas down the mountain."

"I heard you. But you're still struggling with that decision. Trotsky doesn't have to walk off this mountain for you to file your reports. All it will take is a visit to the bishop of Innsbruck or a call to Chad Kaminsky at Langley."

Drew had grown accustomed to the wind sweeping down through the passes, but this morning a gentle spring breeze whistled through the leaves. Even some winter wrens had awakened to the dawn, swooping above the trees warbling and trilling the songs of a warm May morning. One tiny songbird swayed on the limb above them, its musical gurgle coaxing a smile to Drew's face.

The smile faded when Pierre asked, "What's it going to be, Drew? You're not dealing with a Russian agent any longer."

Drew shaded his eyes and watched the exploding streaks of day light the mountaintops and send their brilliant pink glow over the chapel and rectory. The warbling winter wren kept singing, a hundred separate notes, it seemed.

"I've stood here often," Nicholas Caridini said. "Always listening for the sweet music of the phoenix bird."

They turned. Nicholas had slipped up on them stealthily like the dawn with feathered steps, the doctor just behind him.

"And did you ever hear the phoenix bird?" Drew asked.

The priest's sleepless eyes stared back. "We always hear what we want to hear, Herr Gregory."

Johann, wearing his lederhosen and boots, stood by the priest—stoic, silent, on the brink of despair, the smell of liquor on his breath, the German shepherd nuzzling his hand. His wary eyes were fixed on Nicholas—and no wonder. Nicholas looked lost in his jacket, even thinner than the evening before. He wore a blue turtleneck sweater beneath his priestly garb, the solid blue emphasizing the jaundiced hue of his skin. His words were raspy, short-winded, as he said, "I'm sorry I'm late, but I wanted to go inside the chapel one more time."

"To pray?" Drew asked scornfully.

"Yes. Erika was there praying for her Grandmama and for you, I might add. She's quite fond of you, Gregory. But she's worried that she let you come up the mountain."

"I would have come anyway."

"I know. I recognized you when you first came to the parish. And I knew something else, Gregory. You wanted more than to thank Jacques for saving your life. You were a man in quest of peace."

Drew didn't deny it.

"I had the answers, but to help you would have risked my own fragile security. I'm sorry, Gregory. And now—with that said—I have a few things to pack, and then I'll be ready to leave."

Drew faced Heppner now. "Doctor, could we talk alone for a minute while Nicholas packs."

Heppner nodded and led the way back into the rectory, the dog at his heels. The sitting room had the peculiar smell of death and stuffiness. Girl reared back, lifted her head, and howled in the doorway. As they stepped around Dimitri's draped body, Johann said, "The *polizei* will be here around ten."

"Will it go well for Ian Kendall and his friends?"

"I'll make certain they're back in London in a few days."

As Drew stooped at the fireplace and kindled a new fire, Johann said, "There's no need to light the fire. The place will be empty as soon as you take Nicholas down the mountain. Well—empty as soon as the *polizei* come and take Dimitri away."

"Heppner, your priest will need a warm place when he gets back from his morning rounds with Frau Schmid and Frau Helmut."

Johann seemed locked in space. He took his tobacco pouch from his pocket and filled the bowl of his pipe. "Gregory, you said you were leaving now."

"We are. My son-in-law and I. Like you said, Nicholas would never make it down the mountain. Now—I want to exchange envelopes with you." He pulled one from his jacket. "Johann, I've enclosed a check. It should be ample to carry out the instructions inside."

Johann shoved the pipe into the corner of his mouth and read Drew's note. "More than ample. What do I do in exchange for this?"

Drew brushed past Johann and went to the desk, jiggled the broken lock, and retrieved Nicholas's letter. He dumped the letter and replaced it with a blank sheet of paper. As he sealed the envelope and put it back in the drawer, he said, "I thought we could burn Father Caridini's confession."

"But Nicholas—"

"To the people here, he is their priest. What he was—what he did happened a long time ago."

Johann hunched in front of the logs. "May I?" he asked. He lit his pipe, drew on it contentedly, and as the smoke curled from it, he lit Nicholas's confession and watched it turn to ashes.

🌑🌑🌑

When Drew and Pierre reached the crest of the hill, the priest and the doctor and Girl came hurrying up behind them.

"Wait," Nicholas called. "I'm going with you."

"I've been trying to tell him that he's staying here with

me for another game of chess. I don't like to stop any game before it's finished. You know that, Nicholas."

Caridini gripped Drew's hand. "It's true? How can I thank you?"

"Don't. When I return to my post, you know I have to file a full report on the deception at Sulzbach. Someone may come back for you. Troy Carwell, our new station-chief in Paris, or perhaps the bishop of Innsbruck will come for you first."

Caridini smiled again. "I will be here. I won't run."

"You're out of shape for running," Drew reminded him.

"I could flee to Brunnerwald in Herr Schmid's sturdy milk wagon. But, no, I won't run. Time is running out for me." He glanced at the picturesque Alpine setting, his gaze lingering pensively on the tiny cemetery behind the church. "One way or the other, Gregory, I'll be here waiting."

His relentless gaze held Drew's. "I would not have been so kind if the boots had been on the other feet. But the village of Sulzbach, its people, and God are all that matter to me now. Perhaps, Herr Gregory, you and your son-in-law would allow me to offer a prayer, a blessing, before you leave."

"No. You may be a priest to these people, Nicholas. I won't rob you of that. But you will always be Colonel Trotsky to me."

👁👁👁

As Drew and Pierre turned and stumbled over the first part of the mountain trail, Pierre asked, "Did you mean that back there? Do you only see Nicholas as Colonel Trotsky?"

"I really don't know where truth begins and ends, Pierre."

"At different bends of the trail for each of us. If the plane hadn't crashed fifteen years ago, Nicholas would not have changed. That accident was the beginning of truth and peace for him."

"Does a letter of confession blot out his deception?"

"He may have settled the matter in another way—on his

knees." Pierre cocked his head toward Drew, grinning. "By the way, I saw you and Johann make ashes of Nicholas's confession. So why did you do that if you can only see him as Colonel Trotsky?"

"I paced on that one all night long."

"Yes, you kept me awake, Drew. Men can change. Colonel Trotsky did. Somehow I think the real Nicholas Trotsky died when he took on a role and a robe." He stopped hiking and faced Drew head-on. "It's all wrapped up in forgiveness, Drew. Right now Caridini has only a few months at best. If he has anything to straighten out, he can face it up there on the mountain with the people who love him."

"I think it's more like a few days or weeks."

"Do you plan to give Nicholas that long, Drew?"

"I think I'm taking the coward's way out. I'm going to let the church deal with the deception first. Then the Agency can move in."

"Have you considered writing your reports in shorthand and forgetting to stamp them? Delaying them a few weeks maybe?"

"You've been reading my mind, Pierre. But isn't it odd? I have in a way forgiven my worst enemy—yet I cannot forgive my brother. Tell me, what can I do about my dislike for Aaron?"

"I only know one way to get rid of hatred."

Gregory sat down on the ground and stretched his lanky legs. "Go ahead, Pierre. Tell me about your God. I'm listening."

An hour later Drew smiled wanly. "You make it sound so simple. God. God's Son. Forgiveness. I'll think about it."

"Don't wait too long, Drew."

Drew laughed. "Look, I was an altar boy a long time ago."

"I know."

"And I was confirmed."

"So Robyn told me."

"When Mother divorced Dad and married David Levine, she pulled us both out of church. That was the end of it for me, Pierre."

"Then why do you think about those days so often?"

"I keep wondering why it slipped away from me so easily." He raised one hand, palm out. "No more, Pierre. I'll chew on what you've already said for a while."

"I think it's time to stop chewing."

"Pierre, I'd like to hassle this one out alone."

"All right. I'll go on ahead and wait for you."

Time ticked away as Drew sat on the trail under a canopy of clouds and evergreens, his back and head resting against a tree trunk. For the first ten minutes he just sat there, trying not to think at all. Then the memories rushed him. Since boyhood he had not been a man of prayer. He was all too often a man of few words, reserved and stoic, but he felt tears sting his eyes the way they had stung on the day he found his daughter again—the day Robyn forgave him and they became family once more.

Drew guessed as he tried to sum up God—as he tried to recall the prayers of confession memorized as a boy—that finding Robyn again was a bit like finding God. He had, after all, believed in God once, had known that God's Son hung on a cross. Drew was simply finding his way home.

Pierre was nowhere in sight now. He had rounded the bend in the trail, allowing Drew the privacy of the mountain. The ground felt cold on his buttocks, his hands clammy, but he glanced up toward the clouds in what he believed to be the general direction to God and said, "Lord, if You're there, I need You."

The wild thumping of his heart cut off the sound of his words, but he tried again. "God, I'm a man in need of forgiveness."

For an instant he considered signing off as he would a letter or a report to the Agency with "sincerely" or "case closed." But words and phrases from the missal and the liturgy of the Eucharist piled on top of one another. *Lord, I have sinned against You. Lord, have mercy. Christ, have mercy. Father, I celebrate the memory of Your Son.*

In his thoughts, he was an altar boy again, standing

beside the priest, solemnly listening to the words: "The parish is a recovery ward for lost sheep and struggling sinners. So welcome, my children." And then Robyn's words thundered across the valley: "God is just waiting for one stubborn man to follow Him."

Drew understood now what had happened to Nicholas Trotsky. Nicholas had touched truth and could not let it go. He knew now why his own mother had not been alone in the hour of her dying, for here in the Tyrolean Alps something more than the awe of the scenery gripped his heart. Something holy. Something good. Slowly, reluctantly, Drew got to his feet, ready to follow, and realized with a burst of joy that the weight and tightness in his chest were gone.

🜲🜲🜲

When they reached Brunnerwald, they went straight to the Gasthof Schrott. A startled Consetta met them as they came through the door.

"Herr Gregory, is Father Caridini with you?"

Drew glanced at his Rolex. "I'd say he's still making his morning rounds. I believe he was taking Communion to Frau Helmut, and he was going to spend some time with your Grandmama."

Relief swept over her face. Her lip quivered as she said, "Will you be back again, Herr Gregory?"

"Someday perhaps. To visit. I'd like my wife—my ex-wife to see your village. There's no place more beautiful."

Pierre followed him upstairs to Erika's room on the third floor. His luggage still lay untouched in the corner, the balcony window open to the mountain view. They walked over and stared up at the majestic peaks, tracking the run-out of the old avalanche.

"Sulzbach is to the left," Drew said.

"That's where I figured it." Pierre shaded his eyes against the dazzling white of the mountains. "It hasn't been an easy last assignment with the Agency, has it, Drew?"

"I lost a friend up there fifteen years ago."

"Yes, this visit stirred up a lot of pain for you."

A crooked, contented smile touched Drew's lips. "I left my worst enemy up there. But I found my best Friend on the way down."

"God?"

"Yes."

"I thought so." Awkwardly Pierre put his hand on his father-in-law's shoulder. "We haven't always been in agreement, Drew. We've had our differences."

*A host of them,* Drew thought. *My work in intelligence. Your faith. Our political differences.* "A lot of them," he said. "But we've both loved Robyn intensely."

"More than you'll ever know, sir."

They went back downstairs to check out of the *gasthof,* Drew banging the wooden rail with his handbag to alert Consetta. She waited for them, standing businesslike behind the desk. Drew put his cases down and opened his wallet to settle the account.

She shook her head. "The balance is zero," she said quietly.

Before he could protest, she added, "If I had told you the truth when you first came, perhaps those three people would still be alive. Especially that young cyclist."

Her businesslike calm slipped. Tears welled in her eyes. "I should have told you. The description you gave—I knew it had to be Father Caridini, but you didn't ask me about a priest. You asked about a stranger in Brunnerwald, a tourist, who might have stayed here at the *gasthof.* And Father Caridini was not a tourist."

"You were just trying to protect a friend."

"And I was frightened. I thought you were involved with the men who had beaten me."

"They have names now. Werner Vronin and Yuri Ryskov."

"Did you catch them?"

"No, but we have full descriptions. We'll go through Interpol. Perhaps they'll help us." He didn't add that Vronin and Yuri were undoubtedly safely on their way back to Moscow, but not strong enough on their own to stir the ashes of the PHOENIX PLAN.

She still looked troubled. "The other two—the woman and Mr. Kermer—meant you no harm," Drew told her. "They both tried in their own ways to protect your priest."

The bell on the *gasthof* door rang as a middle-aged couple entered. "We were hoping to get a room," the man said.

Drew stepped back from the desk and hoisted his suitcase. "It's a good place to stay—and your hostess most hospitable."

Consetta smiled and whispered, "Preben said to thank you."

&#9883;&#9883;&#9883;

The next few hours were a maze of paperwork and interviews, the first stop at the *polizei*. Drew promised to return if he was needed in connection with the death of Kermer or the young Grecian. At the *postamt* he sent a fax to Troy Carwell in Paris and placed an international call to Chad Kaminsky in Langley. He gave a sketchy report on his time in Brunnerwald and his side trip to Sulzbach, promising that written reports would follow—especially on the identity of Ben Bernstein. It took him another forty minutes to form the words for a wire to Alekos's father in Greece—to convey his sympathy in the accidental death of his son.

Father Caridini's name was never mentioned.

On the commuter train to Innsbruck, Drew struck peace with himself regarding his decisions. "I decided not to contact the bishop in Innsbruck," he told Pierre. "Not yet."

"That's a wise choice."

"And let's bypass Lyle Spincrest's hospital bedside. I'll have time enough to renew Spincrest's friendship at the tennis court in the months ahead."

"You won't be as angry with him then either."

"He's not the one who got Kendall and his friends involved."

It was late afternoon before they reached the airport in Geneva and took a taxi to the Courtland apartment. Drew reached out to press the bell. "Don't," Pierre said. "Let's surprise them."

They stole up to the second floor, a couple of grinning conspirators. Pierre turned the key and the knob of his apartment at the same time and swung the door open.

"Sweetheart," he called, "I'm home."

Robyn faced him, her auburn hair aflame in the late afternoon sun. Fear shadowed her blue eyes. "Pierre, is Dad all right?"

"Ask him yourself," he said stepping aside and letting Drew frame the doorway with his broad shoulders and towering six feet.

Drew winked at Robyn, then allowed his gaze to meet Miriam's. Miriam's eyes were wide and deep-set, thickly lashed, full of love. Her lips parted, not to that familiar half-smile, but to the whispered words, "Drew darling, you're home. You're safe."

Miriam moved in slow motion, her beautiful sculpted face radiant with welcome, more brilliant than any painting he'd ever seen. She eased from the cushioned chair and wiggled her narrow feet into Italian pumps. She came gracefully across the room to him, her smooth, bejeweled hands outstretched. Drew opened his arms, and she stepped into them willingly, naturally. As his lips found hers, it seemed as though sixteen and a half years of their lives had never slipped away.

# Epilogue

Drew Gregory leaned against the bulkhead idly watching a heavy traffic of tugs and pleasure boats cruising the Thames. Across the way the towers and spires on the Houses of Parliament stretched into a cloudy London sky. The monstrous bell of the clock tower on the northern end struck the hour as Dudley Perkins joined him.

Without looking up, Drew said, "Lyle Spincrest likes this spot. I've met him here more than once."

"What Lyle likes is the power that those buildings represent. But you didn't invite me here to discuss the scenery, Gregory. What's so important that couldn't be settled in my office?"

"Perkins, Marta Zubkov is dead." A horn blast on the river almost drowned out Drew's words. "She was carrying your name and phone number in her hand when we found her."

"The fool."

Drew kept his eyes on the Thames. "Did you send your men to Brunnerwald to protect her or to find Nicholas Trotsky?"

"Both," he said quietly. "I've used her before."

"Knowing that she was a Russian agent?"

"She was well-informed, Gregory. Believe me, she was nothing to me personally—if that's what you're wondering."

Perkins hooked his umbrella over the rail, his face a rigid

mask. The seconds stretched to three minutes before he said, "There was something captivating about Marta Zubkov. Under that cold, cynical facade there was a beautiful woman."

"Nicholas Trotsky thought so."

"I wondered about that. I met Marta at an embassy dinner. My wife and I were standing in the receiving line when Marta came down the stairs in a lovely formal. As our eyes met, I thought, *Taste not, touch not, Dudley, old boy.*"

"Spincrest says you're happily married."

"I am. Molly is my strength. But given the right set of circumstances Marta Zubkov would have been a temptation."

"But you knew she was a Russian agent."

"Of course. She was there with the Russian delegation. So her usefulness to MI5 clicked into play. As we danced that evening, I asked to see her again for dinner the following week."

"Your poor wife."

"Molly never questions my motives. But Marta Zubkov was a clever woman, Gregory, intending to use me as well."

His attempt to smile stretched the pachydermal skin and reset the facial muscles, making him even more homely. "Marta could have been a good dancer, but she was rigid in my arms, more interested in mocking England than in enjoying herself. She took great pleasure in telling me that she had met Philby and Burgess in Moscow when she was young. She thought all British alike, capable of betrayal," he said bitterly.

"And you wanted to prove her wrong?" Again Drew turned away. "Odd, Perkins, you haven't asked me how Miss Zubkov died."

"I'm more interested in Nicholas Trotsky. Did you find him?"

"Yes, but you first, Dudley. How did you get involved?"

He didn't hesitate this time but said, "Miss Zubkov called me two weeks ago with the strangest offer. She wanted to help MI5 find Trotsky before the Russians found him."

"So they wouldn't ship him to Siberia or execute him?"

"I didn't ask. This Trotsky—is he still alive?"

*Barely*, Drew wanted to say. "Give me a month, Perkins, and I'll fill you in on the whole story as best I can."

"So you can scoop the story? Under the circumstances, I can't wait that long. I meet with the prime minister in an hour."

"To report on this conversation? In a month," Drew repeated.

"Then we'll find our answers somewhere else."

"Don't play games, Perkins. MI5 had no right to be in Sulzbach. That was out of your jurisdiction. Yet you sent Lyle Spincrest and a team of inexperienced kids. We know Spincrest is in the hospital with a badly fractured tibia. And putting those kids at risk cost a curious twenty-two-year-old his life."

An inconsolable mourning darkened Perkins's eyes. "My son died young, too."

"I'm sorry about your son. The Falklands, wasn't it? But at least he died for his country. Alekos died for no reason at all. I hope you can live with that, Perkins."

"I can't change what happened to him. Zubkov was another matter. We know the risks in this business. So did she."

A rumble of a sigh exploded from his throat. "When we dug into the archives on Trotsky, the PHOENIX PLAN kept coming up. A revival of the PHOENIX PLAN meant a threat to England."

"To all of us. But to use those young kids . . ."

"Zubkov was mixed up in the plan, wasn't she?"

Another blast on the river forced Drew to silence. He faced the Thames again. "Zubkov knew more about Trotsky than she did about his PHOENIX PLAN. But for a while up in the mountains, Perkins, you gave me a fright. I thought we had another Philby or Maclean on our hands—someone with red running through his veins."

"I could kill you for an accusation like that."

"But you're a gentleman. Lucky for you, the doctor in Sulzbach didn't argue with me when I pocketed your name and phone number. He was too busy examining Marta's broken body. Otherwise the *polizei* would be on your case now for your association with a Russian agent."

"So I'm at your mercy, Gregory? How ironic when Zubkov was merely useful to MI5. To both of us. But you're holding out on this Trotsky affair. Is your Agency interrogating him?"

"Nothing like that. I assure you, Nicholas Trotsky will not be rising from the ashes. And if Dimitri Aleynik is on your files, Perkins, you will be glad to know that he is dead. Otherwise I would have missed my own wedding."

Perkins frowned. "If those two men are out of the way—"

"The PHOENIX PLAN is dead. As far as I'm concerned, Perkins, the rebellion has been reduced to a legend, like the bird."

"So what do you want from me, Gregory?"

"The name Zubkov stays sealed between us—on one condition."

"I'm listening."

"That you seal your file on Ian Kendall's grandmother."

Perkins remained motionless. The wind barely whispered. "It's too late, Gregory. An article is scheduled for the morning paper. Just a reminder to Ian that more could follow."

"You may have ruined Ian's career. What happened to Alekos could keep Ian from the race."

"I had no choice, Gregory. I have to keep young Kendall from turning Alekos's death on MI5."

"You'd better pray he never reads that article." Drew bit his tongue at the vengeance in his words. No, he wasn't going to let go of the peace that had engulfed him on the mountain. "Forget it, Dudley. That's not the kind of game I want to play anymore. Just take it easy on young Kendall. Whatever you hold against Ian's grandmother is not his fault."

"She was no better than Marta Zubkov." Loathing rose in his voice. "She was an enemy agent, Gregory. A threat to Britain."

*Uriah's wife, an enemy agent?* "Dudley, Olivia Kendall is dead. Ian loved his grandmother. Whatever she was, he misses her." He faced Perkins. "You lost your son. Don't take the past out on Kendall. He's just a kid trying to win a race."

Perkins's facial muscles twitched uncontrollably. "The prime minister may want to talk to you. How can I get in touch with you about this Trotsky affair? At the embassy?"

"Not right away. I'm flying to Geneva in the morning."

"When will you be back, Gregory?"

"In six weeks. I'm taking my bride on a honeymoon."

Perkins picked up his umbrella and whacked it against the bulkhead. "It would take an extraordinary woman to marry you."

"Miriam *is* an extraordinary woman. But, Perkins, I'll keep in touch with you."

Perkins stalked off, the ends of his hair whipping around his bowler hat, the crook of his umbrella hooked over his arm.

As Drew watched him go, a well-groomed woman rose from the wrought-iron bench and stepped forward to meet him. Molly Perkins's plainness disappeared as she smiled up at Dudley, her smile wide like the brim of her hat. She took his arm, her stately bearing proud like her husband's as they merged into the crowd.

*And there,* Drew thought, *goes another remarkable woman.*

🌹🌹🌹

The last Saturday in May dawned in all its splendor with a brilliant sun and a cloud-free sky. Outside, Mt. Blanc looked a dazzling white, the forests beyond Montreux a jaded green. Inside, the elegant home of Pierre's friends was once again bustling with preparations for an afternoon wedding.

Robyn Courtland had met the delivery trucks and signed for the flowers and food and a three-tiered cake. She had given last-minute instructions to the French caterers in the kitchen and overseen the transformation of the living room into a tiny chapel. Now the sweet smell of dozens of pink and white roses permeated the room where her parents would marry.

Her hostess met her at the foot of the spiral staircase and smiled. "You're almost as happy as the bride," Anita said.

"I've waited for this wedding for a long time."

"Then you'd better get ready. I'll keep my eye on things down here and welcome the guests when they come." She glanced around her home and then patted Robyn's cheek. "No wonder your parents are so proud of you."

Robyn had reached the third step when Anita called out, "Oh, Robyn dear, this letter from Austria came for your father." She held it out. "In the excitement I forgot about it."

Robyn flew up the steps, breathless as she burst into the room where she and Pierre were staying. He was already dressed, striking in the dark tuxedo, a white rose in his lapel.

"You'd better hurry. You don't want to be late for this wedding."

"But everything's gone wrong, Pierre," she said.

"Everything?" He cupped her chin. "What's wrong, sweetheart."

She waved the envelope at him.

"What's that?" he asked.

"It's a letter from Dr. Heppner."

Gently he took it from her and checked the return address. "It may be important. We'll have to give it to your father."

"Not before the wedding," she said, tugging on her dress.

"You'll have to give me what?" Drew asked as he came from the adjoining bedroom that he shared with Vic Wilson.

Pierre squared his shoulders. "It's a letter from Sulzbach."

"Father Caridini?"

"No, sir. It's from Caridini's doctor."

"Heppner?" Drew held out his hand and tore it open and read.

He groped for a chair and sat down. Robyn was there at once, leaning over his shoulder, her cheek to his. "What is it, Dad?"

"Nicholas died in his sleep ten days ago."

"Dad, I'm so sorry."

She scanned Johann's letter.

*I ordered three stones like you suggested, Gregory. The peo-
ple of Sulzbach are grateful to you. As I am.*

She fastened her pearls. "What does this mean? What stones?"

Drew glanced up at Pierre and then chose to share it with them. "I left funds for matching headstones for the two priests of Sulzbach. It was the least I could do."

She'd never seen her father cry, and now she reached up and brushed a tear from his cheek. "For Nicholas and his brother?" she asked softly.

"I did it for the people. I thought it was a good idea."

"You made the right decision, sir," Pierre said.

Drew nodded as he yanked at his bow tie. "Get Vic Wilson in here so he can fix this thing. Otherwise I'm going to be late for my own wedding. If that happens, Miriam will think I ran out on her again."

"She won't let you." Pierre stepped over. "Let me tackle that tie for you. Drew, was the third grave marker for Marta Zubkov?"

"Yes. She had no family nor friends."

"In a way she had Nicholas."

"It was too late for them, Pierre."

"Dad, how can she be buried in the church cemetery? She was a Communist—she didn't belong to the church. She didn't believe anything. She didn't even belong in Sulzbach."

"I can't judge her, Robyn. She and Nicholas talked at great length the night before her death."

"She was still a stranger in Sulzbach. Won't the people of the village oppose her being buried as one of them?"

"It was what their priest wanted. Marta paid a high price for loving Nicholas Trotsky. And an even higher price for loving Nicholas Caridini."

"There," Pierre said. "Don't touch the tie again. It looks great." More seriously he asked, "And Trotsky—or Caridini—whatever you called him, did he care as much about Marta?"

"She was the only woman Trotsky ever loved."

DORIS ELAINE FELL

"Except for his widowed mother in Russia. Will someone notify her that he's gone?" Pierre asked.

"Vic's working that out with our station in Moscow to see whether she's still alive. For her sake, I hope not."

Sounds of the old traditional wedding march peeled from the organ. Drew stood and strolled toward the door. He looked back at Robyn. "Princess, come kiss your old dad and wish him well."

She flew across the room to him. "One more question. If they find Nicholas's mother, what will they tell her?"

"That her son was a priest when he died."

"But that would be an outright lie, Dad."

"Princess, to the people of Sulzbach he was their priest."

"What about the letter—his confession to his people?"

"You said one question, Robyn," he teased. Still he answered, "There is no letter, Robyn."

Pierre came up beside them. "Sweetheart, your father and Dr. Heppner burned the letter just before we left Sulzbach." He touched his finger to her lips. "As long as Nicholas thought the doctor would deliver it, he could die in peace. He lived his role well, Robyn. They didn't want to take that from the people."

"Dad, does Troy Carwell know that you found Trotsky?"

"I haven't mailed in the final report yet." Drew glanced at Johann Heppner's letter. "I can send it in now."

"And what will you tell Carwell?"

"That Nicholas Trotsky really did die in Sulzbach—that he's buried there. Carwell will be glad to officially close the case."

She heard a catch in her father's voice as she brushed a thread from his collar. "Dad, I thought Trotsky was a violent man, a political assassin."

"He was once. For years Nicholas fought a war for world domination. Men kill in wars."

"Aren't you making excuses for him?"

"I'm just trying to understand a complex man. Whatever he was, he changed. It's difficult to say when he ceased being Nicholas Trotsky and became instead the brother of Jacques Caridini."

"You really think he was genuine?"

"I think it was more like he was forgiven."

She studied Drew, perplexed. "You're different, Dad. You seem to be at peace with yourself."

"I am."

The organ music grew louder, persistent. "Robyn," Pierre said gently, "let the questions go. Your mother is waiting."

Robyn stood on tiptoe to kiss Drew's cheek. "Mother will think you're as handsome as I do. Where are you taking her?"

"I promised Miriam Paris thirty years ago."

"That's crazy, Dad. What if you run into Troy Carwell?"

"How much sightseeing did you do in Paris on your honeymoon?"

Pierre's pleasant, sun-bronzed face crinkled with laughter. "I think we had a perfect view of the Seine from our bridal suite, didn't we, Robyn? By the way, I booked you there, Drew."

Before Robyn could answer, the phone in the adjoining room rang. "Wait, Drew," Vic Wilson called as he poked his head around the corner. "Troy Carwell is on the line. Says it's an emergency. He's got to talk to you."

"Tell Carwell he has the wrong number."

"He heard that, Drew. He wants to know when you'll be back."

"In six weeks."

Vic covered the mouthpiece. "You expect me to tell Carwell you'll call him back in six weeks? Maybe he's got your retirement papers on his desk."

"Good. Tell him to mail them to me."

Vic eyeballed the phone. "Troy, the static on this line is terrible." He dropped the receiver into place and grinned as he walked over and clapped Drew's shoulder. "Now go on and get that wedding ceremony rolling before Troy Carwell calls back again."

Robyn's father winked at her, then turned the doorknob, and led the way into the sun-lit hall. Her mother stood at the top of the stairs waiting for him, looking lovely in her delicate blue gown and matching veil. As Drew reached her,

Miriam broke off the twelfth rose from her bridal bouquet and slipped it into his lapel.

Drew looked like the happiest man in Montreux. Those intense gray-blue eyes—sad just moments ago—sparked with love for her mother. He seemed even taller, stronger, his noble face vital and vibrant as he bent and kissed Miriam.

He tucked her arm in his, and together they turned once more to glance at Robyn. "We love you, Princess," Drew said.

And then with the organ playing, her parents went down the spiraling stairs to stand beneath the arched trellis of a hundred pink and white roses to renew the vows they had made so long ago.